"Always mine," he said huskily as he drew the sheet down to her waist. Bending, he touched his lips where they had not been able to touch before. Meridel yearned toward him and whispered—she knew not what. He loosened her hair, spreading it in a bright veil across her bosom, and trailed his lips through the silken strands.

"Wherever we go, whatever life brings, remember I love you," he murmured as he uncovered and kissed her everywhere, exclaiming at the silken texture of her skin and the beauteous curves of her small body. His hand found her most secret places, and all her being responded as a flame swept through her—a wild call of abandon.

PRAIRIE FLAME

PRAIRIE FLAME

JESSICA HOWARD

A JOVE BOOK

The author wishes to thank the many people who helped build a framework of truth for this work of imagination. Special thanks go to the staff of the Kansas Collection in Lawrence, and the Lecompton Historical Society in Kansas.

PRAIRIE FLAME

A Jove Book/published by arrangement with the author

PRINTING HISTORY
Jove edition/March 1983

ISBN: 0-515-04729-5

PRINTED IN THE UNITED STATES OF AMERICA

Part I

Life Was a Golden Apple

Chapter One

The queen had commanded, so the peers and peeresses of the realm had come in their coaches to the grand ballroom of Buckingham Palace. Sequined gowns billowed and rustled and jewels flashed as the ladies strolled about, nodding to others of noble rank, while the black-and-white elegance of titled gentlemen formed a background for their magnificent array.

Victoria Regina, when at last she arrived, would gaze upon nobility of all ages—the reckless young, the dependable middle-aged, and the skillful but elderly courtiers left over from the Georgian era. But always the queen would smile on the youngest of her guests, the yet-untitled maidens around the age of seventeen, most of whom were of noble birth.

Like the few older women who had not yet been presented to the sovereign, each debutante wore a demure white gown and a headdress of three curling white plumes, worn in honor of the Prince of Wales since the fourteenth century. But unlike the older women, who wore jewels—as befit married women—the debutantes remained unadorned; they were considered the real ornaments of the occasion. Aware of the admiring glances thrown their way, they stayed close to their parents and fluttered their fans shyly.

One girl drew more than her share of warm male glances, earning her the resentment of the mothers of other debutantes, who considered her a mere commoner; worse, she was an Irish American. Besides, what was so wonderful about masses of coppery hair above the girl's smooth forehead? And why must their own daughters wish they could have obtained the same effect?

But Meridel McGraw turned male heads with more than her striking tresses. Even other females could not deny that her petite figure was lovely, nor that she appeared uncommonly graceful even when she merely stood, waiting with the others for the queen to appear. In fact, Meridel did not feel quite so nervous as the other ingenues. At Miss Whittaker's Academy for Young Ladies in London, she had been noted not only for her scholarship but also for her poise.

She had never before been inside Buckingham Palace, yet she cast no more than a blue-eyed glance around the ballroom's glittering opulence. No oohs or aahs came from her. After all, she was no longer a schoolgirl. She had reached the age when she could put to use her knowledge of French and of dancing, of how to daub watercolors and manage servants and curtsy to royalty and pour tea while chatting entrancingly with an eligible man.

She had learned something of the classics, too, and of geography and history and the like. But, as everyone knew, the stylish "dame schools" prepared a girl first and foremost to find a husband. In fact, at the moment a girl rose from her curtsy to the queen she also rose in status from debutante to social butterfly. She would see and be seen at balls, parties, dinners, and "afternoons," where she counted on finding her future spouse. Once betrothed, she spent months collecting a trousseau. And at last she discovered certain secrets that a proper young lady never was supposed to find out before her wedding night.

Not that—as Miss Whittaker used to sigh—every girl who

4

was presented found a husband. But Meridel had no fear of becoming a spinster. Rather, she counted on marrying soon and marrying well—possibly into the English nobility. Yes, why not marry a handsome lord and preside over his big house surrounded by five thousand acres? Lifting her small round chin, the petite charmer watched the unfolding ceremony without doubting her right to be there.

Nevertheless, to some degree Meridel envied the other girls. They had attended the court with their parents, while her own half-British mother, Dianthe Cabot Blakiston McGraw of Boston, was dead; she had died whispering how dearly she hoped her daughter would attain a title. Meridel still had her beloved father, but . . . oh, she couldn't *blame* Finnian McGraw, but she wished he hadn't stayed home in order to be able to travel between New York and Washington on one of his never-ending "deals."

But at least Meridel had been brought to the court by excellent sponsors. Childless Lady Anne Blakiston, faded but stately, took her hand and whispered, "Now, dear, be patient, the queen will arrive shortly." Her husband, Viscount Hubert Blakiston of Wend, Meridel's distant cousin, bent to murmur, "Sticky wicket, but every debutante so far has survived."

Patience, then. Meridel smiled to a classmate and waved her left hand slightly. The other girl, winking, also moved her white-gloved left hand. Yes, both knew that after one curtsied to the queen, before long—with a bit of luck—a gold band would ring one's left finger.

But meanwhile the queen's curtsy loomed closer in every young woman's mind, and soon trumpets blared. On cue the lords and ladies, commoners and diplomats turned in unison to face the throne dais. A quaintly costumed procession, walking straight out of history, entered. Two seargeants-at-arms, swinging outsized ceremonial maces of silver gilt, were followed by a small, heavyset woman draped in priceless Alençon lace—Victoria in the nineteenth year of her reign. Walking beside her, his hair and curly whiskers salted with gray, orders glittering on his coat and sash, Prince Albert cut a handsome, youthful figure.

When the royal couple had been seated, the court opened

with sundry announcements before the lord chamberlain, robed and pompous and wearing a large golden key on a matching chain, stepped forward and unrolled a scroll.

In a deep clear voice he rolled out the names of foreign diplomats, among them James Buchanan, minister of the United States and Finnian McGraw's friend, who at the mention of his name elegantly strode forward to kiss the queen's outstretched hand, before retreating to make way for other prominent men on the royal roster. Then, in the order established by ancient custom, the peers and peeresses, the knights and dames of the realm all performed the same ritual, some more or less clumsily than others.

After awhile Victoria began to look a bit weary. Shifting in her chair, she nodded to the lord chamberlain, and he began to read the last group of names—the debutantes'—each of whom paraded to the dais on the arm of her sponsor, curtsied and received the queen's smiling nod and murmur, before retreating and allowing the next in line to have her "debut."

Meridel knew her name would come last of all. At sixteen and a half she was really six months too young to be presented, and her father was a mere builder of railroads in America, hardly someone to impress landed British aristocracy. But Meridel had graduated with honors from Miss Whittaker's Academy, and Buchanan had pressed over the objections of minor officials until someone high in the crown's hierarchy—the lord chamberlain—had given the nod.

Meridel heard one of her classmates gasp, "I'll faint, I know I will. Miss Whittaker said we must curtsy like a flower in the wind, but I simply can't."

"I'm sure you'll do beautifully, Gwendolyn," Meridel whispered to the girl.

The pudgy Gwendolyn did not faint, face to face with Victoria, but she did manage to trip over her short train, turning crimson with mortification. The queen and the prince merely gazed straight ahead of them, as if not catching the gaffe.

Portly James Buchanan, also ignoring the girl's stumbling, gave Meridel his arm and walked her to the throne where he bowed to the royal couple and drew aside.

So far every debutante presented had been nobly born and

introduced as the Honourable Miss This-or-That. This time the lord chamberlain declared, "May I present Miss Meridel McGraw, Your Majesty," and the assemblage stared.

Then the diminutive American with the plain Irish name not merely advanced toward the queen, she floated like thistledown, and bent like a flower in a breeze when she curtsied, managing her skirts so well they formed a perfect disc of ruffled white on the polished floor. When she lowered her gaze to show the royal couple the respect due them, her red hair topped with nodding white plumes transformed her into a red-centered, white-petaled blossom.

Victoria came to life. Prince Albert leaned forward.

Later a feverish buzz would race through the ballroom— some of it quite indignant. The well-born wondered what had made the difference to Victoria, that she would converse at length with one of the debutantes. Had it been the surprise of meeting a plain Miss? Relief at coming to the end of the line? The welcome contrast between Miss Meridel and the Honourable Gwendolyn? Or, having been warned in advance, had the queen decided to pay special attention to the one American girl she'd meet that evening? Relations with the United States had been strained for years, and the queen's gentle welcome might be seen as more than courtesy—but an instance of international relations, carried out on a small scale.

When Meridel looked up, she showed the royal couple a nymph whose lips seemed touched by nectar, whose heart-shaped face bore glimmering eyes of a magical blue, whose whole air marked her as a queen in her own right, able to deal with heads of nations on the same level. Rising lissomely, Meridel wondered why some called Victoria a crosspatch. Not with that friendly smile! Nor did the queen regnant seem at all tired as she asked with genuine interest, "Tell me, Miss McGraw, in what part of the United States do you come from?"

"New York City, Your Majesty," Meridel said without hesitation.

"A great city, surely. Do you think it will be as large as London one day?"

"Perhaps so, Your Majesty." Before she could stop herself, Meridel added, "The city is growing uptown." She wondered if she said too much. After all, others had curtsied and moved on.

But Prince Albert was smiling and said, "New York is not so foggy as London, I am told."

Meridel wondered how to respond. Remembering the cold fog outside and the chill in the Blakiston carriage, she hazarded, "It's less foggy in June, at any rate, Your Royal Highness."

The Prince seemed delighted with her insight. The buzz was beginning to spread through the ballroom. Titled parents wondered in whispers why *their* daughters had not been held in conversation with the royal couple. Who *was* that American chit anyway?

Victoria asked, "Have you traveled to other parts of England?"

"Yes, Your Majesty. I've spent some time in Devon and I've visited the Cornish coast."

"Were you surprised to see the palm trees?"

"Indeed I was, Ma'am," she said without hesitation. She had learned at Miss Whittaker's that she could drop royal titles during conversation so long as a good substitute was found. "I never thought a palm could grow outdoors in England."

Prince Albert nodded. "That's because our south coast is warmed by the Gulf Stream as it comes across the Atlantic. One might say we import warm water from America as well as all those valuable shiploads of cotton."

Victoria gave him a look of fond appreciation for the jest. Meridel had heard they were a loving couple; how true this moment proved the legend to be. She remembered another fact gleaned from her history classes at Miss Whittaker's: that it had been Victoria who had proposed! But then she was already the queen of England and Albert merely the crown prince of Saxe-Coburg-Gotha, and it would not have been proper for him to make the proposal.

The prince knitted his brows together and displayed his famous memory, one Meridel had heard of often. "Miss McGraw, are you not the young lady in the guardianship of Hubert Blakiston down at—let me see—Wend, isn't it, in the Devon hunting country?"

"Yes, sir," she nodded.

"And didn't a branch of the Blakistons go to America some time before the Revolution?" He cocked his head slightly, gazing over her shoulder only a moment. "Yes, they went to the royal colony of Massachusetts."

Meridel was shocked almost speechless before she found her reserves. "Yes, sir, to Boston. It was my mother's family, and they went over in 1755—just a century ago." Proud and wealthy; her family in Boston lived in splendor until the first part of the nineteenth century when they became poor as church mice, but refused to leave their crumbling mansion on Beacon Hill. How could the daughter of such a proud family have married a poor immigrant Irishman, Finnian McGraw? Not for the first time, Meridel puzzled over her ancestry.

Queen Victoria interrupted her reflections, saying briskly, "Well, then, Miss McGraw, you are having a family reunion at Wend. How pleasant! We trust you will enjoy your stay in England." Meridel knew she had been dismissed, though very graciously.

She gave a smaller curtsy, as required, and retreated backward, gracefully managing her train. At the proper moment she turned and faced the assemblage, almost stumbling at what she saw—rows of hostile eyes staring her way. Remembering her poise she straightened herself and waited for her escort to appear, but as she did so, her eyes briefly locked with those of a very tall blond man who was peering over other people's heads. An expression not of hostility but of utter astonishment was on his knifelike face. A most striking person, she thought. Like a Viking.

Buchanan finally appeared at her side for what seemed minutes, and taking his extended arm, she strolled down the aisle, not knowing that she appeared to think her chat with the queen and the prince was nothing more than the normal order of her day. The statesman leaned her way and whispered, "Look here, young lady, do you realize what a triumph you've had tonight? Right now your status has soared so high you could choose the peer who'll put a wedding ring on your finger."

Meridel unlocked her fan of ivory strips and fluttered it open gently. Mr. Buchanan was a dear, she knew, but he was exaggerating. Nevertheless, how had her father put it? "Mucashla, 'twas your mother brought you up to be a lady, and when I hand you over to an English lord you'll become a lady with a capital *L*. Why, marryin' noble will only be a wee bit of advancement, after all."

The strikingly tall blond, sharp-faced man had had trouble entering the palace. His credentials were in order, only he had arrived late, and no guest was allowed to enter the court after the queen had been seated. It was considered disrespectful.

Bloody hell, thought Harald Wayne, stranded in the palace doorway. He should not have dallied at White's, but how was a man to pass by the famous card house and not go in? He had spent only an hour there before he had risen from the table fifty pounds richer. "I say, chaps," he had murmured, "I'm to attend court. A bore, what? But one has one's duty."

For a moment he had savored his new, honorary title of baron—and his new status as an earl's only son—an *heir*, by Gad! On top of that, it felt so good to be no longer a younger son! No longer an embarrassing appendage to a noble family, reared as a gentleman but left without money or title, never refused his bed at home but always made to feel subtly and unmistakably as though he belonged far away. Ponsonby, the familiar flunky at White's door, had brushed his tall silk hat before handing it over to Harald: "Fearful sorry to 'ear about Lord Didrick, sir."

"Ah, yes, yes, death waits for all of us, and we never know when or where," Harald had said in the appropriate tones while glancing at his mourning band. He'd been wearing the band since his elder brother, in the excitement of landing a fish in a Norfolk river, had overturned their skiff and been drowned.

"Is my cloak straight, Ponsonby? There's a good fellow." Silver passed between hands. "I'll be coming down to town more often—now that I've finished my term in the diplomatic corps."

If a younger son did not become an army officer in India or go gold mining in Australia he took refuge in the diplomatic corps, a haven for the well-born but penniless, Harald Wayne had not remained penniless for long. He was a younger son for sure, but one who possessed an extraordinary head for business and he'd used his abilities to make a small fortune while in the corps.

"Been far away, your lordship?" asked the steward at the door, conversationally.

"Off in a little country called San Tomás, Ponsonby. In Central America. Snakes, fever. Hot as bloody hell with a pitchfork," he said, then waved at the smiling lackey who bowed in a manner reserved only for an heir, not a younger son.

Though he'd gloried a moment, his mood soured when he encountered trouble at the palace door. Barred from entering, he felt his temper rise before an elderly usher arrived, perhaps feeling that ex-younger sons needed time to learn palace customs, and let him slip into the ballroom through a side door.

Calmer, Harald could enjoy the effect his well-tailored evening clothes made on the assemblage. A young and comely woman noticed him—sidewise, slyly. Because she wore jewels, he could tell she was married. He flashed his most charming smile. The round-bellied husband, standing nearby, sidled nearer after catching the exchange and glared, but despite the strained moment, Harald's mood this time would not be soured. He went on displaying his top-to-toe elegance, his short, clipped golden mustache and beard and his long hair, swept back and pomaded. Women often had told him he looked like the commander of a Viking ship.

Glancing around, Harald's thoughts turned to an unpleasant duty to which he had better attend. The roots of the matter lay some years back in San Tomás, where Harald, as a junior consul, had rendered valuable aid to a railroad-building Paddy. Of course, anyone who ever conversed with red-haired Finnian McGraw had to listen to his stories about his red-haired daughter, Meridel. It seemed that the brat had grown up, and old Finnian, who always made friends in high places, had arranged for her to meet Victoria. In a letter he had explained this to Harald, saying he'd be tremendously obliged if Harald would attend the court and make himself known to the girl.

For once McGraw's spelling had been accurate, most likely because he had dictated the letter. He had ended:

You'll find Meridel in the care of Lord and Lady Blakiston, whom you may know. She will recognize your name because I often have spoken highly of you. I wrote to her that you might be there. Believe me, my dear Wayne, I would not ask this favor save that I hope soon to put you in the way of an excellent business proposition. I plan to build a railroad in the western part of the U.S.A., where every new railroad earns a huge profit. You know I have won a reputation by putting the first rails across the Isthmus of Panama. This helps, and if I can make the proper arrangements in Washington, I shall be glad to have your own special talents once more on my side. Please tell Meridel I feel badly about not being able to take the time for the round trip to London, but if I can't give her her papa, at least you come as my very special and trusted friend who has every interest in her welfare. . . .

Good enough. It had given Harald an excuse to come to town and get away from his nagging father. And of course, the family estate, Danemead, needed money and Harald himself always required more and more for his personal extravagances, gambling being foremost among them. McGraw's hint of good business and high profits were just too irresistible, and for this reason, he had come to charm a stubby redhaired debutante named Meridel. But what could the girl look like? he wondered, grimacing as he studied faces. Anything fathered by Finnian McGraw would be ugly as a pig. But he would endure the girl and remember the prospect of making good money—far away from the earl, his father. It was fortunate, too, that Viscount and Viscountess Blakiston were old friends of the earl, having visited Danemead to admire the blooded horses before Harald had departed for San Tomás.

The lord chamberlain—pompous ass—had been making the ballroom echo with the names of the various debutantes he introduced. It amounted to a string of Honourables, each more awkward than the other. Then—good timing!—the lord chamberlain intoned, "May I present Miss Meridel McGraw, Your Majesty."

Excellent. Harald pushed his way through the crowd toward the throne dais, nodding here, nodding there, smiling dazzlingly at people who thought he was being rude. Finally he saw her. Vicious Vicky and her German darling were chatting with a petite, red-haired debutante. Even with her back toward him, the girl displayed a marvelous grace. He wondered if this vision could really be the daughter of a potato-eating Paddy who resembled a bullfrog.

When the queen had finished with Meridel, the girl retreated prettily enough, forming her gown, her train and her plumes into one flowing line of motion. When she turned her head he saw her in profile and noticed her gardenia skin and a piquant ear beneath coppery hair that glinted as though alive. And most of all he noticed the swelling of proud little apple-breasts.

Their eyes met. Harald's jaw dropped in astonishment. Finnian McGraw had sired a charmer, an entrancing elf! As she moved away Harald studied the sway of her slender hips, and felt weak in the knees, trembling when her dress fleetingly clung to a limb before billowing in swirls of soft silk. She carried herself like a princess. No, like a ballerina. He wanted to push away the United States minister and lift her light arm to his own. He asked himself, "Come, you're not smitten with a mere child?" But his racing pulse and his sweating palms told him how badly he had been struck, and for the first time in his life, Harald Wayne wondered if he had fallen in love. He rejected the notion as the merest sentiment. Still, no other woman had ever shaken him so—no Norfolk milkmaid tumbled in the haystack, no sophisticated London debutante, no moody, fiery *señorita*. He ached to strip away the silk hiding the girl's limbs, her lap, her breasts, and to possess that small gorgeous body from twilight to dawn and around the clock till dawn again. He must bring her to his bed or die!

But he reminded himself, this white vision of loveliness *was* Finnian's daughter, and he wanted no trouble with the old man. Noticing two other men moving in the same direction, he stepped ahead of them, and in the genial tone that belonged to a titled country squire, he called, "I say, it *is* Blakiston?"

The viscount spotted Harald and lit up with delight. "Wayne, my dear chap!"

A handshake, a bow to Lady Anne, expressions of joy at renewing old acquaintance, a moment for looking long-faced when sympathy for Didrick's death was offered. And all the time the elf stood gazing up at him, shaking his foundations, making him believe it was love at last, after all. Never had he seen anything so exquisite, so fresh, so glorious, so delightful!

The introduction. The soft sunrise of an elfin smile appeared. "Lord Harald Wayne! Papa has mentioned you so often—although as Mr. Wayne, you understand."

"Quite."

"And he said if he hadn't had your financial advice down in San Tomás, he'd never have gotten that railroad built. And he told me how much he liked you and . . . He sent you to see me? I'm really overjoyed, Lord Harald."

The elf's voice outdid the tenderest note of a violin. Her tilted eyes had been made for sorcery, her lips to madden. Most marvelous of all, despite her delicious femininity, something about the sprite said "unawakened." Unquestionably virgin—but that was to be expected. She was more than virgin, this girl—she had remained innocent. Where had she been finished? Then he remembered. Miss Whittaker's, one of the best of the dame schools, famous for turning out girls who needed instruction from their husbands. Perfect, incredibly perfect!

Husbands. The word stayed with him. *Wife* came with it, and Harald Wayne caught his breath as he realized that the heir of Danemead must have a wife. Didrick before he had drowned had been scheduled for marriage to a large, dull Lowestoft heiress now left sniveling over her wedding gown. The earl, although still desperate with grief, had hinted that Harald after a year of mourning might well consider an alliance with the buxom Ethelreda. Ethelreda be damned! Catching his breath, Harald realized that the lovely creature smiling up at him was Finnian McGraw's only child, that he himself might soon become McGraw's business associate, and that if he married Meridel he would also be marrying the McGraw fortune.

Meridel, meanwhile, noticed that Lord Harald had shaved parts of his chin to form a point beneath his lower lip; he looked quite dashing. One of the girls at Miss Whittaker's had had a brother who wore his beard that way, and she had said she was sure only wicked men wore them that way because Bobby was such a rake.

But surely, thought Meridel, this engaging bachelor, whose age was no more than twice her own, could not be wicked. Not when her father had spoken so highly of him!

She exclaimed, "Why, you're the man who found ways to get more money out of Commodore Vanderbilt!"

"Yes," Harald said proudly, smiling at her. "Vanderbilt finally had to see that his original loan was not enough. Now he's running the San Tomás railroad, you know, and although I believe your father made plenty out of laying the rails, the Commodore will make five times as much by shipping cargo across the Isthmus instead of by going around Cape Horn."

Meridel's blue eyes flashed at him. "Now I remember even more about you, Lord Harald. Papa has said how lucky he was to have a British diplomat dealing with the *presidente* of San Tomás—a man named Acevedo, wasn't it?"

"Quite right." How could he bear to stand so close to the nymph without grabbing her? Gad, her perfume was unsettling.

"So Papa was able to bring in his shipments of rails without having to bribe everybody."

Bending close as though speaking in confidence, Harald murmured, "Only the captain of the port, who was Acevedo's brother-in-law."

Laughing with Harald and the Blakistons, who had overheard, Meridel felt quite the woman of the world. "And Papa has told me so much about the mountains and the jungles and the headhunting Indians! It's a wonder he got those rails laid at all. He said a canal would be more efficient than a railroad, but it would take thirty years to build such a canal, if it could be done at all."

Harald arched his brows, surprised. "Quite impossible, Miss Wayne. You'd know what he means if you had seen the country."

"I did want to go down there with Papa and take care of him. I so wanted to meet you and another man whom Papa could not have done without. It was someone named Daniel

15

Forrest . . . no, Forrester. Daniel Forrester. Wasn't he the construction engineer?''

"Yes," said Harald a bit shortly. Not that Forrester had ever stood in the way of his various schemes; but the man had such unsettling deep-set eyes, and when he looked at you, he seemed to look *through* you. He was a rock-solid American, six inches shorter than Harald but much broader in the shoulders. Harald had spoken to Forrester only rarely, and their talks had mostly centered on horses because the engineer had wanted to go into horse breeding somewhere in the American West. He had heard of the Danemead breeding stock.

"Papa said that Mr. Forrester had to fight bandits all the time he was building roadbed or hauling locomotives out of the mud, leaving him with permanently scarred hands.''

The fellow seemed to have taken hold of Meridel's imagination, Harald thought.

"What about you, Lord Harald?" she continued. "Did the bandits shoot at you too?''

Harald had to laugh at the girl's wide-open stare. The truth was that he had avoided danger whenever he could. The one exception was when a planter sent an armed guard to escort him through the jungle to a far-off coffee *finca*. There, as a broker, he was treated like a king, discoursing all the while on the virtues of English railroad stock before putting some up for sale.

Nevertheless, if Meridel wished to hear alarming tales of bullets whistling around him daily—he'd feed her eager curiosity. "But," he warned after colorfully describing a precarious existence, "I did return to Danemead in one piece. And now, Miss Meridel—" he paused, intimating he wanted permission to use her name, and she smiled devastatingly—"I trust you like the theater?''

"Oh, I do.''

"In that case," Harald said, turning to Lord Blakiston and Lady Anne, "I hope you will all come with me to the theater before the season runs out. In fact, why not tomorrow evening? There's an excellent production of *The Tempest* at the Theatre Royal.''

Meridel's face lit up and she cried, "I've read the play— and I'd love to see a performance.'' She almost had said,

"I've read the play at school," but that would have been gauche!

"Then allow me to make arrangements with your guardians."

Lord Harald obviously knew the rules of propriety inside and out, Meridel reflected. He was so charming and urbane! He seemed the kind of man Miss Whittaker had always said was the best kind—a man whom a girl could trust to take care of her.

Yes, as a marriageable young lady of fifteen minutes' standing, she had maintained a most satisfactory conversation with an eligible man. More than merely eligible! A baron, a future landed earl, all her mother had ever dreamed of for her. A man not too young and not too old, of striking appearance, elegant in dress and marvelously tall—for she, like other petite women, was drawn to tall men.

She could see her ex-classmates eyeing her. Jealous, every one! And yet she felt slightly uneasy. But she quickly ascribed it to inexperience. The "men" she had known so far had been callow youths from Oxford or Cambridge. She could forgive herself for being a bit at sea with a worldly, mature, and titled gentleman.

After they had agreed to go to the Theatre Royal tomorrow evening, Harald had leaned down and whispered, "I hardly dare take you to the theater without your guardians. But I'd much rather be with you alone."

Startled, she tapped him with her fan—a sophisticated gesture of mock reproach. Inwardly she felt greatly pleased that Harald Wayne knew how to be both proper *and* daring.

Was it possible that within a few minutes after her presentation at court, just when a girl should start thinking of marriage, she had already met her life partner?

And yet, why not? thought the girl who held life like a golden apple in her hand.

At the theater Meridel watched the stage, but occasionally, when she turned to smile at Lord Harald, she saw him watching *her*. She wore flounced taffeta that would have been too much for her if she had not stopped the seamstress at three flounces—Lady Anne wore ten—and if she had not known better than to wear a crinoline. Small as she was, a great wingspread all around her would have made her resemble a tea cozy. And, now that she had made her debut, she had moved her decolletage downward, though, being unmarried, she wore no jewels beyond tiny pearls in her ears. She saw the ardor in Harald's eyes, but she did not know how completely he approved of her as the future Lady Wayne. Or how much he wanted to drape the Wayne emeralds around that lovely throat, and ached to see the largest emerald blaze between the two swells of pearly flesh which he dared not touch . . . yet.

After the show, Harald took them to Perrine's for oysters. Never before had Meridel stayed up so late. Oh, how she liked Harald—liked him deeply! When the Blakistons, who she caught winking at each other, went to speak to acquaintances at another table, she chatted easily with Harald, her face close to his striking Viking features. She was telling him about her father's trouble with servants in the big house he had built on New York's fashionable Union Square, when he drew in a breath and asked, "Tell me, Meridel, do you think you could manage a household now . . . or at least a few months from now?"

Her heart fluttered. "Why, I—"

His voice very low, his face almost touching hers, Harald said, "It's difficult for any young matron who starts with a new house and a corps of untrained servants. But when a bride comes into a household that is already well staffed with faithful people—that is what I mean, Meridel." His hand touched hers and lingered a moment.

Properly she drew away her fingers. But she knew her face had flamed. This seemed close to a proposal! Confused, she thought she should pretend to misunderstand him. "Yes, one household can be easier to manage than another, but I daresay that servants can always be a trial. Like my own maid, for example. That Plunkett! I'm definitely going to lose her. She's heard that it rains only half as much in the United States as in England, and she's announced that she will stay in England because her complexion needs the moist air."

Harald frowned, drumming his fingers on the table. "You're returning to New York?"

"Yes, before the end of the year. I promised Papa."

"Then you'll stay in London for some time yet. So tomorrow let's go and see—"

"Oh, dear! Auntie and Uncle"—as she called the Blakistons—"are about to take me around Europe, and we'll be dreadfully busy shopping and packing from now on." She felt sorry and yet—relieved? She wasn't sure.

Lord Harald's mind rang out an oath: *bloody hell!* "When will you return?"

"Sometime in the fall," she said, lowering her eyes, not in modesty but because he showed his disappointment so clearly. When the Blakistons rejoined them he forced himself to be genial, becoming genuinely warm when he discovered that both he and the viscount had attended Exeter College at Oxford. They chatted of student days, Harald being careful not to mention that he had been sent down without graduating, accompanied by heavy gambling debts for his father to pay. As he talked, he schemed: he must capture Meridel before the end of the summer.

He turned the conversation to Danemead, with its historic house, its rolling pastures, its prosperous tenant farms. He neglected to mention that these days the tenants were more prosperous than the earl himself. He went on to talk of Norfolk and the watery wanderings of its famous broads and fens. He took note of Meridel's interest when he described a harbor that went dry at low tide, where vessels unloaded into wagons that came out onto the sand. He also spoke of his profitable experiences with securities, and of how the Age of Steam had multiplied the ways in which an enterprising man could get rich.

"Because, of course, we of the nobility no longer think it proper to go threadbare rather than soil our hands with trade."

"Quite! I myself have bought an interest in a Devon creamery," said Lord Hubert Blakiston. Meridel saw him glance at his wife, who catching his meaning, invited Harald to attend a bon voyage dinner at the Blakiston town house, a gracious Queen Anne mansion in Belgrave Square.

Harald had been hoping hard for just such an invitation. Accepting with pleasure, he calculated quickly and asked

Lady Anne if he might arrive early on the day of the dinner. His room at his club, he told her, was to be painted that day, worse luck. Of course they'd all be busy dressing and such, but he asked only to be allowed to sit alone in the library, quite out of the way, where he would happily immerse himself in Virgil or Catullus.

Lord Hubert had mentioned the pleasure he took in his second-floor library overlooking the square. And Meridel no doubt would have the best guest room, which could be nowhere except on the second floor.

On the day of the dinner Harald had no trouble with Plunkett, a saucy cockney with a full-busted figure. A pinch, a pat, a shining new silver crown flipped down her bosom left her giggling, protesting and wriggling until the coin dropped to the floor. "I'll stand guard, and don't you fret, milord. I'll run now and whisper in Miss Meridel's ear. Ooooh!" She giggled. "She's so young to be 'avin' a gentleman caller."

Arrayed in a simple tea gown of sprigged muslin, the radiant elf floated into the library and stood looking up at Harald with a silent question in those faerie-blue eyes. The apple-breasts rose and fell quickly.

"Meridel, I take a great liberty because we have so little time. And I owe you more time—time in which to assess me as a person, and not merely as your father's friend. But very soon you'll be far away. So let me say it now, begging forgiveness for my haste, begging forbearance if I offend you . . . but what am I to do? At least know I speak honestly when I tell you, Meridel, my dearest Meridel, that my heart is full of thoughts and dreams of you."

He saw her lovely lips part in surprise and something more. Perhaps uncertainty.

"And my heart is filled with pain, too," he went on, ignoring her reaction, "because if I see how sweet and desirable you are, other men must see it too. Beyond a doubt you'll meet many men on the Continent. I fear you'll return engaged to be married."

How would she reply? Would she dash his hopes by saying, "But I *want* to meet men!"

Instead, stuttering a little in her confusion, she said, "No, I

20

n-never would become betrothed without Papa's knowledge. And—and his approval, too.''

Delighted at her reply, Harald very nearly kissed her. She detected his impulse and pressed her hand defensively against her face. He moved a step backward. "I . . . Please trust me. But tell me, do you like England?''

"Yes . . .''

"Remember, if you are attracted by some German *Graf* or Italian count, please, dearest Meridel, remember how well you fit among us here in England, and that if you go to live on the Continent you will always be a foreigner and a stranger. And wherever you may travel, remember this . . .''

He paused so long and gazed at her so earnestly that she asked, her voice trembling: "What is it, Lord Harald?''

"Remember that your father and I expect to do business together. In America. I shall likely be speaking to him within the next few months, in New York. At that time I hope and pray to be able to speak to him on a matter far more important than mere business. To me, it's a matter as important as life itself.'' He extended his arms in a pleading gesture. "But when the time comes, I shall need your permission before I dare say a word.''

Did he mean. . . ? She could not speak.

"Yes, with your permission, when the time comes, I want to speak to your father about your possible future as Lady Wayne . . . as mistress of Danemead . . . as my honored and beloved lifetime partner . . . as my wife.''

And now she had been offered a golden apple from a golden bough. Every wish, every dream had come true—depending upon her father's consent, of course, though he would never object to her marrying a man he liked and trusted and admired.

Watching the play of emotion upon that heart-shaped face, Harald released his trump card. "My beloved, why wait? Instead of going to Europe, stay with me. We can rush across the Atlantic and have your father's consent in half a month's time.''

Her eyes widened. One word—the only word she need say—quivered upon her lips. Here stood a handsome, loving, titled man who wanted to marry and cherish her forever. Nobody said a girl *had* to flirt and search and wait and hope before marrying.

One word!

But what stopped her from saying that word? What frightened her?

Meridel had long ago rehearsed the little speech. She had learned it at Miss Whittaker's Academy and she recalled it now. "Sir, I am sensible of the honor of your offer, but I must consider a matter so important to a woman and to a man. If, in the future . . ."

But what came out was a strangled cry, "I need time!"

Well, thought Harald unhappily, he had tried. But a virgin is a virgin and an innocent is a virgin doubly wary, and he could only hope he had not spoiled his chances by rushing her. He begged her pardon humbly, dwelling secretly all the while on the thin layer of cloth that intervened between their bodies and the loveliness of her skin and the curves of her form. . . .

Plunkett popped her head into the room and whispered that someone was coming up the stairs.

"I must dress for dinner," said Meridel, fleeing.

Chapter Two

Paris turned out to be as delightful as everybody had said it would be, and was exceeded only by Versailles, which was simply dazzling. Returning to the heart of the City of Light, the ladies left the viscount resting at the hotel while they attended to a very important matter—a visit to Monsieur Worth's, whose salon was becoming a foremost center of fashion.

The couturier took three fittings to finish the canvas forms of Meridel's figure—all the while murmuring appreciative remarks—and Lady Anne's more opulent contours. With the canvas models, he could tailor any number of gowns for them—so long as Madame and Mademoiselle kept the same measurements. They could even order by mail if they also sent along sketches of fashion plates.

Could she order gowns from New York? Meridel asked. *Mais certainment*! the couturier had cried, throwing up his hands dramatically.

The women ordered gowns on the spot. Meridel's first choice was perhaps a bit old for her, but she could not resist a "society gown" of a fine periwinkle-blue brocade in a delicate flower pattern. A less skilled dressmaker might have gathered the full skirt, but Monsieur Worth draped it into unpressed pleats at the tiny waist, and the skirt billowed out smoothly. The neckline, although cut low, cunningly avoided baring the shoulders, and was edged with a soutache and ruching of pale-blue silk. Long silk tassels at the backs of the elbow-length sleeves called attention to the lovely arms of the wearer as she moved.

After Paris, Meridel and the Blakistons journeyed to the Riviera for the last of the season, thence to Rome, where Meridel wanted to linger and absorb the wonders of the ancient capital until they learned that a fever had struck the city and if they remained they would expose themselves. Instead they found themselves before long in Switzerland, which offered snow-capped mountains, but not—as Meridel had believed when very young—a one-toothed old woman who sat on top of a mountain biting the holes into Swiss cheese.

Steaming down the Rhine, they were enchanted by the fairy-tale castles that clung to the steep hills. They visited the cathedral in Cologne and eventually arrived in Berlin, a grim city bustling with men in uniform. Then they went on to Holland for a shipping excursion, and Meridel who had been sending her father souvenirs all along, sent him a pair of wooden shoes. They returned to France and the Bay of Biscay and after journeying northward through yellowing leaves and ripening vineyards, they finally embarked again on the wallowing ferry that crossed the channel. The last time, rain and mist and heavy waves had made nearly everyone sick—except for Meridel. Even during her rough Atlantic crossing years before, she had not felt a bit queasy. This time the sky stayed blue, the sun shone, and she spent most of the trip leaning on the sunward rail where she was joined frequently by one of the ferry's officers for a chat.

Alone for a moment, she heard Lady Anne say as she approached with her parasol, "Why, Meridel, you're not being posh!"

"What's posh, Auntie?"

"On a Channel ferry it is considered posh to stay on the port side going over and on the starboard side coming home. P-o-s-h. It always keeps you on the shady side."

"How veddy British to have so little sun anyway and then stay out of it," said Meridel, laughing. "Why, the fall sun in Europe is so low it wouldn't tan a baby."

"Perhaps so," smiled Lady Anne, who kept her parasol open even though she had to struggle with it in the wind. After a while she said softly, "Meridel, a penny for your thoughts."

"Well, Auntie, I've been thinking about Papa. He isn't entirely well, you know. And, oh yes, I've been wondering whether Mr. Buchanan will really run for president, as Papa says. And . . ." She decided to try to lighten the conversation. "And why ship's officers who come off duty smell of beer."

Lady Anne laughed, then murmured, "Tuppence for your real thoughts."

Meridel gave up. "Oh, Auntie, it's Harald. And Harald. How do I know if I love him? How do I know if I should say yes to him—because he's asked me already—or whether I should wait?"

"Well, to use an American expression, why not keep company with Harald for a while? It's so important to love the man you marry."

Meridel raised beseeching eyes. "Auntie, did my mother love my father? They never quarreled, but sometimes I thought, old Boston money and an Irish immigrant? How could they be comfortable together?"

"They weren't, entirely. But they did love each other. Imagine yourself as your mother. Old Boston money, yes, but it's all gone, and the family does with one servant, and the roof leaks, and all winter they huddle at a single fire, the men talking about family pride, the women straining their eyes while they remake their dresses. Dianthe told me in her letters that she envied girls who were allowed to work—even in the codfish plants—because at least they had friends. And then, somehow, she met an Irish immigrant who—I remember how excitedly she wrote about him—called himself Lucky McGraw—"

"He still does!"

"And who had made five thousand dollars in his first year in America, and who was always brimming over with energy and confidence and invention. He carried the model of a locomotive he always wanted to build, all the way from starving Ireland to America, you know."

Finnian McGraw's model, Meridel remembered, had contained a novel idea on how to improve the efficiency of a locomotive's driving wheels, and when he showed the train to a wealthy Philadelphia locomotive builder, his railroading career was born. Meanwhile he courted the beautiful, proud daughter of a Beacon Hill family, and struggled to make himself a gentleman acceptable to the bluebloods, with the daughter, Dianthe, showing him how. It was when her brother told him in her presence, 'A gentleman is *born* a gentleman,' that Dianthe took Finnian's arm and walked out of that house altogether. Only a sister, Penelope, came to the wedding and was forgiven for being a widow and thus independent-minded.

"So mama married Papa because he saved her from—from practically rotting away?"

"Much more than that, dear, much more. She loved him. Never ask why anyone loves anyone. No one knows the answer. And she loved Finnian all her life, though she did sometimes think—you're old enough to be told—that her brother might have been right. Finnian did try."

Meridel sighed. "He's still trying."

"—and I think I see why your mother always wanted you to marry an English nobleman, as a kind of apology to her family. Perhaps, too, she wanted to be known as the one who returned Blakiston blood to its English roots." They gazed silently at a red-sailed fishing smack till Lady Anne went on. "But your mother would have wanted you to love your husband, no matter whom he was."

"Papa's worked with Harald and likes him . . . but how does a girl *know?*"

"Keep company. Get to know him as a person. Now, Harald intimated at dinner last June that he might come up with an invitation from his father for all of us to enjoy the autumn fox hunting at Danemead. That would give you a good chance to—Ah, here comes Hubert with a wrap for me. That's one sign a man loves his wife. He doesn't leave everything to her maid."

They all watched the terns skim the water. Meridel remembered married "old girls" who had returned to visit Miss Whittaker's Academy. Some had bloomed. Some had withered. Some had glowed with inner joy. Some had sent off vague signals of despair and fright.

The clanking paddle wheels pushed the steamer across the water. Nearing England, they ran into heavy fog, which suddenly parted as they approached the white cliffs of Dover. When they landed, they had to wait while Lady Anne's maid Vesey, Lord Hubert's man Cason, and Meridel's ever-complaining Plunkett, untangled the party's luggage from that of the other passengers. In sudden, blazing sunshine they followed their trunks and portmanteaus to the train shed. And there in the steamy bustle, wearing a gleaming silk hat, a gray-piped frock coat and an elegant cravat held closed with a simple onyx square, stood Lord Harald Wayne. Freshly barbered, his beard clipped to perfection, he bade them good afternoon, and though he greeted them all, he had eyes only for Meridel.

"Are you betrothed?" he said, pulling her aside.

"No. Of course not."

He smiled. She saw passing women turn to look at him. But his gaze never left hers. He whispered for her ears alone, "You have become lovelier, an incredibly lovelier creature."

The Continental trip had taught Meridel a few responses. She said, "You are dazzled by the sunshine."

He laughed and kissed the air so that no one saw him do it but her. He took charge of the luggage, haughtily ordering the cartmen about in a lordly manner. As they bustled about, unquestioningly, he begged Meridel to forgive him while he drew her beaming guardians aside. They agreed quickly to something, and Harald swaggered as he returned.

"Lord and Lady Blakiston will come to Danemead in two weeks for the fox hunting. Of course you'll come with them?"

She remained silent.

"I hope you ride?"

"Ride?" said Blakiston, coming up from behind him. "At Wend I have seen her take fences that I rode around even when I was her age."

"It's settled, then. I'll meet you at the railway station—it's the last one on the line—two weeks from today."

"I didn't say I would go!" Meridel cried.

Lady Anne said, "We can hardly leave you alone in London, my dear. But if you'd rather we all went to Bath to take the waters . . ."

"A pity," said Harald in his cultured drawl. "There's been no sort of festivity at Danemead since my poor brother Didrick's death, and a bit of gladness would benefit my father. I saw to it that the hounds were taken cubbing during the summer, so they'll now be hot on the scent. And the county gentry are looking forward to having guests from Devon."

He waited, his eyes gazing at her intently.

Meridel looked away and reflected how a girl could go visiting in the country without committing herself. And yet . . . and yet—

Well, she would see more of Harald—but keep him at his distance at the same time.

"I really would enjoy a good gallop after the hounds," she admitted, and Harald grew charming again.

Two weeks later he met them with the Danemead tally ho at a little country station piled high with grain sacks. The station smelled of fresh paint. A mile beyond, gangs of navvies could be seen laying down tracks which would stretch all the way to the Channel.

While Harald again saw briskly to the luggage—the stewards scurrying about at his command—and while his coachman directed Meridel's three servants to their seats in the tallyho, Meridel wandered toward the front of the train. The coal-smudged driver, who sat in the open air, showed his astonishment when she identified his engine's wheel splashers and the beehive firebox of burnished copper. She told him that if her father were there he would surely pay a pound for the privilege of driving the huffer-puffer back to the next station. She further amazed the man by telling him that in Amer-

ica railways were called railroads and that American locomotives wore cowcatchers to push livestock off the tracks.

Turning to see what had made the man look alarmed, Meridel found that Harald had come up behind her, frowning. "If
you don't mind, Meridel," he said stiffly.

Contrite, she took his arm. She should have realized that at
a station where every woman bobbed and every man raised
his hat to the heir of Danemead, one did not chat with a mere
engine driver.

Everyone had told her that Norfolk was flat, but Harald's
part of the ancient kingdom of East Anglia turned out to be
pleasantly hilly and once they left the little village of mill
smokestacks behind, Meridel found the country autumn-
tinged and peaceful. Danemead lay at the end of a mile of
curving drive that cut through a river and horse-grazing meadows. The house loomed before them suddenly, seeming to
have sprouted from its orangerie and swan pond, gazebos and
gardens naturally. Peaked turrets clung to the stone walls, and
a crumbling tower, where a thousand years before Saxons had
shot arrows at invading Danes, stood off to one side. A low
battlement, peaceful now in its smothering of ivy, had been
connected to the house with an ell that bore a handsome balustrade. Harald explained that the eighteenth-century balustrade led out from French windows in the master chamber,
making a private walk for the lord and lady.

A tall, sharp featured old man stood on the barbican and
waved them on with a brisk gesture, part of an ancient tradition that if followed to the letter, called for the lord of
Danemead to either identify his guests or blow a ram's horn
calling his men to battle stations.

Catching a quick glimpse of the earl, Meridel noted he
might once have been as blond as his son; he now looked
gray but sturdy, his ruddy countryman's face still showing the
ravages of some secret sorrow. "Come ye in peace?" he
asked jovially enough when he joined his guests in the mar-
ble-floored reception hall. Nevertheless, Meridel thought he
acknowledged her more correctly than warmly, and he certainly gave her a sharp glance beneath the thick hedges of his
white brows.

As they dined from mellow old silver dishes in a huge, vaulted hall with a minstrel gallery at one end and suits of armor at the other, the earl informed them that warm weather would delay the hunt a few days. He spoke of his work as a magistrate, and his duty to attend the quarterly assizes, where serious cases were judged. Landed peers such as himself received no pay, but this duty to the Crown was balanced by being allowed to exercise some influence in politics.

Later the earl escorted them through a portrait gallery of ancestors wearing everything from Plantagenet brocaded robes, to Elizabethan lace collars, to full-blown Restoration wigs, and he used the portraits as capsules of history to lecture them on the ages of English history. Before long, everyone weary, the earl apologized for his "longwindedness" and the need to discuss a most pressing estate matter with his son, Harald, in private before rejoining his guests.

"Aha!" whispered Lord Hubert to Meridel. "Harald still has to learn that running an estate brings responsibilities with it."

They drifted into the music room, where the Blakistons sat down to cribbage while Meridel leafed through sheet music she found in the piano. Abruptly the quiet room was invaded by angry quarreling that came from behind a paneled wall.

"No, Harald, you must go, and first thing tomorrow."

"But our guests, Father!" Harald said sharply.

"I can only beg their forbearance. You *must* go."

Harald's voice rose in frustration. "Why the devil did you have to buy that stinking swamp?"

"I've already told you I thought it could be diked and drained at low cost, like the rest of the fenland."

"Someone pulled the wool over your eyes."

"Perhaps so. But while you were idling in London I had an offer. You will *kindly* meet the man on the land and talk price. I say you must, Harald!"

Appalled and embarrassed, Meridel and the Blakistons could only gaze at each other.

Harald growled, "Oh, I'll go, I'll go. And what with unwinding your mistakes which are making the estate insolvent, I daresay I shall have no time for—"

Meridel, crashing a chord, began playing Chopin's "Pol-

30

onaise in A'' loudly. Lady Anne nodded her approval of the noise.

So Danemead's finances were not in good order. But what bothered Meridel was Harald's display of bad temper. Though he did have reason to be annoyed—sent away by his father on business when they were entertaining guests! Especially herself, whom the earl surely realized her son had an interest in—which might be why Harald had been sent away.

Meridel shuddered.

Despite herself she was beginning to suspect the old earl's motives.

At breakfast the following day the earl said that Harald had rushed off at dawn and might be away for two days. He himself took his guests out in a high-wheeled dogcart and showed them the ruins of a house built by the Romans, who had been present in Britain hundreds of years before they were recalled by troubles at home. Meridel exclaimed with delight over a broken mosaic that still spelled CAVE CANEM—Beware of the Dog. They found the open atrium, the *cubiculai* for sleeping, the *cellae* for storage.

Later that day, Meridel had Plunkett help her into her riding habit. Jennings, the head breeder, found her a suitable mare and took her to see Bluebonnet, the estate's Cleveland Bay stallion.

"Deep-chested and barrel-bodied, ye can see, miss. Not a true saddle horse, the Cleveland Bay ain't, but good for pulling light freight or for coaching on rough roads."

"You keep him well, Jennings." The snorting, prancing stallion's coat gleamed in the sun.

"'E's worth a bit, Bluebonnet is, miss. For stud mostly, beggin' your pardon. 'E was sired by Pilot Lad, with three crosses to Sultana and a cross to Silver Maid, which gives him powerful blood, miss."

Quite incomprehensible to her, but she knew bloodlines were dear to the breeder's heart. "What's that old house showing through the trees, Jennings?"

"It's the Dower House, miss, or is now, but it was the manor house once. Built in King 'enry the Eighth's time.

Countess Grizel lives there, miss—the dowager countess, you know. The earl's mother.''

"And Lord Harald's grandmother?''

"Righto, miss.''

"I'll drop in and get acquainted.''

"Er . . . p'raps not, miss. 'Scuse my sayin' so, but you'll meet the dowager when she's ready to meet you, miss.''

The old lady must be quite an autocrat.

But Meridel did not have long to wait. As she cantered past the house, noting its ancient exposed timbers, high gables and extensive gardens, a middle-aged domestic in a spotless white apron rushed out and hurried toward her.

"Miss! I'm Persis, Miss Countess seen you and says to come in,'' the woman said in a frenzy.

"Very well, Persis.'' Meridel realized she'd been summoned to the throne!

An elderly groom helped Meridel dismount and waited while she gathered her voluminous skirts and draped them over her left arm. Entering the front garden, Meridel saw no shabbiness as in the present manor-house garden, where a one-armed cherub gazed into a pond full of algae or a satyr from whose mouth water had ceased flowing. At the front door, an ancient butler bowed langorously to her, then escorted her through low-ceilinged rooms arranged with heavy oaken settles and chairs. She glimpsed a spacious kitchen lined with racks of battered pewter dishes and tankards, and towered over by a cavernous fireplace that rose to the exposed beams.

At last, in a long sunroom, she faced an unsmiling woman whose wizened face was framed in flowing ribbons, the style of another age. Withered though she was, she filled her wheelchair with the furbelows of her old-fashioned morning gown.

"You curtsy nicely,'' cried a sharp voice, somewhat slurred. "And I've heard about your curtsy to the queen. Why haven't you been carried off by one of the young Lochinvars who lusted after you that night?''

Odd language from a lady! "Perhaps it was because we went to the Continent so soon after, Countess.''

"Hmmm. You don't seem to doubt what it would have

happened otherwise, eh? Well, you don't chatter, anyway. And you do know how to walk in a riding habit. Any goose of a girl can look good on a horse, but when they're off the horse they look as though they're wearing a draper's shop. Not you. I also hear your mother was a Blakiston. The blood shows, despite the unfortunate American blood mixed in it.''

Unruffled, Meridel smiled as she remembered the phrase "powerful blood.''

"Poised little thing, aren't you? Hmmmmm. And so, rich American railway builders send their daughters to London to marry titles.''

"At least one of them has done so, I daresay,'' Meridel said coolly, lifting her chin.

The dowager glared, drawing back to favor her farsighted eyes. A reluctant smile appeared on the withered lips and spread through the maze of wrinkles. "I have never before been so definitely put in my place. Perhaps it's time. Do sit, child.''

She rang a bell attached to her wheelchair. Not waiting to see if a servant had appeared—although a maid had fairly raced into the room—the dowager snapped, "Tea. Extra cookies for Miss Meridel. Now tell me, how has my son been treating you?''

It took a moment to realize the dowager was speaking of the old earl. "Very well, thank you,'' Meridel said.

The ancient woman startled her with a crackling laugh. "Bah! I know he isn't having the servants snub you, nor is he keeping you out in the rain. But I also know he isn't warming up to you at all. Oh yes, little American, my son's servants tell my servants, and my servants tell me everything. Why do you suppose my son has sent my grandson to see about selling that fenland? To keep him away from you! He'd like Harald to marry Ethelreda. You don't seem to know whom Ethelreda is. She was Didrick's fiancée.''

"Oh . . .'' Meridel cried, her suspicions confirmed.

"And titled, you see, which you are not, even though you're prettier and smarter. But I've a good notion that Harald wants to get *you* into bed and draw the curtains. Oh pooh, don't look so shocked!'' Again the dowager cackled her bird cry of a laugh. "Nor would I object, for I'd much rather have you on the estate than Ethelreda. Yes. You and I would get along." Lady Grizel paused, seeming to wrestle with an unpleasant thought. "But if you're considering marrying Harald—or else why did your guardians bring you here?—I don't see why you shouldn't know as much as the servants do about certain family matters."

"Really, Countess, I'm not one of the family—"

"Yet. Besides, *I* am head of this family, and I can tell you whatever I please. Do you understand the law of primogeniture? All of an estate's land and buildings and cattle and such go to the elder son?"

"Yes," Meridel said, once again thanking her lessons at Miss Whittaker's.

"Then you know that such property is called entailed property. But my son also owns a good deal of property not entailed, outside the estate. That property earns good income. It's all that keep Danemead going. And he can leave it all to anyone he pleases—for example, to his daughter Claudia."

"I didn't know—"

"She married a Northumberland baron and seldom visits. Doesn't like Harald, anyway. My point is that Claudia doesn't need the coal mines, the interest in the local cotton mill, and other such nonsense. But Harald does. And if he keeps on quarreling with his father, he may find he has inherited a big house, plenty of land and horses, and little else. Harald will be left very short of cash. You may have noticed that my grandson is exceedingly fond of money."

"Why, no, he never—"

"He's trying to impress you. Wait till you know him better. He is also very fond of his new title." Something that might have been the shadow of bitterness crossed the dowager's face.

Tea came rolling up on a table furnished with beautiful old Spode. "You may pour, child. Two lumps and no lemon, please. I had a stroke and it still bothers by arms, while my lower limbs"—she would not say legs—"have become useless. A second stroke will finish me."

"Oh, I trust that—"

"You don't know what to say and neither does anybody else, so say nothing," she snapped, eyeing Meridel as she prepared the tea. "You pour well, child. You are more a lady than many a lady to the manor born. Are you seriously thinking of marrying Harald?"

This came so suddenly that Meridel almost spilled tea on a Maltese cat that had come prowling around her chair. "I don't know yet, Countess."

The old woman brooded over her cup. "Well, he's handsome enough, and competent enough when he wants to be, and he always does find some way to bring in money. Only . . ." She fell silent, before adding, "I only mean I preferred Didrick, as everybody knows. My poor Didrick. You know what happened?"

"Only that it was a boating accident."

"Yes, yes. They were fishing in our little river, Didrick and Harald. They'd fished there a hundred times before. But this time the boat turned over. Harald could swim. Didrick never learned how, and he sank and he was . . . gone, gone. Ah, me." Her eyes glazed over, and her voice grew distant. "Harald dove so often to rescue Didrick that he almost drowned, too. Someone found poor Didrick's body downstream. Ah, I remember, I remember how Didrick promised to bring me his babies when they came—my great-grandchildren—and put them in my lap. Ah, to see a grandson dead." Meridel kept silent as the dowager stared at nothing. "But so it goes. My only quarrel with poor Didrick was that he looked down his nose at Harald. Not that Harald didn't cause a good deal of trouble when he was young. When he grew older, too—the kind of trouble one has to expect from males past sixteen, I suppose." The *grande dame* seemed to notice Meridel again. "You don't seem to know what I mean."

"No, I—"

She put down her tea. "Child, it's simply that men are driven by their natures to sow wild oats. Virtue in a man fits more loosely than virtue in a woman. But they don't teach you that in dame school."

"No, ma'am." Meridel had heard more than once that men sow wild oats, but she never had found out what that meant. The girls had only whispered their giggling guesses.

The dowager took another sip. "I hope you are not as

poorly informed as I was when I went to my marriage bed. Fortunately I had a kind husband. Still, Harald is no fool. If you marry him he'll treat you like the prize you are. I hope. What a dear child you are! I like you. I like you very much. But . . ." Again that hesitation and reserve. "There are other fish in the sea, dear child, and you have the best of bait— your beauty and your poise and your intelligence and your excellent figure. I also hear that your father has money. I don't mean you *shouldn't* marry Harald. I mean . . . I mean that marriage is to be taken very seriously, which is all I am trying to tell you."

She handed back her cup, not caring that her spoon clattered to the floor. "You may go now. I have enjoyed your visit, and if I had not I would say so. I should like you to visit me again." She rang her bell and said, without looking to see if anyone heard her, "Tell Shallcross he is to bring Miss McGraw's horse around to the mounting block, and be quick about it."

"Good afternoon, Lady Gray." Meridel rose, both puzzled and amused at the decisiveness of her dismissal. "It was a delicious tea."

"I will employ no servant who cannot brew good tea," said the old woman sternly. But fondness for Meridel showed on her worn and weary face.

Later that morning Harald returned. Everyone in the manor house heard him with his father, their tempers blazing. "You sent me on a wild-goose chase! That man has lost his interest in your worthless swamp."

"I had no way of knowing—"

"Kindly don't bother me with your mistakes again!"

As the angry words clanged through the house, servants averted their faces and scurried from the vicinity of the earl's office to pursue chores, whether their tasks were urgent or not.

At dinner, Harald and his father refused to speak to each other. Later, however, Harald recovered his poise and sat at Meridel's side, turning pages of music for her while she played the rosewood piano. She thought she should not judge him harshly. She came from an Irish household and knew how tempers could flare. But an unbidden fear that this was

36

no small spat between loving relations, surfaced to mind, and before she could upset herself, she buried the uncomfortable feeling away.

Harald spoke tenderly to her, telling her how much he had missed her. Arranging pages of music, he contrived to touch her hand. "Don't worry about how the guv'nor and I shout at each other," he whispered. "Merely a family thing."

Later, while the gentlemen had brandy and the ladies had lemon-squeeze, he said affably, "I've had a note from that chap Forrester. You recall, Meridel? Your father's construction engineer in San Tomás."

"Yes indeed."

"He's in England on business, and he's coming to Danemead in a day or two for breeding stock. I believe he's going ahead with his plans for a ranch in your West."

"Is he a gentleman?" asked the earl.

"Near enough. We shan't have to feed him in the kitchen."

Going up the stairs with Meridel, Lady Anne whispered, "See, Harald didn't stay angry at his father very long. Anyway, don't you fret about the male temper. Men simply like to roar sometimes. Even my own darling does it on occasion."

"Quite so," said Lord Hubert, obviously making light of the matter. "A man is like a steam engine. Every now and then he has to pop the safety valve and roar away." But even though Meridel appreciated her relations' efforts to excuse Harald's behavior, she still felt a strange discomfort.

Chapter Three

Wishing to have some time alone to think, Meridel rose early the next day, determined to explore the far reaches of the estate and the neighboring area. She found the little river, followed its border of thick bushes beyond the estate, and soon saw the tall mill chimneys that smudged the sky with their smoke. She turned her mount back along an old pack road, long ago cut through the forest for horses and now barely wide enough for a wagon's passage.

She had a lot on her mind as she rode, wondering what love was. If a woman loved a man did she accept him with all his faults, calling him only human?

She imagined sleeping at Harald's side in the great master chamber opening out onto the balustrade that allowed the lord and lady of the manor to stroll in private and to view their dew-spangled lawns. Meridel knew that sleeping at a man's side led to something more, and whatever it was, that something could only happen with a husband. Some of Miss Whittaker's undergraduates had heard that those moments when a man and woman were alone together brought love into a marriage, even if love hadn't been there to start with. But Meridel also remembered the "old girls" with tight lips who never mentioned their husbands, and it seemed to her that there must be marriage in which love never came.

Lacking guidance from its rider, the mare ambled along. Meridel became aware of men building a new section of the railroad through the woods. She gave the construction scant attention. On a straight stretch of road she wanted speed and urged the mare into a gallop.

Where the woods thinned and the navvies worked on a high embankment, a different kind of motion caught her eye. A plank runway had been set down on the embankment's steep side. A muscular fellow at the bottom of the runway had hooked a rope to his heavy barrow-load of earth and stone, and was using a pulley to pull the barrow up the embankment at a fast clip. Meridel's eyes caught sight of the young man's struggle, and because she watched as she galloped by, she kept her eyes from the road an instant too long. She felt her mount surge into a sharp turn. Before she could slow down, an uncovered chaise—stopped and blocking the road while its driver also stared at the navvy—seemed to leap at her from nowhere.

Frantically Meridel reined leftward, hoping to miss the chaise by inches and to stop on a small, clear space at the side of the road. But mud lay beneath a drift of fallen leaves. The mare skidded and staggered as Meridel gave it a loose rein to help it save itself. Sliding with braced forelegs, it stopped so short that Meridel was flung sidewise over its head. She fell flat on her back, gasping.

"You're plumb lucky you landed in mud."

Breathless, Meridel stared up at a man—Harald's age—whose wavy brown sideburns stopped at a strong jaw and a smooth-shaven chin. She did not know how she knew he was an American. Later she realized she had heard it in his speech.

He crouched alongside her. "Better hold still while I see if anything's broken."

He felt her limbs. She slapped away his hand. "Don't you dare touch me!"

"We-ell, Miss," he said, unperturbed and slightly drawling, "at least go and move your near leg. Move your off leg. Move your arms. Bend your knees. Elbows. Wrists. If everything works, chances are you're okay." The stranger used a wearily patient voice, as though he were dealing with a child.

Nevertheless she did test her joints—and realized with a gasp that her skirts had flown up above her boot tops. Frantically making herself modest, she cried, "You could have killed me! Stopping in the middle of the road!"

"Seems to me that a gal doesn't go galloping around blind turns if she wants to grow up to be a wife and mother." At her glare, he added: "Judging by your age, you're neither yet."

"What do *you* know about my age, sir?"

"Nuhthin'," he said, exaggerating the drawl that told her he came from the mid-South. "Nuhthin' 'cept what my eyes tell me—that if you were one day younger you'd be young enough to spank, but as it is, maybe I'd better not. Anyway"—he chuckled as she sputtered her indignation—"it's hard to get real peeved at such a pretty face."

He had strange, dark blue eyes, nearly black. Wrinkles at their corners and the cordovan tan of his cheeks revealed that he had spent much time in the sun. He had a wide but sensitive mouth.

"How dare you block a public road!"

"I s'pose I dared think that people riding around a bend will look where they are going."

"I *did* look where I was going." But a strength of gaze in those searching eyes made her remember she had been looking at the navvy and his barrow. She muttered, "I mean, I used reasonable care."

"We-ell, I'll own I *might* have stopped before the bend if I had thought of it." He jerked his chin toward the raw-earth railroad embankment. "Haven't seen that technique with the horse and the runway used in the U.S.A. So if it makes you feel better, I'll accept forty-nine percent of the blame. Now tell me where you live."

"Tell you where I live?" she cried. "Do you think I'm going to invite you for tea?"

"No. But in case you faint, I ought to know where to bring you."

"If I haven't fainted by now—"

"After a shock, there's often a delayed reaction."

She rose shakily. "Well, I am not going to faint, sir."

"I believe it. Now turn around."

"*What?*"

"I said I wouldn't spank you. Well, never mind." He walked around her. "Not much mud on you. The leaves kept most of it off."

He picked her hat up from the ground and, doffing his own stovepipe, held the two hats together and grinned, causing her to snatch hers from his hand. He chuckled. "Your hair needs fixing first. I've a shaving mirror."

"I don't need a mirror."

Nevertheless he walked to the chaise with a swinging stride, displaying broad shoulders and a square-cut figure, thick but not fat, very solid. She thought him not as tall as she liked men to be. When he unstrapped a huge valise of heavy leather she saw it had been branded "D. F." He found a small mirror.

"I said, sir, that I don't need your mirror."

"And I'd believe you except that the entire history of women tells me otherwise."

"You are most insulting."

"Born that way, I s'ppose."

She glared. He grinned. She put her hands behind her back, but when she realized it was a childish gesture she relaxed and extended a palm toward the looking glass.

The stranger found one of her fine tortoise-shell hairpins in the leaves and wiped it with his kerchief before giving it to her. Despite her annoyance he watched her rearrange her snood, hat, and veil.

When she slapped the mirror back into his hand, he asked, "No thank-you? Then let me thank you for this experience. A sixteen-and-three-quarters-year-old girl acting the haughty dame. Never saw the like of it."

He wore a checked traveling jacket and had opened his waistcoat and collar. It occurred to Meridel that Harald never would have done that; Harald would rather have been correct than comfortable in the sun and the dust. Oddly, she also realized that Harald never grinned. He smiled; but that was different. The stranger grinned at her broadly and frankly, as though waiting for her to say something.

But of course! How could he have known her age? He grinned all the more when he saw her bite her lip rather than ask him.

"You're not going to ask how I know? Rather stand there high as a rabbit and freeze me? Well! Stop chilling me, I don't have my buffalo robe. But now I do recollect that your mother came from high-toned Boston folk. Nobody higher-toned than a high-toned Boston lady— 'cept her daughter maybe."

"How did you—" Meridel stopped herself.

"Not howdy? Just how?" he chided, as if he'd never seen or heard anyone so humorous as she. "Howdy, Miss Meridel McGraw who's staying at Danemead up the pike."

She stamped her foot and cried, "You came through the village and heard all the gossip!"

He laughed. "Such as—when you were six years old and lived in New York City, you had a pony named Buttercup?"

She could only stare.

"Or that you could read when you were four, and tried to help your father with his spelling? Or that you used to sneak up behind your governess and pull out the bow of her dress and run away?"

"Oh! How. . . !"

"You haven't grown much taller since, you know." He eyed her up and down. "Although you've grown more . . . decorative."

Suddenly Meridel understood. The initials "D. F." on the valise flashed into her mind. "You're Mr. Forrester!"

"Dan Forrester, at your service."

"And down in San Tomás my father told you. . . !"

"More than I ever wanted to know about his cute daughter. Your father told me you'd be at Danemead when I saw him recently as I passed through New York."

"Is he—"

"Middling fair and full of big plans. Now, whyn't you get into the chaise with me and we'll lead your horse back, seeing's we're both going to the same place."

"I'll find my own way back, thank you," she said, straightening her hat again.

"We-ell, do as you please, Miss Hoity-Toity. But remember, you have mud on your back. But you can always say some fool galloped past in a muddy spot and spattered you."

"Or I could say I had a most unfortunate encounter with Mr. Forrester who should not be allowed to travel the public roads. But since we'll both be guests in the same house, I'll say nothing."

He smiled. "That's very grown-up of you, Meridel,"

He thought her a child! "I don't like you, Mr. Forrester!"

"More's the pity, because I like you fine. I like the way you can take a tumble and jump right up with fire in your eye. I don't like the way you endanger other innocent travelers but I do admire your presence of mind in giving your horse its head. And the way you kept hold of your reins even when you went flying. That took real horsemanship. I'm going to stay at Danemead a few days, looking to buy horses, so we're bound to meet again. If I took fifty percent of the blame for your fall, would you talk purty to me?"

She turned without a word and tried to get up onto her mare. But she never had been able to mount anything but a pony without help. Dan Forrester effortlessly appeared beside her, his clasped hands held open to give her a boost up. When she decided to accept his offer, he tossed her up onto the saddle as though she were as light as a feather. For an instant she felt oddly warm toward him. But he infuriated her by obviously enjoying the flash of petticoats as she arranged her skirts.

He asked, "How about riding ahead and showing me the way to Danemead?"

"Straight ahead. Look for big beeches on either side of an iron gate. You'll see unicorns on the gate." She turned her mare the other way, and though she felt Dan Forrester watching her, she let him see no other feature but her disapproving back.

She gave him plenty of time to reach Danemead. When at last she returned she saw the chaise in the coach shed. Meridel slipped in through the kitchen door and up the back stairs to her room. She warned Plunkett not to say a word about the mud on her riding habit, simply that Miss Meridel felt fatigued from her ride and wished a luncheon tray sent up. She'd rather eat alone than face Dan Forrester, who had so deeply, oddly annoyed and disturbed her.

Pacing her room so rapidly that her French cambric peignoir lifted revealingly and floated after her, she recalled that her father held the man in high regard. She *should* speak to him, if only for her father. However, she would certainly not have to be very warm.

At dinnertime, bathed and rested and redressed, Meridel came downstairs. She found the family in the green drawing room where the walls were covered with green Spitalfields silk, a bit shabby but still handsome.

Harald stood at the cigar chest, rolling one cigar after another in his fingers to test for the proper crinkle. Dan Forrester, like the other men attired in evening dress, made a bulky presence in a leather wing chair. She heard him tell Hubert Blakiston, who listened with interest, "Yes, McGraw needs help from Jefferson Davis, and I think he'll get it."

"Eh?" said Blakiston, turning his head to favor his good ear. "But how is Mr. Davis involved with a railroad across your state—no, *territory*—called Kansas? Is Davis not your secretary of war?"

"Yes. But you see, Lord Hubert, Jeff Davis also has great influence with President Pierce, and he has many friends in Congress, too. The government has to make the land available for railroad building, and so—"

"Ah! I see. Politics is politics everywhere, is it not? But your Mr. Davis—is it true that he imported camels to carry army freight in remote areas?"

"He did, but it's too soon to tell if they'll be a success. I hear they're harder to handle than mules, even though any Kansas muleskinner will tell you there's no animal more ornery than mules."

Lady Anne looked up brightly from a book of pressed flowers. "Imagine, camels in the United States! Oh, here comes Meridel."

The gentlemen rose. Meridel tensed as Dan strode toward her, but observed at the same time that his span of shoulder made him magnificent in an evening suit.

He winked. She had to return the wink because it meant they must pretend never to have met before. Lord Hubert made the introduction. Meridel murmured distantly, "Mr. Forrester? I do think my father once mentioned your name."

"And I *think* he mentioned yours to me. Yes, he said he enjoyed having letters from you when he and I were in San Tomás." His dark eyes twinkled. "Of course you were only a child . . . at the time."

She glared, noticing also that Harald glared—straight at Dan's back.

"Well!" said Lord Hubert. "You two Americans must have a good deal to say to each other."

Trapped, Meridel remained with Dan. But as her guardian walked away she lifted her chin and observed, "I quite talked myself out the first time we met."

"But that was horse talk, of a sort, and now you are dressed for a different type of conversation." His gaze roved to her décolletage, which the French couturier had cleverly swathed in satin. "Or at least so I assume, because I can see so much more of you than I saw this morning. I guess you don't have any bruises from your fall, or they would show."

"You are being improper, Mr. Forrester," she snapped.

"*I* did not design your dress. Do women wish to be seen but not noticed? Or noticed but not seen? By the way, did anyone notice the mud on your back?"

Keeping herself from glancing down to see if her gown had slipped, Meridel snapped again, "Only my maid."

"If you want to see real mud, come to Kansas Territory."

"Seeing mud is hardly a reason to go anywhere."

He grinned. "Touché. But if you ever do go, you'll like the land's broadness—unlike England, where everything's squeezed together. The eastern part is full of untouched forest that swarms with game. And the great mountains in what the Spanish call Colorado are surrounded by ruddy land. I wish you could see them, snow-capped all year, scraping the sky.

And in between—the prairies. There is nothing on earth like the American prairie. In the spring it's an enormous painter's palette, filled with the colors of tiny flowers. And a different color in the summer and again later in the year, and then—''

"Have you perhaps been appointed poet laureate of Kansas?"

In triumph she watched the barb hit hard. But again he grinned above his spotless white stock and evening ruffles. "In return for that remark, I am going to tell you a story about yourself when you were three years old."

She said mockingly, "When I must have been at my darlingest."

"I'll leave that part up to you. Anyway, your governness had been supervising your bath. You heard your father come home and you jumped out of the tub, naked as a jaybird, and ran downstairs to meet him. He told me you looked like a pink tadpole."

Meridel felt herself flush. "That is hardly a—an interesting story to repeat."

"Perhaps not. I don't suppose these days it's likely to happen. A shame. You'd certainly make an eyeful."

She gasped. But whatever she might have retorted was lost when Vane, the Danemead butler, announced that dinner was served.

She saw Harald start toward her, then saw the earl call him back. A thundercloud took shape on Harald's face when the earl asked Mr. Forrester to escort Miss Meridel in to dinner. She had no choice but to take Dan's very solid arm and walk with him into the great hall lined with suits of armor.

He turned out to have good stories to tell about the western frontier. They were rough, strange stories for an English country house, and yet the man who told them had been raised as a gentleman, quite at home with the array of napery, crystal, and silver. Meridel never had seen or imagined such a man—battered but polished, muscular but well-groomed.

The baron of lamb had scarcely been served, piping hot, on its nest of asparagus and tiny sausages, and the Château Ausone had hardly been tasted and approved, when the butler hastened in and whispered to the earl.

The Lord of Danemead seemed displeased. "Ahem!" he

said to the table at large. "The dowager countess is doing us the honor of joining us for dinner."

Lady Grizel appeared, being pushed by a steward in her wheelchair; she looked like a vision of the 1830s grand style. Ordering Forrester to move over, she took up space between him and Meridel.

"Americans are so refreshing that I couldn't resist seeing two of them at once," she cried to the assemblage. Noticing that no wine goblets had been set at her hastily arranged place, she began shrieking orders, making the servants scurry about her. When the earl demurred that her doctor had told her to drink nothing stronger than tea, she scoffed huskily and would not be still until a goblet had arrived. Before long the wine began showing its effect on her.

She said to Meridel, "Even with your complexion, don't be afraid of a little rice powder, my dear." And to Forrester, "Bother the introductions. I know you're Daniel Forrester and you know I'm Lady Grizel and that in the days of George the Fourth I ran this house. I hear you have a piece of land in the American wilderness. Tell me about your estate. You must have a brave wife. Why did you leave her home?"

Dan stifled a grin. "Lady Grizel, out there we call sixty thousand acres a ranch. And I don't have a wife. I guess I worry more about my crops and herds that I do about home cooking."

"Is that all a wife is good for in America? Home cooking?" Lady Grizel cackled wickedly. The earl frowned, and Lord Hubert cleared his throat several times.

Lady Anne, who had gone a bit wide-eyed, offered: "You must have left a good steward in charge of your ranch, Mr. Forrester, before you took such an extended trip."

"Well, I've a mighty good *foreman* and a good crew all around. All I need is a few very good horses, and I hope I'll find them here. I don't mean your racers," he said to Harald, who had scowled at his plate during most of the meal. "I know they have Arab blood going back to the Byerley Turk, but it's the Cleveland Bays that interest me. I want to breed them for the Kansas climate."

"Turk?" questioned the dowager.

Harald grunted. "The Byerley Turk was a famous Arab stallion that was brought to England long ago."

"Turk!" Lady Grizel cried, spilling wine. "Isn't it a shame that England's ally in the Crimean War is Turkey? Why couldn't we have been allied with a Christian nation like Russia?"

"Because we've been fighting Russia, Mother," the earl said.

"Yes, yes, I know. I read the *Times,* young man. But your Bluebonnet must have Arab in him too, because he certainly has a harem. You men ought to be envious of Bluebonnet. One stallion and a dozen mares!" Continuing to sip wine, the old woman obviously relished her wicked talk. Meridel, sensitive to impropriety, inspected the ceiling. The dowager said suddenly to Dan, "Just like the Mormons you have in Kansas."

"Uh, the Mormons have all gone west to Utah, ma'am." He explained that Kansas so far was nothing more than a road for people moving westward—Mormons and Oregoners and forty-niners. But the territory was becoming settled, at least in the eastern part. "You'd be surprised at the number of settlers who come up the Missouri."

Lady Grizel hiccuped and said indignantly, "The Missouri isn't a river. It's a Slave State."

"It's a river and a Slave State both, Countess. The Big Muddy—that's its local name—runs between parts of the state of Missouri and the territory of Kansas."

The dowager shook a finger. "Don't you tell me that Kansas isn't full of slaves too, young man! You look to me like the kind of man who'd whip his slaves while they were picking cotton."

Patiently Dan replied, "You can't grow cotton that far north. And I don't have a slave on my place, although I do have some free Negroes."

"But I know human nature, and I know you are going to turn your free Negroes into slaves as soon as Kansas becomes a Slave State!"

Harald coughed and said, "Now, Grandmother—"

"Don't you 'now, Grandmother' me, you ill-behaved rascal!" she grumbled. "Tell me, Mr. Forrester, have you read

Uncle Tom's Cabin? Didn't it make you ashamed of yourself?"

"No, Lady Grizel," said Dan with some force, "reading *Uncle Tom's Cabin* did not make me ashamed of myself. If you really care to know, I thought Simon Legree was a caricature of evil and Little Eva was nothing but sweet treacle."

"Yes!" cried Meridel. "I read it and I thought the same. But still, the book's message is what really counts. And I did like the message because I am very much against slavery."

Dan Forrester turned to gaze levelly at her. Expressionless, he said, "I see," and turned to Lady Grizel again. Then Lady Anne spoke up, declaring herself against slavery and her husband, cupping his ear, nodded his agreement.

Meridel waited to hear Dan Forrester's stand on the issue. But he said nothing, and the subject was dropped when the earl, flustered, pleaded, "Mother, be more gentle with Mr. Forrester, please."

"Mind you manners, Derwin. *I* am senior here. Well, Mr. Forrester, the United States should be ashamed of itself. England got rid of slavery at home and in the colonies long ago. And I'll have you know I helped. Where is my reticule?" Somewhere in her wheelchair she found a big old bag done in petit point and held it up for all to see. Above the date 1828 they all saw a black family, scantily clothed and dancing.

"They seem happy," said Forrester, amusement curving his lips. Meridel felt sure he knew he had said the wrong thing.

"Happy!" screamed Lady Grizel. "They're happy because they're home in Africa before *you* went with your slave ship and—"

"But I've never been in Africa."

"You expect me to believe you?"

The earl held out both hands helplessly toward his other guests, then asked, "Mother, can't we please get on with dinner?"

The old lady subsided, mumbling something under her breath. She finished her wine, pausing only to shake her finger at Dan who ate his dinner heartily. Soon she became groggy and fell asleep, snoring. A footman, keeping his face wooden through all this, wheeled her from the hall.

Eventually Lady Anne and Meridel rose, and the men followed suit as custom dictated. The ladies went to the music chamber, which was separated from the dining room by two other rooms so that the ladies would not be bored by the men's chatter as they discussed business and politics, drank port, and traded coarse stories. The custom had begun to disappear, but, Meridel reflected, perhaps in Norfolk the custom was changing slowly.

After a while the men rejoined the ladies. Harald sat on the piano bench beside Meridel, turning pages as she played a lovely Clementi sonatina. But something was bothering Harald. He scowled, forgot to turn a page, and dropped another.

At length, as everyone applauded—Dan Forrester's hard hands making a sound like a thunderclap—Harald muttered into Meridel's ear, "That fellow Forrester—what does he mean to you?"

"Why . . . he's merely an old friend of my father's."

"Is that all?"

"But of course that's all!"

"Well, I don't like the way he eyes you. He keeps giving you a certain look. Any man knows what he is after."

"Harald, really!"

"I tell you, don't encourage him. Remember, you are going to marry *me*."

Meridel bridled. "I never said so."

"Oh, you need time, but you will, you will."

"A girl does not like to be taken for granted, Harald!"

"Hmmmm. I daresay. At any rate, we hunt tomorrow. Make very sure you ride with *me*."

"If I see fit, I will." But of course she would, she thought as she followed the others upstairs, still angry at Harald's presumption.

Plunkett seemed happy that night, humming to herself as she brushed her mistress's hair and plaited it into two night braids. Meridel, still bothered about Harald, had been keeping a sober face but at length she smiled at her own in the mirror. Nothing much had changed these past months, except for an older, wiser look in her blue eyes; she was able to think now more on her own, relying less on the flashes of lessons learned at Miss Whittaker's to guide her. And when she thought about it, many women would be pleased to be in her dilemma; to be sought after by a lord wasn't such a dreadful thing, really!

"Norfolk is pleasant, isn't it, Plunkett?" she chimed to her busy maid.

"It's frightful quiet, miss. But proper damp, 'tis."

"Proper damp" for her complexion was what she meant, Meridel reflected then smiled to herself. They said nothing more till they exchanged a good-night.

A while later, as Meridel hovered on the edge of sleep, she heard her maid slip stealthily from the tiny room where, country-style, she slept close to her mistress. Perhaps the girl had a tryst with a handsome groom behind the stable. A kiss and a giggle. A pinch and a slap. Or . . . more? Meridel had barely pondered the question when she drifted into sleep.

Chapter Four

Long sideboards steamed with a vast hunt breakfast. The ladies and gentlemen of the hunt chatted cheerfully as they shared ham, bacon, North Sea kippers, broiled kidneys, cod-dled eggs, thin curls of brown bread, butter with the dew on it, sturdy cheeses from the springhouse, cups of tea, and flagons of ale.

The earl, having ridden out early with Dan Forrester, promised to return in time for the start of the hunt. Harald too was missing. Cursing his luck, he had gone off on another estate matter that his father insisted could not wait, involving another lord's coal mine whose pump had failed and was in need of being replaced. He had raged that the estate steward knew more about machinery than he did, which Meridel sus-pected was true. The earl's request only proved the earl wanted his son far away from the railroad builder's daughter. Putting the thought aside, Meridel inspected the sturdy break-fast and smiled at the two young men who hovered around her.

"Really, Miss McGraw, you must ride over to see my father's little place near Swaffham. We make do with only fifteen servants, but we've a wonderful view." Flushed with eagerness, the younger squire's face almost matched his pink coat.

The other heir had already confided his disappointment in not having gotten out of school in time to serve in the Crimean War against the Russians. As though to compensate he had assumed a military manner and had grown a great black Guards mustache. He said stiffly to Pink Face, "You know quite well that your view can't compare with ours," and waited as though expecting a challenge to duel over the matter. Turning with hauteur, he confided to Meridel, "Pater is a fancier of art. We have a Winterhalter."

Meridel nodded. "Oh yes, the artist who paints the queen," she said, and watched the youth's face light up with pleasure.

Just then Dan Forrester entered the hall. He was dressed in a borrowed hunting coat that was too tight across the shoulders, and his boots sparkled wetly with morning mist. Why did her heart leap? Why did two eligible young men, each practically forcing his father's estate upon her, fade away when Dan smiled? He strode in with the earl, who told him jovially, "My dear Forrester, you've no need to worry about English saddles. Not the way you ride!"

Dan chuckled. "As long as I don't have to rope a steer. That's when I'd prefer a Western saddle." The earl and he had obviously relished their morning ride.

"My dear," the old earl cried, "our good friend Forrester rides like a centaur, but he's been wondering if someone—you, perhaps—could instruct him in the technique of pursuing the fox. I assured him you are quite expert, so you will become his tutor, won't you?"

With that, the earl turned on his heels and bounded from the room, leaving Dan and Meridel alone. She could only glare his way until Dan, trying hard to hold back laughter, let it loose, filling the room. "Tutor me, do, and you may slap my wrist if I scamp my lesson," he said.

Trying to ignore him, Meridel said, "We assemble near a

covert, the kind that foxes like and then the whippers—'' She stopped, indignant at his grinning manner.

''Meridel, I deceived our host,'' he said by way of explanation. ''Down in Carroll County—that's in Maryland—where I was brought up, we had fox hunting aplenty. I learned when I was very young.''

''Then how dare you—'' She stamped a foot.

''Simple enough. I wanted to have you near me.''

''I shall leave now, if you please.''

''Wait! Pretend to be teaching me. Would you expose me as a fraud?''

She hesitated. ''I suppose not.''

''And later I must ride very close to you and listen carefully.''

''You are an impostor, sir.''

''You do not seem overly annoyed, miss.''

''If I must put up with you, then I must, if only for the sake of not demeaning a fellow American in the eyes of the British. But I warn you that if you watch me instead of watching where your horse is going, your tumbling will be one hundred percent your own fault.''

''Touché again. And now I know who you remind me of.'' He grinned as he crossed his arms. ''It's one of our local schoolmarms out in Kansas.''

He waited wickedly till she took the obvious bait and asked, ''Why?''

''She knows how to put naughty boys in their place.''

''I think you should have some breakfast, Mr. Forrester. You need some sobering.''

''I wish you'd call me Dan.''

''Really? Am I old enough to become so familiar?''

''Lawks-a-mighty! You leave me speechless. But as for our winning esteem in British eyes—yes, I will join you over—ugh!—tea and kippers.''

Together they rode out with the hunt to the top of the slope. At first Meridel kept silent, puzzled by this brawny, handsome but disrespectful man who could disarm her so. Before long however she found herself remarking on the beauty of the silver mist as it hung above the distant river, and discovered she shared Dan's interest in an ancient hedgerow sparkling with autumn berries.

Flasks passed hands. Dan accepted a cigar. The questing hounds appeared and disappeared as they ranged over the covert. And before long, a horn blast sounded in the air. Meridel tapped her hat to settle it firmly on her head, and watched as Dan, who was accustomed to drier country, snuffed out his cigar before tossing it away. A rapid series of notes blared, and a fox streaked from the bushes, rushing away through the stubble with the hounds on its heels, baying. As the earl waved "Go," Meridel's and Dan's horses sprang forward together in the excitement of the chase.

The world became a galloping and shouting melee as clods of earth from the horses' hooves flew past their faces. Although surrounded by other riders, Meridel and Dan seemed alone as they raced through a stretch of woods, ducking branches, spraying each other with water as they splashed through a stream. Meridel kept her eyes firmly ahead, but all the time she knew Dan was gazing at her. He rode like a centaur—half man, half horse.

The hunt paused as the riders milled about at a gate, waiting for it to be unlatched, and when it was, the fox streaked beneath the fencing, with the hunters leaping in pursuit soon after.

For a time the hounds lost the clever creature. Then, "View halloo!" sounded. The panting hounds rushed off in the direction of the call, the hunters following close behind.

Meridel watched as two or three riders held back their mounts. Up ahead, Fowler's Leap—an overgrown stone wall in the valley below—often took its toll among reckless horsemen. Now, side by side without breaking their stride, she and Dan rushed at it, though the fox and hounds had had the time to skid around and avoid it. Meridel gathered herself for the dangerous leap, rising into it at the same instant that Dan, stretched over his horse's neck, rose. He glanced her way. She saw how a branch snatched away his hat, how his brown hair was tossed by the wind. For a glorious instant in mid-jump, the two seemed to hang between blue sky and green earth as one. And in that moment Meridel gave up denying her feelings. She knew she wanted no other man in the world flying beside her.

When the hunt was over, Meridel was still caught in the exaltation of that flying moment when something wonderful had happened, when something utterly new in her life had awakened.

She said not a word to Dan, nor did he speak to her. But together they fell farther and farther behind the others until the group, returning toward Danemead, rounded a bend in the road, and left them by themselves.

Heart had spoken to heart. They were glad to be alone.

Still without speaking, they entered a glen on their horses and stopped along a tall hedgerow in a secluded corner. The world stood still. Meridel whispered, "I'll call you Dan," and silence, broken only by their breathing, closed around them.

Dan's mount obeyed his unseen command and he edged closer to Meridel. Their boots touched, and she realized she could have leapt into his arms from her sidesaddle position, he was so near.

"Meridel, there is something I want to know."

She nodded and hoped he wouldn't see her trembling.

"Are you looking forward to becoming Lady Meridel?"

The question struck home. Instead of answering directly, she gave him a Miss Whittaker response, "I couldn't be Lady Meridel, only Lady Wayne, because I wouldn't be bringing along my own title."

He laughed. "Interesting. And as the wife of an earl you'd be a countess?"

"Yes. Odd, but there are no English counts."

The silence grew between them. All she could think of was how close he kept his horse and how the only sound she could hear in this glen, filled with the sights and sounds of a forest, was their boots squeaking.

Finally he broke the spell. "Your father showed me the newspaper clippings—about the American girl who had made such a triumph in Buckingham Palace. He said you'd certainly catch a peer, which would make him very happy. And he said you'd never be content to be one of those peeresses who only entertain and gossip. Tell me, Meridel, considering that you'd have a butler and a housekeeper to do all the managing for you, how would you keep busy in that big house?''

She heard his words rumble deeply from his chest and felt the power of his gaze, knowing this was no idle question. Her heart beat so rapidly she could hardly reply, but she managed some control, saying, ''First of all, I would do the basic household management myself, or else I'd feel a dreadful idler.'' This brought a gleam to Dan's dark, searching eyes. ''Also, I'd certainly contribute my time and money to the local orphanage the way Auntie—Lady Anne—does in her parish in Devon. I'd work with the vicar on other charities, and most of all I'd speak to my member about—''

''Member of what?''

''Member of Parliament. I'd speak to him about getting children out of factories and mines. It's dreadful. As a boy, my father worked in a mine. It ruined his health.'' She waited for Dan to speak. He only gazed at her. ''Dan, why do you ask me about . . . about . . . such things?''

''Because I wouldn't want you to come to Kansas and just fade away, as some other women have done—the kind who expect to be constantly entertained and coddled.''

''You mean, visit you in Kansas?'' she asked.

What he said then came as no surprise, nor did his hand grasping hers. ''Not visit, Meridel. Come to stay.''

His hand felt warm, and something more. She wanted both to flee and be embraced at the same time, and all she could do was look here and there as if seeking rescue.

''Meridel.''

Her lips moved but she could not speak.

''Meridel, I love you. I want you to come to Kansas as my wife. I've loved you since the moment we met. Marry me, Meridel.''

In the stillness she watched the dark blue eyes draw closer to her's. Her lips parted as he caught them in a kiss. Had she too been in love with him from the moment she rose from the mud and looked into his face? Her lips opened upon Dan's, and she found her question answered.

Her mare's restless motion broke the kiss, leaving her with the hand that had clutched Dan to her empty and she dropped it to her side. The space between them widened and suddenly

57

she became afraid, not of Dan, but of herself. How could one believe in such love? Who was this man who left her hotly yearning and strangely helpless?

She tried to act as though she did not take him seriously. "Come now, Dan, knights don't gallop off with maidens anymore."

He answered harshly, letting her know how unfitting her words had been. "Meridel, I spoke from the heart. Marry me and come to Kansas. Come and share my ranch with me, Meridel. Help me build the new world that is being made out there. I'll cherish you and our children, because I cannot imagine any kind of life, any other way of living. I don't have the words to tell you how deeply I love and need you. Come with me, Meridel."

What was she to say? All her being leaped into a great awakening, and she felt as though she had not really lived until that moment.

She dared not say yes. She could not say no.

Something inside her whispered the ready-made Miss Whittaker answer: *Make him wait.* Although her own silent cry of need strangled the words from forming on her lips, the innocent girl in her, frightened to lose her innocence, kept her arms from reaching out, and froze her face into a mask of propriety. "Dan, because I'm not bespoken is no reason for you to steal kisses. And besides, you are rushing me dreadfully, and you know you must ask my permission to speak to my father for his permission to propose to me."

Dan, dark-faced, said, "That's the worst damn-fool idea that—" But he stopped himself. "Your father's consent," he muttered, looking beyond her. The turmoil in his weathered face seemed to disappear a moment until suddenly his horse—one with him—moved close to hers again. "So simple," he whispered, his face darkening again, "to grab you up and run away with you."

She shocked herself a moment by allowing a wild desire he do it. "Come now, this is the nineteenth century," she said instead, trying to steady her voice.

He threw back his head and let loose a bitter laugh. "No, I must *win* you. And not by slaying some competing knight with a lance. All right. Shall we keep company?" Auntie had

called that an American phrase. "Come with me tomorrow—
oh, bring along your maid, of course—and let me show you
an interesting combination of railroad and canal I happened
upon. It's something you might want to describe to your father. Whose consent I will need."

Meridel consented though his words made her flush red,
and as they headed back to join the others, she saw that his
lips were set in a grim line.

At the imposing, aged house, they slipped into the noisy
crowd. Three musicians had arrived, and with fiddle, cornet,
and reed organ held between the knees, they struck up a dancing tune. Everyone paused between rounds for ale and wine.

Dan had been content to allow Meridel to dance the old-
fashioned minuet and a traditional morris with her lovesick
young men. But for the waltz, which followed the first two
rounds, he led her away, not bothering to ask her permission,
and encircled her waist with his arm.

"One-two-three, one-two-three," he murmured as they circled together. "Pretty tame stuff," he added.

She smiled, excited to be in his embrace.

"Wait till you try a Kansas hoedown," he said. "First you
get oiled up on rattlesnake juice. Then—"

"I prefer to dance *without* arrows flying around me," she
retorted.

He chuckled. "The hostiles aren't that thick in the eastern
part of the territory, where I have my ranch."

"My father did have some notion of building a railroad in
Kansas. Is your ranch anywhere near where he wants to
build?"

For several moments Dan seemed lost in concentrating on
the unfamiliar dance step. Massive though he was, he had a
light step. Without warning, he whirled Meridel off her feet
and held her in midair, leaving the yards of her riding habit
trailing behind her.

"Everyone's watching!" she gasped.

"Excellent. Let them see how well we do together," he
said, resuming the dance steps. "Yes, your father does have a
Kansas railroad in mind, and he's the right man to build one.
But much depends on where the transcontinental line is laid—

a matter by no means settled. I'm sure your father knows how much he can gain by making his line part of it. But never mind railroads. All I want to know is that I'm dancing with you.''

She pushed against him as he drew nearer. "Not so close, sir.''

"You've acquired some kind of English accent that I find hard to understand,'' he said, laughing and ignoring her gesture. "Wait, now I have it. You really said, 'Hold me closer, Dan dear.'''

"No!'' she cried. "Dan, the music is over—let go of me,'' she cried, struggling to be free. But when she finally shook herself loose, she felt strangely lost and deserted.

Hours later, when Plunkett drew the bed curtains and said good night, Meridel huddled under the blankets, afraid. What was this yearning she was feeling, all centered on Dan as though no other in the world. Worse yet, her body yearned so much that her mind was overpowered. Did she at last feel passion? But until a girl married she dared not feel passion! And some said no decent woman felt it even then. When she sat up, she pressed her hands to her face, then quickly thrust them away, embarrassed. Her arms had pressed against her thin nightdress and she had felt the swollen nipples.

Worse yet she seemed hardly able to remember Harald's face. But her mind could re-create every feature of Dan's rugged, desirable one.

For a while she stood at the window, trying to calm herself, then crept shivering back into bed, praying blessed sleep would overcome her, and quiet the turmoil boiling inside her.

In the morning, feeling somewhat rested, Meridel thought of pretending a headache, then decided against giving into self-doubts. She did not know whether she wanted to stay near Dan or away from him. She simply did not *know*. But she knew she shouldn't remove herself from the presence of the others, whose company she could enjoy.

Going to the breakfast room, she hesitated on the threshold as she saw that everyone had been seated and were being served homecooked eggs, bacon and sausages. They hailed to her, and even the unnaturally reserved earl seemed warmer in his manner as she took her seat. She found conversation with Dan, though trivial in subject matter, not so restrained as she expected.

At Dan's mention of a trip to the canal, the earl became very excited and offered them the use of a barouche and his own coachman, Wilmot. Nor did Lord Hubert and Lady Anne have any objection to Meridel's sharing the barouche's rear seat with Dan so long as Plunkett, prim as could be in her mouse-gray cloak, sat facing them.

The weather had warmed, reminding Meridel of an Indian summer. She savored the freshness of the morning air as they made good time along the main road, then lurched onto a lane that led to an old canal wharf.

She had taken along her sketch pad and some soft pencils. Every dame school taught sketching, along with watercolor, because both were dear to Queen Victoria. Now, as Plunkett let herself down from the barouche, ready to help her mistress descend, Dan slid the pad and pencils beneath the lap robe and winked at Meridel.

Puzzled, she said nothing. Meanwhile, a fisherman with a peg leg they'd spied on the whàrf, came clumping toward them, his belly, cinched by his military belt, quivering like two mounds of gelatin. The breeze reeked of gin, the source no doubt being an empty bottle lying next to the spot where the fisherman had been sitting.

He touched his cap and revealed in his wheedling singsong how thoroughly the gaucheries of the gentry had filtered down to the country people. "My respects, lady, but 'ave ye a copper for one who has lost a leg in 'er Majesty's service? An American coin will do if you don't 'ave an English one, miss."

Dan tossed him tuppence and said, "Now off with you."

"I will, sir, I will. Just let me pick up my fish, sir, for a poor man needs a mite to eat. All I was doin' was sittin' and fishin'. Poor Stumpy Bailey, your servant, miss, sir, and known to Lord Harald, I am, and was known to Lord Didrick too, may he rest in peace. Only poor Stumpy Bailey hisself, who would never harm a soul. Just sittin' and fishin'. Quiet I am and peaceful, and if I ever can be of service to ye, look for me here at the public canal.'' He finally went stomping off.

"Good riddance," said Dan. "Now, Wilmot, you'll want to stay here with the barouche and the horses. Plunket, come along with us. Your mistress and I are going to have a closer look at that trestle.'' He pointed to where crisscrossed beams spanned the canal.

They walked together down the hardened towpath, Plunkett following at a discreet distance behind them and carrying Meridel's cloak at the ready should she need it.

"Why did you hide my sketching things?'' Meridel whispered.

Dan's answer only left her puzzled and oddly excited: "All's fair in love and war.''

A barge drawn by a horse on the towpath on the other side of the canal lumbered underneath the trestle's arch, bearing a heavy load of gravel which the horse seemed to pull as effortlessly as it carried a young boy on its back. Where a small cabin perched in the bow of the barge, a woman watered geraniums, cocking an eye at the laundry fluttering from poles on the cabin's roof. Meanwhile her husband—one could guess—sat puffing his pipe in the stern where holding the rudder he steered the listing craft.

"That's the past,'' Dan said. "The railroad trestle marks the future.''

Meridel looked puzzled. "What do you mean?''

"A horse can pull a floating load of fifty tons at four miles an hour, and until now a man could build a barge, buy a horse, and have his home and his freight business in one package. But now freight moves on rails at forty miles an hour, and railroads require a huge public investment, millions of dollars—or pounds.''

"Yes, Papa has explained all that to me. And so has Harald.''

Dan's voice went dry, his tone cooly cautious, as though he didn't want to reveal too much. "Yes, our mutual friend, Lord Harald, did very well selling English railroad stock to tropical planters.'' Something like bitterness had entered his voice. "The man who sells paper makes a tidy sum in commissions even if the railroad never gets built. However,'' he added briskly to lighten his tone, "I see this one's running all right." He pointed to the trestle towering above them.

A plume of smoke that had appeared in the distant countryside moved closer until a train came into view, chuffing and clanking as it thundered across the bridge. Meridel noticed that the little locomotive did not pull a tender loaded with coal. Travel distances in Britain were shorter than in the United States and a train here could carry smaller loads to fuel itself.

Dan was looking at the barge. "See what I mean?" he said, pointing. The captain was shaking his fist at the steam-spouting contraption. They laughed.

Dan, having been at this spot before, easily found a log a few feet off the path where Meridel could sit and sketch. "You'll want to show your father how the crossbeams are linked to the curved girders. It's quite unique. But"—he stopped, then added in mock amazement, "Where's your sketchbook?"

Her heart leaped. Now she understood—and smiled. "Oh dear, I left it in the barouche."

"Perhaps Plunkett can get it," Dan said.

"Yes," said Meridel. "Plunkett, go back and find my sketchbook and pencils, will you? There's a dear."

"It's such a long walk," Plunkett muttered as she sighed heavily, lifted her skirts and trudged in the direction of their carriage.

"We've half an hour." Meridel heard the excitement in Dan's voice. "Sit down with me, Meridel, here on the log. I have photographs of my ranch to show you."

He spread his kerchief for her to sit on. She remained aloof another moment, realizing that once she sat on the log, behind the bushes, she would be out of the servant's sight. And she had told herself she would not allow Dan to see her alone! Nevertheless she sat down beside him, her hands unsteady as she smoothed her loose walking skirt around her.

"I call it Rainbow Ranch. A photographer came by . . ." He took out a flat package of metal plates—daguerreotypes. "Here's a view from the barn."

She saw stretches of woods and fields going back into the distance. Kansas certainly had plenty of distance. She felt afraid to look up from the picture into Dan's face, especially when he peered closely at the daguerreotype and his hair brushed hers.

His voice rumbled in his chest. "It's hard to believe the ranch really belongs to me now. All the years I worked and saved for it . . . and now it's mine, mine!"

The wandering man at last had put down roots. She was the daughter of a wandering Irishman. She understood.

He took another plate from the package. "Here's my house. I began with a log cabin. I added on."

The original log cabin looked cramped and forlorn against the homey two-story dwelling of a dozen rooms or more. The wide veranda bore rocking chairs. Someone had nailed a handsome set of antlers above the shallow front steps, and young shrubs—not yet the size of the ancient yew hedges at Danemead—had been planted around the house. Some day they would mature and help give the two-story house lush surroundings.

Still averting her eyes from Dan's, Meridel asked, "Did you build the house yourself?"

He straightened, a warm look in his eyes. "Myself and my men, except that neighbors came to help with the framework. We had a grand house-raising. Biggest house for a long way around."

Too big for a lone man, she thought, flushing. She could not name her feelings, except that she felt nothing like the fear that Harald at times inspired.

Near the house, in a blur, roamed a half-dozen saddle horses that had obviously moved as the photo was snapped. The people leaning against the house had known enough to stand still. Their faces were tiny, but Meridel instantly recognized Dan, who wore overalls tucked into his boots. Of the three other men, one had black braids that fell to his waist— surely an Indian. Two women also stood against the house. One, who seemed middle-aged, had no more figure than a potato sack. But the other woman . . . Meridel peered closely. She, who stood next to Dan, also wore a stayless dress and clumsy sunbonnet. But she was young, and her dress had fitted to her body well. She posed in an easy, lounging stance, her arm against Dan's. Her face, lost in the bonnet, was turned toward his . . . and yes, her lips were parted in a bold smile.

A very shapely woman. And she had fitted her dress to show it.

Dan said something.

"What?" She looked up at him.

"I said, not many people in Kansas have ever faced a camera, so everyone got into the picture. That man here is Fritz Mueller, my foreman, and here"—he pointed to the shapeless woman—"is Bertha, his wife. The Indian is Low Sun. He's taken a prairie sort of name, but he's descended from Shawnee who were moved to Kansas from Indiana. He's got a farm on the edge of my ranch. I should mention I'm an agricultural adviser to the Indians. The other man is Cassidy, my blacksmith. Now, this"—he pointed to the shapely woman who seemed to hover possessively over Dan—"is the schoolmarm who knows how to put naughty boys in their place. She—"

"Is she married?" The question came breathlessly.

"No, schoolmarms had better be spinsters." He showed her the next picture. "Now, here's our main corral. The black man is Henry, my best herder."

In the photo Dan stood at the rail fence and next to him, touching him, smiling at him, again stood that woman.

"She seems a very graceful person, your schoolmistress." What else could she say? Why did Meridel hate this woman she had never seen, of whom she knew nothing? Or did she know something—something that somehow was connected with her desires of the night before, something she found hard to name?

"Graceful? I guess so." He seemed bothered by the comment, and quickly moved on. "Now, here's my prize Hereford bull. The photographer posed me admiring him." Only Dan and the stocky bull appeared in this photo.

"And here are cattle at a water hole. Often you can see deer there of an early morning." The schoolmistress once again! She was paying no attention to the cattle, standing almost obscenely close to Dan.

"Here's the prairie, looking westward."

At last the fabled sea of grass, which rolled and rolled till the eye stopped at the horizon; only a single figure on a far-away horse punctuated the vastness.

"That's probably an Indian scouting to see if he can steal my horses. They're all branded, but it's an awfully big prairie. Let me show you my brand." With a stick Dan drew on the ground three arcs, one within the other. A rainbow for Rainbow Ranch. "Out in Kansas, when a gal catches her fella, we say she's put her brand on him."

Meridel said nothing.

In the next picture the schoolmistress again stood possessively close to Dan, her hand clutching his shoulder as they stood before his steam sawmill. She had caught up her skirt to keep the hemline from touching wood scrap, and the shape of a leg showed clearly.

"Does she live nearby?"

"Our schoolmarm, you mean? Mile or so."

"I suppose she boards with a local family?"

"Boards? Uh, no, she lives alone. Has a cabin and a vegetable patch about as close as she can get to the schoolhouse." Dan laughed awkwardly. "But in Kansas pretty close can be pretty far."

Odd that a schoolmistress should live alone. It sounded absolutely dangerous. On the other hand, no one would know if a man dropped in—Meridel watched her own wringing hands. She wished Dan had never shown her the daguerreotypes. For the first time in her life she knew the stinging whip of sexual jealousy, driving her onward, even when instinct told her she should drop the matter.

Dan was speaking earnestly. "Meridel, living on the ranch will never be as comfortable as living at Danemead. It has been dangerous at times, and lonely. But new houses are being built nearby, and every settlement in the territory keeps growing. And whether Kansas enters the Union as a Free State or a Slave State, it will become the breadbasket of the nation, covered in wheat, and what's not wheat will be cattle. I'll have an endless market for my light workhorses—the Cleveland Bays—and I'm thinking of breeding Clydesdales for the real heavy hauling. And don't forget my Herefords. And the stands of wheat I've put out to see which kind will grow best, and my special strains of corn for hog feed. I'm pioneering in many ways, Meridel. I expect to reap the reward."

Meridel said in a dull, stained voice, "I see." But she could only think of the insolent woman in the photos.

"Nor am I a poor man. My wife won't have to chop kindling or break the ice on the well to draw water. And she can go to St. Louis with money enough to buy what she needs. She can do the house over from top to bottom, and . . . Meridel?"

She stared at him.

"My wife will have the best piano in America, and a man will keep it in tune for her if I have to bring him five hundred miles to do the work. And my wife is going to be an important woman in Kansas. Because I'm going to be an important man. I can do it as long as I have you beside me." He turned her face to his, his big hands gentle on her cheeks. "I want you to be mine, I want to be yours. We'll have children."

When he kissed her she uttered a wild sound that fell between ecstasy and terror. She hammered at him wildly with her fists. Unhurt, he drew away.

"What's wrong?"

The awful question was wrenched from her. "Dan, who is that woman?"

Had he been innocent he might have asked, "What woman?" *But he knew*, meaning he had probably slept with the woman as she suspected. She certainly invited him to do so in the photos. "She's our local schoolmarm, just as I told you. Her name is—"

Meridel cried, "I don't care what her name is. I want to know what she is to you." Her words and tone were meant to sting.

She watched Dan's expressive mouth set grimly before he said harshly, "She's a neighbor."

"A neighbor? *Is that all*?"

His manner and reply revealed his guilt. "I don't want you to ask that question, Meridel. When you're a little older you'll understand."

But his words brought from the tortured girl only a low, angry whisper: "I am old enough now to realize you have taken her to bed as though she were your wife."

Dan Forrester scowled. "It is very foolish for any woman to notice the hairpins on a bachelor's dresser."

"Then you admit you've—you've—slept with her!"

He jumped up from the log. "Damn it, do you think an unmarried man devotes himself to chastity? My past is my past. It has nothing to do with my future. I want you to marry me and no one else—"

"After the way you flaunted her at me!" she cried, leaping to her feet to face him.

"No! I only wanted to show you my ranch, my house, my stock. I told you everyone got into the picture."

"But she stands there, telling the world she owns you."

"I'm done with her, I tell you! Now will you give up this foolishness and—"

"And you want me to lie in bed with you and know she's been there before me, in your arms?"

"Damn it, why must you—"

"A spinster schoolmistress by day, and at night a . . . a . . . wanton woman! She obviously goes to your bed—or . . . you go to hers."

Dan glared at her, then wiped his hand down his face in an effort to calm himself. "Look. I admit certain things passed between us. But it's all over, I tell you. I promise you I'll keep her out of your hair and never touch her again."

Meridel thrust a fist to her hip. "You mean no matter what she is, what she was, she'll go on being your neighbor, *our* neighbor. Meanwhile, I'm supposed to forget what she was to you—because schoolmistresses are scarce in Kansas?"

Dan banged a fist on his knee. "Damn it, she has hurt no one. She's a valuable member of the community."

"You defend her?"

"Call it what you will," he roared then groaned more to himself, "everything would have been all right if you hadn't asked such a schoolgirl question."

Floundering beyond her depth, shaken to her soul with love that warred with jealousy, Meridel found refuge in her pride. Deathly cold, she whispered, "If I still act the schoolgirl, then I am too young to speak of marriage." She brushed smooth the folds of her skirt. "I hope you'll find your—your very good friend waiting for you when you reach home."

"Meridel!" he cried in agony. "Don't you see—"

"I see everything. Quite clearly," she said, struggling to maintain her dignity. "Allow *me* to make clear that Lord Harald Wayne has done me the honor of asking for my hand, and I shall give his suit every consideration."

"So that's it! Playing one man against another!"

"I owe you no explanation."

"Because you have none. I see it, I see it," he said.

"Finnian McGraw's daughter must marry an English peer and she will—not neglecting in the meantime to sport with the Kansas stockman. But wait. Harald will only become an earl. Why aim so low? Why not bide your time and catch a marquis? Or a duke, for that matter?" Dan furiously kicked a stone into the canal and watched it sink. "Whatever made me think you'd have the courage to live on the frontier? A hothouse flower, that's all you are."

Meridel in a flounce of skirts whirled around to go. He grasped her wrist, and she almost relented when she heard his voice break. "Meridel." His strong body shook as he turned her to him, crushing her against him. "But I tell you, you are mine! Don't go away from me."

But her anger swelled up again as she noticed the photos clutched in his hand. She broke away, slapping Dan's face as hard as she could. Watching the red imprint appear on his cheek, she told him, "I will—I will marry Lord Harald."

She could hardly see through burning tears as she stumbled away. But she did make out Plunkett coming down the towpath with the sketchbook and pencils in hand. "I am sorry I made you walk so far for nothing, but I have decided to return," Meridel said, as calmy as she could manage. The pretty maid looked puzzled but kept her peace.

Dan Forrester came up beside her, and they walked together in silence, mostly to keep the servants from talking about the two Americans quarreling on the old Norfolk towpath.

Chapter Five

The old earl could not understand why Dan Forrester left
Danemead so abruptly. He had enjoyed Forrester's company;
and they had almost agreed on terms for his buying three
mares and the horse Bluebonnet. Then, without warning, Forrester had announced he had to leave immediately to see his
London banker. Not only did he drop the matter of buying
horses, but he hardly took time to say good-bye.

Everyone appeared startled by his leaving. Everyone but
Meridel. As Dan drove off in his hired chaise she watched
coolly from the croquet green. Very well! she reflected. Let
him go in such an angry state. When she bent to strike a ball,
she missed the wicket by a wide margin.

Well, she told herself, she could be forgiven for being a bit
upset. She cared not a fig for Dan Forrester, she'd forget him
soon enough.

Nevertheless, as the day wore on she restlessly paced the
Danemead gardens, angry and strangely desolate, until to end

her torment, she made a decision: she would go to the Dower House for a visit with Countess Grizel.

In the time of Cromwell, the Dower House had sheltered Cavaliers, and bullets fired by Roundheads pocked the walls, many of them still buried in the masonry. Though later generations had lived in peace they had maintained a hidden path to the house that wound from the gardens through a brush-choked gully. Once a month old Lady Grizel sat patiently at the top of the path in a sun-warmed crook in the garden wall, waiting for two people, each of whom would arrive separately and by way of the gully.

Only Persis and the countess herself and her lawyer knew why the people came and what she gave them. Sometimes, in stormy weather, Lady Grizel sent a shivering Persis to crouch there in her stead—for the matter could not be neglected.

On the day Meridel sought her out, the countess had awakened feeling poorly. Persis, bringing the money from the iron chest, had wanted her to stay in bed, and was thanked for her concern by a thorough scolding. In the sunny crook of the garden wall, the countess sat, waiting as usual. She leaned her head on her hand, her flesh feeling like feathers. She could recall a time her skin was as lovely as the skin on that young American chit—what was her name? Oh yes. Meridel Blakiston—no, an Irish name. McNaughton, McPhee, Mc-Graw. Yes that was it, McGraw.

The sun occupied the place in the sky that indicated it was time for a village woman named Sarah to come up the gully. Lady Grizel dropped her feeble left hand into a pocket of her coat and felt for the bank note that Persis had placed there, then in the right-hand pocket for the other bank note. They were both in place, as usual.

From off to one side, a gleam of coppery-red caught her eye. As she peered closely the nimble figure of that Irish beauty—no, American—came into view, picking her way through the garden from the front gate. She'd never find the countess if that was whom she was looking for unless Lady Grizel called out, but she did not have the strength and sank back into her chair to watch Meridel's beautiful red hair vanish behind the thick hedges lining the walk. Perhaps this was as well, the countess reflected, for by the time Meridel found her hiding place, the stealthy visitors would have come and finished their business without any additional outsider, other than Persis, knowing the family secret.

Shades of blackness rose and fell before Lady Grizel's weary eyes. She wondered dimly if Harald would marry Meridel. What a delicious tidbit the scamp would bring to bed if she was foolish enough to consent! Of course Derwin wanted him to marry some British whey-face who bore a title, someone who carried her hips and bosom all wrong. Meridel, like herself, could give any of them lessons. But did the girl have strength to handle Harald?

Again the old countess's head sank upon her hand as the pain lurking in her chest grew stronger. Was it an ache of conscience? One did not grow up north of the Tweed without developing a conscience, strong and grim and relentless as a weed.

Suddenly, the sounds of cracking twigs interrupted the countess's thoughts. A comely, slender woman of five-and-twenty was leaping up the banks of the gully onto the path and within moments she loomed over the wheelchair, curtsying to the old gentlewoman and smiling with a flushed face. "Good even, milady." Afternoon and evening were the same to the cottagers.

"Good evening, Sarah dear," the dowager said in a more gentle voice than most people knew she possessed.

"I hope you are well, milady."

"Well enough, thank you." But a black shadow kept flapping like raven wings in front of her eyes.

"Let me tuck in your coat, milady."

Lady Grizel acquiesced. Sarah had a little girl and an older boy. The girl, born two years ago, was her husband's. The boy, now almost five, was, as her husband knew, another man's child, born some time before Sarah had married.

"How tall is he now?" the countess asked faintly.

Sarah indicated with her hand: more than waist-high. "He grows whilst you watch," she said, smiling shyly.

He'd be tall, like his father. "Is his hair turning darker?"

"No, milady. It's staying yellow," she said.

Lady Grizel sighed, then fumbled in her left-hand pocket

before handing Sarah the pound note. "Remember, Sarah, if anything happens to me . . ."

"Yes'm, your ladyship. I go to Mr. Farnham, the solicitor, near Erpingham Gate. But I pray you'll be spared for many years, milady."

"Thank you, Sarah. God bless you. And kiss . . ." She concluded faintly, "Kiss the child for me."

"I always do, milady."

Sarah scurried out of sight. The ancient woman remained with her head leaning heavily on her hand, her eyes gazing blankly at a point in front of her. It didn't mean much that a young aristocratic scalawag had sired a by-blow here and there. Milkmaid mothers knew that such children received no inheritance. What had made the situation grievous was Harald's refusing to acknowledge the child, much less contribute so much as a farthing toward its support. She recalled Harald's indignant reaction at the idea. To him, a girl who made an easy tumble for one man made an easy tumble for another. Like as not, he'd sputtered, Sarah had lain with half the younger sons in the parish and no doubt some of the older sons as well.

The countess gasped for breath as an invisible hand seemed to squeeze her heart and let go. By the time she recovered her breath, Stumpy Bailey the fisherman, aided by a crutch, made his way out of the gully. When he stood before the dowager in his filthy scarlet jacket, he poised himself as if he wore the plume, doublet and accomplished sword of one of Dumas's three musketeers.

"I'll 'ave wot's in the right-hand pocket," he said.

"Curse your impudence!" the countess cried.

"If you say so, your ladyship," the man sneered. "No hurry. I only stopped by on my way to go fishin'. Mebbe on the canal. Mebbe on the river."

"Be sure you don't trespass on Danemead land, you poacher."

"Never poached on Danemead land but once, and never caught anythin' that day anyway. Ye know what day that was."

"I know," she croaked. The pain in her chest had crept

down her right arm. She could not slide her hand into her pocket. "Take the money, you dirty wretch."

Bailey nipped the five-pound note from her coat as cleanly as a pickpocket and after examining it, winked and tucked it out of sight.

"Good-bye, you piece of filth," the countess cursed.

"Orrrewoor, hain't it? And don't forget Christmas is comin' and a man wants 'is plum puddin'. Ten pound for Christmas wouldn't hurt yer ladyship. Might help, even, to keep things goin' the way they are." He turned and whistling insolently under his breath, began kicking through the brush on his way to the gully.

"Skite! Rankster!" the dowager called after him like any fishwife. Or thought she did, for her sagging mouth made only weird, incoherent sounds. Again the raven flew before her eyes, clouding her sight and battering its wings against her temples. She could barely make out the copper-red hair and lovely, frightened face that swam before her.

"My lady, are you ill?" a gentle voice cried.

Half of the old countess's face twisted in vain effort to speak while the other half appeared smooth as pond water. A second stroke! Grasping the withered form to keep her from toppling over, Meridel eased the countess from the chair to the grass. "Lie still, Countess. I'll run for help. You'll be all right."

All right? No, dear girl. Not in this world. The last light collapsed in funnels of whirling blackness. Some bodily feeling penetrated the dark—the precious girl's arms around her, her gasping breath. Yet the countess could not find the strength to utter some few last words. And she must utter them or die evil. She must warn the girl, the girl must know . . .

Bending over the dying woman, Meridel tried to read the wavering lips. But no distinct sound formed, and whatever the dowager countess had wanted to say went with her to her grave. Meridel gasped and sobbed as the older woman's face went ashen, and never having faced death before, she rose to run for the help no one could give.

The day after the dowager's funeral, Harald had gone to

see Meridel and the Blakistons off at the little country station. Eyeing her pallor, he had said, "I didn't think you'd be so affected by my grandmother's death."

He did not know the other and greater reason for the dark circles under her eyes. She said quickly, "But I had grown so fond of her."

"Yet you scarcely knew her."

"But I liked her so much. And she died in my arms."

"Yes, of course," Harald had said, somber in his dark clothing. Yet he watched Meridel as though he wondered whether she was telling him the truth.

The Blakistons, too, wondered at Meridel's condition. She dared tell nobody that the shock of Lady Grizel's death had only deepened that of another loss. Dan.

She had refused his love and only now realized how much she had fallen in love with him, his absence doubling the sense of grief that had descended on her like a lead weight. And yet she had allowed a small slight to drive him away. True it had been more than a slight but a hurt she had let crush her, unreasonably so.

Dawn touched her bedroom window before she fell asleep. She awakened at the harsh sounds of Plunkett protesting to someone outside her door: "Nah, nah, I'm not waking the miss. You just give me that letter and I'll 'old it for her, I will."

A man said plaintively: "But the gent'man give me a sovereign, 'e did, to give it to Miss Meridel personal."

"I'll peek then. But you stay right 'ere."

Meridel parted the curtains and sat on the edge of the bed, blinking her sleep-shrouded eyes. Who could have sent her an important personal letter? Plunkett ducked her head into the room, and exclaimed as she saw her mistress sitting on the edge of her bed, wide awake. Apologizing profusely, she turned to the unseen man in the hall and whispered loudly enough for Meridel to hear, "Now you scat, the miss's awake but it won't be you who give 'er the letter—you go tell your master you done your business. Now be off wi' you." Turning once again, Plunkett closed the door and handed the letter to Meridel. Moments later she could hear Plunkett quarreling once again with the man in the hallway, but by then Meridel had forced herself to don her peignoir, go to the writing table and find the paper knife. Of course the note could not have come from Dan, she told herself. He'd be on the high seas by now, bound for home, and if he thought of her at all, it was to remember the chit of a girl he was better off without.

Indeed it might be a letter from Dan saying exactly that.

Tear it up! a voice inside her urged. But another made her slit open the seal and unfold the letter and look at the signature. She leaned dizzily against the wall as she glanced down again, barely believing what was lying at the bottom. "I love you. Dan."

Her hands shaking, she read how he'd seen her coach in town, made inquiries, discovered she was staying at the Wayne house in Belgrave Square, and known he had to reach her. He apologized for the way he had treated her and begged her to meet him the following day at a place he indicated in the letter. He urged her to give the waiting messenger her reply.

"I love you, I love you. Meridel," she wrote at the end of her triple-sealed reply. She kissed the letter and when she went to the door saw that Plunkett was still arguing with the messenger. "It's alright, Plunkett—this man is to return with my reply." The maid, her hands on her ample hips, merely frowned and bit back some oath she had been about to utter to the messenger. He grabbed up the letter from Meridel's hand, and scurried past Plunkett to the front door, but the maid followed close behind, making sure he didn't linger anywhere. When Meridel, smiling after Plunkett, turned to her window, the sun was shining and the birds were singing merrily in the square.

Next day she arrived very early at a certain shop on Regent Street. She needed a stroke of luck not to arouse Plunkett's suspicions. She found it when she spied a seventeen-year-old girl in the care of a woman who looked like a dragon aunt, and told Plunkett that the girl was a school friend. The maid returned to the house in the coupé and explained that Miss Meridel had met a dear friend with whom she would visit before returning home later in the day.

Dan was to arrive at eleven, and Meridel could not make

the clock go faster. She spent a long time buying gloves and was examining another pair when a hush fell over the store. A man had entered. In that frilly, powdery, perfumed shop, a man was rarely seen.

"Why, Uncle Dan!" Meridel cried.

"Come now, Niece! I arrived a bit soonish in order to save you from spending your entire allowance on frippery." His tall, rugged frame filled the doorway.

"Isn't he handsome?" whispered a female voice from behind her.

Meridel approached Dan and took his arm. Her feet seemed to glide above the floor as he swept her outside and whisked her into the hansom he had engaged. "Drive—just drive," he said to the cabman who looked down inquiringly through a trapdoor in the roof.

As the trapdoor closed, Dan held Meridel's fingers to his lips. Unsteadily he asked, "Can you forgive me?"

"My dearest," she cried, a slight tremor in her voice, "I had no right to say what I did."

"You call me dearest?"

"Yes, dearest, dearest, dearest, dearest!" She touched his face and caressed his rough cheek a moment.

"I was so—broken to bits—when I thought I'd never see you again."

"You were hardly out of sight when I realized what a silly 'schoolgirl' mistake I had made." She kissed him. "Now I know I love you—have always loved you, have never stopped loving you."

"You loved me at the canal?"

"With all my heart."

"Tell me again."

"I love you, Dan, I love you." She knew her tears came from overwhelming joy and relief.

They held their kiss a long time as the cab lurched through London streets, though they felt not a thing, lost as they were in their own private world.

"Will you marry me, Meridel?"

"Yes, yes!"

"You'll live on Rainbow Ranch with me?"

"How can I tell you it's the only place in the world I want

to live? 'Entreat me not to leave thee or to return from following after thee; for whither thou goest I will go, and where thou lodgest I will lodge.'"

"So beautiful and appropriate," he smiled, drawing her to him again.

After a time, Dan murmured, "You do realize that I didn't flaunt her in front of you?"

Meridel looked away, saying in a low tone, "Don't talk about her anymore, Dan. As long as you'll never again—"

"Never," he said quickly.

She smiled and asked, "Did you say there are deer on the ranch?"

"Plenty. In winter I can get them to eat from my hand."

"Oh, I'd like to try that. Oh, Dan! *You* feeding deer from your hand! And I'd heard you were so rough and tough."

"Shouldn't believe everything you hear."

She laughed. "And I want to see the buffalo."

"Won't have to go far."

"And the Indians."

He grinned. "The peaceful ones, yes. But Meridel—"

"Yes, my dearest?"

"You've been brought up to expect luxury."

"Then, sir, I'm glad I am young enough to be flexible."

He chuckled. "*I* wouldn't dare be the one to tell you that."

"Better not!"

"Anyway, I must write to Mueller to have certain improvements made in the house before you arrive."

"Such as?"

"A bathtub."

She laughed in delight. "Dan, tell Mrs. Mueller I'm going to take all the advice she wants to give me and then I am going to run your house for you."

"And bawl me out for tracking mud in?"

They laughed, and kissed. For a moment Dan held Meridel at arms' length, gazed with glowing eyes. "Mine," he whispered, his lips coming down on hers, seeking, finding, possessing. Meridel felt no shame as sweet need spread through her body.

Dan's breath came strong and quick. She closed her eyes,

swaying, when his fingers found the buttons of her blouse and exposed the upper curves of her high, small breasts.

"Dan you . . ." But the word "mustn't" faded into a sigh as he drew his lips along the pearly skin. Farther, farther, he nuzzled down into her underclothing toward her taut nipples . . . then drew himself away.

He moved away awkwardly and motioned to Meridel to cover herself. He tapped the scuttle and told the downward-looking face to drive to a number on Burnham Road. Then he sat down again, drawing his hands down the length of her body with infinite delight and tenderness.

They arrived at the address—an establishment of rented rooms—and went up to Dan's quarters. Meridel liked seeing that huge valise again with "D. F." branded on it. She liked the pipe left on a table and the cravat dangling over the back of a chair that made the rented room not just any room, but his.

She felt only love and longing when he swept off her cloak and bent to kiss her deeply. Before long, he was fumbling with her buttons again, and when one became stuck she knew that he wanted to rip her dress from her body. She crossed her arms over her half-exposed bosom and whispered, "Dan . . . it's not that I'm afraid of you . . . but all her life a girl is told . . ."

Reluctantly he held back. "You are my bride, and modesty becomes you. I'll go into my dressing room. Five minutes?"

"My corset laces . . ."

"Ten."

She undressed without hurry, laying her clothes carefully upon the settee until Dan's mirror—only a man could endure so small a mirror—reflected her pink, naked flesh. With a strange mixture of emotions—fear and trust, excitement and contentment—she pulled away the bolster from Dan's bed and slid between the sheets. Never before had she lain naked in bed. The very touch of the cool sheets upon her skin signaled that she was about to enter another stage of womanhood. She felt as though she had lived all her life for the sake of this moment.

Dan knocked at the door of his tiny dressing room, opening

it at her inviting murmur. He wore a fine silk gown in a paisley pattern and as he sat down his weight depressed the bed, sliding her to him. "Are you mine?" he asked.

"Always."

"Always mine," he said huskily as he drew the sheet down to her waist. Bending, he touched his lips where they had not been able to touch before. Meridel yearned toward him and whispered—she knew not what. He loosened her hair, spreading it in a bright veil across her bosom, and trailed his lips through the silken strands.

"Wherever we go, whatever life brings, remember I love you," he murmured as he uncovered and kissed her everywhere, exclaiming at the silken texture of her skin and the beauteous curves of her small body. His hand found her most secret places, and all her being responded as a flame swept through her—a wild call of abandon.

He whispered, "Now you *are* mine in a way that comes only once," and though she gasped at first, the flooding tide of pleasure swept over her, and they began a motion as natural as the waves of the sea until she soared somewhere far above the earth, enveloped in a great golden flare of sunlight and glory.

Gradually she returned to the world and lay at Dan's side, breathing with him in quiet bliss. Was this what a "decent" woman was not supposed to know? This utter ecstasy after an initial twinge of pain? This oneness beyond her wildest dream? "Dan," she cried, and welcomed his hand's return to her.

He nuzzled her cheek, nibbled her ear. "The man who marries you becomes the luckiest man in the world. Which means I shall become the luckiest man in the world—ten times over."

They lay a long time, their lips seeming to have melted together, while his hand wandered up and down her back and stroked her buttocks, pinching her. She cried, "Oh!" and moved away.

He laughed. "I'm ready again."

"I really shouldn't stay here any longer." Even so, she rested on his shoulder and wound her fingers into the wiry hair of his chest.

"I s'pose you're right," he said reluctantly as he got out of bed, lifted her, and set her down in the rough wicker chair, chuckling as she squirmed. He helped her dress, stopping to kiss every bit of skin before she covered it. She told him she would never recommend him as a lady's maid.

As she put her hair up he stood behind her, watching her face in the mirror. At first he answered her reflected smile, but gradually his mouth set tightly and his eyes narrowed.

Tucking in the last tortoise-shell hairpin, she asked anxiously, "Darling, what's disturbing you?"

"I hate to mention it," he muttered.

"Dan, tell me. If you have troubles, they're mine too."

He turned and strode across the room before returning, brooding all the while. Meridel braced herself for the worst. "Meridel, isn't it rather silly to postpone our marriage until I can speak to your father?"

She sighed with relief. "No, dearest, it's really necessary. Of course—" she flushed—"neither Papa nor anyone else must know about . . . the way we love each other. But I do want you to ask him, mostly for his sake, because he feels that a good father should certainly approve the man his daughter wants to marry. There's not a chance in the world that he'll object to you."

Somberly, Dan said, "No, there is a chance he'll object to me."

Silence followed.

Meridel wasn't sure she had heard correctly. "What are you talking about? If you think it's because you have no noble title—no! Papa wants his daughter to be happy."

Dan did not seem to know what to do with his hands. They reached for Meridel, then fell away. At last he gripped his lapels. She saw his knuckles whiten. "It's time I told you that your father and I . . . oppose each other in a business matter."

"I didn't know you were doing business with Papa!"

"I'm not, but he—" Dan faltered, unable to find the words to explain.

"But if you've had a misunderstanding with Papa, I'm sure it can be straightened out."

"Don't be too sure about that," he said .

The words fell harshly upon her ears. Frightened now, she asked quickly, "Dan, what is it?"

The lines in his face deepened again, showing how much he was suffering, holding back something significant. "I can't tell you everything, but I'll tell you this much—your father wants me to sell him something I own. It's important for him to own it."

"You're not saying what it is?" she asked.

He shook his head grimly.

Determined to remain cheerful, she asked, "But whatever it is, is it really so terribly important?"

Again he turned, his face pale, and paced the room. He stared out the window, then whirled suddenly around to face her. "Meridel, if your father can't buy from me . . . what he wants to buy . . . he may be ruined."

"Ruined?" She could not comprehend.

"Bankrupt, very likely."

"Dan, what are you saying!" Fear, worry and confusion crossed her face.

"Listen. You are used to thinking of your father as a rich man. But while you've been in England he has had business reverses. He told me that Lucky McGraw may not be as lucky as he used to be. Now he has committed his resources and a great deal of borrowed money to a plan—an enterprise—that could make him another fortune."

Dazedly, Meridel asked, "Dan, are you standing in his way?"

"Well, let me make clear that I had nothing to do with his enterprise. It was only after he made arrangements—after he was over his head in them—that he asked me. Just a little while ago, when I saw him in New York, he asked me to sell something I own. I had to refuse."

"Couldn't you . . . whatever it is . . . lend it to him for as long as he needs it?"

"No. I'd be willing to sell it some day, but I don't know when. Unfortunately he needs it now." Dan ran his hand across his face and said painfully, "Meridel, I don't *want* to see your father ruined. Do you believe me?"

"I believe you, Dan. But . . . he might . . . I mean . . ."

"Under the circumstances, he might not allow us to marry."

"Dan, we *must* marry!"

"Dearest Meridel, I want desperately to! Look, let's marry today, write the news to Finnian and ask him for his blessing. Whatever he says, you'll still be my wife."

Her hands shook helplessly. "Not have Papa at my wedding? I couldn't do that to him. No, no, we must go to New York and you must ask him—"

"And what will you do if he says no?"

She only stared, feeling torn and terrified.

Suddenly Dan's mood darkened. "We must have it understood that if he says no, you'll marry me anyway. Do I have your pledge on that?"

"Dan, I . . ." She remembered her father holding her close after her mother had died. Sobbing, broken, he had told her, "Macushla, darlin' daughter, you're all I have left to love." How *could* she deny him the privilege of giving her away at her wedding?

"But, Dan, he might say yes. He does want me to be happy. And he wants to give me the biggest wedding New York has ever seen!"

Dan said, his face grim, "Big wedding or small, I still won't sell him what he wants to buy from me. I can't. Do you understand?

"Y-you mean you'd marry me and still let my father go bankrupt?" She clenched her fists. Suddenly the space between them seemed cavernous.

"I tell you I am bound by a very strong obligation not to sell. I am as strongly bound not to tell why. If I did, and you knew, it would only make matters worse."

Frantically she tried to temporize. "Things do sometimes blow over. And . . . oh, Papa did say that when I came home from England I could still have a year in New York society if I wished. Why not? And meanwhile the trouble might straighten itself out."

His glare chilled her. "A year in New York society!"

"But Dan, I'm really rather young, and if it did some good for us to delay—"

"A year in New York society!" he shouted. "Damn it, Meridel, you're nothing but a child playing at life. You still haven't comprehended what it means to live on a ranch at the frontier. I doubt if you really could. You'd rather parade in your gowns and glory than be a rancher's wife."

Tears streamed down her cheeks. "Dan, there is no other man for me. All I want in the world is to be your wife! But, don't you see, I don't want to hurt my father. Dan, tell me *why* you won't sell so I can understand, please!"

"No. I am bound by oath . . . and by honor."

"Dan, I beg you to tell me. I beg you."

"No," he repeated.

"Only tell me what Papa wants to buy, not why you won't sell it to him."

"No. Especially if you're to live with me in Kansas, you are better off not knowing."

What did he mean? If he loved her, why couldn't he confide in her? She gazed at his face through the blur of her tears. Suddenly a realization dawned on her. She cried with wild bitterness, "I see how you've trapped me. First you take me. Then you tell me you may ruin my father."

He bit his lip. "No. Finding you again . . . hearing you tell me you loved me . . . There comes a time when a man— No, I did not mean to trap you!"

"But you did!"

He passed his hand across his face. "We should be married, yes, but what happened here today is our secret. You are no more obliged to marry me than . . . I don't know!" he shouted desperately. "But I do know that if you insist on making our marriage depend on your father's permission, it can't be." He paused. "I've an idea. You have a painful decision to make. Sleep on it. Beloved girl, go back to Belgrave Square. I'll visit there at four tomorrow afternoon— teatime. Natural enough. And I'll expect to see you downstairs. *Please* be downstairs at four o'clock, my dearest. You'll act surprised to see me. And glad, I hope. Because your being downstairs when I enter the Blakistons' house will mean you have decided to marry me."

"And if I remain upstairs?"

"It will mean you are still tied to your father," he said

bluntly, walking to the window and gazing at the London street scene below.

"Meridel, Meridel," he sighed, twisting around. "I don't know what else to do. I must leave London very soon to see about horses for the ranch because the first snow has likely already fallen in Kansas, and if I wait much longer I may not be able to reach my ranch for weeks." Searching for words, he added awkwardly, "Remember, you have two choices. Either marry me now, or promise me that you'll marry me in New York no matter what your father says."

"And then you'll go ahead and ruin him?"

There was a long pause as his eyes roved around the room searchingly. "Meridel—"

"All right!" she cried, and strode to the door, regaining her composure. "I'll sleep on the question. Come to Belgrave Square at four tomorrow and you'll have my answer." Her voice broke briefly. "And Dan, if I didn't love you, I wouldn't let you treat me like this." Then, as he moved to embrace her: "No! Don't touch me!" And she swept out in a flurry of skirts.

She entered the Blakiston house cheerily, waving her new gloves at everyone. Had she enjoyed her visit with her school friend? they asked. Delightful, she responded, the lie sticking in her throat and her heart beating painfully. Pleading fatigue, she went to bed early—a mistake as she found out when she spent half the night tossing miserably. Plunkett found her hoarse and red-eyed in the morning. Perhaps Miss should stay in bed? the maid suggested. No, she would dress, she would pretend nothing had happened to her, she would live the day as though four o'clock only meant one more teatime.

In the early afternoon, a man arrived at the house. Meridel knew by his voice that the guest wasn't Dan. A few minutes later she paused at the drawing-room door and saw Lord Harald Wayne, chatting with her guardians. Strange that she had put Harald so far from her mind that she had not recognized his voice!

"Meridel!" He came toward her smiling, both hands extended.

Hardly knowing what to do, she offered only her right hand

and murmured how pleased she was to see him again. She hoped the earl had recovered from his new bereavement; he had, nearly, he replied. She hoped Harald himself had recovered from the loss of his dear grandmother; he nodded with a brief solemn look that turned to a smile as he gazed at Meridel and scanned her from head to toe.

He was dressed as elegantly as usual in the kind of coat that the prince favored—called a Prince Albert in his honor. He told her he had come to town on estate business that dealt with more than which tenant grew rye and which grew mangel-wurzels. "That's a kind of rough beet used as cattle feed," he explained for Meridel's benefit. Indeed, once she had entered the drawing room he spoke only to her. The Blakistons, noticing it, smiled, and making excuses, left them alone together. Meridel wished they hadn't departed. She still did not know if she could make herself marry the man who might ruin her father, but she knew quite certainly that she would never marry Lord Harald Wayne.

Before long, she pleaded a headache and returned to her room. Remorselessly, the clock on her dresser ticked. At quarter to two she felt that heaven itself wanted her in the arms of the man she loved. At five past two she told herself it would be naive and schoolgirlish to trust mere instincts and emotions. But the next moment she felt guilt for betraying her gentle rearing and all the teachings of her church—oh, how Dan Forrester had brought her low! She hated him, she hated all men, but most of all she hated the convention of society that said she *must* marry Dan, after doing what she had done.

"'Scuse me, Miss."

"What is it, Plunkett?" Meridel asked wearily.

The maid crept close, looking around with exaggerated care, smirked then finally whispered, "Lord Harald gave me a con-fee-dential note for you."

Meridel wished Harald had merely slipped it beneath her door. Plunkett was not the kind of maid who inspired one to share secrets.

The note said that Harald must see her on a most urgent matter. He trusted that in this quiet hour she would meet him again in Lord Hubert's library, and had taken the liberty of asking her maid to keep watch. He assured her that the matter was of the utmost gravity.

At least it would take her mind off Dan, she decided, and descended the stairs.

As she entered the library, Harald replaced an unopened volume of Catullus on a shelf and turned to face her. "I don't think you really have a headache, Meridel. I think something else has upset you."

She sensed danger, but only said, "What do you have to tell me, Harald?"

"Lady Anne has the impression that you really didn't have a very good time with your old school chum yesterday. You seemed to return not yourself."

He watched her closely. *What did he suspect?*

"Come now, Meridel. I know Dan Forrester is in London."

"What of it?"

He trailed his hand down her forearm. It was not Dan's touch, and she felt unmoved. "What of it? This: that I have offered you my heart, and Danemead too. That you are all I can think of or dream about. That I saw the way Dan Forrester looked at you—"

"You have no claim on me!"

"Why so nervous, Meridel? Everything about you bespeaks the girl who has had a lover's quarrel."

"I tell you it is none of your affair!" The words burst out of her mouth, and she wished she had not let them. She lifted a hand to her forehead. "Harald, I am not feeling well, and you are most unkind to speak to me like this."

"Perhaps so," he murmured, his eyes taking her in from head to toe, this time very slowly. Drawing a letter from his pocket, he glared at her. "This is from your father. It was delayed by storms on the Atlantic."

"It came to Danemead? For me?"

"No, it came to me. But certain matters have made me want you to read it." He held the wrinkled envelope out to her.

Uneasy but curious, she grasped the letter and glanced at the writing. She saw immediately that her father had not dictated his message to his secretary since the scrawling was his own, so he obviously had wanted the message kept confidential.

My esteemed Wayne:
I rite in great distress and hope you can do something with Forrester before he bankrupps me. As you know, the only good rite-of-way for my Kan. railroad is through his ranch. I have made him an ofer of five thousand dollars for the strip of land that is not worth even one thou but he says he wont sell.

Meridel lifted a shocked face. "Go on," Harald urged.

He wont give any reson but I know his reson. Which is he knows I must have the rite-of-way. So he will make me up my ofer and up it till maybe fifty thou is only my gess, maybe more.

Wayne, you know if you come in with me on this there will be baggs of money for us and I hope the connect. with the transcon rr but remember Congress will only OK a good strait rr if there's a reason for extra miles and if I have to lay iron all around Forrester's ranch it means I must go around more miles of Indian farms either side too & Congress wont bother those Indians any more account of already they got pushed out of the east states into Kan.

Alreaddy I owe heavy dett to Vanderbilt for rolling stock and rails etc & will need another construckshun loan before the new rr opens up new farm land & starts errning. Meanwhile very bad luck in real estate etc. If must pay fifty thou to Forrester I will default on payment to Vanderbilt & he takes control so Forrester makes me a ruined man.

Forrester admits he sees good rite-of-way across his ranch, sure he does, he is a rr engineer. So he has a gun at my head. Now he saw me in NY & sed he is going to England to buy horses from you. I authorize you to bargain him on my behaff 20 thou maximum. You are good with money and good salesman & it is in your own interest becos I want you in with me to handle all kinds of extra matters while I build the rr.

Friend Wayne I have to leen on you. Also I am grateful you saw my darling child meet the queen and she writes she is visiting Danemead with my dear dead wife's cousins so please tell her I miss her but remember she thinks I am still rich so say nothing about money.

I remain most faithfully . . ."

Meridel's blue eyes stared at Harald, unseeing. She saw Dan, heard him telling her about his oath, about how he had to honor an obligation which he could not disclose to her, yet.

No wonder. He had not wanted to mention a right-of-way because he knew a right-of-way was the lifeblood of a railroad builder! Imagine, he had sixty thousand acres! Why, that was a hundred square miles! And he was refusing to sell a mere strip of land to her father, no more than a hundred feet wide. Oh, he had an obligation, did he? His only "obligation" was to wait and drive up the price of the land before selling. He'd get rich at the expense of her desperate father who needed the land immediately.

Oh yes, the entire foul scheme became instantly clear to her, a railroad man's daughter. Thank God she had not married him and then found out too late!

Not that her father should be excused for buying cars and rails with borrowed money before he knew whether he had land on which to set them. But Finnian McGraw had made his fortune by taking risks. She remembered his saying, when the money was coming in, "Business? It's nothing but taking chances."

"You did meet Forrester here in town, didn't you?" Harald's question brought her sharply back to the present.

"It is none of your affair!"

"The only possible answer, I realize. But now, *if* you met him and *if* he means something to you, I did my duty by showing you how he holds a gun at your father's head. And Meridel, as you know, Vanderbilt will have no mercy."

"But couldn't Papa go elsewhere to borrow the money to—to—"

"Pay Forrester? Chances are, he has already tried. And chances are that Vanderbilt has let it be known that a Kansas railroad looks like a good thing and he wants it for himself. Nobody will oppose him."

"He—Vanderbilt—will take over all the cars and the rails . . ."

"And he'll pay Forrester fifty thousand or a hundred thousand and get that railroad built. Forrester profits either way."

And Finnian McGraw, Lucky McGraw, would be left out in the cold. Bankrupt.

"No!"

"Pardon?" said the handsome, charming, elegantly dressed heir of Danemead who surely had no trouble reading the emotions that raced across her face. And yet he had done her a great favor.

"Th-thank you for—for—showing me the letter."

He watched and waited.

"Harald, I'm sorry . . . M-my headache had grown so dreadful . . . Excuse me, please."

He went to the door. "Plunkett, help your mistress to her room." Turning back to her, he said, "I have been invited to stay for dinner. I hope to see you then, Meridel."

Alone again, Meridel stood at the window and watched the shadows lengthen across Belgrave Square. Liveried footmen walked dogs. Crested carriages rumbled by.

And she had thought herself in love with Dan! A man who could crush her father with one hand—while he seduced her with the other!

Strangely, then, the word *seduce* aroused her body's memory. She tried to fight the intimate tinglings and nameless yearnings that crept through her limbs. She fought herself with words: "Whore! Strumpet!" She remembered sitting in Paris at a sidewalk café where certain painted, bedizened women had sauntered by, giving every man an inviting look—even Lord Hubert. And now at last, she felt she understood them. "I am no better than they!" she cried. It did not help. Her body remembered. Her heart remembered.

The little clock on the dresser chimed, reminding her that in an hour Dan would arrive.

"No, no. I hate him!"

But that was only her mind speaking. Her heart told her she was bound to Dan forever—even if she never saw him again.

At quarter to four she saw Dan Forrester stride across the square. She reeled from the window in horror as she realized how drawn to him she was.

The rap of the big brass knocker sounded on the front door,

followed by the butler's voice. Then Lady Anne's, pitched high with delight, rang out. "Why, Mr. Forrester, such a pleasant surprise! Do come in! We're having quite a Danemead reunion!"

Meridel sat in her chair and gripped its arms while voices drifted up through the walls and the clock indicated that five minutes had passed. Ten minutes.

It chimed four o'clock.

Five after.

Ten after.

Meridel leaped from her chair as someone knocked. She flung open the door, and for many days afterward was to ask herself what would have happened if Dan had been there. Sometimes she thought she would have bounded into his arms. Sometimes she thought she would have simply fainted.

But she faced Lord Blakiston, his head cocked so that his good ear was turned to her, his lined face filled with kindness and concern. "Meridel, my dear. We thought you'd surely come down. Do you know Mr. Forrester has dropped in? Dan Forrester—you remember—the man who came to look at horses? And Lord Harald is still here, and we do need you among us."

In panic she asked, "Is Mr. Forrester staying for dinner?"

"No, he has to go. He's not even staying for tea. But he would be so glad to see you, if only for a moment."

"Tell him . . . please . . . I really feel dreadfully ill . . . so ill that I may ask you to call the doctor if I don't feel better later on."

"Then I'll ask Plunkett to—"

"No, please. I'd just like to be alone. The spell may pass. If it does, I'll come down, I promise you."

She sank into her chair, praying Dan would leave before she did anything rash. Now and then she sobbed dryly.

She heard them chatting at the open door on his way out and his voice drifted up to her: ". . . might come back and talk again about buying Bluebonnet . . . but I'll be going to eastern Europe now . . . there are some excellent Polish stables—"

She leaped up from the chair and ran to the window, watching his broad shoulders sway as he crossed the square.

He never looked back and disappeared from view. Something went with him, and a deep groan wrenched from her. She had to get a grip on herself, pull herself back together. In the middle of her mind, which felt as hot and dry as a desert, a thought took root.

She suddenly knew exactly what she had to do.

She called Plunkett to send word that she would come down for dinner.

She kept Plunkett busy for two hours, dressing her, coiffing her, changing her hair this way and that. After an hour they began all over again, because she felt her organdy gown made her look trifling, like a girl enthralled by an ice.

Harald had never seen Monsieur Worth's "society gown." The clever, expertly tailored, unpressed pleats made her seem sophisticated, while the delicate flowers wrought into the brocade emphasized her femininity. And the bodice that made it clear that, as Lady Grizel had put it, *this* young woman knew how to carry her figure.

Floating down the stairs, she remembered her parents' dream of having her marry English peerage. She wondered how many girls lived to see such a dream come true.

Pausing in the doorway of the drawing room as a lady should, she saw nothing rough-hewn in Harald Wayne. Rather she saw generations of aristocratic breeding, exactly suited to match the breeding she had inherited from her mother's side.

His eyes widened as he saw her. She glided into the drawing room, where two parallel rows of gilt-framed mirrors created a hundred reflections of her pale face.

Harald rose, his eyes still wide with surprise and delight. Lord Hubert murmured, "I say!" and Lady Anne seemed transfixed with admiration. Step by step Meridel rustled toward Harald, toward Danemead, her back a willow, her thoughts very still.

Harald escorted her into a chair and bowed before taking the seat next to her. She sat as Lady Wayne would sit, with grace and place and dignity, and when Harald gazed her way, she mustered a small, surrendering smile as she turned her face to his.

Chapter Six

On the *Atlantic*, a huge paddle-wheeler of nearly three thousand tons, the coats of arms of all thirty-one states composing the Union had been fixed to panels between the cabins. An oil painting in the grand salon showed the figure of Liberty trampling a feudal prince. Harald said he found little in the ship to comfort an Englishman—but he said so tongue in cheek, and all during the voyage he remained affable and charming. Meridel was relieved at his behavior. Perhaps he really did need a wife—or at least to be affianced—to settle down.

He had his own quarters, of course, while Meridel shared a cabin with a widow, Mrs. Agnes Uttley, a friend of Lady Anne's who was crossing "the Pond" to visit a married daughter. Mrs. Uttley thought it marvelous that Meridel's father would give her a year in New York society before her marriage. It would work wonders for a girl's social standing to gad about with a titled fiancé at her side.

And somehow it would avenge her on Dan Forrester,

thought Meridel. Except . . . did she really want revenge? She would rather have forgotten him, but she had come to know how despairingly she would remember Dan Forrester all her life.

For her seventeenth birthday Harald arranged an elaborate party at the captain's table. But the dreaded North Atlantic winter came down from the Arctic and the party was forgotten while the ship staggered through a raging storm that coated the decks in ice. Meridel spent her birthday for the first time groaning with seasickness. She recovered before the vessel made its landfall and eagerly stood at the rail as the battered ship pushed through the slush and ice of New York Harbor and got nudged into its slip by a red-and-green tug.

Meridel peered eagerly at the waiting crowd but could not single out the small, heavy figure of her father. Only after they had followed their luggage out onto the street did she see Standish, the McGraw butler, waving from three hansom cabs which he had obviously hired for their landing party. One cab was for Meridel and her maid, one for her luggage, and one for Lord Harald—who of course could neither stay at the McGraw house nor call until Meridel's father came home. Standish had a note for Meridel. Her father pleaded with his daughter to forgive him for not meeting her, but he had been called to Washington for a conference "of the most urgent kind."

Cheerfully enough, Harald took a suite at the St. Nicholas Hotel near Wall Street, where all the curtains were made of satin damask and even the embroidery on the mosquito nettings had been copied from netting used in a European palace.

Miss Whittaker always had counseled her girls to keep their distance with servants. But Meridel hugged every servant at 42 Union Square. The house seemed terribly empty without her father, but still it was home with its mansard roof, pink marble stairs, wainscoted walls, and curio cabinets. Now mistress of the house, Meridel decided to have her meals in the morning room, always the mistress's special domain.

She did what she could with the household accounts, then turned with relief to the daily newspapers, brought to her warm each morning after the creases had been ironed out. She found it most interesting that a Madam Demorest had invented a method for making dress patterns of thin paper that could be sold through the mail at low cost. She wrinkled her nose at an advertisement for something called the Imperial Dress Elevator, which discreetly raised or lowered a hoop skirt at the wearer's whim—such as at a muddy crossing.

She read about fighting in Kansas where scores had been killed in the battles between Slave Staters and Free Staters. She read about the famous Brooklyn minister, Henry Ward Beecher, who thundered from his pulpit against slavery every week. And there was an item about an American soldier of fortune named William Walker who had conquered Nicaragua in Central America where politics were as wild as in San Tomás. Ah! Walker was said to be backed by Cornelius Vanderbilt! So, despite the successful San Tomás railroad that Meridel's father—and Dan Forrester—had built, Vanderbilt wanted a still quicker way to haul goods across the Isthmus of Panama.

She had been trying hard not to think of Dan but now he possessed her mind and awakened her body with a tingling memory. She cried out against him with a low, desperate, almost animal sound that also expressed a deep fear that had been gripping her of late. Her monthly cycle had been off, and she could only console herself with the thought that all her school friends had laughed and said such things happened all the time, and that one day the normal course of things resumed—

But another day passed and another, and not all of her running around town, shopping, and ceaseless walking could subdue the worry that had grown into a haunting fear.

One morning, when the smell of breakfast made her not hungry, but nauseated, she had to face the truth.

Huddled at the morning-room stove, she could not get warm. She puttered aimlessly in the conservatory, where snow drifted along the huge windowpanes, asking herself: "Me, with child?" Her bitter laugh turned into a sob. "Dan!" she cried, staring out the window.

No! She would not summon the man who heartlessly wanted to make himself rich by ruining her father.

And yet—if she didn't immediately let Dan know that she was carrying his child, and that he had to marry her, what

95

then? She had no choice. Thank heaven, the telegraph wires had recently been extended to St. Joseph, Missouri, right on the Kansas border. Frantically she scrawled an unsigned message that Dan would understand: PERSON YOU MET ON NORFOLK ROAD DESPERATELY NEEDS YOU HERE ON CONFIDENTIAL MATTER. URGENT YOU COME AT ONCE.

But how far away did Rainbow Ranch lie from St. Joseph? Even if she paid in advance for a horseman to carry the message to the ranch, how many days would he have to push through the drifted snow? And then how many more precious days would go by before Dan could reach the railhead somewhere in Missouri? The thought that each day lost meant that much more difficulty in making people believe she had had a seven-month baby, sickened her.

And she did not know if he would come at all. No, she must go to him—today, at once. She would go and find Dan and marry him and live in Kansas, no matter if he did ruin her father. Living on Rainbow Ranch, she would be envied by the neighbors because she didn't have to chop her own firewood—and she would invite the wanton schoolmistress in for tea!

Seven-month baby . . . seven-month baby . . . seven-month baby . . . tolled in her mind as she tossed the draft of her telegram into the stove, trying to think clearly. How soon did a train leave for the West? And what about money? She'd have to pawn her mother's jewels. She rushed to her father's study. In his desk, in the third cubbyhole to the right, behind a sliding panel, she'd find the key to the wall safe where the jewels were kept. Quickly, quickly!

As she was struggling to push open her father's rolltop desk, she heard the wheels of a vehicle clattering through the snowcovered street, and stop outside their home. As she fumbled for the key, the front door opened and Finnian McGraw roared up the stairs, "Meridel, machushla! Where is my precious? I'm home!"

He burst through the study door and without pausing swung her into his arms, kissing her heartily and hugging her as though she were still seven. When she really could see her father through her confusion of panic and joy she found him balder, grayer, more sallow. But his genuinely ugly face, framed in ginger-and-gray whiskers, beamed like a sunburst on his only child.

"Faith, and is it not a peril for a man to send his wee one away to school? How is he to know her now, the grown woman?"

"Oh, Papa, Papa!" What to do, what to say? she wondered. Now that he was home, it would be next to impossible for her to run away to Kansas.

Woman or no, he took Meridel upon his lap to talk to her. "Macushla, do you know why I went to Washington? To shake the hand of President Pierce. And that I did, and I've more to tell." McGraw put a stubby forefinger against his nose and winked portentously. "But a long story it makes of itself, colleen, and I've to tell Wayne, too. I've already sent Briscoe," he added, referring to his valet, "to the St. Nicholas to fetch Wayne for dinner."

Harald! What was she to do—*what was she to do?*

"Then I must dress for dinner," she muttered through the haze of panic that clouded her mind.

McGraw chuckled. "Spoken like a finished lady. And don't think your Papa isn't waiting to see those Paris gowns!"

When she came downstairs in green-sashed creamy satin, Harald's admiration and her father's delight in his admiration only added to the leaden weight in Meridel's breast. In the big formal dining room that Standish had happily reopened at last, she hardly knew what dishes were set before her and, with her stomach churning, she feared to eat. At the end of the meal she would have been glad for the chance to exert a lady's privilege of exiting. But as she rose, her father roared cheerfully, "Sit down, sit down, stay here with us. We need someone pretty to look at."

"Hear! Hear!" said Harald Wayne.

"And anyway, you've smelled my cigars before."

She sat, smiling a smile that went no deeper than her quavering lips. A footman brought a spirit lamp with which the two men lit up their cigars, watching her smilingly.

Finnian McGraw leaned back, knowing the suspense he had created; he looked like an aging, happy leprechaun. "Well, sir and miss, do I have your attention? For I have something to—ah—what the divil is that Boston word? I've something to impart."

He took a moment to get his cigar drawing, and said, "So I had your letters, and here I sat waiting to meet my daughter precious the chirruping instant her ship touched the pier. And a telegram comes from my dear friend Jefferson Davis—come see him in Washington, it says. Most important. Och, it hurt in the heart o' me, it did. But off I took meself.

"'Well now, Mr. McGraw,'" says Jeff Davis to me when we'd passed a few fingers o' bourbon in his Washington office, "'you are aware o' the shooting in Bleeding Kansas, as they call it?'

"To be sure, everyone knows that whether Kansas comes in as a Slave or a Free State is to be decided by squatter sovereignty, meaning the settlers are to get the vote. 'Och,' say I, 'Kansas could be settled in peace as a Slave State, an extension of the old South, if the abolitionists didn't send in so many Free Staters, each with his Beecher Bible, meaning a gun.'

"Which pleases the secretary of war. I'd known 'twould. And he pours me another bourbon and he says, 'And do you know that the first territorial governor, Reeder, had to be withdrawn after much shooting and trouble, and that the next governor we sent—Shannon's his name—ordered out the troops when he should not have and we'll withdraw him soon, too?'

"'The man who could keep the peace in Kansas is not born,' I tell Jeff Davis. He explains that in between governors there's always a lieutenant governor to take the chair till a new man is sent out. Then he says—Are you well, Macushla?"

"Quite all right, Papa. Just . . . excited."

"Ah, wait, you'll be more excited yet." McGraw patted his well-filled belly and continued through the cloud of blue smoke. "So Jeff Davis tells me that President Pierce and himself want to send a different kind of man to Kansas. They have cooked up a new title, all in the hands of the White House so Congress won't butt in. And with no salary but with certain advantages in the way of—eh, well, a man on the spot in Kansas, a man of experience and business judgment who might take advantage of opportunities bound to open up."

Harald now sat on the edge of his seat. "Did Davis mention railroads?"

"In a manner of speaking, he did. That he did." Taking pains to speak to the glowing end of his cigar, McGraw went on, "Now, the name of the new office I hold, confirmed to me by the President of the United States, is Commissioner of Boundaries for the Territory of Kansas."

"Papa!" In her pride, Meridel put aside her worry and ran to hug him. Harald, beaming, shook his hand.

"Which," continued McGraw in obvious pleasure, "will send me to live in Lecompton, now the capital city of Kansas. I'll confer with Governor Shannon and others and report to Jeff Davis and Mr. Pierce. I am to consider the boundaries of the future state of Kansas and"—he drew an impressive document from his pocket, found his spectacles, and read— "'perform other such duties as may properly fall within his province, according to his judgment and the exig—exig—' The divil! 'The exigencies of circumstance.' Hah! And wherever I go I'll have troops to protect me. And if in seeing whether Kansas should go all the way to the Rocky Mountains or end somewhere in the plains, for instance, I happen to take note of where a railroad could run, well, Jeff Davis knows I'm a railroad man ready to lay iron."

Harald Wayne said, with more excitement than he usually showed, "And the territory certainly needs a railroad! And I have heard that Jefferson Davis swings great influence at the White House and on Capitol Hill. McGraw, you could not have done better!"

"Why, I'm Lucky McGraw again, I am," said the formerly penniless immigrant complacently. "And let me tell you a bit more. I am to learn all I can about everything in Kansas. So that when Shannon is recalled—why, no need to hunt for another man when I'm there all ready to move in."

"Papa! You'd be territorial governor!"

McGraw poked a thumb into the armhole of his waistcoat and pretended to weigh the matter before reaching a decision. "Now begorra if I would not. I would! And later, being known as a fair and just man, if the people elected me governor of the state itself, why, 'twould be the success I came to America to make. And a padded chair for a man who will soon need his comfort. Oh . . . ah, Jeff Davis did happen to say, concerning a Kansas railroad, that he had a few sundry provisions, if I agreed. I agreed. Now he's to swing the land grant through Congress. Barrels o' money, friend Wayne. Barrels piled on top o' barrels.''

Harald glanced at Meridel. ''But McGraw, what about that right-of-way trouble with Forrester?''

Finnian McGraw winked at the plaster cupids that frolicked on the ceiling. ''I'll have influence in high places. There'll be no trouble about that right-of-way. No trouble at all.''

''Champagne!'' cried Harald. ''Let's drink to your success.''

''Why, thank 'e. And next I must send a telegram to St. Joseph, Missouri.'' Not noticing that Meridel had gasped and gripped her chair to steady herself, McGraw went on, ''Which someone out there will get to my chief engineer, Henrick, who waits down near Forrester's ranch for word to lay iron. Good man, Henrick. Keeps me informed on all sorts of matters. Even lets me know that our ex-friend Forrester is still somewhere in Europe on that horse-hunting expedition of his.''

Meridel felt ice-cold though she was perspiring. Suppose she had gone to Kansas to find Dan! Not that her situation was now any better than before. Her shaking hand touched her abdomen beneath the table.

As though from far away, she heard: ''So you see, my esteemed Wayne, I need you to manage finances on the Missouri and Pikes Peak Railroad.''

''Papa, that's a beautiful name.''

''High, wide, and handsome, say I. And Wayne, you're also the man to run notices in the newspapers and bring in settlers to start farms along my iron. And once we lay a hundred miles of rail, which will take us well beyond Forrester's ranch and out into Indian country—listen to this! I've had Vanderbilt's hand on it that he'll back me for all I need, for I'd make his profit sure, then. And ours, too. Eh, Lord Harald? You can lose on Wall Street but you can't lose on a Kansas railroad, and in a couple of years you can go home wearing a solid-gold suit. We've worked together before and made money. Are you with me in this?''

Harald rose, glowing. He held out his hand. "I am honored and proud to be able to work once more with . . . Lucky McGraw!"

"Ah, you've said it, lad, you've said it, for the wheel of my good luck has come 'round again. Standish. More champagne!"

Meridel only pretended to sip. How clever of Jefferson Davis to put her father in Kansas as the White House's own man! She frowned, however, when she recalled that Davis came from Mississippi and Pierce was said to look kindly on the South which meant they expected her father to favor the slave-staters, a dilemma repugnant to the freedom-loving Meridel. But she knew one thing they didn't know—her father was a businessman, not a politician.

"And now, daughter darlin'," he asked in his blustery voice, "how'd you like to come to Kansas, too?"

Meridel gasped. She heard her father say after a moment that if she didn't come along with him she might not have a place to live, for he feared he'd have to sell 42 Union Square. She could, he supposed, stay with her Aunt Penelope in Boston, but wouldn't she rather come out West with him as his hostess? "'Twon't be a year and I'll be running Kansas," he said gleefully, chucking Meridel beneath the chin.

Lucky McGraw had rebounded from his recent setbacks and Meridel realized that nothing she said would make her father doubt his future success. And why should it? In many ways, his bluff nature had won him his privileged station in life. Her thoughts turned to Dan Forrester. He lived in Kansas. But suppose she did meet him—it would of course be far too late by then for an honorable marriage. In any case, would he acknowledge the baby? She did not know the answer. Insofar as she could see ahead, she knew what she could count on: in Kansas in the spring she would tell her father she was pregnant, and out of bitter pride she would refuse to name the man. Then it would be best to leave before she "showed." She could take a steamer down the river and go to, say, New Orleans and pose as a heartbroken pregnant widow. . . .

But she did not know if her father would ever want her to return.

She said in a very low voice, "I'd be happy to go to Kansas and take care of you, Papa."

This greatly pleased him. "Good, good. Let's all get ready then because President Pierce wants me on my way in a week. Och! And here I promised you a year in New York society."

"It doesn't matter—" Her heart cried at the fate which fortune had meted out to her, though she masked her pain, "—the least little bit."

Excited discussion broke out between the two men, and then Meridel became aware that Harald had stopped speaking and was watching her. He nodded as though signaling—she knew not what. But something inside her *did know*, and her blood ran cold.

Smiling, the tall, blond-bearded man said, "Now is the time to bring up another very important matter. Sir, for many months I have been in love with Meridel."

"Aha!" McGraw's joy smote Meridel's heart. "Not that I didn't read it between the lines!"

"Sir, I believe my qualifications as a husband are known to you, and I ask your permission to speak to your daughter on the subject of marriage."

Meridel wanted to cry out "No, it's impossible," but she found herself simply looking on, in increasing horror.

"So-o-o-o!" said McGraw, gazing delightedly from Harald to Meridel and back again. "If only her mother was here to know it! Macushla! You heard? He has my permission to speak to you, to be sure, so tell him your answer whilst I go look at my mail, which is piled to the ceiling." Chuckling, the excited man rose and began to leave the room.

At the door he turned, red-faced. "Now, daughter, there'll be no time for a grand wedding, but a decent small wedding, that you shall have—if you say yes. And we'll get Father Weems at St. Thomas's to do it. He's Episcopal, Harald, for the McGraws went Church of England in my grandfather's day, so we'll have no trouble there. And I'm thinking, Macushla, that a married woman would make the best kind of hostess at the Governor's Mansion. Nor would I be bothered in my government business with every young swain in Kansas galloping to my door. But it's up to you, girl, whether my friend from old San Tomás days, a man I trust and like more than any other in the world, is to be my son-in-law. Excuse me while I see to my mail.''

Harald Wayne·came around the end of the long mahogany table. He took the seat beside Meridel and captured her cold hand in his own.

Her other hand toyed with a teaspoon that did not match the rest of the ornate silver setting. Her mother always had used those chaste old coin-silver spoons made by Paul Revere. She watched the spoon make reflections in her hand because she could not look at Harald.

She heard him declare his undying love and formally ask her to marry him. When she did not answer, he whispered, ''I want you at my side as long as we live in Kansas. And later, I see you beside me at Danemead, welcoming our guests, the most beautiful woman in Norfolk—''

She found her mind racing with thoughts and feelings that only raised questions with no answers. How could she even consider marrying Harald while she carried another man's child?

But then she recalled that Harald wanted, needed an heir desperately. True, she would suffer all her life with her secret, but it would remain hers alone. She would never allow anyone else to be hurt. Not her child, not her father, not the Earl of Danemead—no one but herself would suffer. Why not marry Harald, then, while she was able to pretend he had given her a seven-month baby?

Instantly she hated herself for the thought. How terrible to use Harald that way! At least let her baby have an honest mother.

Honest mother! Much good that would do a child brought up fatherless by a mother estranged from everyone she loved! And when at last she had to explain to the child that it had been born a bastard—what then? Her own child would hate her. Turn on her. Or, at best, would always resent having been made the victim of her sin.

If she did not marry Harald, *everyone* would suffer.

Her soul cried out for the father of her child. But she had no way of finding him, and she dared not wait. Her mother's instinct surfaced now and a little voice cried out, "Protect your baby."

Turning to a man she did not love, she whispered, "Yes, Harald, I will marry you."

Chapter Seven

In the small chapel at St. Thomas's, Finnian McGraw blinked and sighed as Harald Wayne slid a wedding band upon Meridel's finger and made her Lady Wayne, mistress of Danemead. He lifted her veil of virgin white and looked down into the blue eyes of his bride. Perhaps something showed on her face that should not have been there, for Harald's gray eyes widened, and a furrow appeared upon his brow.

Ignoring the change in his features, she did what she'd learned at Miss Whittaker's, lifting her face to his, and letting him kiss her cold lips.

All night the train rattled westward, slowing as they ascended the long climb over the Allegheny Mountains. Harald, having helped himself twice to his bride's body, told her for the third or fourth time that he loved her. She had not had to pretend pain. She had felt it, caused by Harald's failure to make her ready, and she had given him the difficult entrance he was entitled to expect.

In time she slipped from the fold-down bed and blew out the lamp that Harald had insisted on leaving lit. But the mountain air blew cold, and she had to lie down again beneath the blanket, keeping as far away from her husband as she could. She didn't want him waking and beginning another unsatisfying round of lovemaking.

At least, she reminded herself, she had found safety and respectability. She and Dan's baby. *Her* baby.

She stared at the dimly seen paintings of Elysian fields on the walls of the sleeping compartment. When she fell asleep, the upward-slanting train caused her to roll against Harald. She shrank away to the edge of the bed and drowzed for a while, then rolled against her husband's naked back again. But Harald seemed completely to have satisfied himself and was sleeping like a baby.

So ended her wedding night.

The newlyweds occupied a magnificent private car upholstered in the purple plush that railroad men called spit-and-varnish. Beside their sleeping chamber they had a dining nook, a sitting room, and a kitchen where a fine black chef presided. They even had a bath, fed by hot water from the heating system, and at one end of the car, the servants slept in tiny, cramped quarters.

Harald spent hours every day working with a huge portfolio of advertisements and other material. Meridel sat at a window and read a new book of poetry called *Leaves of Grass* or watched bare-limbed forests and snow-streaked farms as they rushed by.

Her father was riding with his man Briscoe and his secretary, Frank Llewellyn, in the private car behind their own. The day came when Finnian thought he had waited long enough to join the newlyweds at dinner. He was so excited about a work train he had sketched, that he took Harald back to his car to see his drawings of a bunk car, a mess car, and so forth. Left alone Meridel decided to explore the coach ahead. She brought a blast of cold air with her from between cars, and this she regretted, for the shabby coach held dozens of foreign immigrants trying to keep warm. They were a poor, dazed lot, having to sit and eat and sleep on hard wooden benches amid their squalling babies and their bundles of clothing and food. The coach had no bath, not even a sink, and reeked of unwashed bodies.

Meridel smiled tentatively at a young black couple and an imposing older woman, also black, who was obviously a matriarch of great dignity. Her proud, handsome face showed the imprint of decades.

In the center of the car, several people huddled around a coal stove and stared at the fine lady who had come to visit. One, a good-looking woman in her early twenties, did not look like an immigrant. Meridel took note of the woman's fitted, stayless dress which had not yet been streaked by soot caused by the chuffing train, nor by days of not being able to bathe or change into fresh clothing. Surely she had not boarded with the others on the Atlantic coast but at some way station along their route west.

Noticing Meridel's curiosity, the woman indicated with a motion of her sleek head that Meridel might come and warm herself if she wished.

"Thank you," said Meridel, moving to the stove and holding out her hands to the warm glow.

After a few silent moments, during which time she noted that the other woman was quite pretty, Meridel remarked, "Who are these poor people? I've heard their language somewhere, but I can't understand it."

"Germans going to settle on farms in Missouri."

"But—in the dead of winter?"

The woman shrugged her shoulders, as if to say the season did not matter. Meridel detected signs of education in her voice along with a Western tang as the woman continued, "Might be getting in with one of the Mennonite settlements, I s'pose." A sniff. "Whew! Isn't that smell awful? I'm glad I don't have to spend a night with this bunch."

"Did you get on in Illinois?"

"Yes, just a bit back."

"But, if you don't mind my saying so, aren't you afraid to travel alone?"

The woman snorted. "The railroads *say* their trains are safe for female passengers. Anyhow, when one lives in Kansas, as I do, she can't be as particular as females in the East from where I suppose you hail."

"Yes." So she had better not be too "particular" in Kansas!

"Whatever made you come in here from a private car?" the woman asked. "Don't you know when you're well-off?"

Really! thought Meridel. But conversation with another woman was too precious to be spoiled by getting offended. She said, "One likes to stretch one's legs."

"Nobody here is going to introduce us, so—I'm Miss Lucy Barth."

"How do you do, Miss Barth? I'm Lady Wayne. Meridel Wayne," she amended, her title still sounding strange to her own ears.

"You don't sound English."

"I'm not, though my husband is."

"Englishmen are coming out to the West in droves. It's because England brings in so much money from exports and America is a good place for investment. I s'pose you tagged along to see the Indians?"

It appeared that Lucy Barth was not the most tactful person in the world. Nevertheless Meridel answered, "No, we're traveling out with my father, and we'll stay a while. My father has been appointed commissioner of boundaries for Kansas."

"I hope he lasts longer than the governors have. Anyway, count on it, Lady Wayne, you're bound to be the best-dressed woman in the territory. But you'll soon get rid of all those petticoats. Kansas shakes things down to the essentials, as you'll see."

Should she say "thank you?" But the locomotive suddenly shrieked several warning whistles, and the train jerked to a stop. Staggering, Meridel almost fell. A woman screamed, pointing through a dirty window. Outside, rough hewn and armed horsemen galloped down the track toward them. "Bushwackers," cried Lucy Barth, and mockingly added, "That's how safe the trains are."

"But . . . where are the soldiers?" Meridel peered desperately into the distance.

Miss Barth snorted. "Polishing brass at Fort Leavenworth, I'm sure."

The men who had straggly beards and wore dirty heavy

clothing leaped from their horses with rifles slung across their backs. Some of the men pointed their unholstered revolvers at the passengers, then laughed as the immigrants reeled away from the windows. Others took chains and fetters from saddlebags. The conductor came running up to them protesting. They tripped and kicked dirt at him, and then from either end, stormed into the immigrants' car.

"Thar they be!" roared a half-drunken bushwhacker who had tucked a tomahawk in the belt of his sheepskin coat.

He pointed. The three black people shrank down in their seat. The young woman gave a long and terrible wail. But the matriarch lifted her heavy arms and face heavenward and in a deep contralto full of resonance and power sang:

> "Go down, Moses,
> Way down in Egypt's land.
> Tell old Pharaoh . . ."

As a bushwhacker dangled chains before her, she shouted the last words with the strength of despair:

> "Let my people go!"   •

"Sho 'nuff, you kin go," the ruffian chortled. "Straight back to your marster." He displayed a handbill that bore a crude woodcut of a black man running from bloodhounds. Meridel saw its headline: $500 REWARD FOR RETURN OF RUNAWAY SLAVES.

In a flash Meridel remembered seeing Lady Gray showing Dan Forrester her reticule with its picture of Africans dancing before the slave ships came. Somehow she also recalled that Dan had not declared himself on the issue of slavery—but did that matter now? She choked with horror as she saw the bushwhackers jerk the black passengers to their feet and slap fetters onto their wrists, clamping them tightly.

Shame swept through Meridel. The German immigrants had come all this way from Europe to their own promised land to see this! "No!" Meridel cried out, running forward then.

But Lucy Barth grabbed her arm, warning, "It's a crime to interfere with slave catchers."

The grand old matriarch, hearing, gave them a glance that contained a world of sadness. Raising her chains as though before the sight of God, she again rolled out the spiritual in her deep, majestic voice:

> "Go down, Moses,
> way down in Egypt's land.
> Tell old Pharaoh
> Let my people go."

"Shut up before we shut you up," growled the group's leader, a bull-necked giant who wore a brass badge in his raccoon cap.

As the slave catchers pushed their victims to the door, Lucy Barth whispered to Meridel, "Likely they're runaways from Kentucky trying to reach the Mississippi. Underground Railroad people might have slipped them aboard a keelboat heading north."

"But they're being captured in Illinois, a Free State!"

The bushwhackers' leader turned and growled at Meridel, "It says in the Fugitive Slave Law that's okay, so mind your own business, woman." His long, greasy hair did not conceal the fact that his face had been slashed and his ear was missing. "And if you're one o' them abos"—Meridel knew he meant abolitionist—"stay outta this afore one o' me buckos gets trigger-happy." He grinned and peered at her. "Nah, you ain't no abo. Too purty. And dressed mighty fine, ain'tcha?"

"T'other's purty, too," said one of the men, coming close to Lucy Barth. He wore a cap with turkey feathers and carried a bowie knife in his boot top. A knotted rope of black hair swung at his belt and Meridel almost screamed when she realized it was a scalp.

"Whyn't we take 'em along to cook for us?" suggested another bushwhacker.

"Doggone," said yet another man, scratching his beard. "Wish I'd shaved this week. I ain't really this ugly, y'know."

"Toss you for the redhead," said another. "Hey, she's got jools."

"Wouldn't keep her from freezing outside."

"I know how I'd keep her warm," said the leader amid whoops of laughter. With an elaborate bow he told Meridel, "Sam Vickery at your service, ma'am."

Meridel seized the stove lid's handle and raised it above her head, daring the man to come closer. But he was too quick and in a flash slapped the piece of iron to send it flying from her fingers. He loomed over her, an ape of a man, his grin showing stumps of tobacco-stained teeth. "I got an ambition now. To warm you up good."

Suddenly the door to the car was flung open. Meridel gasped with thankfulness as she saw her father in his shirt sleeves. Yet he looked quite ill, and she instantly wondered how he was going to prevail against six or seven armed bandits.

"What's the meaning of this?" McGraw shouted at the nearest bushwhacker. "Logs piled on the track to stop the train! I represent the United States government, and I demand to know what's going on.

Vickery, stopping one of his men who made motions to smash McGraw with a blow, became surprisingly mild. "Reckon you're Commissioner McGraw. Heerd you was comin' and you're a friend of Jeff Davis's, which makes you a friend of ourn."

"Friend be damned."

"Now, Commissioner, we had to grab these niggers afore they got off and we lost 'em. Here's m' paper from the marshal. I'm Vickery, and me and my good men, we're Vickery's Raiders, doin' our bit for law and order when we can."

Glaring at a document and still not noticing his daughter, McGraw growled, "I've heard nothing good about border raiders."

"Commissioner, someone's got to hold down the abos and the Free Staters. They want squatter sov'reignty in Kansas, but they don't want no Slave Staters to squat."

"Well, you've got your runaways, so bring them back where they belong and treat them decently, I'm telling you."

"Yes, sir." Vickery turned to his men. "Go on, you rowdies, get the logs off'n the tracks. You heered Mr. McGraw. Yes, sir, Mr. Commissioner, we'll soon be back in Missouri right near the Kansas line, and if'n you have any trouble with them Free Staters, you send for Vickery's Raiders, day or night, and we'll come ridin'."

Swaggering to the door, Vickery lifted his cap to Meridel and Lucy in mock deference, and at that moment the deep contralto voice outside once more sounded its lament:

> "Go down, Moses,
> Way down in Egypt's land. . . ."

Meridel managed a shaky smile as her father spotted her, telling her sharply, "Meridel, this is no place for you."

"We'll be all right now. Do tell Harald I'm taking a moment to chat with this lady from Kansas." She presented Lucy Barth.

"Pleasure, ma'am. Now, where did Harald go?" muttered McGraw, looking outside. "Thought he jumped from my car right behind me to help me give these hooligans what-for." Had he not been brave enough? The thought flashed through Meridel's mind. "Well now, Miss Barth, hope you'll come see us in Lecompton. And Meridel, don't you be long. We're near the Mississippi and ought to be getting packed up."

"I hope you don't live far from Lecompton," said Meridel, although she felt little fondness for Lucy Barth.

"Thirty miles or so. I might get to Lecompton if the Raiders aren't making trouble. There are a good many groups, you ought to know, and one gang is worse than the next. They have their own definition of law and order. And then," Lucy continued with emphasis, "there's John Brown and his sons. When they're out looking for a fight it's better for others to stay home."

Meridel had read of John Brown, who was known to be a stern abolitionist who had raided Missouri and freed slaves, believing himself to be the avenging hand of God. Osawatomie Brown, they called him, after a Kansas creek where he had settled. Some feared him. Some revered him.

A German woman, who had been standing with her face pressed to one of the windows, uttered a cry of horror. Meridel turned and saw that Vickery's men had mounted their ill-groomed horses, and that one of them led the three Negroes, linked together on a chain by a rope. Grinning back at the woeful trio, the Raider kicked his horse into a trot and the prisoners found that if they too didn't trot, they'd fall and be dragged over the rocky terrain. Even the old woman had to shamble at a dreadful speed, gasping to find the breath she needed to sing. Meridel looked on, too stunned to utter a cry of horror.

As the train clanked forward, she finally found her voice and said with deep emotion, "Those poor people. And yet one hears that the South would be ruined without slaves. What is one to believe?"

"Don't ask me," Lucy Barth said curtly. "I'm a teacher."

"But I don't understand what being a teacher has to do—"

Lucy let loose her mocking laugh again. "Lady Wayne, a schoolmarm in a small Kansas community never knows how her pupils' parents think on the goose. That's a local phrase for how one thinks on slavery, for or against. So any territory teacher had best stick to her three R's and not take sides."

Schoolmarm. Where had Meridel heard the word? She gasped as she remembered. But . . . oh, no. Impossible. She remembered the woman in Dan's photos and compared the two—but that woman had been bonneted and her features fuzzy because of the photo quality. From their size and shape, though, they could be one and the same woman.

She made herself ask, "Do you live in a farming community, Miss Barth?"

"Yes, right on the edge of the biggest ranch in Kansas, and I daresay in Nebraska, too. Ranching is a new word this far north. As I tell my pupils, it comes from the Spanish word *rancho.*"

Meridel remembered where she had heard the term *ranch.* Growing frightened, she said, "You mentioned that Englishmen are buying up land in the West. I wondered if an Englishman owns that ranch."

Casually looking at the stove to see if it needed coal, Lucy Barth replied, "No, he's an American, a Marylander. But he's in England right now, as it so happens."

Meridel could hardly repeat, "England?"

"Or—no, someone said he had written to his foreman that he'd be looking around in eastern Europe for just the right kind of horse. He wants to breed a light draft horse that will do well in the Kansas climate.''

"I . . . see.''

"He raises blooded cattle, too, and he's growing various kinds of wheat to find the right kind for the prairie.''

"He s-seems quite enterprising.''

"He certainly is, and handsome besides.'' Lucy Barth's smile filled her face with secret pleasure.

Meridel forced faint, painful words. "Guess I'd better go back and see that my maid packs properly.''

"Must be nice to have a maid,'' Lucy Barth said with a hint of acid. But the secret smile returned. "Still, if all goes as I plan, I'll have one of my own some day.'' Briskly, she went on, "Well, Lady Wayne, I hope Kansas dust won't be too much for you, or Kansas blizzards. 'Bye. I'm stopping for a few days in St. Louis.''

In spite of herself Meridel went on, as though twisting a knife in her own heart, "You know us married women—we're all at heart matchmakers. So tell me—that man who owns the ranch, is he married?''

"Married?'' Lucy Barth became soft-eyed. She tilted her head, and thrust out one hip, just like the bonneted woman in Dan Forrester's daguerreotypes. "Oh, no, my friend isn't married, not yet,'' she murmured, giving Meridel a knowing smile.

Great cakes of ice floated down the Mississippi River which reached as far north as Philadelphia. Winter had struck hard on one of the sides of the turgid river, and on the other, only slightly more mild.

When slaves rowed the ferry to the opposite bank of the mighty river, Dan Forrester's mistress, to Meridel's relief, left their party for her own destination. Meanwhile the immigrants trooped to a sternwheel steamer where they would be taken a hundred miles up the Missouri River to St. Louis. Meridel received a shy *danke* when she handed one German woman a warm bonnet.

River traffic jammed up at the St. Louis levee which no one complained too long about since the commercial activity had made the city what it was today, bustling and prosperous.

McGraw excitedly explained that no railroad bridge had yet been built to span the river, but it was only a matter of time since tracks had already been laid westward from St. Louis to Jefferson City, halfway across the state. It was along those tracks that the party proceeded, this time—with apologies from the railroad superintendent—in a passenger coach. No berths; no bath. The water froze in the pipes and they could not even wash their faces.

At Jefferson City, two heavy stagecoaches provided by the secretary of war waited to take them onward. Meridel looked only once at the round-bodied, deep-chested Cleveland Bays. Brawny drivers saluted them with their whips, and the guard beside each driver patted his shotgun, held at the ready.

Already worn down by a night spent dozing on each others' shoulders, they felt no better as they jounced and swayed across a snow-draped landscape on roads of frozen slush and mud. Long after dark, each endless day, they stopped at miserable inns where they slept on the floor in buffalo robes, leaving again in the frigid grayness that comes before dawn. They had their first taste of buffalo meat, half-cooked on one side, charred on the other. They shivered at the low, two-note call of the coyote and the long-drawn-out howl of the wolf.

Plunkett did nothing but snivel for London while the others tried to cheer each other. They scratched at tiny things that had come to live in their clothes. Yet Harald, dirty and disheveled despite all that his man Prager could do, still drank the "right" wine out of the sizable cellar he carried with him all the way from England. He might accept a portion of antelope steak cut with a Bowie, but of course he would not speak to the utterly low-class vagabond who owned the knife. Meridel knew that he would have dressed for dinner if it hadn't made him look ridiculous. And even beneath a smelly buffalo robe he made up for one night they had missed in the passenger coach. He complained of Meridel's lack of response, pinching her to make her writhe against him. She tried her best to endure his demands, but was only too pleased when they reached the boom town of Westport, which some people called Kansas City.

The young bustling port town roared with traffic and clanged with blacksmiths' hammers and the scraping slither of wheelwrights' tongs. Meridel was told that all winter, men would be preparing wagons for the rush westward in the spring. Wealth showed itself in diamond rings and heavy gold watch chains. Handsome dwellings near the river boasted cupolas with a view. The city also provided headquarters for the Raiders, Blue Lodge, and other proslavery groups, many of them discharged Mexican War veterans who made the city a nest of drunkenness and lurking crime. The veterans patronized a type of woman who sauntered through the streets bedizened in finery that would never rival the dress of their Parisian counterparts.

The travelers took another ferry across the Big Muddy to the Kansas side where they were greeted by twenty dragoons sent by Jefferson Davis from Fort Leavenworth to escort the commissioner and his party through the wilderness between Kansas City and the town of Lecompton—where Meridel's party were heading—since Indians and outlaws thrived there. Meridel watched the trees pass swiftly by as they moved out. Occasionally they met on the road other wayfarers—a hungry-looking family in a wagon pulled by a broken-down mule; a band of armed men who, riding single file to allow space for the passing coach, offered no greeting, bowing their heads to keep their faces hidden under their hat brims.

As the day wore on and the party passed snow-covered meadows and wooded hills, Meridel bundled herself in furs and climbed to the top of the coach, where the driver and the guard pushed aside the mountain of luggage to clear a space for her. She enjoyed the fresh air until her disturbed nights caught up with her, and needing sleep, she curled down between the trunks. In lieu of a pillow, her gloves placed beneath her cheek made the roof just a little softer.

She had almost fallen asleep when the dragoon leader, Lieutenant Hugon, stopped the procession and bade scouts ride ahead to check for danger. At least the coach stopped jouncing against Meridel's ear. Once again she drifted toward sleep, but roused when she heard voices within the coach. The roof had become a sounding board, and she could hear clearly everything that was said.

Harald was saying to her father, "Now sir, we're alone, so let me spread out this map. Here is Forrester's ranch—"

"He'll give in on the right-of-way, don't worry," said McGraw.

"I trust he will," Harald said with emphasis. "But I want to remind you that we'll be laying iron out into empty prairie. We'll have to wait a long time for our trains to bring in revenue, whether it's from passengers or freight."

"Aye, it's not as though we'll be laying iron in New England, say, where the cities and farms are already in place. But I remind *you*, lad, that we're getting a government land grant along our route to make up for that. And as soon as our track reaches sight of the Rockies we can say to the world, 'There's your railroad!' and the settlers will come flocking so fast to buy farmland and town lots that—"

Shocked at herself, Meridel realized she was eavesdropping. But then she heard Harald say impatiently, "That will be well over a year from now, and suppose Vanderbilt gets tired of waiting for his money?" sudden alarm made her press her ear even closer to the boards.

"Harald, before I left New York the Commodore gave me his hand on it that he'd wait."

"And what did he give you in writing?" McGraw made no reply. "What good is a gentleman's agreement with someone who is not a gentleman?"

"All right, all right," said McGraw, then paused as he was seized by a fit of coughing. "I'm sure Jeff Davis will find me other credit if I need it—because I agreed to run the rails to bypass Free State settlements like Lawrence and favor Slave State settlements like Lecompton. Sshhh, that's a secret—but 'twas worth it for help from the White House. Och! Where's my medicine?"

"Here." A pause followed, then Harald's voice resumed. "But, my dear father-in-law, if you'll pardon my saying so, I've gone over your figures, and I see you've taken a frightful chance."

"Business is built on taking risks."

"But it could be as much as two years before the rails reach the Rockies. Given a couple of bad winters, Indian trouble—"

"Don't fash yourself. My luck's returned, lad, you know that," said McGraw. Meridel frowned at the weakness of his voice, his coughing. There was a pause, a rustle of paper. McGraw said edgily, "Lad, you're leading up to something."

"Yes, sir, I am reminding you that in San Tomás you were paid to lay rails from one ocean to another. You did your job and left. But in Kansas you're going to run your own railroad. And once the rails are down and the farms and towns spring up and you control the shipping rates for all the produce that goes to market, you'll pile up your profit. *But you can't wait till then.*"

"I tell you my luck has—"

"Luck won't pay your notes." How right Harald was, for once, thought Meridel grimly. She had heard her mother say the same thing to her father, but that been back in the days when he had always won his gambles. Harald went on, "You must make money *now* by selling the government land *now*, even if the sure right-of-way is not yet laid out. That's how the Illinois railroad builders did it."

"That bunch of thieving—" McGraw's voice turned surly.

"They made a mint while they brought in half a million settlers, and everybody gained in the end. I've told you before and I'll tell you again: your first order of business is not laying iron—"

"Now by all the kinds of Tara, 'tis nothing else."

"No. Absolutely not, sir." Meridel heard contempt in Harald's voice. "First we go into the land business. Then we lay rails when we can. And we don't pin down the route across the prairie until we must. Why, in Illinois, counties sold bonds and bribed the railroad builders to make sure *they* got the tracks and not the county over the hill. Land along tracks—*promised* tracks—is what will put us in clover. Let me read you an advertisement I've written. There'll be a woodcut of a horn of plenty and the words 'Come to Kansas, the cornucopia of the universe. Kansas soil will grow bumper crop after bumper crop of every grain, vegetable, and fruit known to temperate regions. Buy land cheap! Buy now! Soon the western United States will hold a hundred million people, ten million of them in Kansas—so imagine what your land will be worth then, in this happy, healthful, prosperous garden spot of the world."

Meridel hardly knew her father's voice—a voice of defeat—as he muttered, "Now, if that isn't the father and mother of nonsense. Western Kansas lacks rain, it's full of hostiles, and—"

"Listen: 'Right now the salubrious plains of Kansas lie like a treasure chest unopened. But as plowing breaks the soil, hidden moisture will arise to the sky and attract more moisture, beginning a cycle of rain followed by sunshine, then rain again, gently falling, the answer to a farmer's prayer.'"

"Poppycock," said McGraw. "Nothing can increase rain in the dry plains. The average farmer will be lucky if he—"

"But by the time enough farmers find out by trial and error what they *can* grow on the plains, and cities get built, and you start making a profit, what then? I'll tell you. Vanderbilt will forclose, and he'll own everything, lock, stock, and barrel."

McGraw's voice had become barely audible. "My good friend Jeff Davis—"

"But you risk everything by waiting and you gain nothing. Never mind farmland—what about city lots, which are bound to rise forty times in value?" Ignoring McGraw's groan at the exaggeration, Harald went on, "Here's my plan for a great new city. The City of McGraw. See? Every tenth street is a broad boulevard. A park here, a parade ground here. City Hall here. And the Missouri and Pikes Peak depot right in the middle."

"But where would you build—"

"Take this pencil and make a dot on the map. It doesn't matter where. The plan for the city is what sells the land, not the city itself. If the railroad happens not to run through that city later, never mind. We thought it would. Meanwhile we sell lots, and that's what counts."

"You'd sell lots on the basis of a few surveyors' stakes?"

"Of course. Didn't you say business consists in taking risks? Settlers know they are gambling. We could lay out the City of McGraw and the City of Wayne a few miles from each other and let them bid against each other to get the rails. Now also let us not forget the very considerable amounts of money to be made meanwhile by selling our stock. I have a

New York printer ready to run off thousands of certificates with bank-note borders. . . ."

McGraw groaned and complained that his head was spinning. He coughed miserably. Harald merely went on explaining how adroit selling could force stock prices down. A railroad could then buy back its stock from the public at low cost before letting the price go up and be sold again. "You know you can leave that part to me," Harald said in a confidential tone.

Lying motionless three feet above their heads, Meridel wanted to hammer her small fists upon the coach roof, but instead swallowed her despair. Yes, her father could leave "that part" to Harald. In the end he would have to do everything Harald's way because he had no escape from bankruptcy and disaster.

What was Lucky McGraw saying feebly to her husband now? "But my good friend Jefferson Davis—"

"Will put you out on your own to sink or swim. What Davis wants is rails to connect with the rails coming up from St. Louis; he wants to make a pathway from the South into the West. He won't care who builds the railroad—you or Vanderbilt. Maybe he'd even prefer Vanderbilt, because Vanderbilt could buy out Forrester at any price and push iron to the mountains without even dipping into his reserves."

"But consider what I'm doing for the South."

"What *you're* doing? Vanderbilt's man William Walker had already suggested that Nicaragua enter the Union as a Slave State."

Meridel felt her father's silence, black and bitter. In her own silence she begged him: Don't give in, you'll find the money *somewhere*.

But she expected the worst—that the aging man, whose health had seemed to be steadily declining, would not be able to find his former courage. She could not really expect him to give up this one last chance to recoup his fortune.

She blinked away tears as she heard him surrender. "Son-in-law, do it your way. But remember, I remain president of the company," he muttered, trying to keep a shred of pride.

Harald must have planned it all carefully for a long while, Meridel reflected miserably. He must have spoken to her father several times before about the need to make money by selling land before a rail had even been laid, then hit him hard at the last moment, when he was fatigued, ill, and had little hope of help from any source. So the Missouri and Pikes Peak would become, like so many other railroads, mainly a real estate promotion that impoverished thousands and made a very few rich. Not that it seemed to matter to Congress who gave government land away. The laws were kept loose, for the one sure way to get railroads laid was to show some entrepreneur how building one would line his pocket.

Lieutenant Hugon gave the signal for the coaches to go on. Meridel sat up. She agreed with the young officer riding alongside that it would soon snow, for the sky looked heavy and leaden. She didn't care what she said, she felt so miserable.

The dragoons showed their joy in escorting an attractive woman. They danced their horses to impress Meridel and played a game of passing a hat from saber to saber. Meridel cheered up a little when a deer bounded across the road. But she saddened again when they passed farms owned by Shawnee and Delaware tribes and she saw black slaves working around the corrals and barns. Indians keeping slaves! Doubly dreadful. She remembered the matriarch in the train and shuddered again at her first experience of slavery.

The coach's team slowed to a walk on a long, curving incline, where a dragoon waited at the top looking colorful against the lowering heavens. The tree line receded into the distance, then disappeared from view altogether. Meridel gasped as she viewed the ceaseless brown-and-white, rolling space of the tall-grass prairie under the endless sky.

Across vacant miles a thin layer of snow stretched to the western horizon, and in brown islands sere, long-stemmed grass poked up. Nothing—not even Dan's daguerreotypes— had prepared Meridel for this incredible view that went on and on and on. What were those tiny dark dots out there, miles away? Surely a herd of buffalo! Where were the Indians? Thousands of savages could be lurking in lairs just beyond the horizon, unseen.

At one point they passed a burned-out cabin where blackened beams lay mangled and splintered inside the crumbling columns of four thickly-sodded walls. A broken wheelbarrow had been left leaning against a tree, and a child's doll was lying facedown and twisted in the muddy snow.

"Raiders did this, Lady Wayne," the lieutenant told her.

Meridel shuddered, remembering Vickery's crew. "Then Dan had been right in telling her that in Kansas even a woman dared not be weak or idle. She would make herself as strong as any pioneer woman, and she would bear her baby fearlessly and never take time to feel sorry for herself!

The coach topped the rise, lurched downhill with squealing brakes, and after a while, crossed the width of the prairie "finger" until they met forest again. Meridel's thoughts returned to other matters. She certainly did not favor the South, but her father did—if only for business reasons—and of course Harald always would because he was an even bigger opportunist. So right there in the family, she realized, they mirrored the basic conflict that had brought so much death to Kansas, now known as Bloody Kansas. But neither her father nor her husband would ever change her feelings of outrage against slavery. If the matter came to a family quarrel, so be it. She remembered the magnificent black matriarch in the train, holding her chains to the sight of God. To *that* vision would she remain faithful.

She wondered if she would meet other runaway slaves coming north through Kansas. She wondered what she would do then.

Lieutenant Hugon galloped up and shouted, "Kaw River, Lady Wayne. Lecompton is just out of sight, on the other side."

Meridel put her hand to her forehead and peered ahead at the sparkling Kaw, a tributary of the Missouri, now frozen from bank to bank. A shabby little sternwheel steamer lay iced-in against the far shore, and the only way they could cross the frozen water was on foot.

"Everybody out, if you please," the lieutenant called. "We can't take the heavy coaches across the ice."

Briscoe came running to help McGraw. Meridel slid down the roof of the coach by herself and found her gray-faced father squinting at a large log cabin which was distinguished by panes of real glass, and graced a bluff on the other side of the river.

"What's that shanty up there?" he wanted to know.

Lieutenant Hugon said cheerily, "Why, Commissioner, that's the home of Governor Shannon."

"What? You say the territorial governor of Kansas, appointed by the president with the consent of the Senate, lives in *that*? I understood the governor lived in a mansion."

"Yes, sir, he will, only it hasn't been built yet."

"Bloody hell!" swore Lord Harald. "If the governor lives in such a godforsaken hovel, then where are *we* to live?"

Plunkett, in her misery, uttered a wail that echoed along the black-mud riverbanks. Briscoe and Prager, gentlemen's gentlemen, glanced at each other in dismay.

Meridel thought, What are we waiting for?

She stepped out upon the ice, never looking back as the others followed. The first flakes of the coming storm stung her cheeks. Bits of rough ice caught at her skirt, and the slush soaked through her shoes. But she strode firmly on, and if her world no longer resembled the golden apple in the fairy tale her father had read to her as a child, she did not care.

Part II

Life Was a Child Lost

Chapter One

For two days and nights the blizzard raged on, flinging snow with an awful fury so that when at last the sun broke through, the little city lay smothered under a layer of snow. Low buildings showed only their peaked roofs. Taller buildings had lost their bottom floors to the swirling drifts, and for an hour or more, as Meridel watched from a window, not a person could be seen. Although Lecompton was full of danger, it looked like one of those toy villages nestled in cotton wool under a Christmas tree.

At length she saw a man climb through an upper story window, put on snowshoes, and go off to shoot wild turkeys stunned by the cold. A shovel broke through a drift, and a fur-capped head appeared, followed by another, and soon several paths were cleared, growing toward the town's saloons—for Lecompton was "dry" only in theory. Another cleared away path led toward the all-important Land Office and the next broke a way to rescue the prisoners in the snowcovered jail. Off beyond, on a slope called Hungry Hill, blue smoke meandered above the buried tents and shacks that held the city's drifters. Storekeepers pushed their way outside to brush snow from signs that proclaimed: HARNESSMAKER or FEED AND GRAIN or GENERAL EMPORIUM and the like. Since it was a southern custom to shade the walks, each store had a wooden canopy that projected over the plank sidewalk before it. Again Meridel was reminded of how far the South had spread to influence its western neighbors. One southern-style canopy had collapsed beneath its weight of snow.

Shivering, Meridel thought of returning to bed but remembered Harald, still asleep in their room on the third floor of the new Nevins Hotel. Pitch oozed from the raw plank walls, but at least Meridel had been able to persuade the hotel's chef, a privileged slave, to use less grease on the food he sent up from the kitchen. She had forced Plunkett to put up curtains. She had found her father a rolltop desk that, although it took up room in his bedroom, gave him the "office" necessary to appease his pride. So McGraw, the newlyweds, and their servants were able to settle down—after a fashion.

But McGraw found troubles pressing in upon him. His high-placed Washington friends had given him a title that carried no real weight, and Kansas officials—not all of whom favored a railroad—frustrated him at every turn. True, Governor Shannon thought Kansas was ready for a railroad; but he would not risk giving a private builder any public assistance; no, the territory's woes had already given him trouble enough.

McGraw vowed that he'd get started somehow. But until Dan Forrester returned from Europe Finnian could do nothing about the critical right-of-way. Vanderbilt had turned very sour and wanted his notes paid immediately, while Jefferson Davis had answered McGraw's appeal for funds by saying that *he* was no financier.

While McGraw brooded, growing gray-faced and thin, his son-in-law strode through Lecompton's streets like a conquering hero. He hardly had to seek local business deals, because dazzled businessmen brought them eagerly to his attention. At business offices he allowed Prager to explain that he was generally to be addressed as Lord Harald, though "milord" was to be used by inferiors. For a time Meridel expected that someone would shoot him. But no; in his insolence Harald became the very symbol of English money and, to some, the trusted herald of the rails who would surely enrich the community a dozen times over.

Meridel preferred her husband to go about without her. But there were times when he demanded she accompany him, and she understood it was not out of love but because she enhanced his standing in the community. Once he had her lend style to a meeting he had called at Legislature Hall, a skimpy, drafty building. Keeping her at his side on the platform—the very image of what an American girl can aspire to, she supposed—he spoke with his usual hauteur to a couple of hundred shabbily dressed men on the advantages of working for the Missouri and Pikes Peak Railroad. He told them about "his" invention, a work train, a village on rails full of food, drink and comfort. He described how wagons would load rails at the flatcars and gallop them to the spiking gangs and how the men would grap the heavy lengths of iron two by two and lay them in place. Thirty seconds to place two rails on the ties, four rails to the minute, three strokes to the spike, ten spikes to the rail, four hundred rails to the mile.

"A mile a day across the prairie—that's what I'm going to pay you *three dollars a day* to do," Lord Harald said while the men leaned forward eagerly. They whistled appreciatively when he told them they'd get three meat meals and half a pound of free tobacco every day. "But I want you to stand by and be ready when I need you, so I'll pay you three dollars a week—right now—just to stay in town and be ready to go."

Cheering, the men crowded forward to sign their names or to make an X on the document Harald had brought to bind them to his project. Then they helped themselves to the keg of "clarified" whiskey set aside by the Englishman in back, which was sure to have a good color because plugs of chewing tobacco had been steeping in the barrel for a week.

"Thank you, my dear," said Harald grandly to his wife. "Your presence helped me keep those beasts in order. I'll soon have need for railers, gangers, spikers, and bolters."

You? Meridel resented the slight to her father. She only said, "But Forrester's not home yet, so what about the —"

"Forrester returned to his ranch last week, my dear."

Meridel forced herself to appear calm. "Will he . . . ?"

"No, damn him," growled Harald. "I've thought of getting the governor to invoke the right of eminent domain—the right of a government to buy land that's needed for the public good. But Shannon says Congress would have to approve any such notion, which is unlikely because too many Northerners think the railroad's good for only the South. We'll just settle things locally." Harald slapped his leg hard. "Damn Forrester! He had bloody hell better watch his step, I'm telling you."

"Watch his step?"

"Watch his step because he's in danger. Settlers have been known to shoot anyone who stands in the way of a railroad."

Meridel tried not to let her fear show. How easy it would be for Harald to have Dan killed by one of those mysterious shots that came from the Kansas forest! She must warn him! But two loyalties clashed in her heart. She loved Dan helplessly, and yet if she protected him, she would only be helping him to ruin her father.

Torn and terrified, she wrestled with that painful knowledge, failing in the end to reach a decision. Then fate worked in her behalf. Since Plunkett's cockney accent—the girl called it her proper Henglish—made her hard to understand, Meridel went shopping by herself at the General Emporium. There, a woman who came from somewhere across the Kaw—a woman who did not know Meridel—told her that some filthy-rich skinflint Eastern promoter was trying to buy a railroad right-of-way across her neighbor's land. And people had warned her neighbor, Dan Forrester, that such questions were solved with a bullet. Well, Forrester had gone and fixed that railroad promoter. He had made a will that said that in case of his death his ranch would go to a Maryland cousin; the cousin had already bound himself not to sell or lease any part of the land for any purpose for ten years. So there, Mr. Railroad!

When Meridel told Harald what she had heard, he swore so foully that even McGraw asked him to hold his tongue.

At any rate, rails could not be laid during the wild winter. So the months of snow, ice, and merciless cold wore on while

Harald made himself an important figure in local business, McGraw's health went from bad to worse, and Meridel frantically tried to keep busy, knowing all along that she had yet to come to terms with Kansas, her pregnancy and herself. She knew she had to act soon.

Fearful of her husband's reaction to the news, she counted, counted again, and at length revealed to Harald—who still used her every night and damned her for not responding—that he was going to become a father. Overjoyed, he became almost tender for a few days, while her delighted father overwhelmed her with advice. Meridel tried to appear happy, knowing she had to accept what fate had brought her. When Harald wrote to his own father, she added a postscript telling the earl how dearly she looked forward to bringing his grandchild to him. With a sigh she tried to resign herself to the fact that until the day of her death she would remain Lady Wayne of Danemead, rich and envied . . . and loveless and lost in the desert of her heart.

With the approach of spring the sun rose higher, and Meridel had cause to remember Dan's words: "If you want mud, come to Kansas Territory." That brought to mind the dinner at which Dan had fenced with Lady Grizel and she herself had declared for abolition. She knew the "trains" of the Underground Railroad had been stopped, but as the mud dried they would run again. She knew as well that the hidden black passengers who were referred to as the "freight" were often driven by "conductors" to secret "stations" where they waited till the "track" had been cleared—made safe—for the journey northward.

Suddenly it came to her. The Underground Railroad—that was where noble work and self-respect awaited her. With determination she set herself to find the "station" that must exist.

She began to go out twice a week with food and clothing for the destitute on Hungry Hill. Harald at first objected, but she pointed out that his wife's charity could only add to his own good reputation, and she promised not to overtire herself. On Hungry Hill she met other charity-minded women, several of them Quakers, and proved that Lady Wayne could work steadily at their side, help nurse the ill, and not turn away from the pungent odors that often choked the air around where they worked.

Gradually she found out that the phrase "Let my people go" meant much to these women. She deduced that Lecompton itself harbored a secret Underground Railroad station. It might more logically have been placed in Lawrence, the Free State core not far away; but Lawrence was a well-planned city, while Lecompton, in a wilder corner of the territory, contained stretches of woods and overgrown lots. Meridel soon guessed that her first connection with a "switchmaster" would be made in one of those woodsy secluded spots. And sure enough, as she worked beside a Quaker woman in a miserable tent where those struck by dysentery had been quarantined, her companion whispered, "Come up here tomorrow without thy maid." Plunkett had been carrying Meridel's bundles. "Then go home along the ravine. Thee will be safe enough from rattlesnakes if thee watches closely, and as for men, most men respect decent women as long as they can find the other kind."

In the twilit heavily wooded ravine Meridel walked with care, holding her skirts close and keeping a wary eye out for any unexpected movement. When she finally made out the leathery old man who stood in the trail, she realized how well he had mastered the art of fading into the background. Now he straightened himself by tucking his long beard into his ragged shirt and by buttoning the holster of his heavy old "Sam Walker" six-shooter lest the gun's accessibility make Meridel feel threatened.

Everyone knew Horse Hurlbut. He walked with an odd, clumping gait and claimed to have hooves instead of feet. He would bet strangers ten dollars that if they drove their knives into the forepart of his boots they would draw no blood. He won those bets. But the fronts of his boots were empty not because Hurlbut had hooves but because he had been a mountain man, trapping beaver for Jacob Astor, and all his toes had frozen and been cut away in surgery as primitive as the surroundings.

He doffed his hat, saying most respectfully, "'Scuse me, Missus Lady Wayne, but Missus Dempster, over at the blacksmith shop—she said to tell you she wants to give you a recipe for hoecake."

Meridel knew no Mrs. Dempster. "I see," she said.

"Whyn't you drop over to the blacksmith shop tomorrow 'bout four? But hide your red hair, 'cause Mrs. Dempster, she's agin red hair. You got a big ol' bonnet?"

He meant Meridel should try not to be recognized. "I'll be there, Mr. Hurlbut," she said.

"Just call me Horse." The old man turned his hat in his hands, as embarrassed as a small boy.

"I'll be there, Horse, depend on it," Meridel repeated.

"And y' see, I mean, mebbe you shouldn't talk to anyone on the way over. They could stop you, and Mrs. Dempster, she's agin her callers bein' late."

Either Mrs. Dempster was a formidable woman or—more likely—this was Horse's way of saying that Meridel should keep her visit to herself. "I'll be prompt, never fear." With those words they parted, Meridel already finding new strength at the thought of entering this secret world.

A draft horse pawed the smithy's solid oaken floor while Phineas Dempster hammered a horseshoe in a clangor of steel that sent sparks flying. A boy who looked like Dempster's son worked the leather bellows and let air sigh into the fierce heat of the forge. When Dempster pulled the horse's forelock, the animal raised its unshod hoof and appeared bored as the man set the hot shoe in place, causing pungent white smoke to appear on contact. Meridel noticed that even while the smith hammered in horseshoe nails and clinched their ends tightly, the horse remained relaxed.

Dempster had so far scarcely acknowledged Meridel's presence. Then, without lifting his head, he said, "I hear from up Hungry Hill way that you've a skilled needle."

"I've learned fancy needlework, but I can also sew a patch," she said to his bowed head.

He let the horse loose and stood back to watch it try out the new shoe, thumping it on the floor. "You got any interest in railroads outside of the one your father wants to build?"

"I'm interested in all kinds of railroads. Now, in New

York City when they built the railroad up into Harlem Village, they had to tunnel right through a hill, so they had a kind of underground railroad."

Dempster flicked a swift glance her way. "Harlem's north of New York?"

"Yes, on Manhattan Island, but *north*."

"Like Canada's north of the U.S.A," he asked.

"In a sense. And I've heard that Canadian weather surprises some people who have lived in the South." Runaway slaves often headed for Canada since Queen Victoria's decree that in any British Dominion slaves were free and beyond recapture. Meridel went on swiftly, "Mr. Dempster, I know that if anyone happens to be sending *freight* to Canada, I can help." She leaned forward. "I swear to that," she said quietly.

For a time Dempster frowned at a big, twisted barn-door hinge that he held like a toy in his gnarled hands. Then at last he faced Meridel squarely. "You'll now speak to Carrie, my wife. She has the gift of knowing honesty in people. And now I tell thee in the old way of speech that a Quaker neither takes an oath nor asks it of another. But if thee should breathe ought of what thee seeest or hearest here, only God might forgive thee for the great harm that would come."

He nodded to his son. The youth went to a rack of heavy iron bars and moved a pivoted section to reveal a secret door. Meridel passed through into a corridor built behind the back wall of a long wagon shed. At the corridor's end she found a woman in a plain dress who sat sewing beneath a skylight.

"Look upward, please, Lady Wayne."

Meridel held her face to the light while Carrie Dempster examined her. She was invited at last to look down into a surprisingly apple-cheeked, motherly face. Carrie asked softly but pointedly why one of the British aristocracy would be willing to risk arrest, injury or even death for the sake of carrying freight to remote regions.

"I bear a title but I'm an American after all. And, Mrs. Dempster, I want to do some good in the world."

"We know your father is Jeff Davis's man."

"He is, but it doesn't matter."

"Your husband must show a liking for the South to get along so well in Lecompton."

"Yes. All true. But *I* am against slavery and *I* can keep secrets."

"You have met a woman named Lucy Barth."

The woman's knowledge surprised her. She said nothing.

"Miss Barth travels a good deal. We have reason to believe when she spots runaways, she leads slave catchers to their car. She does it for a share of the reward."

A reward for returning that frightened young couple and that dignified matriarch to degradation and chains! And what did it say for Dan Forrester who had taken such a woman to his bed! "I've met Lucy Barth once. I hope I never meet her again. Mrs. Dempster, whether you accept me or not, I want to give you this." Meridel held out a gold-and-ruby brooch. "Sell the jewelry and use the money to help your work."

Light glittered richly on the precious gems as Carrie murmured, "This is a fine piece." Her intense eyes again met Meridel's.

"It was my mother's. I can give you one or two other pieces, but no more. My husband would notice. And I must tell you—I am with child. After I begin to show I'll have to stay home, but I can still sew for charity. Your charity. Please, Mrs. Dempster."

"This could be a clever scheme to put a spy among us."

"Oh, no, no!"

"Look again at the light." Meridel did, and after a few moments the Quaker woman said, "Welcome to the Club. Call it only the Club. At most, call it the U. R. It goes far and wide. This is the Lecompton station. You may never meet more than one person from any other station. We've borrowed the idea from the European revolutionists of 1848, to guard against treachery."

"I see."

"Never come here if you think you are being followed, and never mention the Club unless you are alone with my husband, my son, or myself."

"And I must dress inconspicuously and wear a deep poke bonnet," said Meridel, sighing and smiling in her gratitude.

Returning the smile, Carrie patted her hand. "What a shame to hide that lovely red hair! Now you'll need a Club name. Our learned New England leaders favor names out of mythology or history."

"Well, since I do feel a bit British, I'd like to be called Boadicea. She was a queen of ancient Britain and she fought the Romans."

"Boadicea it shall be. I am Ariadne."

"Very good! She helped Theseus escape the labyrinth! Oh! I'd wager your husband calls himself Theseus!"

"He does. You are bright. You should know one more person who is pivotal to our club—the leader of our group in Kansas, Leonidas. You may meet him in the future." Carrie rose. "I am about to take you through another secret door. Once you pass through it you are bound as no mere oath can bind you. Do you want to go?"

"Take me through the door, please."

Carrie slid aside a plank in the wall, then pressed a hidden stud. "Come, sister," she whispered, and led Meridel into a station of the Underground Railroad.

The heavily built, low log cabin—Meridel found out later that it had been made to look wrecked and unused from the outside—contained two rows of berths against the walls, stores of food and piles of well-worn clothing. She saw a skinny black girl younger than herself, huddled in a blanket and fast asleep, and one other in what looked like a bundle of rags but which was actually a baby wearing the shreds of a potato sack.

"Look at those poor little rickety legs!" she exclaimed. "And it doesn't weigh half what it should."

Carrie said, "One of our sisters is bringing it fresh-drawn milk. The mother is dry, and no wonder. She's carried that baby two hundred miles in thirty nights, and she's eaten mighty little."

"She didn't dare move by daylight?"

"No. And she waded through creeks and swamps to hide her scent. Her clothing rotted off her body."

"But how did she ever find this station?"

"Mostly by luck. All she had to go on was a few directions she had memorized—that and the Drinking Gourd."

136

"The Big Dipper? That points to the North Star?"

"These days, slaves learn young how to find the North Star."

Meridel whispered, *"Follow the Drinking Gourd. . . . Follow the Drinking Gourd."*

Carrie added the second line of the spiritual: *"'Cause the Old Man's a-waitin' for to carry you to freedom,"* and nodded as Meridel bent to pull the blanket up over a black shoulder wasted to nothing but skin and bone.

Chapter Two

Like Topsy in *Uncle Tom's Cabin*, the city of Lecompton had "just grown." The Rowena Hotel, which was being erected across the street from the Nevins, would be the biggest hotel west of the Mississippi. Employing a good number of builders, it also attracted the town's loafers, who hung about whittling, grumbling, and cadging drinks.

Sometimes Horse Hurlbut could be seen there, clumping about, stopping strangers and offering the toe of his boot. When Meridel saw him from her window, she knew "freight" had arrived at the smithy during the night.

By now she had invented a couple of critical charity cases who lived out near the so-called State House, which never had been built beyond the bare stone walls of its first floor. Dempster's smithy also stood there amid wagon yards and an odorous tannery. There, whatever Meridel had learned about fancy sewing soon gave way to the roughest of tailoring, patching, and making do. She learned much about illness and its remedies, and—gritting her teeth—she learned about treating gunshot wounds. For the town doctor could never be called; he was known to be strongly pro-slavery.

Unless the Raiders were out in force, only invalids stayed more than a few days in an Underground Railroad station. Somewhere not far away, on the other side of the Kaw, they all passed through a highly secret "switching yard." No one knew where it was or what it looked like, but it served as a key station on the road north. Its reputation had grown to almost biblical proportions. Some called it the Land of Gilead, as in the place Jacob met Laban and David for refuge from Absalom, and some confused it with the Promised Land across the Jordan. Only two "conductors" were trusted to take "trains" in and out of this Land of Gilead, for, if slave catchers ever found the refuge, it might spell the end of the Underground Railroad in Kansas.

When Ben, a favorite child of Meridel's, had to go, he wept and clung to her, pathetically pulling out her big tortoise-shell hairpins and pushing them back into her beautiful red hair—his favorite game. At length she asked Mercury, the conductor, if she couldn't go part of the way with the child. He agreed reluctantly, and Hurlbut went to tell Finnian McGraw that his daughter had been forced to stay overnight with a woman giving birth. Meridel huddled with Ben and three black adults beneath a wagonload of firewood. Protected by a low frame, they could not be seen, but she worried about her unborn baby as the wagon jolted on.

Yet she could not spare herself. After midnight she helped the others pull the watertight wagon across the Kaw with a rope. The horses swam across separately, and one was almost lost when hit by driftwood, forcing the horse to turn around and swim back to the other side. At length the party stopped in thick woods. Shivering in the night wind, Meridel joined the others in a dinner of cold beans and bread. They drank river water that had stood in a bucket till the mud settled, then slept a little, huddled close together on the damp grass to keep warm.

At dawn Mercury insisted she must not go any closer to the secret Land of Gilead. Fortunately Ben still slept. She closed his little hand upon one of her precious hairpins and went away, hours later slipping through the back door of the Nevins Hotel. Fortunately Harald had gone away overnight with four armed guards to dicker with some lurking prairie Indians called the Skidi Pawnee. A deal in buffalo hides, her father supposed. McGraw had his own troubles. Frank Llewellyn, his secretary, had tired of doing almost nothing and gone off westward on the Oregon Trail.

"Plunkett, come and take care of your mistress!" McGraw roared with a bit of his old spirit. But he didn't seem well at all.

Huddled in bed—alone, for once—and warm at last, Meridel felt her still-slender abdomen. There was no tenderness. Carrie Dempster had assured her she was the type who could conceal a pregnancy right into the sixth month. But concealment was the least of her worries. She wanted the baby to be born on time and in good health. She knew she should better not press her luck by over-exerting herself, yet also she couldn't help feeling proud that she'd grown far beyond being Dianthe Cabot Blakiston's pampered daughter. She felt she could handle setback, no matter how large or how small.

Little did she know how soon her strength would be tested.

Later that spring, having seen Hurlbut watching the new hotel go up, Meridel had slipped off to the smithy. But she saw that one of the curtains at the Dempster house did not hang straight down, a signal that something had gone wrong.

She quickly turned back home. She knew that her father, who had been feeling better, wasn't there, having gone to speak to one of the Indian agents on some pressing matter. Harald was at home, saying earlier how much he wanted to catch up on his accounts, and he would welcome the few hours alone.

Not feeling pressed for time, Meridel paused to admire the blooming redbud and the fresh new grass. At the Rowena Hotel she shook her head very slightly at Horse Hurlbut, then strode around to the Nevins Hotel's rear entrance, where she stopped to speak to Big Robert, the slave chef, about finding early salad greens. She felt pleased at his sunburst smile.

She proceeded slowly up the three flights of steps that zigzagged across the back of the building to the McGraw's living quarters. Prager, a pair of Harald's shoes in one hand and a blacking brush in the other, was walking between rooms when he saw her enter. Stopping as if in shock, he turned pale, and gasped, "Didn't think you'd return before dusk, milady."

She brushed past him, pausing to look back into his startled face. "Oh . . . ah. . . ." he said rather loudly, "there's a burr on your dress, milady. Allow me." He took it off, and as she nodded her thanks he said almost in a shout, "Milady, do be careful going down the corridor. More of that resin has been coming out of the walls . . . all the way down to your rooms, milady."

What ailed the man? she wondered as she strode down the shadowy corridor, peering at the poorly painted walls, but she could see no resin. As she rounded a corner she heard a door slam somewhere ahead. A figure flitted across the corridor, opened another door, and disappeared inside. Meridel had caught a flash of bare legs; could she have seen a kilted Scot? How odd! And the dim figure's arms had been bare too.

Harald was not at his desk but napping on the bed, wrapped in a blanket and his back toward the door.

Tiptoeing, Meridel took a dress from the armoire and thought she would change in the tiny sitting room they shared with her father. Should she call Plunkett? Oh, bother Plunkett. But then, as the dress she carried fluttered against her, she realized that the shadowy, bare figure also had been carrying clothes against her body. Yes, *her* body. A man didn't move that way.

Feeling neither panic nor shock, Meridel suddenly *knew*.

Standing very still, she remembered a night at Danemead when Plunkett had kept a tryst with a groom. No, not a groom, she realized—a higher-ranking lover. Plunkett had had her own reason for risking her complexion in the dry American air!

Walking swiftly into the bedroom, Meridel snapped at her husband, "Get up!"

"Wha—?" His mouth opened in an elaborate yawn. He had not been asleep, she knew. "You're home early, my dear."

"Yes, I am home earlier than you expected me, am I not?

141

Do speak to Prager—he uses such a loud voice. And by the way, where is Plunkett? Oh, of course," said Meridel with contained fury, "she is dressing. But whatever possessed the girl to *un*dress in the early afternoon?"

Harald raised his brows. "Oh? So?" He had the audacity to smile as he murmured, "Well, well, caught *in flagrante delicto*." His blanket slipped down his naked chest as he added with put-on charm, "I must commend Prager, really, for trying to protect me."

Meridel flung the dress she had taken from the armoire at a chair. "Plunkett leaves on the next stagecoach."

"A pity. She did so much to compensate me for your coldness. Where will you find another maid?"

"I'll do without."

"But your condition—"

"I am not likely to bring on a miscarriage by dressing and undressing myself!"

"Quite. But do give me a son, not a daughter. A son will be worth twenty thousand pounds to me by putting the earl on my side." Harald had begun in a light tone, but ended on a note of fear. "You're not planning to get on that stagecoach, too?"

"No, I shall stay with Papa."

"And incidentally with me? You know, I do enjoy my dear wife's beauty and charm and I shall give you due honor as the future countess of Danemead."

Ah, she had learned much these months since her debut before the king and queen of England. "Danemead, yes—where I'll be expected to look the other way while you pursue the upstairs as well as the downstairs maid."

"And the 'tweenstairs maid," Harald said lightly. "And the milkmaids, too. But, my dear, you'll still have your enjoyable position in county society, where we shall be the top family, don't forget."

Yes. And she, elegant and envied, a doting mother, would support the local church and charities and work to help the factory children. And she would live side by side with Harald till death did them part, never allowing the breath of scandal to sully his noble name.

She had not expected a happy marriage. But now she knew

how terribly unhappy and false it had become. Harald saw the thought reflected upon her face and smiled, relieved because she apparently accepted his picture of their future.

"Well," she said, "we agree that the child must be born safely, so I shall henceforth sleep on the chaise longue." The chaise stood at the foot of the bed.

"And a little celibacy is good for a man, isn't it?" Harald laughed aloud as she turned and walked out. Both knew how very uncelibate he intended to be.

Shortly after Meridel gained this knowlege, she was reminded of the beginnings of her marriage, of the day Harald had asked her father for her hand. For a letter had arrived for McGraw. He glowed and winked and laid his finger alongside his nose to show he knew a secret.

"Take out your most gorgeous gown," he told Meridel. "And tell Harald to dress for dinner, and so will I. For nothing less will do for the good news I am about to impart."

Meridel found it pleasant enough to be festively arrayed for the first time in many weeks and to sit with men dressed elegantly in their evening clothes. Never mind that poor Prager served mere pork and beans on her mother's trousseau dishes. She made no pretense of leaving the men alone with their brandy as McGraw, grinning his old frog-mouthed grin, drew a paper from his pocket.

"Now, here is a letter from my dear good friend Commodore Cornelius Vanderbilt, and the fine old chap has seen the light." He read the letter. Meridel brightened. Yes, Vanderbilt had agreed that a short delay in building the railroad would not matter, and he was giving McGraw an extension on his notes.

"We're saved! And what think ye of this old Irish potato-eater now?" asked Finnian, sticking his thumbs into the armholes of his waistcoat and cocking his cigar in the corner of his mouth.

Meridel couldn't feel happier for him. "Oh Papa, wonderful!"

But Harald had bought into too many businesses whose profit depended on the railroad's getting started. He showed no joy. "What's the good if we still don't have our right-of-way across Forrester's ranch?"

"Aoch!" said McGraw with his broadest grin, "don't fash yerself. I've had chats at the land office. About floats. You don't know what a float is? Let me tell you." Through a cloud of blue smoke, he went on. "'Tis a floating patent to a section of land, a square mile, y'know, and 'twas given to Indians who helped the government. Then, if they wished, they could put the section up for auction. A white man would buy it, and the land office would make sure the Indian got the money. Lecompton stands on an old Indian float."

"What of it?" Harald asked glumly.

"Aha! You know little, laddie. I'll tell ye. Now, Agent O'Hare at the land office—he, like meself, comes from County Offaly—he said he's always wondered how Forrester put his e-nor-mous parcel of land together. And he did have in his memory, did the good O'Hare, that many a time Shawnee came to the land office with a good white friend, very drunk. Suppose"—his voice dropped to a whisper—"suppose that Forrester plied half a dozen Indians who owned floats with whiskey y'see, and each, drunk, made his mark and Forrester bid on the land. Eh? Well, it's been known for an auction to be canceled later, when an Indian plied with liquor has said afterward he wants his land back because he was cheated. Now, what with Congress favoring Indians who smoke the peace pipe, and what with a palm greased here and there at the land office and the right Indian found and, ye might say, reminded, so that a question about Forrester's entire title arises—well, rather than lose his ranch . . ."

"I see," said Harald tensely.

"And two weeks from now we'll be seeing Dan Forrester—"

Meridel started, her heart caught in her throat.

"And I'll say to the lad: 'Now, Daniel, you were once my good right arm down in San Tomás, so let's shake hands on it.' Then I get around to telling him about the land office's discovery. He gets flustered and I say to him, I say: 'It doesn't have to happen. You sell us our right-of-way at the standard dollar and a quarter an acre and you've naught to fear. And don't worry about our trains scaring your stock, for it's been shown in the East that stock gets used to trains in their pasture, and that's what was on your mind all the time, wasn't it, laddie?''

Meridel, catching her breath, managed to say, "But Papa, couldn't Mr. Forrester have acquired his land honestly?"

Her father winked. "He's got to prove it, and he'll see he has as much chance as a snowball in—as a snowball stuck on the devil's pitchfork.'' McGraw turned to Harald. "Well, my good partner? Here I've persuaded Vanderbilt to give us leeway on the debt. And here I have the foolproof scheme to make Forrester eat crow and sell us our strip and have done with it.'' McGraw rubbed his hands together with satisfaction. "Tell me, do you doubt we'll have rails laid soon and stretching fast, and with no debt to bother us for months yet?"

For a moment Harald hesitated. Then he smiled and lifted his glass. "Sir, forgive me if I seemed to doubt you. Meridel, my dear, join me in a toast to your father. I drink to the health of a man whose astuteness and business ability I have yet to appreciate to the full.''

Had Meridel heard a thread of sarcasm in her husband's voice? But her mind dwelt on something else. "Papa, you said we'll soon be meeting Mr. Forrester. What do you mean?'' she asked.

"Eh? Oh!" McGraw displayed a printed white card. "Governor Shannon will soon be replaced by a new governor. He's giving a farewell ball up at the''—McGraw made a face—"mansion, and everyone important is invited, including Forrester 'specially. For do ye not think I've put a bug in the governor's ear—that he should talk to Forrester about co-op-er-a-ting in building the future of Kansas?''

Meridel gripped her hands together and twisted them as a wave of anxiety swept over her. She was going to have to meet Dan again.

As the men talked, she toyed with a Paul Revere spoon and tried to read her unsettled mind in her reflection. Should she warn Dan that even the governor was taking the railroad's side? No . . . she could never be disloyal to her father. Her only consolation was that she would see Dan again, her need to see him at least one last time, to touch him, to speak to him, growing desperate, despite a fear of what might happen.

Chapter Three

The cabin on the bluff, once its furnishings had been stacked outside, offered a hardwood floor that volunteers could wax to perfection. To make extra space, dragoons from Fort Leavenworth had brought a large mess tent to pitch on a platform made of sections of plank sidewalk "borrowed" from Lecompton. Rats had nested in some of those hollow sections, but the governor appointed a committee to straighten the warped boards and scare the rats away. Lanterns swung from the tent frame, glowing almost glamorously on that uneven dance floor on the bluff above the river.

Although the governor was a married man, his wife had long ago decided she could not bear to live in Kansas, and left, leaving the hostess role to be played by Mrs. Lecompte, the judge's wife, in a fantastically wide-hooped gown. Nevertheless, Meridel's pearl-gray taffeta worn with grace over the clever wire cage stole the show. She did not relish outshining the many women who simply had no way to dress adequately for the occasion, but she *was* Lady Wayne, like it or not, and she had to dress the part.

She promised a dance each to her old friend Lieutenant Hugon and his superior, Colonel Sumner, both resplendent in their dress uniforms. She chatted with Albert Boone, Daniel Boone's grandson. She charmed Colonel Jefferson Buford, a polished old Southern gentleman who had won his colonelcy in the Mexican War. She tried to avoid "General" Jim Lane, who had commissioned himself by taking command over a couple of hundred Free State militia. This scholarly but evil-looking man had been responsible for an astounding resolution passed by the Free State Convention: When Kansas entered the Union it would not tolerate slavery, but it also would not permit Negroes to live within its borders! Fortunately, Meridel had heard, the resolution had no chance of being made into law.

Someone had brought a church's small foot pump organ up the hill. But the church organist did not attend dances, so Meridel, noting the resemblance of the organ's keyboard to that of a piano's, volunteered her services. She had time to practice since the raging river had temporarily stopped the ferry and a number of guests were stranded on the other side, waiting for the right moment to safely cross. Meanwhile her father chatted with the governor, who was affable for once. Harald made himself agreeable to all the ladies who had influential husbands, and Jim Lane waltzed about with an imaginary partner, sometimes tripping on his sword.

"Ferry's comin' across!"

Meridel lost her beat. Dan might be among those passengers.

Soon the newcomers came pouring in, laughing and waving, and the men were muddy to their knees because they had had to carry the women ashore. Governor Shannon proclaimed that muddy trousers were full dress, causing more cheers and laughter. But Meridel only stared down at the organ, afraid to glance around.

Then gradually she became aware that a man stood beside her. Slowly her eyes traveled upward from his mud-smeared trousers, pausing at the ruffles of his dress shirt, which she recognized by the way they were sewn. Frightened but exalted, her gaze continued upward to the strong, clean-shaven chin she knew so well, then to the wide but sensitive mouth until she met those twin midnight-blue eyes, so intense in the force of their gaze. "Dan!" she gasped. When they'd first met on the road in Norfolk, why hadn't he swept her up and carried her away? "Harald is watching us," she whispered, quickly lowering her head.

"Why not? He's your husband, after all." The harsh words stung, as they were intended to. Dan turned, holding out his hand. "Good to see you again, Wayne," he said without a smile.

Harald did not hide a sneer at the condition of Dan's clothing. "Forrester," he said. "Heard you finally found a stallion somewhere."

"So I did. Rumak is a beauty, let alone a powerful stud."

Meridel tried to ease the obvious tension. "Rumak?" she asked.

"In Polish it means noble steed, more or less. Wayne, let me tell you I'm sorry I had to leave Danemead so abruptly. I wrote your father, explaining I'd had to rush off on a . . . personal matter." Harald nodded with cold suspicion. "I trust," said Dan in a more formal way, "that it is not too late to offer you both my felicitations on your marriage."

"Thank you," said Harald.

"Thank you," said Meridel, wanting to be gathered into Dan's arms but moving closer to her husband instead.

Jim Lane proclaimed the first dance, an old-fashioned pavane, really a promenade past the governor. Meridel fumbled at the organ, hoping she could manage "Guadeloupe March."

Harald stopped her. "Get up and promenade with me."

"But—"

"You will promenade with me, goddamn it, and show Forrester you are my wife and beyond his reach once and for all. The way he looks at you—as though he wants to take you straight to bed!"

But Harald could take Plunkett to bed and laugh about it, she thought bitterly.

At least the fiddler and the flutist knew a march. Later Meridel played the organ and sometimes danced—with her father, with the governor, and with the dragoon officers who showered her with compliments. She begged off from other dances, saying she had a duty to keep the music going. She tried to stay away from Dan, who had proved himself a popular dance partner. Then, just as Harald went off into a corner to talk to Daniel Woodson, the territorial secretary of state, the fiddler struck up a waltz. The flutist joined, glancing at Meridel—but alas, they had lost the aid of the organist. Dan had stolen off with her, practically lifting her from her seat.

"One-two-three, one-two-three . . . Seems easier than last time. But on that occasion I wore riding boots," he said before continuing in a very different voice. "Meridel, I've missed you. I can't tell you how I've missed you. And you've been so close all these months, but you married Harald. *Why?*"

She could not speak, and tried to lose herself in their whirling and swaying and forget the nearness of his too-well-remembered muscular body. Dan's arm tightened around her. She resisted, but he drew her close. Even when the music ended he still held her pressed against him for a moment. Fear gripped her and she whispered, "Dan, no!" But he only released her when slaves appeared carrying trays loaded with turkey, roast duck, river oysters, and other wild game along with the strong drinks needed to digest them. Meridel noticed that the governor ordered plates and bottles for three brought to his office, then beckoned her father and her husband to join him there.

Alone, she chatted determinedly with the other women, refusing to acknowledge Dan's silent pleas and his nods toward the door. But he came over, and taking her arm skillfully, told her friends that Lady Wayne had promised to continue a discussion begun long ago in Norfolk about English herbal teas. He led Meridel away and through the door in the company of others who wanted a walk outside. She hissed that they never had said a word about herbal teas, but Dan acted as though he had not heard, and instead piloted her strongly through a soft night ablaze with stars to an abandoned rose garden. The untrimmed bushes hemmed them in and a few half-open early blossoms greeted them with a faint perfume.

Dan's great warm hands took Meridel by the shoulders, forcing her to face him. "*Why* did you marry Harald?"

Why could she not find the strength to fight him, to wrench herself free? She tried to be stern and said, "Because Harald showed me a letter from my father explaining how you refused to sell the right-of-way until you could squeeze a huge sum out of him and ruin him. And I hated you. And—" She bit her lip. But he was ignoring her and his eyes were blazing as they peered into her own.

"Tonight," he hissed, "I danced with you, and held you close. No my dear Meridel, I know you had another reason for marrying our Lord Harald."

He caught her to him while she pounded her fists at him—uselessly. His hand at the small of her back pushed her against him. "My dear, you are carrying my baby."

She wanted to scream and cried, "No, it's Harald's," but her words rang false to both their ears.

Dan slid his hand to the telltale curve beneath the folds of her dress. "*Our* baby."

She cried, "Please, please!"

"I know the date when you married. I see what you mean to claim. Don't sacrifice yourself, Meridel!"

He kissed her wildly and did not have to seek her lips as she yearned up toward him, and in hot passion they kissed long and deeply. She finally tore herself away from the sweetness of him. "Don't you see I had no way of finding you, and I *had* to get married?"

"If only you had waited for me to return to London—"

"How could I *know*?"

He looked away. "I'm sorry. And you're right. At least," he seemed to ask of the bushes that promised roses, "can you forgive me?"

"I love you. How can I *not* forgive you? Or forget my baby's father? But Harald must *never* know."

She could feel him quivering, battling against giving her that vow. But the scarred fighter in him had principles and he said, "It has to be your decision," and his head sank upon his chest. Nevertheless, after another painful moment, he tried to sway her. "Dearest, we can slip back into Lecompton and I'll get a rig, and we'll ride to Rainbow Ranch and live together. Harald will have to divorce you."

From a deep gulf of misery, Meridel said, "Harald and I were married in church."

"Does that mean—you really want to go on being Lady Wayne?"

"Don't be so blind!" she cried furiously. But they caught desperately at each other, knowing the wretchedness that had prompted their outburst. Finally, she began to speak. "Dan, I love you, but I married Harald of my own free will. Not for love, not for money, not for any reason except that I needed to protect my baby. I cheated him, used him, deceived him. Dan, I'll always love you and I'll always . . . hurt, but I cannot end my marriage, and Harald certainly won't end it."

"But I've told you how we can force his hand," he pleaded.

"No, Dan. My dearest, my dearest, promise me you'll never tell anyone. . . . promise me that the secret of our baby will die with you and with me."

For a moment he stood with his eyes closed, his mouth bitter. He opened his eyes and said, "I promise."

The kissed long and deeply. And then, reluctantly, they returned to the brightly lit dance floor, seeing nothing but darkness ahead.

Governor Shannon called, "Ah, there you are, Forrester. Come into my office, we'll all talk about the matter of the railroad right-of-way. Give a little, take a little—that's how bargains are struck."

Meridel strolled to the organ, turning down requests by several men that she dance with them, and played once again to everyone's approval. After an eternity, she was again aware of a man standing beside her, and gazed up into dark blue eyes that now looked hollow. She tried not to sob.

He said, "They can't void my deed with their Indian float schemes. I never dealt with an Indian unless I had two witnesses swearing he was sober. You know all this, I s'pose?"

"I couldn't help knowing. But Dan, really, why even take

the chance of losing your ranch? Harald is very clever. Can't you just sell that narrow strip of land?''

He glared. ''I'll sell it when I'm ready. Before that—not at any price.'' His large, muscular hand gripped the edge of the organ until his knuckles turned white.

She saw Harald and her father approaching. Rising, she steadied herself on the organ. Could one live on and on with a broken heart? She did not know, but at least she remained on her feet, breathing. ''Are you ready to leave, Harald?'' she asked. ''Papa looks dreadfully tired.''

Dan said good night abruptly and walked away, ignoring the presence of both men.

As Meridel grasped her husband's extended arm she stumbled at the thought that she and the man she loved would never meet again.

Chapter Four

And still he visited her dreams, leaving her to awaken before morning to toss in her bed with helpless yearning. Worse yet, at this of all times when she felt as if her heart were being chipped away bit by bit, she could not keep busy enough. The Underground Railroad had stopped carrying its freight for a while because Kickapoo Rangers had captured a wagon full of hidden slaves and had killed the conductor. One success made the rangers hungry for more and daily they sent out a large troop of zealots to scour the countryside for more runaways.

While everyone stayed low to wait out the bad turn of events, Meridel fretted, for she could not bear to remain idle. Meanwhile Harald was planning to pick up a coach he'd ordered at the railhead, visit Henricks at the supply depot, and "attend to other matters" before spending a week traveling into Missouri.

How Carrie Dempster found out that Harald would be away a week Meridel never knew. But the Quaker woman summoned her, brought out buttermilk and salted pumpkin seeds, observed that Meridel looked peaked, and asked her if she felt up to making an overnight trip to Lawrence where she would meet an important member of the Club on Massachusetts Avenue, the town's main street. The New Englanders who had built the Free State city had dubbed all their streets with the names of New England states.

"I'll go gladly," said Meridel. "But who is the man I am to meet?"

"Call him the man you met on Massachusetts Avenue."

"He must be Leonidas."

Carrie frowned. "Canst thee not be a woman who can speak to a man and name him not?" But she turned her sternness into friendliness again, patting Meridel's hand gently. "Hurlbut will drive thee. Traffic moves safely between the cities. Commerce overcomes politics, my husband says."

"Good. I guess it will be my last expedition for some time. Isn't it silly to have to stay out of sight when you're showing? Where do people think babies come from?"

"I've had four of my own, of which two have lived," said Carrie Dempster, "and would have walked out till the day of birth save that my husband forbade it."

"Men make the rules."

"Merely to test female patience."

"Well, Carrie dear, save sewing for me to do when I return. A mountain of sewing." She paused. "What shall I tell Papa? I know. It's only twelve miles to Lawrence, and I want to visit a certain store and buy materials for a layette." The two women smiled.

Meridel and Hurlbut reached Lawrence safely. Tension crackled in the air and rumors flew in Lawrence about how slave staters were preparing to descend on the town, a neat little city of small homes, and burn the house of anyone supporting the abolitionist cause. Meridel took a room at the Free State Hotel, a four-floor structure that had been built with small windows and thick walls by the Free Staters, who suspected they might one day need a fort. Entering the hotel's lobby with Hurlbut at her side, Meridel was not much surprised to see blanket-wrapped Indians with shaven, red-painted heads and rattlesnake tails in their scalps, sitting motionless in corners. Hurlbut rubbed his chin. A white man hunched over a drink caught the abo signal, scratched his nose with his thumb, stretched, and left the room.

Later Meridel strolled with Hurlbut down Massachusetts Avenue, where she peered into an actual bookstore—unheard-of in Lecompton. Lawrencites even spoke of building a college on a pleasant height called Oread Hill, a wish that no doubt arose from their New England scholarly tradition.

A spare, aging man whose sharp nose seemed to point his way as he ambled from a white-painted house came up to them. He looked as though he had once kept a store where he struck hard bargains and frowned at customers who dipped into the cracker barrel.

Without preamble he asked Meridel to tell him something of London. They had not walked long amid a bustle of immigrant wagons when he said, "Ariadne was right. You have a lovely voice, and your diction is clear."

"And I judge by your accent and manner, sir, that you have gone to Harvard."

That drew a twinkle from behind iron-rimmed spectacles. "Boadicea, you are a perceptive person. And your appearance—if you will pardon my saying so to a married woman—could not be faulted. We need someone who can speak to society ladies. Many people in New York knew you and your father. Would you return there and help us raise funds for the Club?"

She hesitated.

"I know of your condition," said the stranger. "I am thinking of a year from now, when the New England Emigrant Aid Society shall have brought in two or three thousand additional voters for the Free State side. You might even like to take your baby to New York." He paused, as if some disturbing thought had suddenly entered his mind. "Do you think that Lord Harald—"

"Lord Harald will not stop me," said Meridel in a resolute voice.

"I see. Then I'll have reading material sent to Ariadne to help you learn techniques of speaking to audiences and raising money. I refer to methods developed by Henry Ward Beecher.''

''Oh yes, a great man.''

''I agree, but I must say that some of his methods appall me. Still, as Reverend Beecher has written, 'He is the best fisherman who catches the most fish, whatever epithet is flung at him about the bait he uses.' I shall be in touch with you again, Boadicea.'' He searched her face. ''We have hesitated about trusting you too far—after all, we know how your father and your husband feel. But now we do trust you.''

''Please, Leonidas, you may trust me.''

''Why do you call me Leonidas?''

''I shouldn't have, I know, but I was guessing it's your Club name.''

He gazed at her without expression, thanked her for her offer of aid, and left, leaving Meridel with the impression that she had been mistaken, that this man had not been Leonidas, and that she still had yet to meet the leader of the Underground Railroad in this territory, someone who was fast gaining a reputation for his boldness and cleverness, and someone who the authorities favoring the Southern cause bemoaned daily.

Hurlbut showed her the town and took her to visit the two Free State newspaper offices. At the busy *Free State Star*, the editor had no time for visitors. But jovial George Brown, who edited the equally thriving *Herald of Freedom*, proudly showed Meridel his handsome new press with a brass plaque bearing the paper's name. He patted the machine as though it were a favorite child. Handing Meridel a copy of the *Herald*, he said he had more than seven thousand subscribers. There weren't half that many literate people in all of Kansas, but most of his readers were abolitionists back East.

Finally she was able to return to her room at the Free State Hotel where she settled down to read the *Herald of Freedom*. But she had read no further than the second page when her gaze was affronted by a full-page advertisement that showed the work of a familiar hand. The illustrations told the story: a bursting cornucopia (bigger this time), a smug family counting piles of bank notes, an endless steam train that ran through ranks of well-fed, jovial farmers who cheered from their prosperous fields. She sighed and read: "CHOICE LOTS GOING FAST IN BEAUTIFUL MCGRAW CITY, PROSPEROUS NEW TRADE CENTER FOR GOLDEN, FERTILE KANSAS. Amazing deep, rich soil full of hidden moisture produces great crops for farmers while merchants find new paradise on earth."

She wanted to dash back to the *Herald* office and tell George Brown—if he didn't already know—that not a yard of rail had been laid in all of Kansas and that McGraw City consisted of a few stakes driven into the ground in an unmapped part of the prairie. But Brown probably was in bed by now, and anyway, if Harald's advertisement charmed people into coming to the territory, they would mostly be Free Staters or abolitionists or both. Something George Brown certainly knew. Strange world!

She drifted off to sleep, only to awaken when Horse Hurlbut rapped at her door in the early morning. "Look out your window!" he cried.

She looked and gasped, then began to dress quickly, staring out at a hill where early roses and verbena made a pretty show against the blue sky. Hundreds of armed men milled about on top of that hill. Their crudely lettered pennants anounced: WHITE SUPERIORITY FOREVER—KANSAS BELONGS TO THE SOUTH—SLAVERY APPROVED IN THE BIBLE. They had five small brass cannon that winked in the sun.

Hurlbut told her that the force was commanded by David Atchison, former U.S. Senator from Missouri. With him were Colonel Buford, Sheriff Sam Jones, and others who strongly favored the South. A Committee of Safety could be seen riding out from Lawrence to parley with the invaders. Word spread quickly: the force on the hill constituted a legal posse armed with a writ from Judge Lecompte. They had come to subdue treason—the creation of an illegal Free State legislature—by capturing prominent Free Staters, by destroying their newspapers, and by tearing down the Free State Hotel.

The armed men waited while their leaders rode into town, made some arrests, and enjoyed a huge free lunch provided in the hope that they would be pacified—for Lawrence was not prepared to fight. Meanwhile Free State horsemen galloped toward the distant telegraph lines. They wired what they believed would happen. Eastern newspapers spoke next day of the Rape of Lawrence, the Burning of Lawrence, the Lawrence Massacre.

In fact, peace almost prevailed. But fire-eating Sheriff Jones led some eight hundred rowdies into town. They smashed everything in the *Free State* office. At the *Herald* office they hauled out George Brown's new press and while he pleaded with them in vain, he had to stand by and watch as they dumped it into the river.

Meanwhile Sheriff Jones had rounded up everyone and forced them to leave Free State Hotel. Standing outside with a mournful crowd, Meridel saw the sheriff line up the small cannon and shout, "Fire!" She flinched at the smoke and the awful roar. But the fortress-hotel suffered little damage beyond broken windows.

Men ran to the cannon with sponges on long sticks, fresh balls and powder, wads, rammers. Again came the angry cry: "Fire!" Chips of stone flew dangerously, but the thick walls held fast. Even a barrel of gunpowder did not bring the building down. At last, after looters had stolen all the liquor and valuables, Jones set fire to the hotel's wooden staircase and flames reduced the building to a blackened shell.

Dangerous bands of men charged along the streets, insulting women, mistreating men, forcing their way into homes and carrying off whatever pleased them. At last, roaring threats against nigger lovers, the ruffians marched out of town, some wearing stolen tight-waisted "Sunday" coats, others draped in yards of fabric "for the missus" or wearing mock helmets made of buckets and saucepans. Nevertheless, except for the cannon shelling, not a shot had been fired.

At first stunned and ready to flee, Meridel noticed the number of destroyed homes and joined a group of women who went about giving what aid they could. She was sorting out dishes from a smashed set when the man who looked like a New England storekeeper—the man she had mistakenly called Leonidas—took her aside amid the street debris.

"Boadicea, we know that you are expected home shortly, and that your family must not learn of your involvement with us. We would like you though to take a message for us to an important man. We can spare no one else we can trust at the moment, and we need the help of Mr. Hurlbut's strong constitution here. We know that your . . . condition"—he looked down at her abdomen "—is not too far along. Can you journey alone on horseback?"

Meridel reflected but for an instant. "Yes," she answered firmly. It would be a short side-trip, and because she was a good horsewoman, she would get home safely and soon. The important man was John Brown, who with his five sons fought on the Free State side with the ferocity of madmen. When she found him at his cabin she gave him the message— that there had been no Lawrence "massacre" no matter what rumors spread. Anxious though they had been to massacre Free Staters, the invaders had realized that they had to keep some semblance of law for the sake of pacifying Congress. They left in their wake shattered homes, but no death, rape or serious injury. The long-bearded old man before her, how-ever, refused to believe her. Already he was prepared to ride off like God's avenging angel—as he called himself—to take revenge on Slave State settlers along nearby Pottawattomie Creek.

Having done what she could, Meridel evaded Slave State rangers by crossing to the north side of the Kaw. She had set out toward the river on a sprightly roan mare with just enough food to last the trip, and it had never occured to her that she might lose her way. But she did not have a country person's eye for small differences in rocks or trees, and on the second day of her journey she realized she had missed a turnoff. Her food supply, minimal to begin with, coming as she did from the plundered town of Lawrence, ran out completely.

Dismounting to drink at a rill, she thought she smelled smoke, a sign that some settler might be living nearby and offer her some decent food and a bed. After remounting she rode in the direction from which it seemed to be coming. She forded a brook, noticing someone's boundary stake driven into the ground, and finally smelled—yes!—roasting beef, and her mouth watered.

When she broke from the woods into a clearing she saw no neat little cabin occupied by a healthy pioneer family. The smoke and the aroma came from an untidy fire, and a big haunch of meat, spitted on a ramrod, was being more black-ened than evenly roasted. The men who waited to eat it turned at the sound of her coming. As they reached for their guns, Meridel's heart sank.

One huge man wore a greasy raccoon cap decorated with a brass badge. Another had turkey feathers in his cap and a bowie knife in his boot. More than one wore a scalp at his belt.

"Well, jest see the fancy company that's dropped in," said the man who wore the turkey feathers. Meridel recognized him in horror.

"Doggone, I shoulda shaved this week," said the same man who had said it on the train.

Let my people go . . .

Before she could turn her mount and leave, a gun was trained on the animal. "Come in and close the door, miss," said the big leader, Vickery, with his stump-toothed grin. His men laughed. Meridel dismounted with as much dignity as she could muster, and one of the men tethered the roan with their horses.

"Set yourself." Vickery pointed at a rock.

Trying to appear poised, Meridel sat and smoothed the rags her dress had become. "I . . . I live in Lecompton. Was visiting . . . uh . . . up along Stranger Creek. Got lost. Wandered all night. I'd greatly appreciate having a bite to eat if you could spare it."

"Sho 'nuff!"

"Rest a spell," said the second-in-command, the one who wore the turkey feathers, after she had finished the charred meat they gave her.

"Lay down. Take a little nap," said another, winking at a companion.

"Hey!" said Vickery. "I seen this little gal before." He yanked a ribbon, the sunbonnet came away, and Meridel's disordered hair fell about her frightened face. "Aha, you're Commissioner McGraw's daughter. And you're wife to that Englishman who's bossing everybody around in Lecompton. Mr. Baron Wayne. Yeah. And I seen you on a train once." He chucked her under the chin.

"I am Lady Wayne, yes. If you gentlemen take me back to Lecompton, you'll find my husband and my father would—would—recompense you for your trouble."

"What's she mean—recompense?" asked the man with the turkey feathers.

"A reward. We get money."

"Oh, yes!" cried Meridel. "I'm sure of it."

"Yeh," said Vickery, calculating. "But suppose we keep her here and tell her husband and her old man that we've got her hidden and make them bring us money, and *then* we take her home. That way, we're sure we've got the money."

"Ransom!" shouted a short, wild-eyed little fellow who wore two scalps at his belt.

"Ransom it is. And meanwhile . . . well, ain't Lady Wayne a nice piece?" His voice quivered with lust.

"If you dare harm me—!"

"Harm you? Can't harm a married woman. It's only a young girl that gets harmed if you pop her." He laughed in Meridel's face. "It's just that we don't want you to miss your husband."

Eagerly, a man asked, "You mean we're all gonna—?"

"Yup," said Vickery as he slid his hand across Meridel's bosom. When she struck away the filthy fingers he laughed. He grabbed both breasts, growling, "We'll all take our turn. But me first."

Lord Harald Wayne's trip to the end of the rails had been rough and boring. As he had gotten farther and farther from St. Louis the inns had grown worse, if that were possible, and he had to travel without his valet. McGraw's man, Standish, had happily returned to England with another titled traveler whose own valet had been trampled to death by buffalo. McGraw was ailing, so Harald had had to leave Prager to attend him.

Bloody hell! But Harald's temper improved when he saw his new carriage, sheathed in a light-colored birch that would not show the dust too much. Sturdy enough for Kansas roads, the vehicle also boasted doors bearing the arms of the house of Wayne—which actually only Harald's father could properly display.

He was pleased too because Frank Eddoes, his new coachman and personal bodyguard, had polished the coach to a mirror finish and would continue to do so. Eddoe holstered a

Colt on one hip and a bowie on the other and carried a thin knife taped to his spine, where he could whip it out from the back of his collar and the notches on the knife's handle showed he had done so often. The face beneath the broad hat was young, taut, grim-mouthed, and watchful: the face of a killer. Harald paid him well, and Eddoes had said he would do anything for pay.

"All ready, lor'ship," said the gunman, feeling no genuine respect for the title.

Harald leaned back in his handsome coach, which had yet to be paid for. He liked the way Eddoes made a long whip flicker as they drove off behind four matched bays. He reflected with pleasure upon some business he had done at the railhead telegraph office. Using a code that only he and Cornelius Vanderbilt knew, he had asked Vanderbilt to foreclose McGraw's notes soon and make Harald general manager of the Missouri and Pikes Peak Railroad. Yes, Harald Wayne congratulated himself, he had done well in New York when he had called upon the cantankerous Commodore and both had thought McGraw's chances for succeeding were good. Nevertheless, Lord Harald had shown old Cornelius that he had a man on whom he could rely if he must. Over the telegraph Vanderbilt had repeated in code that the rails could wait for spring as long as he eventually made thirty percent per annum on his money.

Good enough. But Harald's self-satisfied smile faded as he took stock of his personal situation. Congress, torn by North-South quarrels, had not yet approved the railroad's land grant. This meant he had sold farms and lots he did not own and could not deliver on. But people, seduced by his advertisements, were flocking out to build houses. So, worming for credit, Harald had been forced to buy good acreage closer east and resell it to settlers only too pleased to live within a day's ride of a city. The added debt however had made his financial situation truly desperate. Bloody hell! Why should a titled English gentleman have frontier traders growl at him, "You pay up on your notes or we'll ride you out of the territory on a rail."

Damn Forrester! And damn McGraw's scheme with Indian

floats. It had come to nothing. But Harald's contingency plan now lightened his mood.

Mexican War veterans had been given quantities of land certificates that allowed them to buy cheap government land. They could sell those certificates to speculators who eagerly bought them for resale. Speculators had also been known to print counterfeit certificates, which they sold to trusting settlers who later lost their land.

Harald had discovered that Dan Forrester had also used land certificates in assembling his ranch, and that Harald's agent—a crooked ex-employee of the Government Printing Office—could print obvious counterfeits and substitute them for the genuine ones now resting in the Washington archives. Then, when the counterfeits were discovered "by chance," how eagerly Dan Forrester would sell the right-of-way rather than see Rainbow Ranch auctioned off!

Calm again, Lord Harald nibbled on tiny wild strawberries that almost equaled the delicate flavor of French *fraises des bois*. His thoughts turned to Meridel. The Plunkett episode had turned out very well. Now his charming wife knew what he expected of her as countess of Danemead. She would merely afford him the cloak of respectability so useful to a man of appetites.

Gad, the life he would lead as the richest man in Norfolk! Planning step by step, he decided to bring Meridel and the child to Danemead, leave them there with his father, and return to Kansas for a couple of years. Yes, he would need a couple of years to clinch his American fortune, padding the earl's wealth, which by then would be safely in his hands. For the earl had relented. Where was that wistful, surrendering letter? He found it in his portfolio and settled back to read for the third time his father's shaky writing on the crested, heavy sheet:

How my years burden me. I pray you not to tarry in America lest I never see you again. I was wrong in urging you to marry Claudia, and I tell you sincerely that Meridel will be welcome here. If at times I have scolded you, it was only for Danemead's sake. I share with you the fond hope that your child will be a son, but, son or daughter, I yearn to see my grandchild and of course your well-remembered wife. I hope she will forgive me for having been cold toward her, and that she will sit with me often and bless me with her charm.

Above all, my son, I wish to make clear that although Danemead cannot go to you until I die, the rest of my property need not wait. I shall have the papers ready to be signed. My mines, my interest in the local mill, my fenlands—the ones that produce, of course—the coking plant, and all else shall pass into your hands as soon as you come home. I live for that day . . .

Harald laughed in triumph. Solid English pounds! As for the solid American dollars, they still depended on Forrester's selling the right-of-way . . . but this time, begad, *he would*.

After several moments of pleasant musing, a birch-paneled cupboard yielded brandy and a good cigar. Lord Harald toasted himself, "Here's to the younger brother whose affairs are going so well." Fragrant blue smoke suggested the image of a little skiff on a Norfolk river—ah, what an inspiration that capsizing had been! Poor Didrick! Harald chuckled to himself.

Occupied with a fish on his hook and his scolding of that contemptible creature, Younger Brother, Didrick had not seen Harald peering closely at the riverbank, cunningly, coldly trying to see if they were alone. The banks apparently clear, Harald had risen to stand on the skiff's gunwale and, throwing his weight a certain way, forced the craft to capsize.

Only Harald had seen his brother's hair plastered across his staring eyes, seen his mouth gaping open to gasp the last two syllables he ever spoke: "Harald!" But Harald, who could swim, neglected to respond to his request for help. Down Didrick went beneath the swirling death-dealing water and by the time Harald reached the river bank he had become the earl's only son. Cleverly he had allowed a tenant farmer to find him on the road, groaning, half dead—it appeared—from diving again and again in a desperate effort to rescue his brother. Poor Didrick. But then, every man should learn to swim.

The carriage hummed along, surely the handsomest equipage west of St. Louis. Harald planned to have a short visit with Henrick, and then he'd return to Lecompton and renew the good times he had been having with the baker's fifteen-year-old daughter.

Chapter Five

With a desperate effort Meridel writhed away from Vickery and ran screaming "No!" But instantly the other men caught her and pulled her back to their leader, a monstrously cruel man as Meridel was learning; he grabbed her by the hair painfully and lifting her head shook his finger in mock-playful warning before her eyes.

"Heh, Vickery," said the little man, whose protruding eye made him look perpetually startled. "Kin I unbutton her?"

"Okay. Long's you leave the rest to me."

Someone chuckled. "That's all Shorty does with the whores in Leavenworth. Just unbuttons 'em and looks."

Again Meridel screamed her terror into the empty forest as she tried to fight off Shorty. He stood with all his weight upon her instep and only after about a minute of torture did he withdraw his boot. She sagged, helpless and in extreme pain while he unbuttoned the back of her dress, slipping it down over her shoulders to her elbows.

"Hey, look at all them underpinnings," he panted.

Vickery grunted. "You're lucky it ain't winter, Shorty. That's when it takes twenty minutes to undress 'em."

"I like laces. One pulls out this way and t' other pulls t' other way and I see skin . . . more skin. . . ."

Meridel begged him to stop, but he pushed her dress down, until she was bare to her waist. While Shorty passed his hand gloatingly along her smooth bare back, his companions crowded to the other side.

"Let's see the real scenery!"

Meridel tried to shield herself, but Vickery grabbed both wrists and held her hands high, his eyes on her tender curves.

The man with the turkey feathers snorted, "Don't she have nothin' below the waist?"

"Prob'ly," said Vickery with an evil laugh. He began to touch Meridel's breasts. She stood silent, with her head hanging, lost in shame—till her stunned mind remembered her pregnancy. She was about to scream a plea for mercy when Vickery whirled with lightning speed and pulled out his revolver, making it seem to leap into his hand.

A man who guided his horse with his knees and held his hands up, palms showing—a man who, in the code of the West, showed he bore no weapons—walked his mount into the clearing. He wore a rancher's broad hat, a long leather shirt and stained old trousers tucked into scuffed boots. Meridel's wild gaze caught the brand on the horse's flank—three arches one within the other. A rainbow. And so she met Dan again—Dan, who swung down without hurry while the Raiders, following the same unwritten code, holstered their guns.

Glancing only casually at Meridel's half-nakedness, Dan Forrester turned to the leader of the men. "Vickery, get off my land."

"Yeah? Listen to the big landowner gettin' high and mighty."

"Yeah. I also object to your killing my calves," he said, glancing at the meat that sizzled over the fire.

"If I kilt you right now, you wouldn't object no more."

"Reckon you're right," Dan replied with a hint of his old drawl, "but it would hurt your name in Kansas. I'm not surprised you turned up here. The fighting is bringing in all kinds of coyotes." Meridel heard Vickery hiss in his breath as Dan walked slowly toward him. "Or maybe you came north to keep company with the rattlesnakes." Dan shoved his hands into his pockets, standing in a relaxed manner. "Let's see. . . . Last time I saw you was in San Tomás."

"Yeah. Where you done me out of a million."

"It was out at a coffee *finca*. You were entertaining the planter and his family."

"Haw-haw," said Vickery without mirth. "Listen to 'im. No, they was entertainin' me—with their screamin'. Like you're gonna be entertainin' me pretty soon."

"Sounds like you want to fight."

"Ain't he smart? Yeah. And then listen to the screamin' and you'll reckernize your own voice afore you die."

"I've no gun."

Vickery said, "Fair fight" and dropped his own gun and gun belt to the ground. "But anything goes."

"What's anything?"

"Punching, biting, gouging, kicking, stomping, butting, and throwing into the fire. That's when you'll call the buzzards with your screamin'."

"When I'm in the fire?"

"When you're in the fire roastin'."

"I see."

"And when I'm finished with you, I'll feel right keyed up to take care of Lady Wayne—a little different, like. Never been on top of no nobility woman before. Looking forward to it."

Meridel screamed, "Dan!" and saw dark blood rush his face. Hoarsely he said to Vickery, "Fair fight and anything goes. No weapons. Winner gets the woman. Loser gets to be buzzard bait."

"But roasted."

"I won't need the fire, Vickery. I aim to break your back." Dan went on in a quiet voice, "I'll tie my horse out of the way and meet you right there." He indicated a patch of bare earth near the fire where a stump stood. The tree had been chopped on a slant, so the stump had a sharp edge of wood projecting upward.

As Dan secured his horse, Vickery rushed without warning, his shaggy head down like a butting buffalo's. Only Meridel's cry saved Dan. He leaped aside, then met the Raider with a blow that knocked Vickery back on his heels. But it would take more than one blow to fell the ox of a man.

"Hey, Vickery," someone said. "I'm takin' the meat off'n the fire. Now you got room to roast Forrester."

The men laughed but the two fighters circled each other warily, not paying attention to the jest. Vickery leaped up and kicked his leg toward Dan's groin, catching him in the thigh. Dan backed away in pain and the Raider, seeing his chance, rushed in, but instead of overpowering his opponent, he was met with a fast one-two that left blood on both sides of his face. His panting mouth sprayed blood.

"Watch this!" he roared at his men and tried for a death-dealing bear hug.

With a sharp twist Dan threw him, then leaped to pin him down. They rolled over and over until Vickery slammed his elbow into Dan's rib, knocking the breath out of him, though only for a moment. Both struggled to their feet and began circling each other again. Vickery roared and rushed, taking Dan's boot in his belly. Again they circled, their faces masks of blood-spattered dust streaked grotesquely by their own sweat.

They clashed with a thud. Vickery jabbed his thumb at Dan's eye, missing because Dan stepped backward only to slip on a loose stone. Vickery leaped close, gripped low, strained upward; he lifted Dan with one arm between his legs, the other hand choking his neck.

Howling like a mad dog, the Raider carried Dan to the fire. Meridel shrieked and tried to run and help the man she loved. But she was caught by the hair, and turned to kick and scratch as Vickery threw Dan at the flames. Meridel saw him in the air, twisting, followed by a shower of sparks. He had fallen into the fire on his back.

He had gripped his legs to his chest and jammed his head against his knees. Only his long leather shirt touched the coals. He leaped from the flames, smoking and blackened, just in time to take Vickery's bull-butting head in the middle. Knocked flat, he seemed helpless as Vickery leaped to land his crushing weight on Dan's chest, but the rancher's own lashing foot tumbled the Raider.

They both struggled to their feet again.

"In the fire." Vickery's words sprayed a thick stream of blood.

"Break your back." Dan slapped at his own smoking back, but he instantly closed the gap between them and punched. They hammered at each other until it seemed impossible that flesh and blood could take such a beating. Vickery retreated. Dan pressed close to him. He grabbed the front of his shirt with one hand while striking Vickery's chin with the other. The impact sounded across the clearing.

As Vickery fell forward, Dan caught him over a shoulder, then lifted him to his feet; he walked the dazed man three staggering steps then flung him, not into the fire, but, back down, across the stump's upthrusting edge. Meridel heard a sickening sound—the cracking of bones. Vickery lay very still across the stump, bent backward.

Dan Forrester turned slowly, staring at Meridel, then sat on the ground.

The second-in-command, the man with the turkey feathers, went to Vickery. He listened for a heartbeat, held a burning brand near the staring eyes. "Back's broke. Dead as a doornail." He unpinned the brass badge of authority from Vickery's coonskin cap, tossed away his turkey feathers and pinned the badge onto his own hat. "I'm captain now."

Shorty still stood behind Meridel's naked back. He spoke in an awed whisper. He told her that the San Tomás coffee planter would not tell Vickery where he had hidden the gold—in fact, he foolishly claimed not to have any. So Vickery took the planter's wife and two small children and tied them backward across the top of a fence.

"Then we tied heavy rocks to their hands and feet. It was the wife's back broke first. The kids were more flexible in the spine, but after a bit they broke, too. The wife was dead. One kid was dead, and the other was like a vegetable—might still be living, I don't know. The planter went mad. Vickery laid him across the fence too, and he screamed something awful when we—but then Forrester came along with a gang of peons and we was outnumbered, so Vickery didn't start shootin'. But he told Forrester he'd kill him someday. Forrester didn't say much then, but you see why he had to break Vickery's back now?''

Meridel, snatching up her dress to her bosom, ran to Dan still trying to catch his breath on a stump. She kissed his torn lips and felt his limbs as once he had felt hers. To her relief, nothing was broken. He staggered to his feet and the code of the West prevailed. A man brought Dan a dipper of water. Another brought his horse as well as Meridel's roan. They wanted to help him mount, but he waved them away and struggled by himself into the saddle.

They rode slowly across a stretch of broken country, then across green land and passed Hereford's grazing in a meadow near a pile of buffalo bones collected for fertilizer. Near the house, in a paddock, she saw the steel-gray stallion, Rumak, prancing hot-bloodedly around its corral as if looking for escape. Dan spoke little along the way but she knew it was because he was in pain.

The shrubbery around Dan's house had grown since the wandering photographer had made his daguerreotypes. The house itself turned out to be white with a neat green trim, the bottom boards painted brown because rain splashed mud. The kindly, elderly man named Mueller helped them dismount. And once Meridel was settled into an ugly zinc tub in a corner of Dan's bedroom, Mrs. Mueller rushed buckets of hot water upstairs. Finally soothed and peaceful, Meridel stepped out of the zinc tub onto a buffalo robe, climbed into one of Mrs. Mueller's nightgowns, the size of three of her, and stumbled into a beckoning bed. Dan's bed.

He knocked at the door.

He wore the paisley dressing gown she had seen in London. One eye was closed and his face was blotched with cuts, swellings, and bruises, but he said, "What you smell is bear grease. Good for burns." Somehow he managed to form a grin, as warm as the first one he ever cast her way. She held out her arms. They clung, saying nothing but silently saying a world and more.

Bertha Mueller, having made up the guest room for Dan, had allowed him five minutes out of bed. "I must know," he asked Meridel, "how in the world did you get mixed up with Vickery?"

She could not tell him about her mission, so she only said, "They kidnapped me, wanting to hold me for ransom, and you saw the rest. Dan, I need to send a note to my father tomorrow, just to say I am safe." She drew her light hand across his face to soothe his battered features. "My love, here I am with you. Here you are with me. Right now that's all I can bear to know and I wish I didn't have to know anything else—ever."

"You mean here we all are together at last—you, me, and our baby."

"Yes, oh yes. And I'll always remember how you risked death for *our* sake."

"That scuffle with Vickery? Nothing but an overdue bit of business to be taken care of."

He kissed her lopsidedly, then blew out her candle. "Tomorrow," he whispered.

It seemed to Meridel that tomorrow would never come. But when it did it came wonderfully when Dan slipped into bed beside her just as the day was dawning. When he brought his lips to her lips and then to her throbbing throat, she had no memory of any quarrel. When he found her breast, and her hand moved in his rough hair, pressing him into her softness, she forgot that Harald had ever touched her. When he kissed the place where the baby was growing, she knew nothing of Free States or Slave States or railroads or rights-of-way. She could not get enough of soothing his bruises and of running her fingers along him and in time seeking his manhood as he sought her softest self.

Afterwards they rested, whispered, touched, kissed. When she told him he was a wounded man and had had enough, he laughed.

For a little while they slept, embracing until the sun bathed their bodies. Dan slipped away lest Bertha Mueller would come bustling into their room from the first floor and be shocked to see the two together. Not that everybody wouldn't know soon enough, Meridel thought.

Mrs. Mueller worked wonders with her dress, and Dan's harness maker restored her shoes. Rested, she strolled about with Dan or rode with him in his gig to see parts of his far-reaching land. She met Low Sun, the dignified Shawnee; Black Henry, the herder; Cassidy, the blacksmith; and several sunburned men who simply "rode range." She met Adalberto, the Mexican in the great sombrero, who served as the ranch's gardener.

Neighbors came from a little nearby settlement and were glad to make her acquaintance, asking no questions of her. When they spoke with Dan about crops, horses, or cattle, Meridel saw their affection and trust. Now and then someone called him governor. They let it be known they expected Dan to become governor of the new state of Kansas.

As they sat at their ease on that cool, bright day, Meridel looked around with only mild interest until she heard a wagon approaching. It was a little two-wheeled conveyance that surely had been put together by a carpenter rather than a carriage maker since the hood was nothing more than an umbrella nailed to the carriage.

Descending briskly at the hitching post, the woman driver tethered her horse in a no-nonsense manner. She seemed a pretty sort, soberly dressed, but she had taken pains to make her dress hug her figure tightly.

The woman turned and walked toward them with an insolent swing of her hips. Meridel drew in her breath. It was the woman she had met on the train, the schoolmistress, Dan's former bedmate.

Chapter Six

The woman who betrayed runaway slaves called out cheerfully, "Why, it's Lady Wayne! Such a delightful surprise!"

Pretending to be uncertain, Meridel said, "It's . . . Miss Barth? Oh yes, it *is* Miss Barth." Meridel turned to Dan. "We met on the train somewhere in Illinois last winter."

Looking distinctly uncomfortable, Dan rose to bring out another chair. Seating herself, Lucy said, "Thank you, Dan, but I'll only stay a minute. The stage left mail for you, so I brought it over."

"Thanks. Uh . . . cup of coffee?"

"That would be nice. Well, Lady Wayne, I hope you are quite settled in Lecompton?"

"Yes." Meridel added reluctantly, "Thank you."

"Your father is well? And Lord Harald? I hear Lord Harald is very active in Kansas affairs."

"He is, yes." Lucy didn't quite manage to conceal her sharp glance at Meridel's patched dress, then at the glint of gold on her left hand where it rested, tautly, upon the table. "Have you been in the neighborhood very long, Lady Wayne?"

"Since yesterday." She did not add, "My husband is out riding" or any other invention about him, and Lucy's avid eyes showed she noticed the omission.

Turning to Dan, Lucy asked sweetly, "Goodness, did you fall from your horse?"

"Fella disagreed with me."

"Try beefsteak on that eye." Receiving no response, Lucy said lightly, "But if I know you, you'd rather eat the beefsteak. Ah, coffee. And strudel, too. You do bake so well, Mrs. Mueller. Do you know if Mr. Mueller has those tomato seedlings for me?"

"B'lieve he has," said Bertha Mueller with no warmth in her voice.

Lucy seemed not to notice. "It's late for putting in vegetables, but I couldn't do much till school was out. Do you know tomatoes are one of the few things that raccoons won't eat? Those awful creatures!" As she spoke her gaze flitted from Meridel to Dan and back again, as is she were looking for something in the way they responded to each other.

"You don't seem to have a very long school year," said Meridel.

"No, more's the pity. The children are needed at home at planting time and weeding time and harvest time, and then, in winter, a blizzard can keep them out for two weeks. I'm training an assistant who's going to open her own school out toward Wabaunsee. But while I was away, what a mess she made of discipline! I had to take my ruler and tan a few backsides, I can tell you. Girls included. But fortunately, since Dan has endowed the school"—Dan looked even more uncomfortable at that remark—"the roof doesn't leak and we have enough books." Lucy knocked a chip off the fist-sized lump of sugar and asked suddenly, "Will you be staying awhile, Lady Wayne?"

"I'm . . . not sure. I . . . was visiting near Big Stranger Creek . . . and I got lost in the woods. . . . Dan happened by."

"I was out riding boundary," Dan added gruffly.

Lucy sipped in silence, her sharp eyes probing. Then she changed the subject. "Well, there's Mr. Mueller down at the cold frames. Oh yes, the tomato is a forgiving plant. You can actually transplant them with tiny green fruit on them already. Dan, I'll put up more of that piccalilli you liked so well last year. And Lady Wayne, since you are"—a tiny pause—"visiting, well, my rhubarb came in nicely and I've jars and jars, so I'm going to bake a rhubarb pie just for you." Lucy laughed. "I'm saying it's for *you* so Dan won't eat three-quarters of it, he likes it so much. So good to see you again. I'll run along."

That night when Dan came to her, Meridel reached for him with a small cry, half want and half fear. She found him fierce and silent as he crushed her to him. After he had tip-toed back to the guest room, when she should have slept deeply, she hardly slept at all.

The sun rose the following day and although another cool bright day might stretch ahead of them, Meridel felt only dread. Lucy's remarks had broken the bubble. Meridel could no longer elude some of the harsh realities she and Dan had been avoiding, such as the fact that she was married, or that Dan had so harmed her father, his health was rapidly declining, or the fact that they always avoided the issue of slavery, knowing they would only quarrel.

In time she sat with her lover in a secluded spot on the shore of a creek that tumbled out of the badlands. A magpie seemed to scold them from its rough nest in a cottonwood. A little bird called a dipper stalked about in a foamy shallow pool. But Meridel, frightened and silent, hardly saw the birds or the creek of the forest.

Dan was saying, "Don't think that because Lucy makes so free around the ranch she means anything to me anymore."

"Does she know I'm the woman you met in England?"

"She does. And she knows I've been approached by your father on—on a railroad matter."

A railroad matter. Meridel demanded, "Dan, *when* are you going to sell Papa that right-of-way?"

Dan's voice hardened. "I tell you again that I'll sell it to him at a fair price when I am able to, but not a day before." They sat in hurt silence. The he caught her to him with strong, tender hands. "Please put that matter aside. It will resolve itself—someday. The important thing is that fate has brought you to Rainbow Ranch, and that you belong here, and that you should stay here. You should, you must! What else can Harald do but divorce you to save his own face? Then you'll be free to marry me."

And what of her father's position? A federal official whose pregnant daughter had gone to live blatantly with her lover? But still that begged a more basic question. "Dan, I married Harald in church, and I can't get away from what I've done. I married him dishonestly, for sure, but—" Harald's cruelty, his loveless, self-centered self in which he was openly unfaithful to her would be borne as a punishment for what she'd done. "No, I am married in the sight of God . . . I am married!"

"For our child's sake, Meridel, stay with me."

"Our child will never know."

"But you and I will know, year after year. And we'll know you could have stayed with me. Dearest, we'll always know what might have been. The three of us can be here. Together."

His words jabbed her heart. After a long, hesitant moment, she glanced away. "Let me think. By myself. I'm going back to the house. No, let me go. Oh please, let me think!"

She began to walk away, then whirled around and ran to kiss Dan, still grim-faced, before again hurrying away from him.

Adalberto stopped her to show her where he had planted crocuses to sprout through the snow next spring. She paused to look around at the blacksmith shed, the chicken coop, the big barn, the corral where Rumak galloped in circles. Why, already this was home, she felt comfortable and accepted and—

She rushed upstairs to Dan's room. Too much spoke of him—a moose head; a beautiful Navaho blanket, woven in earth and sky signs, that had come up the Santa Fe Trail; a row of engineering books; a row of novels—Dickens, Thackeray, Washington Irving. She could not face these things alone and rushed downstairs, outdoors and onto the verandah. But instead of finding solace, from around a bend she saw an odd homemade cart approaching, and watched in anguish as Lucy Barth waved.

She tried to show enthusiasm and cried, "Such a marvelous rhubarb pie, and still warm from the oven—what a treat!"

She invited Lucy to sit down with her for coffee and the pie that, though excellent, ended up lying like lead on her stomach. "May I have the recipe, Miss Barth?" Despite herself, Meridel recalled how smugly the girls at Miss Whittaker's had learned to cloak the same question by asking, "May my cook have the recipe?"

"Surely," Lucy responded. "But be careful when you add the sugar. Some kinds of rhubarb want more than others."

The chitchat went on. About a man who harrowed his fields by dragging a dry thornbush across them. About prairie wolves getting into a henhouse. About a rumor that one of John Brown's sons had been caught and shot, but that Brown himself was still at large. But all the time, Meridel knew the schoolmistress had something important to say. Her hands twitched with the urgency to relieve herself of what she wanted to tell Meridel.

As Meridel, with false nonchalance, tossed pie crust to a fluttering whiskey jack, Lucy asked, "Lady Wayne, have you been in Dan's cellar?"

"Why, no. He keeps the door locked, for safety. An underground spring has broken through down there."

"That's a very interesting story," she said. Meridel merely stared. "Look, I know I'm poking my nose in, but you may thank me in the end. You are married. You have come alone to visit a bachelor." Meridel wanted to force the woman to stop, but the schoolmistress's words kept her silent. "You and Dan have been sleeping . . . on the same floor, anyway, with no one else up there. If all this is part of your planning to leave your husband—well, I realize I'm butting into your affairs, but I'm older than you and I've known Dan longer. Has he ever told you how he stands on the goose?"

"No. Never," Meridel said weakly, bracing herself for whatever the woman was getting at.

"Under the circumstances, don't you think you ought to know?"

After a pause, Meridel said faintly, "Possibly."

Lucy rose and beckoned brusquely. Numb, Meridel followed her inside past the hatrack made of buffalo horns and watched Lucy Barth take down a fine old Kentucky flintlock, open the smaller of the two compartments in its powder horn—where some long-dead hunter had kept his priming powder—and remove two keys.

When Lucy unlocked the cellar door, its oiled hinges made no sound. She lit candles. When they reached the bottom of the stairs, Lucy indicated how far the cavernous cellar stretched around them, its earthen floor completely dry. "Well?" she asked Meridel. Dan, she acknowledged silently, had lied to her.

Weakly she let herself be led to a corner where partitions sectioned off a small room. The other key opened its door. Lucy stood aside. "What are you waiting for? Go in."

Entering slowly Meridel saw some kind of machinery lurking in the depths of the dark. As they approached the murky object with their candles, Meridel made out a rough-hewn table on which were set piles of paper, a box containing rollers, smeary rags and a large can of what looked to be black paint, but which couldn't have been because it had a different odor. Leaning against a wall were slanted, divided racks that held bits of metal. As she studied them closely, she recognized fonts of type, just like the fonts she had seen in the Lawrence newspaper shops.

Meridel realized the black substance she'd spotted earlier had to be printer's ink, and the machinery, a printing press. Its long lever and wooden frame looked battered, with some of its paint scratched away and an iron foot broken and hurriedly repaired.

A brass plaque had been attached to a side. Meridel bent to read it, then cried out as she made out the words: HERALD OF FREEDOM, LAWRENCE, KANSAS TERRITORY, 1857. THE TRUTH SHALL MAKE YE FREE.

"Is this . . . is this—"

"The mob that invaded Lawrence threw it into the river. Other Slave Staters hauled it out, found it still in working order, and brought it here to print in secret. Now you see why Dan doesn't want you in his cellar."

"He—"

"Yes, Lady Wayne, Dan prints something secret. Well? Are you afraid to look?"

Slowly Meridel let candlelight fall across one of the piles of paper. They were copies of a broadside. She gasped at a headline that seemed to leap from the page: LOYAL MEN WHO DEFEND THE SACRED SOUTH! STOP AND SINK THE TRAITOR PACKET *BARATARIA!* DROWN THE ABOLITIONIST RATS WHO WANT TO DECEIVE US!

Lucy said, "He prints these by the hundred and has them tacked on trees in Missouri near the Big Muddy, where Raiders and such will be sure to see them. Go on and read."

The text below the headline, set in smaller type, read that the packet *Barataria* was due to steam up the Missouri River, that abos had loaded the *Barataria* with cannon and powder and chain shot and other armaments, that the vessel also carried three hundred nigger-loving gutter rats from the festering slums of Northeastern cities, all recruited and trained by the New England Emigrant Aid Society to fight against Slave State forces.

Meridel's shaking hand spilled tallow on the broadside. "Dan printed *this*?"

"He did. By the hundred. Incidentally, how do you stand on the goose, Lady Wayne?"

Caught up in the emotion of the moment, Meridel affirmed, "I hate slavery."

"Thought so. Well, go ahead, read on."

Meridel read that armed men must meet the packet at a bend in the river where the *Barataria* neared Missouri's shore. She read that cannon had been mounted on the shore and that a brick oven would heat cannonballs white-hot before they were fired into the wooden packet. She read, "All this and a hail of bullets will send the abo rats to a watery grave."

She could read no more, and asked in a lost, childlike voice, "Dan . . . wants to get bushwhackers to sink that boat full of Free State men and . . . burn them? Drown them?"

Lucy nodded.

Meridel did not know how long she stood staring at the accursed thing, but when Lucy said they had better go, she absently folded the broadside and stumbled after the other woman. It occurred to her that Lucy knew she would renounce Dan, leaving him to turn to his former mistress for consolation, which was why Lucy had led her to the basement in the first place. But nevertheless Dan had told lies, Dan had arranged the deaths of Free Staters, Dan was strongly proslavery, and Dan was beneath her notice from this moment forward.

"Miss Barth, if you don't mind, I want to speak to Dan alone when he gets home."

"I was leaving anyway. I did poke my nose in where it doesn't belong, but—"

"I'm glad you did."

"Good-bye, then." Lucy did not hide her sense of triumph.

When Dan returned to the house Meridel rose from where she had been sitting and met him at the bottom of the steps.

Anxiously he asked her if she had had time in which to think about his proposal she stay on at Rainbow Ranch. In answer she unfolded the broadside and thrust it at him.

Even the range dust on Dan's face did not hide his sudden blanching. "I told you not to go down into the cellar." He waited for her to speak, but she said nothing. Helplessly he asked, "How did you find the key?"

"Does it matter? What matters is that I know you now for what you are. And I despise you utterly."

"Meridel, I . . ." His face worked. His hands pleaded and, finding no softening in her features, dropped away.

She walked around him. "Good-bye."

"Meridel—"

From a black depth of misery she cried, "Stay away from me. It's good our child will never know its real father."

"Meridel . . . someday . . . I'll be able to explain. . . ."

"Dan, once I slapped your face. Now I wouldn't soil my hand by touching you." Shivering with emotion, she strode off down the road, not looking back.

She had gone a mile on foot, tears forming behind her lids, when a wagon overtook her. She glared at Adalberto and Low Sun. They had orders from Dan to transport Lady Wayne safely to Lecompton—and, by the way, she had been walking in the wrong direction. With an incoherent sound of rage and despair she climbed into the wagon. She saw that besides food it carried a trail tent, a portable stove, and other comforts—not for the sake of the rawhide-tough men, but for her. She had no choice but to accept.

But she found her patience worn thin as the men dawdled, slept late and stopped to visit a Shawnee farm. When at last her guardians lifted their hats to her at the Lecompton ferry she demanded, "What's on your minds? Three days to go thirty miles!"

"*Como no?*" asked Adalberto, trying to look puzzled. Low Sun merely peered back beneath his hand as though at the track of an endless journey.

But they had had some hidden purpose for delay. It was not till her friend Frank Avery was pulling her across the Kaw that she found out indirectly why Dan had wanted her kept out of communication.

"You heered about that-there packet, the *Barataria?*" puffed Avery. "Comin' up the Big Muddy? With a load o' abos? Well, our southern boys bushwhacked her down below Westport, yes ma-am, they did, and she's burned and sunk."

Might Dan rot in hell for what he done! "Many dead?"

"Dunno, but plenty. The more the better, say I. They was nothin' but gutter trash from the stinkin' free-state cities."

Killed because Dan Forrester had printed those broadsides. Had she ever really loved him? Or did a woman cling to the first man who had seduced her . . .

At length she reached the Nevins Hotel and found a smile and a kiss to give her worried father. It was good luck, anyway, that Harald had not yet returned with his new coach.

"Then Papa—Harald's excitable, so let's not tell him how long I've been away. I . . . couldn't leave another woman who'd been taken desperately ill after childbirth . . . oh . . . it was a girl."

"But you'll have a boy. Tell Papa."

She laughed with him at his tender, fatherly silliness; she could not see how he tried to rise above the weakness that had again afflicted him. He confessed that while she had been away Jeff Davis had disowned him and slippery Cornelius Vanderbilt had written to refuse more extensions on the notes, and to say that if McGraw could not get the railroad built he would have to make room for someone who could. "Forrester is killing me," old Finnian muttered. "But Harald will get us that right-of-way . . . somehow."

The heir of Danemead returned in very handsome equippage driven by a thug whom Meridel instantly detested. Before long, Harald took pains to parade his wife all over town in the crested coach, trying his hardest to attract investors to his latest railroad project. He still cultivated that rakish "devil's point" of hair beneath his lower lip while his clothing, sent by a Bond Street tailor whose bills were long overdue, always looked elegant. Striking it lucky at faro, he was able to keep at least his Lecompton creditors at bay. And he told Meridel in triumph that he had found a real flaw in Forrester's title to Rainbow Ranch, and that Forrester would be hard put to argue with Washington records!

Meridel tried not to care. She now showed noticeably, and got her sewing room equipped for her seclusion.

Meanwhile Lecompton's Elmer Street became so full of land dealers, brokers and merchants, that people called it the Wall Street of the West. Word reached Meridel through the underground that her handsewn clothing had reached Canada on the backs of runaway slaves, which pleased her. Missourians had brought up cannon from the burned hulk of the *Barataria*, but the entire matter was kept under wraps, for it was feared that Congress would become annoyed and act to resolve the Kansas problem, unilaterally.

Meanwhile, Meridel wrote to her relatives, Lady Anne and Lord Hubert, of the haze and the heat and the dust and the dryness choking the land. She told of the late-summer sunflowers that bloomed by the thousand, their heavy, seed-laden heads bowing under their towering heights. She told how housewives in sod cabins stretched cheesecloth from beam to beam to catch the sod loosened by a storm, along with the mice and the spiders living in the roof. But wild grapes made tangy preserves and new wine, and though they had not yet obtained a right-of-way, she still loved the freshness, the openness, the wonder of it all.

Her hour of truth was fast approaching and Meridel

McGraw knew her baby would have to pass as a seven-month-old child. She had miraculous luck. Jim Lane came storming down from the hills with his Free State militia and bombarded the new fort. His artillery roared from an abandoned quarry whose rocky walls magnified the sound and though the cannonballs hurt nobody, panic gripped the town of Lecompton. Wagons leaving the city crashed into each other, their passangers' shouts and screams adding to the boom of the cannons. It was during this uproar that Prager—his master away again on a trip—ran to get the midwife who helped deliver a healthy boy not long after. She certified the child as being a seven-month baby and rushed off to attend other women who had been frightened into premature birth—though none of those women put an old-fashioned expensive ring into her hand as payment.

"We got away with it," whispered Meridel to the infant who tugged at her breast. Tiny wisps of red hair told of his McGraw heritage. His unfocused eyes were of an indeterminate pale blue, a "baby" color that probably would change with age. For a few precious days the infant seemed his mother's alone. She whispered to her son that he was also the son of Dan Forrester, a strong and wonderful man whom she hated in her mind but whom she helplessly loved in her heart.

She laughed softly and said, "Well, little lord, you'd have loved your real father but if you find my husband rather unlovable, never mind—I'll be there with you at Danemead to help you ride your first pony. In time I'll be dowager and you'll bring me your own children to cuddle, and maybe one day, they'll bring me their children . . . because I'm very healthy like an old woman who lived in a place called Dowager House." Suddenly she burst into tears, for the triumphs, the losses, the promises that would never be fulfilled. "I hope you haven't understood a word I've said. Of course you haven't. Because you must never know."

Harald became so transformed with joy that for a few days he turned almost tender. The new governor, John Geary, attended the christening. Dan Forrester sent a note of felicitation, very brief and correct. And so Meridel's baby became Eric Derwin Didrick Fitzwilliam Bellomont McGraw Wayne, reflecting generations of family history.

When Finnian McGraw returned home from the christening, he took to his bed with fever. He had lingered only long enough to see his grandson. He told Meridel he wanted to be forgiven for not having traveled to London to see his daughter meet the queen. Meridel begged him not to blame himself. He wanted to know how so fine a chap as Daniel Forrester could have turned so sour. He spoke of his many high-placed friends and predicted that good old Jim Buchanan would be elected president in November.

The doctor gave him medicine but shook his head. Meridel bent over her father to hear his last faint whisper: "Macushla . . . if I really . . . meet . . . your mother . . . in the beyond . . . I'll tell her . . . what a fine . . . English nobleman . . . you married."

He said no more. Within a few minutes the penniless immigrant who had owned nothing but a locomotive model and the rags on his back, the young man who had glowed with promise and romance, the rising railroad builder, the new arrival among New York City's rich, the grand schemer, the man who should never have trusted his son-in-law, lay cold and deathly still.

Meridel nursed her baby and mourned her father. But only she knew of the lost love that she also mourned behind her black veil.

•

Chapter Seven

Eric's eyes still had not found their real color, but the hair beginning to sprout on his head took on the exact shade of Meridel's. Harald objected to Meridel's nursing him—it simply wasn't done by a titled woman—but when she threatened violence if he brought in a wet nurse, she got her way.

Still, he wanted his son to have at least a caretaking nurse, so the baker's daughter, addlebrained but well developed for a girl of fifteen, came every day. Every day until she heated her curling iron on a brazier at the same table on which she was dressing Eric, and gave him a bad thigh burn. Harald half killed her with his riding crop and discharged her without a "character"—a terrible thing to do in England, but meaningless on the American frontier, with its shortage of women. Before she left, the girl spitefully told Meridel about another service besides baby-tending she had been performing in the family. Meridel was not shocked.

At least Eric healed well, although he would bear a scar

above his right knee. Harald's luck was turning bad and he decided not to hire another maid. Also, the local marshal came to see him. Meridel heard Harald, gripped by terror, shout that he knew nothing of the thief who had been caught rifling the land office files. The man knew his name? So did a lot of other people!

At this time, too, he found out that Kansas folk in general liked Dan Forrester. Even Slave Staters, who stood to gain most from a railroad line that would link up with the rails in St. Louis, told Harald they thought a rancher could ask any price he wished for a right-of-way. The public was coming to know the extent of the railroads' profits, and—as Harald growled to Meridel—the public liked to see the rich get "stung." He went around with his temper set at hair trigger, and his face lined in desperation.

Governor Geary did not last long. James Buchanan sent out Robert Walker, who faced the same problem of continued violence and of arranging an honest vote. Meanwhile, out on the prairie, the untamed tribes shaped arrowheads from the thin sheet steel of barrel hoops, which they secured from white traders. Far more deadly were the rifles that the traders exchanged for hides and furs and bits of gold. After the long winter when bare streaks grew wider on the dead prairie grass, braves drunk on the white man's firewater danced in a frenzy and boasted of the scalps they would take once the wagons began their westward trek. The wiser of the chiefs worried less about wagons than they did about iron rails and the thundering "iron horse." Wagon-made ruts might fade away, but never the railroad that already to the north at Rock Island was paring down the land until the Indian and buffalo had nowhere to go.

Then the three worst diseases that the white man had brought—cholera and smallpox and whooping cough—struck Indian villages.

Infected traders in their canoes and Indians who now enjoyed traveling by steamboat brought the diseases back and forth. Soon Lecomptonites developed nausea, pains in the lower back and the dreaded eruption of small red spots—smallpox—on the wrists and face. Some rushed to be inoculated. Others said inoculation was nonsense. Still others died.

186

Just when Horse Hurlbut came to warn Meridel about the spreading smallpox, Harald burst in. "There's smallpox all over town!"

Meridel knew his first concern. "I'll keep Eric indoors." She had enjoyed taking the baby out in his pram, sometimes all the way out to the smithy.

"You call that safe? We've got to get him out of town right away." As Hurlbut rose, limping—for a stranger had divined the secret of his "hooves"—Harald roared, "Where are you going? I'll need you to help carry our luggage to the coach."

"Didn't know I worked for you," said Hurlbut with a level look. "But I'll do it for Missus Lady Wayne and the baby."

Eric sucked a toe, uncaring. Meridel asked, "But where can we go?" She thought Harald would arrange to go to Judge Lecompte's farm or some other outlying spot where he did business. Her heart almost stopped when he said, "Forrester's place. Rainbow Ranch."

Steady! Betray nothing! she told herself. "Why there?"

"I have to go there anyway. I've almost certain proof that his boundaries are faulty, and he had better listen. Hurlbut! Go and find a man with a horse. Send him to Rainbow Ranch with the message that we'll arrive tomorrow. Here's—"

"You don't have to pay me for helping Missus."

"It's to pay for the man and the horse, you fool."

"Didn't think you wanted a fool working for you," said Hurlbut, and he stared at Harald till Harald looked away. Despite her confused feelings Meridel enjoyed seeing her husband bested by an uncouth mountain man.

Excitement, longing, love, and fear mingled in her heart. She was going to see Dan again, and with their child. She wondered how he would act toward her. She wondered if she could stop him from looking at her "that way." Did she really want to stop him?

Meridel never knew how many hours passed on the journey. But suddenly Dan was trotting alongside their carriage on his workhorse. He greeted them all cooly and when Meridel lifted Eric to show Dan his son through the small coach window—a natural gesture, she thought—he barely glanced at the infant. Even later, when Bertha Mueller danced around ponderously with "precious little darling" and Low Sun presented a tiny bead bracelet he had made, Dan only gave Eric another look and said, "Yup, there's the McGraw red hair."

Not till they were at dinner did the dark-eyed man betray the heat that ran beneath his cool surface, not by the way he looked at Meridel but by the way he ignored her presence as he spoke in brief sentences to Harald, always in a tight, strained voice. He mentioned that Southern planters in the new Slave State—he took it for granted that Kansas would enter the union on the Southern side—would have to get used to letting land lie idle for several months of the year. He agreed with Harald that the climate would give slave owners a need to get away from the single-crop system into agriculture of a more balanced kind. Dan also said that many in the South would welcome a civil war because their men were used to shooting and outdoor living, so they could harry and defeat any invading Northern army made up of factory workers and clerks.

At any rate Dan and Harald did not quarrel. Later, however, they spread out a map of the ranch and began a discussion in low voices, and for the first time Meridel noticed tension between them. Next morning they went out together on horseback, Harald's horse carrying a hamper of food and Dan's loaded with his surveyor's transit and leveling rod. They were going to look at certain boundaries. Neither man said why.

Dan paused to speak almost too shortly to Meridel from his saddle. "I'll have time tomorrow to show you—both— around the place." His eyes told the rest; he knew this must seem to be Meridel's first visit to Rainbow Ranch, and no one on the ranch would reveal she had been there before. She merely nodded and turned away.

Meridel idled away the day, awaiting the inevitable confrontation with Dan. Finally, near sundown she strolled out near a row of little ornamental trees that Adalberto called his niños, his children. Filled with doubt and apprehension, she caught sight of Dan and Harald riding down the path that trailed through the woods. They were arguing—about her? She did not think so. Most likely about boundaries. And she felt a sudden fear for Rainbow Ranch, which somehow had become home, although she did not let herself admit it. At length Harald turned his mount back up the trail. Dan swung to the ground, unlashed his equipment and gave his horse a light slap on the rump. The tired animal plodded toward the stable to be unsaddled and wiped down by the groom. No one else was in sight as Meridel, standing very still, watched Dan go to the front of the house and disappear inside. Not knowing what to do, she began to roam the grounds, stopping to inspect the beginnings of a rock garden; after a while she looked around as though someone had called her. But she had heard no voice. Had her mother's instinct warned her that Eric had awakened? Anyway, it was time she had a look at him since she had tucked him away in a big wicker basket at the foot of the guest bed. She walked around to the front door, and as she passed the old Pennsylvania rifle that hung on the wall with its powder horn, she noticed that the cellar door was no longer padlocked. She sighed and went upstairs.

From the top of the stairs she saw nobody, heard nobody. Perhaps Dan had not gone upstairs after all. She dared not be alone with him, anyway, she reflected with relief.

But when she entered the guest room she found him standing at the wicker basket, gazing at his sleeping son.

Chapter Eight

He had heard her footsteps, and had turned. Oddly, what she noticed first was the line left across the top of his dusty face by his hat which he had worn in the sun all day. Then she saw a man, stripped of all pretense, whose agony showed like a mask of tragedy upon his face. He held out his arms and she walked into the circle of his strength and rested her head against his chest. "Dan," she murmured. "Dan."

After a time they knew Eric had awakened by the gurgling sound that came from the crib. When they looked he was kicking and smiling at them and banging his makeshift mattress with his tiny hands.

They stood near a window with western exposure. The sun looked like a red ball balancing on the horizon as it painted the sky with fantastic reds and pinks and yellows. Below the riotous clouds they saw a stretch of prairie and tall, gray-green grass waving in gentle ripples to the horizon. With the light on his back, Dan leaned down and kissed Meridel. He rested his head upon her bosom and they shared a peaceful moment together.

The baby gurgled and cooed, making them remember where they were. "Stay here with me," Dan whispered.

She choked out, "Dan, I cannot."

"I'll be the only father Eric will remember. He'll know this house as his only home."

Torn with longing, shivering with desire, Meridel wondered what faithfulness was due an unfaithful, unloving husband. Words of glad surrender wanted to force their way past her lips. But no, no, no! If she had to do penance till the day they found her dead in the Dower House—

"Dan, please understand. When Harald goes back to England . . . we're going with him, Eric and I." A moment of brooding silence enveloped them before Meridel changed the subject. "Did Harald find anything wrong with your lines?"

"No. I ran those lines myself. He's going back to find any fumbled triangulation, but he won't find what he's looking for."

Again silence held them. Eric laughed at reflections of pink light on the nearby ceiling.

At the sound, Meridel froze. "Dan, what if Harald returns—"

"Returns? Damn Harald," he growled. "Who are you? Little Miss Hoity-Toity or a woman who has looked life in the face? You are *mine*."

Meridel turned her face away, refusing to meet his intense blue eyes.

"No," he said, "I have listened to you make our love less important than a veil and orange blossoms. I have heard you make mere ceremony stronger than a father's right to know his child. You punish yourself because as a desperate girl you tried to save yourself from disaster." His hands raised to her cheeks, he forced her to look at him. "All day I rode with Harald and all day I wanted to tell him how it has gone with us—tell him who fathered Eric, let him reach for his gun while I reached for mine. I would win that battle. But it's not the way I want to win *you*. Meridel, it must be *you* who breaks your marriage." He kissed her hard, set her down, and said with abrupt decision, "But whether or not you leave Harald, you are going to be mine now."

"Dan, I want to, but—"

"On this you cannot say no to me." He grabbed the top of her dress fiercely.

"Don't rip my dress, please!"

He let go of her dress, beating his hands together in despair at the part of himself that wanted to force instead of gentle a woman to bed. "Then . . . tell me you are going to be mine, right now, because we may never meet again." She thought she would go mad with inner conflict. "Show me for an hour that you love me," he grated. "Or—go."

A great calm came over Meridel. If Harald returned too soon, so be it. In a glow of love and happiness she said, "I'll stay the hour . . . here where I belong, Dan."

Still perturbed, he drew a hand across his face. "Now I'll tell you—Harald is staying at Gawlty's Inn, so he can get a local surveyor to rerun my lines tomorrow. He won't be back tonight."

Instead of being angry for his testing her, she felt pleased. "Now you see my love for you."

"But do you have the will to make us happy?" She did not answer. "Well then, Bertha is out. Write her a note. Say you want no dinner and that Lord Harald won't come home tonight. She doesn't know I'm here and anyway, they're very discreet, the Muellers." He picked up the basket holding Eric. "I'll take Eric to my room."

Meridel left the note in the kitchen and ran back upstairs. Dan kissed her fingertips, traced his lips along her arm to her throat, to her bosom, where he kissed each breast, then kissed the sweet valley that he found deeper than before. Stroking his hair, whispering to him—not in words but in tiny gasps and syllables of passion—she melted with him into a yearning wildness. Guiding him with her soft, firm hand, she took him deep where her body flamed. They became one flesh and one shared rapture. Love held them secure in a long, ecstatic union. Had an hour gone by? Had two? But no, they had all night! She held him tightly lest he move away.

At length came an interruption they welcomed. Eric whimpered. They laughed and kissed. Meridel rose and put the baby on her lap. As the rosebud mouth sucked in nourishment she saw a glint on Dan's cheek. He turned away to hide his emotion.

When she returned the sated Eric to his basket, Dan lifted her and carried her to the window that faced the setting sun. He murmured, "There lies our land. Forest. Prairie. Sky." She turned to watch a radiating fan of sunbeams make the clouds glow with a deepening, darkening pink. He murmured, "See how pink it makes your skin—or are you flushing?"

"I have reason."

He chuckled, raising her to bring her bosom to his lips. "I'm jealous of my son," he whispered.

"Oh!" She held him there.

Not many minutes passed before Dan turned and carried Meridel to his bed. With hands and lips they warmed each other, the slender white arms and the muscled hairy arms mingling and cherishing the other. Now they could wait a bit, and they surged slowly, again and again approaching the height of pleasure, pausing at the brink, cooling, kissing, going on to warmth and heat and another rhythmic adventure to the quivering edge of bliss. At last they went over the brink, crying out together. For a time they lay in drowsy contentment, side by side.

Meridel had almost fallen asleep when Dan showed her a bright silvery star outside the nearly dark window. "See, Venus is blessing us."

Meridel blew a kiss to the star and returned to Dan's arms for sleep. But Dan couldn't sleep and lay wide awake and searching for a way to keep this woman and this child. It had to be Meridel with valor, not he with violence, who broke that marriage. He might be the only one who saw it that way, but he saw it as the only honest thing to do.

Harald Wayne had ridden out of sight along a forest trail which he planned to abandon soon. No matter what he had told Forrester, he had no intention of returning to the ranch's northern boundary nor of dealing with a surveyor nor of sleeping at Gawlty's. He had not expected to find anything wrong with Forrester's lines but he had had to make sure.

Now he would carry on with an elaborate plan he had been preparing a long time. A dangerous, tricky plan, yes—one that would get him what he wanted and also rid him of Forrester once and for all.

He reined in at a pond and frightened an elk with a forty-pound rack on its head. He whistled a few bars of "Come High Tide I See My Johnny," and in time Eddoes emerged from the woods.

"We're going ahead with the plan, Eddoes."

"The plan, your lor'ship"—Eddoes tossed away an empty bottle—"called blame-it-on-the-Indians?" He belched.

"Show me the railroad flares."

Eddoes reached into a leather sack. "Here, lor'ship. And Hendrick says stuff is gettin' stole. Locals run off with the copper tubing for the locomotive boilers and made whiskey stills."

"I'll talk to him. But what about the whiskey for the Indians?"

"I buried the kegs good. Only the chief—Dry Corn is his name—knows the spot. But the braves had better not know, right, your lor'ship? But when Dry Corn sees my flare tomorrow night, he takes his braves to the barrels, they drink up, and then . . ."

And then the Skidi Pawnee would gallop into Rainbow Ranch and leave it devastated and strewn with corpses.

Harald spoke quickly. "Remember, Eddoes, *you* stay sober tomorrow night. You get back to Rainbow Ranch before the fighting starts and you drive us out of there quickly. But can we absolutely count on Dry Corn and his fighters?"

Eddoes's sharp features grew sharper and a foul odor of whiskey wafted from him. "Sho. You know what horses are worth to prairie Indians. When I promised 'em Forrester's, you betcha they're going in shooting. Let alone they want Forrester's scalp. The chief said the scalp of a man as strong as Forrester would make powerful war medicine."

"Tomorrow night, then. Can I depend on *you*?"

"Long's you pay me good, lor'ship."

Harald rode on, then paused at a branch trail. Forrester's scalp. He nodded grimly, then turned his mind to a more pleasant matter. Chances were that he had a place to sleep away from home that night. Lucy Barth had told him exactly how to find her house.

She had said she would be glad to have him drop in anytime.

That afternoon Lucy Barth had gone to Rainbow Ranch to make sure she met Harald Wayne again, only to learn he had ridden off with Dan Forrester. To try and gain at least something from her trip, she idled behind the house and spied Meridel McGraw Wayne in the tree nursery.

Gladly Lucy saw Dan Forrester and Lord Harald return before Harald rode out again, this time to the north. Dan entered the house and in a little while Meridel went around to the front door and . . . upstairs? Peering from behind a shed, Lucy waited, restless, she knew not for what, only that she had a premonition about the two and with Lord Harald gone, she could confirm or lay to rest her suspicions. The sun touched the horizon, flashing its glow on Dan's bedroom window and as she peered, she thought she glimpsed movement.

She blinked her eyes and stared again. For the space of a dozen heartbeats Lucy watched Dan, holding Meridel in his arms, nuzzle at her beautiful, full breasts. How the redhead loved it—the bitch!

He lifted and carried her off, no doubt to his bed, leaving Lucy to glare after his mighty shoulders. Biting her knuckles the schoolmistress could not curse away the image of Meridel's lovely, pink form and Dan's hairy body—a marvelous one she had so often felt pressing heavily upon her own. At length she stomped off to the stables, found Henry, the herder, and asked him to take her home. As they rode, the western sky darkened and Venus sailed across it low, clear and cold-blue, as if to mock her.

When Henry left with the extra horse, Lucy glumly entered her cabin and had hardly lit a lamp when she heard a tap at her door.

"Who is it?" Some local couple come to ask forbearance for their bruise-bottomed dunce?

"Wayne."

Good heavens!

Months ago, when she had been in Lecompton shopping,

Lucy had met Lord Harald. She had read him well. He had read her excellently. She had invited him to drop in, and had even told him he'd have to stoop through the doorway, because seven-log cabins were not high enough for such a marvelously tall man. She had expected nothing more than a few meetings in the dark; a few gifts too, she had hoped. But now, she wondered what Lord Harald Wayne, who reeked of money, would do if she told him about what she had seen at Dan Forrester's? She flew to her mirror, then to the door, greeting him with practiced warmth.

"A goddess named Venus told me to come here," he said.

He had insisted on having light but had allowed her to turn the lamp low, which she was thankful for. Too bright a light revealed the tiny wrinkles, not to mention the touch of desperation in her face. Nothing had gone well in her life. Teaching and moving westward; teaching and again moving toward emptiness because the man's wife had found out or because some other piece of bad luck had tripped her up. She had to play this one right.

She had lured Wayne—who was not unwilling—into a second coupling. Afterward, panting and pleased, he complimented the quality of the bourbon she brought him. Good. He must realize she was not a peasant. And now that she had him tired and mellow and somewhat tender, she said, "Harald . . . I don't want to poke my nose into your affairs . . . but . . . your wife—"

He demanded with instant suspicion, "What about my wife?"

"Well . . . sometimes a man is better off not knowing, but . . ."

The hard gleam in his eyes told her she needn't beat around the bush.

"Well . . . did you know that while you were off on your trip, Lady Wayne stayed several days at Rainbow Ranch? Alone?"

"*What?*"

"Yes, she did. Slept upstairs where *he* sleeps. Later I found them cooing like a couple of honeymooners, bold as brass."

Good, she thought. Harald had gone purple in the face. His knuckles showed white on his clenched fists. "You are saying that my wife . . . that my wife . . . Gad!" He glared toward the ranch. "She's been deceiving me. . . . I should have known, God damn it!"

"There's more."

"Tell me! Quickly!" he growled, murderous rage on his face.

"I went to the ranch yesterday afternoon and I saw Meridel in the tree nursery, but she didn't see me. Shortly after Dan went inside, she went in, too." Harald moved closer so as not to miss a word. "There was a lovely sunset. I saw them at his bedroom window—yes, I know his bedroom window— watching the pretty clouds."

"*What?* Watching the—"

"Naked," she said with care. "Both naked. Dan was holding her in his arms. He kissed her"—Lucy pointed—"here and here."

"What . . . else . . . did they do?"

"I didn't actually see, but perhaps they couldn't perform it comfortably while standing, because Dan carried her off toward his bed."

Harald echoed, "Bed. Bed." The sound of his hard breathing filled the cabin. He glared at Lucy through the Viking-blond hair that had fallen over his eyes. "Wait. He used to be your man. So you want me to take your chestnuts out of the fire. Take Meridel out of your way. 'Heaven has no rage like love to hatred turned—'"

"'Nor hell a fury like a woman scorned,' and Congreve said it once and for all, but I would never take Dan back. I want to see him dead, Harald."

"So," he whispered. "You know my thought."

"What thought?"

"That I will kill them both tonight while they're in bed. Because they think I'm not coming back till tomorrow."

She hissed, "You have the right."

"No jury would convict me. I'd never even come to trial."

Now she would show him the kind of woman she was, and now she would bind them together. "Let me help you kill them, Harald."

He bared his teeth in a grim smile. "Yes."

He fumbled for his clothing and thrusting a hand into his pocket found a double-barreled, palm-size derringer made for shooting a heavy bullet at short range, as across a gaming table. "Even if someone sees me come in, I can say I changed my mind about staying in that filthy inn." He unloaded the gun, glared madly at it as he clicked the hammers over and over. "Dead. Both of them. Let Kansas and England know I'm a man of honor! And within forty-eight hours Henrick can begin laying iron. . . ."

"Harald, what about Dan's cousin in Maryland who—"

"His heir? I have taken pains," said Lord Harald as he reloaded his derringer, "to promise rewards to telegraphers who'll delay any message that Will Cranston—Forrester's lawyer—sends to Maryland. The rails will be laid. And the record shows that once iron is down it stays while a court fight goes on. Meanwhile trains run, farmers start shipping produce, the public good becomes clear, and the landowner has to accept a price and give in. I'll take the chance."

"Dan's people are very loyal. His men can shoot."

"There'll be nothing left to defend. Twenty-four hours from now Rainbow Ranch will be ruined, its stock gone, its people dead. Tomorrow night a band of drunken, bloodthirsty Skidi Pawnee will gallop in and do that job for me. Come on!" he snarled, waving the derringer.

Lucy rose, at once chilled and admiring of Harald's audacity and skill at hiring the most treacherous, hostile lot of Indians in the territory, the Skidi Pawnee. Again feeling a touch of fright, she observed aloud that she and Harald would ride more quietly if they doubled up on his horse rather than if they took her tumbledown cart.

Outside the night had become overcast. Venus, in any event, would have set out of sight, so its disappearance portended nothing out of the ordinary in Lucy's mind. They dismounted a quarter mile from Dan's house and tethered the horse. But as they stole toward the steps, Mueller rushed from a side door with a shotgun ready.

"It's Wayne and Miss Barth," Lord Harald said softly.

"Beg pardon, Lord Harald. Didn't expect you."

"I'm glad to see, my man, that you sleep with one eye

open. Miss Barth came with me to get some papers, then she'll leave."

Embarrassed in his nightshirt, Mueller retreated. Inside the house Lucy lit her bull's-eye lantern and adjusted the shutter to allow only a sliver of light. They stole upstairs and headed for the guest-room whose door stood ajar. Lucy heard the hiss of Harald's breath as he clicked the derringer ready and held her breath as the wedge of light slid along the floor of the guest room toward the bed.

"Bloody hell! They've taken Eric in his basket and—"

But Lucy knew the only other place they could be. Tiptoeing down the corridor, she led him to Dan's room and slowly pushed the door open. The little beam of wavering light first found the basket. Then it found the end of the bed. Then it found a man and a woman asleep in each other's arms.

As Lucy opened the lantern's shutter fully the man awakened. In the same instant Harald pointed the derringer's short barrels at the couple and shouted loudly—wanting Mueller, downstairs, to hear—"You! Forrester! Sleeping with my wife!"

Forrester leaped naked from the bed, roaring, "Stay low, Meridel!"

But she sat up and flashed into action, hardly knowing what she was doing as the bark and flash of the derringer filled the room and a window shattered. She had grabbed the heavy brass bedside candlestick and, flinging it at Harald, spoiled his aim. Dan, now having time, punched the gun out of Harald's grasp as Meridel rolled out of bed and grabbed Eric up to her.

Mueller roared from below, "What's going on?"

"I'll kill you, Forrester. Seducing my wife!"

Dan kicked the gun beneath the bed. "Come and get me."

But Harald dashed for the candlestick, colliding with Dan. Suddenly everyone heard shots outside, followed by galloping hoofbeats that stopped outside the house.

Lucy Barth screamed, "The Indians!"

Boots tattooed on the veranda. The front door banged open and a man shouted, "Lord Harald, you there?"

"Eddoes, come up here quickly, I need you!"

But Eddoes had lost his revolver, his bowie, and his silver-trimmed hat. He lurched into the room, clutching a bloodied shoulder. "They're comin'," he gasped.

"Who, you fool?"

"The Pawnee—the Skidi Pawnee."

"I told you tomorrow, you goddamned—"

"But the braves—they had a dog they'd trained to sniff out whiskey. Dug it up. I tried to stop 'em and they—"

As Eddoes slumped against a wall, Mueller rushed upstairs with his shotgun, his wife panting after him. Shots rang out close by. A wakened rooster crowed insanely. Then the shrill cry of the warwhoop slashed the night air for a prolonged, chilling moment.

Lord Harald shouted at Eddoes, "Get the carriage. I'll take the baby—"

"No, you won't," Meridel screamed as Dan grabbed a rifle from a cupboard.

A man—one of the ranch hands—shouted up from the doorway, "Boss! They're running out all the horses. Atkins is kilt, but we shot two Injuns. They've got torches!"

Dan, leaping for his trousers and boots, shouted, "Mueller, get the women safe. Take them down through the cellar and out through the back scuttle and hide them with the baby in the trees."

Dressed but unbuttoned, Meridel hurried with Mrs. Mueller to the cellar while the foreman forced Lucy along. As soon as Mueller flung open the scuttle he fired and sent a wildly shrieking, painted and feathered figure flying backward off his pony.

Mueller thrust the women ahead of him into a copse of trees to hide before running back to shoot another feathered rider who galloped drunkenly, and wielded a blazing torch, straight toward the house. But the Indian swerved his horse, knocking Mueller down, and threw the torch through a kitchen window. Bertha ran to save her husband. Other Skidi Pawnee, their heads shaved to scalp locks, a single feather sticking up in back, staggered into the house for loot as smoke poured from the kitchen.

Breathing hard, Meridel found herself and her baby alone with Lucy Barth while the house, now flaming, sent an engulfing, lurid light up into the clouds overhead.

"Our house," mourned Meridel. But Lucy watched only for the carriage as bullets flew and men died in this small-scale battle. "Dan's horses—gone, all gone," cried Meridel. Lucy spied the handsome, birch-paneled coach rolling by and screamed for it to stop. Harald drove, while Eddoes sat half-conscious beside him, his head lying limply on his chest. Harald only cast one wild glance at Lucy and didn't see his wife and her baby as he fled from the whiskey-maddened Indians who wanted horses and forgot the difference between friend and foe.

Flames burst through the roof of the house. They revealed Lucy standing there, and a redskin, shouting to his comrades, forced his mount in among the trees. Meridel recoiled as the bushes parted before the eager brave. Before too long the feather-bedecked horse of an older Indian whose lynx collar, trimmed with bear claws, marked him as a chief, trotted into view. Others followed, laden with copper pots and kitchen knives. One man's belt held a bloody, black-haired scalp, and he wore Adalberto's sombrero. Another wore a valet's bombazine vest.

Rivals for the same man though they were, Lucy and Meridel shrank together. One of the braves motioned to Meridel, then to the half-awake baby. He wanted her to hand Eric up to him.

"No!"

Backing away, she came up against the chief's leg, and he seized her by the hair. For an awful moment she expected to feel his knife slice around her head. Lucy was arguing in a strange tongue, using English whenever she faltered. Meridel heard, "Teacher." The chief spoke to her, and she said to Meridel, "You'd better give the baby to that brave."

"No!"

"We can't escape. They're going to take us to their village, and because that brave has recently lost a child to whooping cough, he wants a white baby to replace his own."

"No, no! Dan!" she wailed. But no answer came. The chief, growling, yanked Meridel off balance, and the brave snatched Eric from her arms.

Lucy told her, half in fright and half in malice, "The chief wants *you*. He's always had four wives, but one died of illness and you're to take her place."

"Dan, save me!" But they bound Meridel with thongs and tied her face-down across the chief's horse behind his riding pad. Since her hair swept the ground and the horse might step on it, a brave hacked it short with his knife.

The same brave picked up Lucy and set her astride the horse behind him. "They don't want Mrs. Mueller—she's too old," said the schoolmistress with a moan of fright.

They pushed out of the woods and joined a group of other Indians, some wounded and lashed to their horses. Meridel could hardly breathe as the chief's horse jounced her. After some time, perhaps because he didn't want her injured, he stopped and lifted her up into a sitting position behind him. The party now moved through endless prairie in grass so high it brushed the horses' bellies.

Toward dawn the chief called a halt where a thread of water ran and cottonwoods had taken root. Reeling with weariness, Meridel slid down, anxious to reach the howling Eric.

His captor gladly handed over the baby to be nursed. He brought Meridel pemmican and parched corn and water from the rill. She ate, drank, hardly believing what had happened to her—though the soreness racking her body told her she was not dreaming.

Now Chief Dry Corn scolded his braves, and Lucy translated: The younger men were frogs jumping, not men thinking. True, Lord Harald had promised to give them repeating rifles, but only if they showed him Forrester's dead body. But Forrester had gotten away. The younger men had barked like prairie dogs and were just as useless.

A brave objected, saying the raid had won them many horses.

The chief folded his arms and glared. Let the frog-brave remember that they had not captured the fine gray stallion. How could they now breed their small horses to give them bigger, stronger, white man's horses?

With faint gladness Meridel realized that Dan was still alive. So, apparently, was Rumak.

After a short sleep the group pushed on. Meridel noticed that they kept the noonday sun halfway in back and to their left, and that later, they faced the sun, still on the left, as it set blindingly. But what good did it do to know one was being taken in a northwestward direction?

When they finally stopped for the night, Meridel nursed Eric again, washed him in a muddy trickle of water, and diapered him with a strip of her petticoat. Leading Fox, the brave who wanted to keep the baby, looked on with approval. He now considered himself Eric's father. Among most of the Indian tribes, children belonged to whoever took care of them, and a woman belonged to whatever man bought or captured her.

Next day the fickle weather of the plains brought sleet in a storm of needles. Meridel shrieked at Leading Fox, but when he showed her how he protected Eric with a hide, she calmed down. Soon they entered drier country, with shorter grass that hid wolves and antelope. They saw buffalo galloping in one great mass, which left a long-lived plume of dust in the very clear, very dry air.

They paused at sunset beside an old buffalo wallow, disturbing prairie dogs who sat upright beside their holes and yelped and whisked their tails because the intruders frightened them. Meridel found a smile for the silly creatures, a smile that faded as a hiss of caution ran through the camp and the horse guards signaled danger.

In this area of gradually rising plains, the grass was patched yellow where the buffalo grazed and on one such patch a man straddled a gray horse with a rifle crossing his saddle. Keen-eyed watchers said he was a white man. Hope stirred again in Meridel's heart. She could not make out his face, but she knew the horseman was Dan.

The chief sent men to kill the stonefaced watcher, but his horse outran theirs. All afternoon it appeared and disappeared like a phantom that haunted the billows of the prairie.

Sometime during the next night Meridel lay listening to owls and a coyote's low, two-note cry. A thin rain came and went, whispering to her, "Dan is alive!" And as she realized later, Dan at that moment must have been walking his horse through the wet grass to muffle his horse's footfalls, for the guards, huddling in the cold and wet, never heard his approach.

Suddenly he galloped through the camp and wheeled in a circle of gunshots as he shouted, "Meridel, where are you?" Before she could utter a sound, Chief Dry Corn had her by the throat. A flash of lightning showed her Dan in the instant that a bullet smashed his saddle horn, and he galloped away into the darkness.

Later, when everyone thought he had gone over the horizon, Dan swooped out of a thunderstorm and galloped through the tethered horses, firing his revolver, shouting, smacking men with his lariat. Within seconds he was gone again. The horses had galloped off in every direction, except for one that the lightning-blinded guards had shot dead when they were trying to shoot Dan.

The next day, when scouts returned with the pitifully few horses that had not been lost or picked up by other tribes, Chief Dry Corn said he admired Dan's bravery. He said more, and Lucy Barth made sure Meridel understood. "He says that Dan will not scream when they capture him and the women chop off his fingers joint by joint and strip away his skin by inches."

Meridel kept watching the empty prairie. Dry Corn could not have stopped her from screaming a warning to Dan if he appeared. But he never did again. They trekked on across the pathless sea of grass, slowly now because they had no change of horses. One day scouts led them into a Skidi Pawnee village of conical tepees beside a small, tree-bordered stream.

Meridel appealed to Lucy. "Have you any idea where we are?"

Turning a dirty face from horizon to horizon, Lucy could see only the same measureless vista of endless grass ruffled by a mournful wind. Probably no white man had ever trod there.

"We'll never get away from here." The schoolmistress tore at her hair despairingly. "We'll rot here, I tell you!"

Turning away, Meridel wondered how many years Lucy and she would be forced to spend in each other's company.

And yet, despite everything, she still saw beauty in the

awesome stretches of land and sky and cloud shadows that sailed across the prairie like floating islands. But Lucy was right. She and her child might live and die in that far country without her ever seeing Dan or anyone else she knew again. Or—it struck her with sudden force—without ever seeing civilization again.

Part III

Life Was a Secret Told

Chapter One

All morning the wind blew hot and dry across their camp, until afternoon, when the air suddenly went unnaturally still. Birds in the cottonwoods ceased their twittering. Clouds swirled in restless layers and thunderheads piled up in the sky like gigantic black fists. The sky at last sent down a twisting, wavering finger that touched the parched prairie and made great veils of dust dart here and there.

Watching from the river bank, Meridel saw the medicine man—his name was Old Standing Bear—bend under the weight of his buffalo-horn headdress and shake a feathered medicine stick at the roaring tornado. At the same time thunder fighters pounded a drum and horsemen galloped out of the village to shoot arrows at the funnel-shaped creature who seemed to be headed their way.

Meridel grabbed up her baby from a branch where he had been hanging all wrapped in soft doeskin and strapped to his board, and only returned him after the tornado lost contact with the earth and pulled itself back into a heavy cloud. When he wakened he would yowl, sending—and this still left an ache in Meridel's heart—a kindly and comfortable Indian woman named Silver Leaf, to run and nurse him. She was Leading Fox's second wife who had lost her baby but still had milk—a convenience, since Meridel's breasts had gone dry. So Eric lived in Leading Fox's tepee and Meridel spent as much time with him as she could, never allowing a day to pass when she did not hold him close and whisper "Mama, Mama" over and over again.

Meridel blinked. Dan had surely died. After he had scattered that group of horses, no one had seen him for many days. Then, suddenly, he had appeared on the brow of a hill. When warriors leaped to their remaining mounts and charged at him, shooting, he wheeled away on his own large, gray horse. But not long after the pursuit began, a one-in-a-thousand lucky shot brought down his horse. Moments later shots sounded from beyond a hill where Dan had run and apparently escaped the braves who refused to follow. The braves had seen a party of Comanches in the distance, and they decided to leave Dan to the Comanches for capture and torture. The Skidis galloped back, carrying Dan's reins and saddle and later retrieved the stallion's meat and hide. So Rumak, the valuable Polish stallion, was dead; but where was his master?

That was when Meridel's milk had run dry.

After the tornado had come and gone, Meridel helped Silver Leaf dig for medicinal roots and herbs on the sandy shore of the little river. Only Silver Leaf knew as much about these as did Standing Bear, and she had given Meridel a bark cylinder containing *has-hak-a-ta-ton-ga*, a vile-tasting herb that kept pregnancy away.

Soon the two friends turned to their second job, making pots from clay they found along the river. Meridel had just removed the clay from a log where she had been modeling it, when she looked toward the village. Her heart sank. Three frowning women in shapeless dearskin smocks were coming toward her.

She knew them well, too well. They were Dry Corn's other wives, and they and the chief and Meridel—with a few children tucked in here and there—shared the sleeping platform that ran around the inside of his tepee. Dry Corn took whatever wife suited him, but he took Meridel most often. So Pumpkin Vine, Pheasant Call, and Leaping Fish hated Meridel, and because she was the junior wife they made her suffer.

Kind-hearted Silver Leaf muttered at them, but they took Meridel away from her task and back into the tepee village.

"Ho, white woman, you must learn to cook, or our husband will be displeased and beat you," said aging Pumpkin Vine.

"You will lie cold all night and listen to him make me another baby. Yes, you must learn to cook, pale weak one," said crow-voiced Pheasant Call, whose arm, broken by a horse's kick, had been set crookedly and pained her often.

"You must no longer act strange and apart-by-yourself. Let your friends help you become a worthy Skidi Pawnee," said Leaping Fish, giggling and pinching Meridel as though in jest but leaving a purple bruise with her strong fingers.

They brought her to where they had tethered a fat little dog near a fire. They knew what made the white woman sick. Gleefully they gave her the killing club. She closed her eyes as she swung the club and only made matters worse, because the dog lay there with broken ribs, squirming and keening.

Meridel gritted her teeth and killed the poor creature with her second blow. Receiving another pinch to speed her on, she took the corpse by its tail and swung it through the flames again and again to singe off the hair. Burning particles fell upon her while the other women mocked her discomfort.

Then they made her skin the dog. Then, worst of all—but grimly accomplished—they made her butcher it, cut the carcass into parts, and put them in a pot to boil.

"See, we have saved you from a black-and-blue-from-head-to-foot beating," said Pumpkin Vine, giggling with the others while Meridel sorted out the syllables of the difficult Pawnee tongue.

At last they left her alone. She was trying to brush burnt hair from her dress when, lifting her sweaty, grimy face, she saw Lucy Barth approaching, Why, she wondered, did she herself wear patches of trade cloth and leather, while Lucy wore a soft, doeskin smock decorated with beadwork? Why did Lucy live alone in her own tepee—and sleep alone, too, although braves guarded her? And she had no duties. And ate the best tidbits, and always looked combed and sleek and smug. It seemed to have something to do with her being a teacher, and indeed Lucy put on a show of learning, compiling a Pawnee dictionary on strips of bark that might or might not reach civilization.

Extra flesh on her hips accented her indolent walk as she went to the pot, peered into it, and sneered, "Well done. And you have become the ideal squaw—hardworking and untidy."

Squaw, a white man's word, was an insulting word to the Indians. "I'm of some use, anyway." But Meridel's retort fell flat.

Lucy scanned the prairie. "Dan's not sneaking around anymore, is he? You've finally killed him."

"What!" cried Meridel.

"Yes, you. He certainly didn't want to rescue me. I wonder how long he withstood the Comanche torture. They push sharp splinters beneath the toenails, set fire to them, and make the victim dance—"

"Don't, oh, please, please!"

Lucy laughed and walked off. "I have the use of a nail file they found in one of the immigrant wagons," she said over her shoulder. "One must look to one's grooming."

After Dry Corn, who really was not a cruel man except when war required it, had finished with her that night, Meridel lay gazing at the stars through the tepee's ventilation flap. Yes, she sensed that Dan was dead. And the dreary years ahead would turn her into a savage with a savage son, and after a time she might even doubt her memories. But no, all her life, when she lay in the dark, she'd be able to feel Dan making love to her. Still, Dan was dead. *Dan was dead.* Wherever Dan's body lay, there lay her love.

Eric now toddled, naked, as he would stay till cold weather came. He called Meridel Mama—and still went for most of his food to Silver Leaf's breast. The Pleiades appeared in the sky, and a baby born that night was named Seven Stars.

Old Standing Bear announced that the time had come to

hunt buffalo for winter meat. The women dismantled the tepees, turning the long poles into drags to be pulled by small horses. For three days Meridel walked with a thirty-pound pack while Lucy Barth rode and lived like a queen. She filed her nails, combed her hair, and accepted food brought to her before any of the other hungry, tired women had eaten.

At last the scouts who had been sent out earlier in the week galloped back signaling, they'd spotted buffalo. Meridel guessed that a whole square mile of buffalo grazed indifferently beneath a cloud of fine dust. Killed, they would not only provide meat but also sinew for stringing bows; their bones would be fashioned into various implements; their hides would make leather for bags and ropes and harnesses and saddles and tepee covers, winter bedcovers and warm robes. The buffalo's bile would become a green-yellow body paint. Its hooves gave glue. Its blood gave strength.

Braves stampeded the great stupid beasts, riding right in among them to shoot at point-blank range, daring the dangerous horns, in order not to waste a single bullet. Meridel saw a horse gored. As it died, its rider sprang upon a buffalo's back, stabbing it until it died. But when the beast, which weighed a ton, fell, the brave rolled off, and a thousand hurrying hooves chopped him into bloody pieces.

When the herd—barely diminished—rushed off across the horizon, all the able women except Lucy Barth got busy on the thirty-odd carcasses that lay scattered on the plain. Braves brought horses to help in peeling off the furry hides. But all of the heavy cutting and disemboweling and butchering, and the handling of the bones and the enormous haunches of meat, was women's work. Wolves waited nearby, their tongues lolling. Buzzards circled. After sunset the women worked by torchlight, until at last Silver Leaf helped Meridel to her unsteady feet.

Now truly heavy-laden, the tribe crawled northward and westward under the broiling sun while the cool nights made them shiver. At last they rested near a typical prairie river, more mud than water, while scouts investigated the route ahead.

But they had to stay longer beside the river than they had

planned, for a child came down with whooping cough. Then another and yet another.

Standing Bear did no good by blowing medicine-smoke into the children's faces. The coughing grew worse, bringing spasms during which the sick children drew in breath painfully, with a whistling sound. But Eric toddled about happily, saying, "Mama" and "New Yor'" and "Ra-bow Rach"—until one morning Meridel found Silver Leaf keeping him on the bed platform in Leading Fox's tepee, wiping him with cool water to lessen the fever. He had gotten the disease, whooping cough.

Already the first child to become ill was turning blue because he could take in so little air. Standing Bear pushed a hollow reed down his throat. It made no difference. Something burst in the child's throat, and he threw up blood and choked to death.

Meridel had heard that whooping cough did not affect white children as badly as it affected Indians. But soon Eric went into a phase of coughing painfully, which continued for three weeks. He seemed ready to whoop out his heart in Meridel's arms while Silver Leaf physicked him with snakeroot. She herself searched desperately until she found some dried-up flaxweed that white settlers used to relieve coughs and asthma.

Meanwhile Standing Bear, tottering about with his medicine stick and his amulets, muttered that the Great Spirit had sent punishment upon the Skidi Pawnee. But the tribe would have one chance to redeem itself. That was because the planet Venus, which had been setting more and more southward of the sun, had begun to track slowly back and, one early evening, would approach the sun. The two planets, along with the thin crescent of a new moon, would form a three-way omen in the sky.

Standing Bear gathered the people together. With much rattle-shaking and scattering of sacred feathers, he told them they must offer a sacrifice to the universe—the selfsame sacrifice he remembered from his youth, before the custom had faded and the white man had become stronger. It would take away the-whistling-fever-that-kills-children and stop the immigrant wagons and break the rails and bring down the telegraph wires and cause constant defeat to the white horse soldiers. All this and more, once the sacrifice was accomplished the next evening. It was necessary that everyone attend, except for one old woman who could stay behind and tend the sick.

Reluctantly Meridel walked with Silver Leaf toward the place of ceremony. She wanted to be able to rush back quickly to the village in case Eric's condition worsened, so she and Silver Leaf stayed on a little rise above the rest.

The braves carried their war bows and bundles of deadly iron-barbed arrows. Each held his clay pipe in his left hand— the sign of war—as they danced around a shallow pit filled with soft feathers. This represented the garden of the Great Spirit where life had originated long ago.

Meanwhile other men erected a kind of short, vertical ladder that began with two stout poles driven into the ground. Across these they bound four crosspieces of wood, representing the sacred elm, fir, cottonwood, and willow. The old medicine man whirled like a top as he chanted of sacrifice and ranted of war. He burned feathers, scattered mysterious herbs, mixed roots and herbs into an odorous brew that bubbled over a fire. When he lifted the extremely hot pot in his bare hands everyone gasped at the magic that protected him. Still chanting, he bore the smoking mixture back into the village.

As snow drifted down, Meridel huddled, a ragged piece of buffalo skin around her shoulders. A great cry arose as Standing Bear appeared again, leading a woman whose hands had been bound. A naked woman. Lucy Barth! Stout, calm, not even shivering, the sacrificial victim had obviously been drugged. She walked barefooted across sharp stones without showing pain. Standing Bear fixed a "creation" feather into her hair while she gazed blandly and contentedly at nothing.

Again the old shaman shook his eagle-feathered stick and harangued his people. Raging, he shouted that misfortune had befallen them because they had been contaminated by white traders. What need had they of iron implements when they could use the clay pots and flint knives of their forefathers? Why did women use the traders' needles when they could make a good needle out of a tiny bone from a deer's hoof?

215

Above all, why use the white man's noisy gun? Let the foolish braves remember that an arrow shot into a buffalo could be pulled out and used again, but a bullet once shot was gone, and no Indian knew how to make gunpowder. "And remember, O my people," shouted the aged man, trembling with fervor, "if we go back to the old way of life we will gain magical protection against the white man's bullets and so our braves can kill . . . kill . . . kill!"

Some braves looked doubtful. But all leaped into a war dance, patting their mouths and howling and swinging tomahawks. Meridel shuddered, watching in astonishment as two men painted Lucy Barth's right side red to symbolize day and the left side black to symbolize night. Silver Leaf whispered, "Very soon we will sacrifice the virgin to the evening star and the morning star."

Meridel puzzled over the Indian word for virgin, then suddenly realized what Silver Leaf had said. Then Lucy was forced to climb the short ladder. When she reached the top rung, her red-and-black body turned to face the group. She showed no emotion as men bound her waist and legs to the uprights, leaving the upper part of her body free. Meridel watched all this in growing horror, then at last demanded, "Did you say virgin?"

"Virgin, yes."

"How do you—" Meridel wondered if she should ask. "How do you know Lucy Barth is a virgin?"

"The white man makes sure that all his teaching women are virgins."

Meridel gasped as she understood. Old-maid schoolmistress! True, the white man's female teachers never—or rarely—married. But . . .

"Silver Leaf, you can't sacrifice that woman. I absolutely know she is not a virgin!"

But Silver Leaf hushed Meridel, told her in fright that the wildly gyrating, bloodthirsty braves would kill her if she interfered. Nor would anyone believe her. So Meridel stood in paralyzed dread, saying nothing, as Standing Bear took up a bow and a sharp-flinted arrow. He spoke to Lucy Barth and she leaned forward, her breasts, one painted black and one painted red, swinging with the motion. But then she frowned.

Her mouth worked. The drug was wearing off. She stared downward and at last seemed able to focus her thoughts on the medicine man. She uttered a wild shriek of surprise and fear, which broke into a shaking cry of agony as Standing Bear pulled the arrow tautly and shot it into her heart. Then she hung like a rag, dead. Her blood flowed down the arrow's shaft, soaking the feathers, and dripped slowly to the ground.

Everyone who could shoot some sort of arrow, toy or real, came forward and shot into Lucy Barth's body. Luckily no one made Meridel shoot an arrow—she felt she could not have done it—and when Silver Leaf came forward to shoot one, Meridel fled.

She wanted to rush back to Eric. But if she returned alone it would seem irreverent, so she slipped into the woods near the river. Snow fell lightly through the early dusk. She kept remembering the terror in Lucy's face when the schoolmistress realized what was going to happen, and she hid her own face in her hands. A quarter of an hour passed as dusk and snow came down together.

She heard a whisper amid the bare trees: "Missus Lady Wayne?"

She stared about. The hidden man again whispered, blending his voice with the wind: "It's me, Horse Hurlbut. Dan's here too. Don't let on. But when I yell 'Run!' you run into the river."

While her heart hammered with hope she pretended to dig for roots with a stick. The snow veiled her, but she heard the sound of many voices as the Skidi returned to their village, and the chilling sound of war whoops. "*Run!*" She leaped into the knee-deep stream, where a man rushed to either side of her to take her by her arms and hurry her across to the opposite bank, then into a thicket where they had horses waiting.

She found herself peering through the half darkness at a man who had grown a short, scraggly beard during the months of searching for his family. "Dan, Dan!" He caught her hungry mouth to his, and she laughed and cried and laughed again as they whispered their joy at finding one another again.

"Where's Eric?" Dan asked at last, still holding her to him.

"He's very ill. Whooping cough."

"Bad?"

"Dan, it's so bad. . . . Dan, I'm so afraid for him!"

"We must do something. And where's Lucy? We brought a horse for her, too."

"She's dead."

"Oh—"

"Dan, we must rescue Eric."

"Yes. Yes, we must. Tell me where to find him."

"He's in one of the tepees. Come, come!" She tried to lead Dan back across the river.

Horse Hurlbut, who had been wiping splashed water from his revolver, cut in, "Listen, boss, missus, we can't sashay into that village where they're all blood-mad and war-whoopin' and every man has a weapon in his hand. I know Indians—after a sacrifice they'll be up till dawn, gettin' madder and madder."

Meridel said bleakly, "They sacrificed Lucy."

"God!" whispered Dan.

Horse Hurlbut grumbled, "White blood. Now they want more. Boss, look, the wind's changin'. If it shifts a little more, their horses will smell our horses and then . . ."

"They'll whinny, sure enough. Give us away. And we're outnumbered thirty to one, and . . ."

At his words, fear ran through her. "Dan, we can't go away without Eric!"

"My dear, if we're all killed, what will be gained?"

"But he's sick with the kind of whooping cough that kills Dan! Something bursts in their throats!" She sensed the wall of male stubbornness and cried, too loudly, "Dan, I won't go without my baby!"

"Hush! How long has he been ill? Three weeks? Then the chances are he'll recover."

"That's right," said old Hurlbut. "That's how whooping cough goes. And the kid's better off where he is than being hauled through a snowstorm. And we can't even build a fire when we camp or the Skidi might find us. Better get on a horse, missus."

"My baby!" She broke from Dan and ran, but they caught her. They threw her astride a horse and warned her to be quiet lest she bring death upon them all.

"My baby, my baby . . . he'll die without me." She whispered, but the wailing in her heart came through. "Dan, don't you see you're killing our child?"

But Dan and Hurlbut, unheeding, had mounted. Urgently they headed all the horses upriver in the stream, hiding the tracks that would have warned the Skidi of white men's presence.

In deep darkness, with the snow clinging to their lashes and half-blinding them, they left the river after they had gone some distance upstream, made a long detour northward, and then turned eastward through barren country. All night they traveled, the howls of wolves keeping them company. They stopped only for a minute while Dan forced Meridel to put on his warm woolen shirt—as though anything could ease her tears and her misery as she sat, head hanging, crusted with snow.

Some time around daybreak they stopped where the wind had scoured a bare spot in a shallow draw and the horses could find forage. Hurlbut did not want to risk a fire, but Dan rigged blankets to shield a tiny flame, undressed the deeply withdrawn Meridel, and made her drink whiskey that put her to sleep.

Morning sun showed a six-inch layer of soggy snow, which Hurlbut viewed with satisfaction. It had completely covered their tracks. They sat for a few minutes over strong coffee. The old mountain man cracked a joke about range coffee: You boiled a pound of coffee in a pint of water for two hours and then you threw in a horseshoe; if the horseshoe sank, the coffee wasn't strong enough, so you boiled it again. But neither Dan nor Meridel laughed or even smiled. She stared across the blinding white expanse, and if she had known where to run she would have run back to find her child.

Nevertheless, when she noticed a puckered scar on Dan's forearm, she whispered to Hurlbut, "That's a bullet crease?"

"Yeah. Comanche. He kilt four of 'em, but in the end they cotched him. They figured he was good for three days of screamin'. But Dan has a way with horses. He stole one of theirs and got away. When scoutin' cavalry picked him up he hadn't et for near a week—but you see, here he is.''

"Did Mueller—"

"Had a bad bust leg but gets around now on crutches."

"Bertha?"

"Lost forty pounds."

"Adalberto? Prager?"

Hurlbut shook his grizzled head. "We buried 'em . . . and four of Dan's hands . . . and what was left of Low Sun, 'cause the Skidi got real peeved at him." Through a minute of silence Hurlbut wrought a diamond hitch across the pack-horse's load. "I work for Dan now, missus. We're gonna rebuild the ranch. Dan, he lost his horses, but the Skidi didn't bother the cattle, and he still has his special wheat strains growin', and that could be the biggest thing in Kansas."

Dan looked up from where he was smothering the fire in snow. "I'm taking you to Rainbow Ranch, Meridel."

"Never! Not without my baby! If he's still alive . . . But Eric is dead, I know he's dead!"

Dan took her hand, held it tightly. "Meridel, listen. If Eric died in that tepee and with a kind woman taking care of him, then he would have died all the sooner out here. He's alive, Meridel. No, let me talk. After three weeks of illness, they recover. They do. And he's a white child. Indian kids get it worse. Winter is around the corner, and that village is more than three hundred miles from Rainbow Ranch. But in the spring I'll go out with my men and bring Eric back with me. That's a promise. I will bring Eric to Rainbow Ranch next spring."

She heard Dan although she had turned away. Huddled there, she wondered if she could ever forgive him. She was convinced they could have hidden along the river somewhere, sneaked back after the exhausted warriors had fallen asleep, and snatched up Eric to ride away safely with them. He would have been with his own mother, well wrapped, tucked next to her, fed with meat soup, medicined with herbs she would have dug up along the way. . . .

"Meridel! You have got to pull yourself together. Trust me."

"Leave me alone. You have killed our son!"

Dan stood there sagging under the weight of her words, until he rallied against the harshness and said, "Get on a horse, Meridel."

Hurlbut tried woefully to ease the tension as they rode on across the sad brown prairie, camped in melting snow, and rode on again. He told Meridel that out in the Rocky Mountains in the 1830s he had met many French Canadians, and he still felt puzzled at some of the strange things those Frenchies had said. First thing in the morning, they would holler, "Avandong."

"*Avancez donc*. It means 'Let's go'—more or less."

"And if there was any danger they'd yell, "Preney gar.""

"*Prenez garde*. Means something like 'Watch out.'""

"And why are so many Frenchmen named Jimmie Pell— and then something else? Like, say, Jimmy Pell Pierre?"

Meridel answered out of utter weariness, yet tried to smile. "*Je m'appelle Pierre*. My name is Pierre." She did not want to talk, but after those few words she could not bear the silence that Dan Forrester seemed to leave in his track as he rode ahead, never looking back at her. "Horse, any news about the railroad?"

"Yup. Lord Harald, he still can't lay them tracks. Got a notion he figured Dan for dead. And he lined up men for track crews, but there was a gold strike around Pikes Peak and that's where everybody went, railroad or no railroad. 'Pikes Peak or bust.' Well, he found more men for crews, but when it got around that Dan was goin' away for a month—to find you and the little boy, I mean—well, Lord Harald was ready to lay iron but Dan's neighbors, white and Indian both, they said they'd shoot anybody who hammered a spike without Dan's permission. Well, uh, missus . . ."

"What?"

"Well, uh, you see what people think of Dan Forrester?"

"He let our son die!" she hissed, knowing her words went beyond reason and yet unable to transcend the outrage that had taken root in her soul. Hurlbut turned away.

They reached taller grass in the High Grass Prairie and rode on and on, the grass muffling any sound and creating a heavy loneliness through which each rode separately, a tiny speck on the face of the land. Starting conversation again, Hurlbut told Meridel that the Rock Island Railroad had won its suit against the steamboat company that had wrecked their bridge and that their lawyer, one Abraham Lincoln, was going to run for U.S. Senator from Illinois. Meanwhile President Buchanan was urging Congress to ratify the Lecompton Constitution; but Northern lawmakers were still thwarting him. And that battle raged on, not only among the lawmakers, but in the Kansas woods. The Underground Railroad ran infrequently and through great danger, when it ran at all.

Camp and ride. Camp and ride. Not a word to Dan. Not a word from him. They began to see hunters and travelers. One day Hurlbut stopped his horse, peered ahead and to the right, and pointed. "You see that blink in the sky?" He meant a barely visible lightening of the overcast sky. "There's long water over there, reflectin' up. It's the Kaw for sartin." He looked at Dan, then at Meridel, who sat straight and implacable in her saddle. "Now, boss," he said to Dan, "if'n we're goin' to Rainbow Ranch we slant a bit north'ard. But if'n we're goin' to the Lecompton ferry . . ."

Dan growled, "We're going to Rainbow Ranch."

"I am going to Lecompton," Meridel said very clearly.

"We-ell," said the old man, tucking his beard into his belt with elaborate care, "you two talk it over whilst I scout ahead."

When Dan reined up beside her, Meridel could not sustain her despairing rage. America's plains became the smaller, softer, greener Norfolk countryside, and time turned backward to make her a dewy girl confronted by the man who would replace her innocence with womanly passion. When his hard, scarred arm clutched her and his lips caught hers, she shook with the intensity of her need. But the long days of ingrained bitterness made her fight him.

"Let me go!"

"You know I love you. You've shown you love me. . . . Meridel, don't you understand that we didn't have a chance in a thousand to—"

"I understand you could have saved Eric and you didn't. Let me go, I say." When he allowed her to sink back in her saddle she told him in a low, hard voice, "I am going to Lecompton. Good-bye."

"You are going to Rainbow Ranch, Meridel." He reached into a saddlebag. "Look!" He brought out small trousers and a velvet jacket that a very little boy might wear to a party. Rougher garments too, that Dan must have borrowed here and there, because they were of assorted small sizes. "I *expected* to bring Eric back with us."

Her pain would not allow his words to soothe her. "Much good that does him now. Move aside. Move aside, I say! I am riding by myself to Lecompton."

Dan reached out and snatched the reins from her hands. "I'll lead your horse to Rainbow Ranch."

She tried to fight him by commanding her horse to stand still. But he had a way with horses. The animal followed him.

As they traversed the last miles of prairie, Meridel hissed at Dan's back—clad in long-sleeved underwear that should have been washed weeks ago—that if he took her to Rainbow Ranch she would not sleep with him. That if he tried to rape her she would scream until everyone on the ranch heard her. That if he wanted the childish satisfaction of carrying a woman away to his castle, very well, she couldn't stop him from having his King Arthur fantasy. But he'd have to chain her in the cellar—the dungeon—to make her stay.

She saw him clench his fists. But she had found out by then that there are two kinds of men—those who will strike a woman and those who will not. His hands clenched and unclenched. His shifting in the saddle confused his horse. The back of his neck grew red as she taunted him.

At last he shouted, raging: "Fire! We're turning south now so you can go to Lecompton, and we to the ranch, and let's not say another word."

Meridel shook her reins furiously and kicked her horse to little effect. Only when Dan's horse started down the trail did her own follow, only angering her more. But she kept her lips tight the remaining part of the journey.

By afternoon they found the Kaw, whose banks were still lined with oak and hackberry, but were now flaunting their autumn colors. They trekked along the primitive road that followed the river until they saw the ferry rope and a well-remembered log cabin, the governor's "mansion," perched on the highest bluff across the stream.

Hurlbut went ahead to hold the ferry. Turning to Meridal, Dan showed her a face so gaunt it would have roused her tenderness if she hadn't needed her rage to help her say good-bye to him.

Strange forces drew Meridel toward Dan, while at the same time she fought against the feeling. Dan began to speak, stopped. The silence seemed to grow louder. It was the kind of silence that was filled with hurt.

Dan looked away, looked back, tried again: "Tell me, because I didn't try to rescue Eric, do you think I am a coward?"

The truth came hard, but she admitted, "No . . . but you could have rescued him, I know it!"

"I understand your feeling."

"*You* do?" She tried to laugh scornfully but could not.

"And it's more than one wound," he said. "It's not only—*your*—baby lost. It's that guilt that keeps eating at you, so that you must punish yourself forever for fooling Harald. And then you feel angry because you were left pregnant, and because of the way I 'flaunted' Lucy at you. I do admit I handled that very clumsily. And—"

"And my father would have lived longer if you had sold him the right-of-way!"

Dan sighed, rubbing at his scraggly beard. But he simply said, "Well, Meridel, perhaps when you cool down . . . If you do and still want me, you know where to find me."

"Never!" As he drew in a hard breath through his teeth, she slipped from her horse. "Here's your shirt!" She yanked it off and threw it at him. It fell to the road, and he let it lie there as he put his own mount and the horse he was leading into a sudden gallop. Meridel turned, stomping toward the ferry that was only a hundred yards away. But she stopped to shout after the retreating figure, "And you support slavery! Go back to your printing press and get out more handbills and murder more people. Never touch me again—you—with blood on your hands!''

She remembered then that the printing press undoubtedly had been ruined when Dan's burning house had collapsed. But in any case he could not hear her above the thundering hooves of his own fleeing horse.

Chapter Two

Frank Avery stared at the woman who had come back from the dead. "But, uh, the baby, Lady Wayne?"

"My baby is dead," she said, and stood in the ferry's prow with her tatters of trade cloth and leather blowing about her. The ferryman dared say no more.

Silence greeted Meridel when she walked like a ghost through Lecompton. Over and over she saw a man or a woman start toward her, surprised, glad—then stopping short because of something prohibitive on her face.

Upstairs at the Nevins Hotel she glided in silent moccasins through the small, well-remembered rooms. She stood a while at her father's old desk. Slowly, at last, she went to the bedroom she would have to share again with Harald, opened the armoire, and gazed at the gowns that Monsieur Worth had made for her. Her mirror told her she had drastic need of her silver-backed comb-and-brush set . . . but no, that too lay, a blob of melted silver, beneath the ashes of Dan's house at Rainbow Ranch.

Other things on her dresser and in the drawers were as she had left them. She wondered if she should inspect the top of Harald's dresser. At length she did. When she saw hairpins lying next to his shaving gear she laughed wildly, uncontrollably, before she caught herself and stopped, wiping away the tears in the corners of her eyes.

She sank into her old rocking chair, only to look up suddenly when she heard footsteps on the stairs. She knew that step and waited silently until Harald, no doubt warned by others, entered the room and gazed at her without surprise.

Elegant as usual, he slowly beat his riding crop into one hand. He had aged, but not the way Dan had—nor as she herself had aged in her soul, for she felt she had grown a century older even though her nineteenth birthday was still some weeks away.

"Where is Eric?" No greeting, only words sharp as broken glass.

"He may be dead. If not, he's still out there with your friends the Skidi Pawnee."

"Dead?" She could almost see Harald's world crumble.

Somewhere she found a store of common sense that made her admit, "I don't really know."

"What the devil do you mean?"

"I—I think he's dead . . . of whooping cough . . . but I don't know."

"You mean you went off and left him? Left a sick child among filthy Indians?"

"Harald, I had no choice."

"You deserted my child out there!"

"No, let me tell you—"

"You had better tell me before I—" He raised the crop ready to strike, and his eyes glared at her, bloodshot.

"Dan Forrester—"

"Ah!"

"Dan Forrester rescued me, but . . . you see . . . I was away from Eric, and—"

"Away from a sick baby! And Forrester wanted *you*, not the encumbrance of another man's child. I see. So Eric could have been safe and well, but you, his mother . . . Admirable. Where is Lucy Barth?"

"Dead. The Skidi . . ."

"I see. Cast-off women become an embarrassment. So Forrester arranged her death." Harald put the end of his crop beneath Meridel's chin, lifting it sharply to make her look him in the eyes. "I've had parties of men searching for Eric and you all over Kansas and Nebraska. And it was Dan Forrester who found you. Why didn't you stay with him? You seem to like his bed."

"And you like other company in your own bed, but nevertheless you and I are married."

"You expect me to believe you came back to me out of a sense of duty? Or is it that Forrester has little left beside a damaged ranch while I have money—or at least a great potential for making money? Or did you have a lovers' quarrel? But never mind that right now. I want to settle a simple question—your seven-month baby. The evasive midwife does not like to talk to me. I know the day you met Forrester in London, and that day happens to have been just *nine* months before Eric's birth. Now, concerning your alleged seven-month baby . . . Well, Meridel?"

She only muttered, "Let me be. I'm very tired."

"Meridel, you will answer me. Is Eric *my* son?"

"Let me be. I must clean myself, take off these rags."

"Meridel, is Eric my son?"

Harald waited one minute. Two. "*Is he?*" Then, with a savage oath, using all his strength, he slashed the crop across Meridel's cheek.

Leaping up with a cry of agony, she tripped and fell face forward. He went at her back, shouting as he whipped her: "Tell me, you faithless bitch, tell me!"

When she tried to roll away he struck her viciously across the breasts. If she had not been desperate she could not have lifted both feet and kicked him where she did. He dropped the crop and doubled over, both hands at his crotch.

Rising, strangely calm, Meridel cleaned her hands and face at the washstand, threw off her rags, and got into a simple dress and light coat while Harald lay groaning. She remembered to take her bonnet.

As she went downstairs she paused to hold a hand to her heart. She thought that if things didn't change, one day she would break. Blows wouldn't break her, but something had worn her heart thin. She drew a long breath, found the old, poised way to hold her spine, and walked through the front-porch loungers, who stared at the welt on her cheek. All through the busy, brawling little city she walked alone, looking straight ahead. At length she cut across wooded lots and found her way to Dempster's smithy. By then she knew what she must do.

Carrie Dempster seemed only to want to hold her close and weep with joy. But as soon as she could she told the Quaker woman that she needed help in getting to Westport and finding the man from Massachusetts Avenue. She told Carrie that she had had to leave her child with the Indians, that Eric might be alive, though she feared he was dead. To her friend's shocked and tearful questions she could only reply that she could not bear to discuss his fate. "But Carrie, I am going to leave my husband. All I ask of you is to get me to Westport. Carrie, please, dearest Carrie, don't ask me any more, or I'll break into pieces."

Carrie admitted the young woman looked tired, and then told her that Mercury, the young conductor, was going to Westport the following day. Meridel said, "Before dawn? I'll be ready. Tell Mercury I'll be taking a lot of luggage—everything I own."

When Mercury arrived, his manner suggested that Carrie had warned him to ask no questions. At five in the morning, he carried Meridel's trunks to his wagon, and they drove toward the rising sun, only pausing at the little cemetery where Meridel spent five precious minutes at her father's grave. They rolled on toward Westport. At one place a group of rough men told them to pull up, but since they seemed only a couple of disappointed would-be settlers returning eastward, the Slave Staters waved them on.

The sun rode low behind them while they crossed the Big Muddy. Westport had grown since Meridel had seen it last. They drove through a section called the barrio where tamed Indians, Mexicans, and half-breeds lived in noisy poverty. Right on the edge of the barrio they came to a more genteel neighborhood marked by big houses that had been built high to have a river view. Shabby clothing gave way to expensive costumes and the glint of jewels, for the border city had acquired a good proportion of the *nouveaux riches*.

Mercury stopped his wagon at a large and handsome house that bore a glassed-in cupola on its roof. Rubbing his ear, he nudged Meridel to perform the same signal. She did, but jumped when she heard a shot from the house.

"That's only Carlotta up in the cupola," Mercury said. "She's a sharpshooter. Hits bottles floating in the river. She's . . . not quite what you might expect, but don't forget she is a faithful member of the Club."

As he spoke, Meridel noticed men drinking and smoking in the company of young women in a glassed-in part of the veranda—flashy young women who wore rouge and whose day gowns achieved an exposure generally reserved for evening.

Young Mercury showed embarrassment. "You—uh—also may not approve of Carlotta's—uh—establishment. But the man from Massachusetts Avenue will know where to find you. And you'll be safe with Carlotta Arguelo."

Meridel's mind immediately fathomed the reason for his embarrassment.

"She's a madam, isn't she?"

Mercury nodded and flushed.

And so it had come to this. Dianthe Cabot Blakiston's carefully reared daughter was about to take refuge in a bordello. Or, to mince no words, a whorehouse.

Wasn't there some other way for her to meet Leonidas, the man she had heard so much about and had yet to meet?

But after all, she told herself, lifting her chin, when she considered all that had happened to her, why should she draw a line? So she walked like a princess into the house of prostitution.

The maid who admitted them might have seemed a pert French girl, but Meridel's schooled ear caught a false accent. They were led into Carlotta's overstuffed plush parlor where they found an oversupply of gilded, bare Cupids and Dianas standing about. Two buxom Venuses in bronze posed on either side of the staircase as though to give their blessing to ascending couples. Perfume hung heavily in the air. The windows were hidden behind purple velour drapes with gold-colored cords that ended in extravagant tassels. Meridel made out a card room to one side and a grand piano encrusted with mother-of-pearl. Somehow the ostentatious display improved her spirits. At least if a well-brought-up girl was going to be a guest in a whorehouse, she might as well stay in the finest whorehouse in town.

Eventually an olive-skinned woman—who was heavier than Bertha Mueller, until then the largest woman Meridel had ever seen—lumbered down the red-carpeted stairs in a costume that bulged in many-colored satin. A high, jeweled comb accented her black hair and her Spanish appearance. A snapping shrewdness in her dark, kohl-rimmed eyes showed that she probably realized she had dressed for her part.

When Mercury whispered to her, she nodded and said in a heavy accent, "'allo, Señora Boadicea. You two!" she said sharply to two girls who had been looking over the new arrival. "*Vamos!* Señora Boadicea will stay here, but she will not work here. *Comprende?*" Again to Meridel, "Ah, *mamacita*, I know. For you—trouble. But we talk quiet. Andreas!"

A huge Spanish-Indian *mestizo* appeared. Carlotta sent him to help Mercury with Meridel's luggage and invited Meridel to follow her up the stairs.

On a landing they met a thin old man who held himself very erect in his short Spanish jacket, silk sash, and flaring trousers embroidered with silver thread down the sides. He was rubbing some kind of cream into his fingers and he seemed very alert, almost as if he had eyes in the back of his head. His odd nature was explained when Carlotta introduced him as Señor Domingo Quesada de Cerisuelo, the house gambler. He was also Carlotta's father. He gave Meridel an elaborate bow, and kissed his daughter, waving as the two women ascended to another landing, where Carlotta confided, "Money from girls, money from gambling, *sí*, beesness ees good."

Puffing like a locomotive, she ushered Meridel down a garishly carpeted and painted corridor where, at this early hour, most of the bedroom doors stood open. In the pleasant, large corner room that was to be Meridel's—proof enough that she was an honored guest—Carlotta waddled about, checking everything. "Washstand, water, soap, towels . . .

but leetle towels you not need. I weel send Fifi with good big ones. You like mirror on ceiling? Don't worry, will never fall on bed. Is with—how you say—bolts made strong—you know?—into big wood—into beams, *sí*."

Something a girl did not learn at Miss Whittaker's . . .

Carlotta waved an ample, beringed hand at a chair, and when Meridel sat Carlotta lowered herself onto another, filling it completely. "So," she said, then went oddly silent, and the moon face, framed in ruby-and-emerald earrings, went wistful and full of questions she did not ask. At last she said, "You are Lady Wayne, Lady Meridel Wayne—I know eet." Meridel saw something show beneath the heavy flesh that was once beautiful, something of the girl who had listened to *caballeros* sing of love beneath her window. "Lady Meridel Wayne." Carlotta did not seem able to say anything more. At last she pulled vaguely at her gaudy satin dress and spoke. Whatever had bothered her had passed. "You are Señora Boadicea always to the girls. Talk. Sing. Play *cartas* with the *putas*—they are not the worst. But speak always careful. They do not know about a certain room in the . . . the cellar here from where a . . . a . . . What ees eet? A *paso subterráneo*—tunnel, yes?—a tunnel goes. Domingo knows. Fifi knows. And my cook, her name is Carmen, she knows when she cooks for *fugitivos*—you know?"

"Yes."

"*Fugitivos* she never sees." Carlotta shrugged, found a fat smile. "Ah, Domingo, Domingo. A good man. Ah *cartas*, his life. But he—" The madam pantomimed the tossing of a drink down her throat. "Too mooch. I import for him the aguardiente. He is a good man. Now, *chiquita*. You will stay inside. Go out only in my back garden, has high wall. Go up, down back stair, servant stair. Sorry. For Lady Wayne should be front stair, but no, customer see you." Carlotta pretended to twirl a mustache. "Ah, pretty *rojo*—red hair, pretty the figure, ho-ho, ha-ha, hey, Carlotta! How mooch this one? No."

"I had better not meet any of your customers? I understand. So I had better stay out of the downstairs parlor."

Yes, but she would find a passage from which Andreas— he was the bouncer—surveyed the parlor through the peephole and stood ready to eject anyone who started a fight. Meridel could peep, too. She might find it amusing. On the other hand, she could stay in her room if she wished—and had not Carlotta heard that she was good with a needle?

After some more chatter, Carlotta abruptly fell silent, and again came that touch of wistfulness. "I hear people, they say 'Lady Wayne.' Now I see Lady Wayne. Because you married the *hidalgo*?"

"I married a nobleman, yes."

Silence again gripped the mountainous woman, and Meridel felt she had to stop herself from saying more. Then, with a change of spirit: "*Mamacita, mamacita*, you weel find the baby. Have hope." Releasing Meridel at last from the vast, strongly scented pillow of her embrace, Carlotta said, leaving, "*Sí*, talk to girls. Good girls. But sometimes pull hair, fight. Ha, I feex." She displayed a pudding fist. "You theenk I only slap-slap? No. I poonch. Rest, *mamacita*." She waddled away.

Meridel took off most of her clothing. It felt good to stretch out on the bed. Rubbing her arms, which still felt sore and swollen, rubbing her hurt face, she recalled that last scene with Harald, when she had returned from seeing Carrie at the smithy, when she had come back to the hotel and had told her husband she was about to leave him. All during the long day she had kept it from her mind. Now, when she was safe, she allowed herself to remember and shudder.

Certainly Harald had heard her climb the stairs. But when she had entered their bedroom he had not turned from his desk, where he sat with his big ledger open in front of him.

"Harald."

Their fight seemingly forgotten, he did not turn as he said, "What do you want? I'm busy."

"Harald, I am going away."

His pen stopped. He watched a blot form on the ledger. Slowly he turned, waiting, hard-eyed.

"What I mean, Harald, is exactly this: I am going to pack everything I own and leave you. I shall make every effort never to see you again."

"So?" His fingers tapped nervously on his knee. "But as you yourself recently mentioned, you are my wife."

"I know that all too well."

"You are a wife who says she will leave her husband's bed and board?"

"Yes, I am leaving your bed and board. Before morning. But I have no fear about your bed's remaining empty."

"Said the adulteress to the adulterer?"

"If you wish. Good-bye. When you are finished at your desk I will need a couple of hours in this room to get my things in order. I'll tell them downstairs to send up my luggage from the storeroom."

Amazed at her own coolness, she had turned on her heel. Harald snapped, "You want me to divorce you so you can marry Forrester. But I never will." He laughed, forcing it. "Remember, Meridel, while I am alive you will not marry your lover. Now what do you have to say for yourself?"

"What I said before."

"What do you mean?"

"Good-bye."

Taken aback, he leaped out of his chair and grabbed her wrist. "Bloody hell, woman! You'll not make a fool of me. And you had better not forget that I have considerable control over your property."

Trying to ignore the crushing force of Harald's fingers, Meridel returned, "The Wayne emeralds belong to the heir's bride, and she presents them to the next heir's bride—and if you don't know that, your father knows it. And you daren't touch my mother's jewels. Outside of my wardrobe, my only other possession is a certain amount of stock"—Rock Island Railroad stock, which had become valuable—"and my father left it in the care of his lawyer."

"Your father can't have left you much, he was such a fool about money."

"I trust it pleases you to insult my dead father."

"God damn it, Meridel, never mind all that—I tell you, you are not leaving me. I tell you that you are going back to Danemead with me—if I have to lock you up and make you do it."

"No, Harald. It's inconvenient for you, I see. But never."

She winced as he grabbed her other wrist, squeezing hard. "Wait, dear wife. You're not going to Forrester, I tell you, no matter how many times he has swived you behind my back. You'll stay with me, you faithless bitch, because I am going to bind you to me once and for all. No matter whose child Eric is, I am going to give you another baby." Suddenly he flung her across the bed. "*My* baby. I'll make certain of that."

She tried to flee, but he punched her, kneeled on her legs, and ripped her dress up from the bottom, sending tatters of underclothing flying after it. She fought him, but he simply beat upon her until agony left her helpless. "We begin right now," he panted. "And no matter how you scream"—he slapped her with all his strength—"a man can enforce his marital rights, remember." He stood up to unbutton his own clothing. "By Gad, you bitch, I'm going to swive you every day for weeks—months—till I see you swelling."

She kicked at him, but he saw it coming and kicked her in the ankle. She managed to say in her desperation, "Your child could be a girl. And Eric is dead. You'd have no son to show your father."

"You admitted you don't know if Eric is really dead. I have men out looking for him. Now, then . . ." He came at her.

"But Harald, even if Eric is alive and even if your men bring him to you . . ." She paused, took a deep and painful breath, and confessed at last: "Eric never can become heir of Danemead, because *he is not your son.*"

Harald snorted. "A pretty confession, long overdue. You expect me to be surprised? He is not my son, but he'll never know it, and more importantly, the earl will never know it." Something occurred to Harald that drew his lips back in a snarl. "But by Gad, if you ever tell—" He stopped, his face going dark. "If I take you to Danemead I can't keep you gagged, so if Eric is brought to me alive, I'll make sure you get no chance to tell. I expect to take you to an isolated country house, and it will be easy to—"

"No!"

"Yes, and I'll miss you. I might even weep over your grave."

If Eric were found alive, Harald would kill her to keep her quiet.

Somehow the word *lawyer* played back through Meridel's frantic mind. She saw a chance. "Harald, even if you kill me, your father will find out that Eric is a bastard." He laughed, not believing her. "But Harald, I mean it. My father's lawyer, Mr. Finch, in New York . . ." Everything hung on the knife-edge balance of her words.

"What?" At first scornful, the tall blond man became frightened. "You mean you've sent Finch a sealed envelope with your sworn statement that—"

"Yes. I have sworn to the exact circumstances of Eric's birth. When, where, who, and I also say in my statement that I intend to make sure you know. If Mr. Finch hears of my death, or if six months go by without his hearing from me, he will send my statement to your father. Your sister will inherit the income-producing property, and you'll inherit the debts and the heavy expenses. You do understand me, Harald?" she said to the pale, sweating face. And may God forgive me the lie, she thought. Aloud, she went on, "You will now let me get up and pack and go. Nor will you ever try to interfere with me, nor ever attempt to see me again. That is the price of my keeping the secret." *But what if Eric were found alive? Had she, in that case, surrendered her child to her husband?* Yet she dared say no more.

"Conniving bitch!" For an instant Meridel thought that Harald would actually kill her. But he stopped. He cursed her vilely, grabbing his clothing and stomping from the room. She had won.

The *putas* made much of Mrs. Boadicea. They copied her table manners and tried to imitate the way she walked. She taught them whist. They taught her poker and keno. She played sentimental ballads at the piano while the "girls" sang softly, often with tears in their eyes, though singing sessions had to be suspended when some customer, generally a local businessman or town official, came in.

Somehow a rumor went around to the effect that Mrs. Boadicea was thinking of buying into the business. But a lanky dyed blonde named Florabelle confided that most of the girls didn't believe it. No, Florabelle said, the girls were sure that Mrs. Boadicea wore a wedding ring simply to make people think she was not a virgin. But she really was a virgin, wasn't she, and being so pretty and such a lady, she would be sold high to some old moneybags who needed her kind of flesh to make him able. Having stated this firmly, Florabelle removed a black beauty patch from her fair cheek and tried it on the other side. She had heard that a century ago women had worn beauty patches, and she thought that living in the eighteenth century would have been exciting—except that the gentlemen must have had trouble with their breeches if they wished to undress in a hurry.

Now and again Carlotta took her up to the cupola. Andreas would have been out in a rowboat to float empty bottles in the river, and as they came drifting down, Carlotta picked them off with a fine old Hawken rifle. Men who passed on flatboats—there seemed not a man on the river who did not know Carlotta—waved and cheered as the bottles were smashed. Meridel tried a few shots but could not put a bullet within five feet of a bottle.

On rare quiet evenings Carlotta would call Meridel into her two-room suite to drink very fine old wine and to hear tales of the glorious old days in San Tomás.

The old gambler, Domingo, sometimes joined them and spoke sadly of his own past there when he had been rich and respected. At other times, when the girls were idle, he amused them with card tricks. He could send a two-foot arch of cards flying from one hand to the other. Name a card, and he made it fly out of the deck by itself.

Domingo and Meridel grew fond of each other. He confided that he had wanted to become a gambler on a Mississippi packet. *Ay de mí*, whole plantations had changed hands across the *Memphis Belle*'s green baize table! But no. Carlotta and he were dear old friends, so he would stay with her. Yes, she would be lost without him.

Once he took Meridel into the cellar and showed her the secret Underground Railroad station. She saw, as she had expected, rough berths, piles of clothing, stores of food, a tiny stove whose flue led outside. There were also scratchings on the walls and bending to peer at the ragged letters, she read: LET MY PEEPL GO.

The secret tunnel led from the station to a warehouse down

the street. Next day the man from Massachusetts Avenue made his way through the tunnel and up Carlotta's back stairs. Fifi escorted him quickly into Meridel's room, where Meridel sat sewing.

The aging New Englander seemed so worn and tired that she wanted to bring him brandy; but he wouldn't have it. Many abolitionists were also prohibitionists, he said. "Now, Boadicea, I have your message. I know you have broken with your husband, that you have some money of your own and a good wardrobe, and I remember our previous meeting very well. Yes, I think it is time for you to go to New York and speak to women of your own social level. And raise funds for us."

"Good."

"In New York, of course, you will be Lady Wayne. Especially since you continue to wear your wedding ring . . ."

"I feel I must wear it as long as I remain married."

"Yes, I see. All the better, because it will show that you are not trying to hide the fact that you left your husband. The women of your class will be scandalized but fascinated and they will accept you because you *are* Lady Wayne and a woman of charm and breeding.

"Keep in touch with Henry Ward Beecher. And also there is a certain black woman in New York who will act as your maid . . . and rather more. By the way, play up your traveling to New York as Lady Wayne, accompanied by her maid. It will help you get the audience you need."

"Where shall I find—"

"She will have to be one of Carlotta's girls until New York. I'll talk to Carlotta." The man from Massachusetts Avenue hesitated as he approached the door of her room. "And yes, do visit Beecher. He is a wonderful fund raiser, and his church sends more money to the Underground Railroad than any other congregation in America. But . . . do you know he is a married man with several children?"

"So have I heard."

"He had a very successful congregation in Cincinnati, and then his friend Theodore Tilton, the religious-paper editor, persuaded him to settle in Brooklyn. That left Cincinnati—

well—full of broken hearts. I have heard that Beecher used to receive as many as a hundred lovesick letters a day."

"But I daresay he can't help it if women like him."

The New Englander frowned. "Some say he encourages that sort of thing. Well, Boadicea, I am only saying that when you go to visit Beecher . . . well . . . you have learned something of the ways of men."

"Yes," said Meridel, remembering herself as a spoiled brat of a debutante.

Carlotta wept over Meridel's leaving, as did the others. Carlotta sent Florabelle to act as Meridel's maid on the trip east, after which time she would return, replaced by the other woman more familiar with Manhattan. Carlotta also told Florabelle Meridel's title and promised Florabelle a fist in the nose if she did not remember to say "milady."

"*Vaya con Dios*," said old Domingo, his eyes moist as he put Meridel aboard a handsome new parlor car, the first one to be used west of St. Louis. "And return to Papa Domingo, whose heart will be empty till he sees you again." He plucked the queen of hearts out of Meridel's hair and presented it to her as a remembrance.

Soon the locomotive gave off its first laboring chuff.

"Gorsh," said Florabelle, who wore three beauty patches in honor of the occasion, "you mean you're a real English lady?"

"I guess so."

"Ooh," cooed Florabelle. "Hey, I mean, milady, do you ever get to wear one of them—what they wear in their hair, all them jools, you know, a band around the head?"

"A tiara. Yes, I guess so . . . on occasion."

"I bet you can wear it in your sleep, even, if you like. I bet *you* got no troubles, milady."

Meridel stood at the window watching the new snow that lay in the Missouri woods. She said nothing.

Chapter Three

New York bustled. New York had shops enough to keep any woman busy and happy. New York grew in giant strides; why, they had even begun to lay out a great central park to make sure that Manhattan Island kept a parcel of forestland free of man-made encroachment.

A film of black soot was often left on clothing, but as if in compensation, the city had spawned "dry" cleaners. New York ladies, far more readily than Boston or Philadelphia ladies, soon became used to remembering what they had available to wear and what was being de-sooted. Oh, New York was so exciting! So why, when she wanted to feel thrilled with her return to her native city, did Meridel go on yearning for the vast Western skies and plains? She had to admit that something had changed in her. She'd become a Kansan.

Yet she was also excited about her mission. She had three days to get settled and then—to work! For her trip to

Brooklyn she donned, over chemise and corset, a corset cover and a couple of under-petticoats that supported a starched and stiffened "principal" petticoat whose circumference measured ten feet. On top of that came a decorated muslin semi-petticoat, which could be revealed if a lady had to loop up her skirt for protection against rainy weather. A narrow fur hat of Persian lamb, tilted rakishly over one eye, added a bit of height and also matched her coat. At the last moment she decided to pin up on the hat a ring of garnets that supported an ostrich plume.

The steam ferry that ran between New York and Brooklyn was ten times as big as Frank Avery's scow and boasted an airtight, overheated ladies' cabin. Here Lady Wayne sat on a small padded bench while Araminta Atkinson, her new ebony-black maid, sat alertly on an unpadded bench. When Atkinson had met Meridel at the depot in Hoboken, on the New Jersey side of the Hudson River, she had already arranged for a suite at the elegant Hotel Brevoort. She had shown Meridel a long hatpin she carried in her coat's padded sleeve to protect her mistress. Silent, watchful, and intelligent, Atkinson knew every place in New York where a runaway slave could hide. She also knew how to look blank and stupid when slave catchers decided she must know something—because she definitely did.

The goodbye with Florabelle, who turned out to be the perfect traveling companion—filled as she was with so many ribald stories, some of which were too daring for Meridel's taste—had been tearful. Meridel gave her one of her rich Parisian gowns in payment for the girl's troubles.

Florabelle had been overwhelmed. "You be sure to come back and stay with us girls at Carlotta's, I'll be missin' yer so, milady."

"I promise," Meridel had said, managing to hold back the tears and wave to Florabelle, who had had to board another train in the same station to take her back west. She hugged the gown which Meridel had wrapped the evening before, and turned at her gate, crying, to wave a last time.

Brooklyn loomed ahead, a pleasant half-rural city of a hundred thousand, hardly to be compared with New York's nearly seven hundred thousand souls who spoke all the world's languages. There had been talk of building an enormous bridge between the two cities, but most people thought such a bridge impossible.

On Brooklyn Heights, in an area of gardens and beautiful trees, they found Beecher's handsome, high-steepled church. Hundreds of well-dressed men and women milled about in the cold air, unable to get in. For today Henry Ward Beecher would give both a sermon and conduct a special kind of auction.

Meridel sent Atkinson to inquire for Theodore Tilton, a very tall and slender editor of religious newspapers, who when he arrived seemed to survey Lady Wayne for any marred features, and apparently satisfied, waved her into the crowded church past those clamoring on the steps to get in. He could not find her a seat, but at least he gave her a box to stand on so she could see over the parishioners' heads.

"Reverend Beecher's resting a moment after his sermon," Tilton whispered. His voice told of the reverence in which he held his famous friend. Meridel noticed that Henry Ward Beecher's congregation had provided him with a pulpit made of olivewood brought from the Garden of Gethsemane. Nevertheless, the eccentric man had just finished speaking from the floor, having abandoned the pulpit, to address his audience face-to-face. Meridel noticed he didn't wear vestments, but instead favored a comfortable-looking suit with flaring trousers in the Western style. Not a handsome man, he was yet a memorable one, firmly stout, hearty, and magnetic. When Meridel's head rose above the crowd he noticed her, and an interrogating quirk touched his oversoft mouth. Something invisible sped from him to Meridel. Oh yes, she thought, this man could cause trouble with women.

Beecher gazed benignly over the many handsomely cushioned pews and family enclosures that he auctioned each year to the rich of Brooklyn. But today his auction would be of another sort. Reporters had been called in. They stood here and there, pencils poised, their notebooks at the ready. When Beecher held up one hand, all the shifting of feet and whispering and recognizing of friends died away. Confidently he surveyed his audience, but still waited . . . waited . . . till the right dramatic moment.

He turned and thundered, "Come forth, Nora, slave in bondage."

From somewhere behind the altar and beneath the pipes of a mighty organ a woman appeared. She wore a plain, faded plantation dress, the usual bandanna of a field hand upon her head, and she held her fettered wrists before her for all to see. But the expected black face was almost white—*almost*—and young, and marvelously attractive with its tender mouth and fawnlike dark eyes.

Meridel heard the whispers: "A quadroon." "One of those," hissed a woman, referring to the fact that beautiful quadroons often became the preferred bedmates of Southern planters over their darker, full-blooded relatives. "But she's hardly to blame," said a softer voice, while a man said with stern emphasis, squelching the women, "This Nora is a slave, and that's all that matters."

Beecher led the delicately formed, sloe-eyed Nora close to the curving pews. Some women drew their skirts aside, but most of the people who sat in the favored front rows leaned forward, intrigued. For a moment the preacher stood commandingly, waiting. Then he began to speak, quietly at first, then with more dramatic gestures until he was thundering and gesticulating madly, spellbinding his listeners.

"Here stands a young woman, virtuous, baptized in Christ." Thus he instantly identified the girl with his parishioners—although Meridel had not seen a black face among them, and Atkinson had been sent to sit in an antechamber where she could hear Beecher through the wall. "And as Nora—who, being a slave, bears no family name—as Nora stands there in her chains she remains as yet untouched by man." The way Beecher said the words brought a flush to Meridel's cheeks, and she saw other women growing red. "And as such, ah yes, as such she will be sold, I repeat, *sold* to some lusty planter who wants her not to labor in his cotton fields, not to wait upon his groaning table, but to be of shameful personal service to him in a way I shall not describe."

Beecher paused for just a moment, letting everyone grow hungry for his next words. Then, waving his arms, his long hair tossing as he gestured, he roared to his audience that a slave dealer now owned Nora as a rare prize to be dangled before the eyes of lustful men. And, fear not, if the auction did not raise enough money to buy the girl's freedom she would again be auctioned somewhere in the South—perhaps not fully clothed, and "subject to close and intimate inspection of every bit of her skin," Beecher hissed. A woman seated next to Meridel clapped her hands to her burning face, and another clutched her husband's arm in terror.

"Yet here stands a Christian soul, and does she not represent all Christian women? *Virtuous* Christian women who outside of holy matrimony would never allow a male to possess their bodies nor even allow the mere thought of such a sinful union to enter their minds? Oh, my friends," Beecher said more softly, almost intimately, as he placed both solid hands upon the railing that separated him from his parishioners, "you know I do not speak of certain black women, and white ones too, who drift from one immoral relationship to another. No. Give but a sigh of sorrow for such women and believe that I"—his voice again began to rise—"speak only of women who know good from evil, and who, their souls having been saved by the immortal Redeemer, wish to keep those souls pure."

Meridel watched, fascinated, as Beecher stamped, strutted, lifted his hands to heaven and to his audience imploringly. A woman moaned loudly. A man cried, "The villains!" to something Beecher had said condemning the South for condoning slavery, which really only gave planters a license to abuse women. Finally, when he'd wound his audience up most tightly, the preacher thundered, "Then *we* must buy her and *we* must set her free!" Giving his magnificent voice the rolling cadence of an auctioneer's, he cried, "How much for this woman who prays and believes? How much to save this soul that still is armored in virtue, but once sent away in chains, will wither in sin? Oh, my dear friends in Christ, shall we harden our hearts and send her back to *that?*"

"Never!" "No! Here!" A man rushed forward with money in his fist.

The church shook with shouts, but Beecher continued thundering above them as he drew a key from his pocket. "Shall I then unlock her chains? Now? This instant? In full faith that this congregation will provide the money to—"

"Set her free!" came the cries. "Keep her here!" "I will find honest work for her!" "So will I!"

While Beecher still stomped back and forth, keeping emotion at fever pitch, Meridel watched people pour the contents of their wallets and their purses into the baskets held by the ushers. Others ran forward to put money into Beecher's hands—money that he dramatically heaped into Nora's apron whose edge she had lifted at his command. He kept up the resonant and persuasive harangue that by now had even Meridel trembling, and he called for more and more money— "Twice and thrice and ten times five hundred dollars!"—to save other girls from the same looming abomination and also to provide "funds for our brethren in Bleeding Kansas, where runaway comely girls like this one face not only the slash of the whip and the tearing teeth of the bloodhound but also the Indians' stealthy arrow."

Finally, the baskets filled to overflowing, Beecher dramatically unlocked the slave girl's fetters to a great cry of approval, flung them to the floor, and ground them under his heel. Other men vaulted the rail to do the same. And Meridel, who had been telling herself that Beecher overblew one aspect of slavery at the expense of more important issues, unpinned the ostrich plume from her hat and dropped the circle of garnets into a passing basket. Nora was weeping with gratitude, and Beecher took her hand and showed everyone the marks that iron cuffs had left upon her wrists.

While the congregation left the church, Theodore Tilton led Meridel into Beecher's study, a large room filled with books and comfortable furniture. He left her, and soon she heard Beecher approaching. "No, sir," he was telling someone, "I realize that since we gave bond for Nora she did not have to wear those handcuffs, but they were necessary in creating the desired effect."

"But Reverend"—the other man had lowered his voice— "how could you say that Nora remains untouched when we know she's been mistress to a merchant in Mobile?"

"The effect, my dear Mr. Willoughby, the effect is everything. No, sir, you may take exception to my methods, but the end, which is holy, justifies any earthly means."

He entered his study alone, brushing back his disturbed locks. "Ah, you are Boadicea. You have come a long way and I am glad to see you." Instead of seating himself behind his desk, he pulled over a smaller chair and sat facing her, their knees almost touching. Again she felt his definite male allure. "I know you are Boadicea because petite, poised, young, well-dressed, charming red-haired women are rare indeed. Who sent you to me, if you please?"

"A man I met on Massachusetts Avenue."

"Very good. We shall not give that man a name, but I'll mention that he was a friend of my father's." Lyman Beecher had been known for his exciting revivals in a Boston church—and for the stern upbringing he had given his thirteen children. Now his son mopped a florid face. "I must say I worked like a ditchdigger on that young woman's behalf."

"And on behalf of the Kansas Underground Railroad, too, and I thank you, Reverend Beecher."

"Ah, you are all very brave out there, very brave and admirable. But how did a sweet creature like yourself—?"

"Railroad business."

"I see. And our mutual friend from Massachusetts Avenue has sent you to tap the moneybags of Manhattan Island, where so many rich ladies live. I shall help you in any way I can. But, getting back back to Kansas . . ." He leaned very close. "I wonder, sometimes, why Lady Wayne, who in every respect fits her title, should have to become Boadicea. All those aliases of the Underground Railroad do credit to New England scholarship, but I do not approve of the secret-society atmosphere. I'd like to see your Underground Railroad run openly in that territory where it is not subject to state laws." His pleasant face set into a mask of anger, and he pounded a fist on his knee. "Each man sturdily public with his rifle and his Bible—"

Meridel's "No, you are wrong" came with an emphasis that startled him. "You don't realize what is really happening out there," she told him. "Conditions in Kansas are hardly conceivable to Eastern folk."

246

He took only an instant to replace his heavy frown with his accustomed warmth. "Tut! I thought only a man's wife is entitled to scold him," he said, putting the correction aside. "But our subject today is contributions, is it not? I hope you've thought about the approach you'll use in speaking to rich ladies. We'll arrange a coaching session—or several," he added with a certain significance. "Meanwhile, think of a good dramatic approach. Then come and see me again and we'll talk it over."

"Thank you, Reverend, but I already have worked out my approach. In fact, you gave it to me when you stamped on those chains."

"Ah! Sit down. Tell me. This could be valuable material for a sermon. The chains . . . the chains that bind us all . . . that make us so much less than what we could be . . . God's unfettered creatures."

"But I want to work out my plan in more detail and try it out first. Thank you for your kindness, Reverend Beecher, and it has been a privilege meeting you and seeing the church in which so much money has been raised for so many good causes."

"As you wish," he grumbled, and rose as she went to the door. But he attempted to keep another kind of door open. Like a god speaking from Olympus he proclaimed, in his deep rolling, voice, "If anyone tries to degrade you because you have left your husband, say that Henry Ward Beecher vouches for you." Then he added anxiously, "Wait. When shall I see you again?"

"I can't say. I must run. I am so very grateful to you, Reverend Beecher."

As she thankfully rejoined the watchful Atkinson, Meridel sternly told herself she must look her situation in the face. She was a young, reasonably attractive married woman. She now had her own money from the stock that Caleb Finch, the lawyer, had sold for her. She had no family in New York, and her husband lived too far away to make trouble. In short, for any man who had a certain gleam in his eye, Lady Meridel Wayne had become fair prey.

But she certainly would not hide in fright. Next afternoon she visited the new A. T. Stewart store, the largest retail establishment in the city. The old merchant remembered her and came personally to point out in his delightful Scottish burr his imported *robes Empire* in fine muslin and silver tissue, to be worn with scarves of satin and gold. Meridel was not really interested in buying dresses, least of all the out-moded diaphanous dresses of Napoleon's day, but she hoped to meet ladies who would recognize her. Sure enough, she ran into Mrs. Gamaliel Morris, who was assisting Mrs. Reu-ben Verplanck in the purchase of a hundred-dollar leghorn bonnet. They greeted her with a certain avid delight.

"We were all so sorry to hear about your darling father's passing. But Lord Harald is now staying to build the railroad? My dear, you married such a dashing man!"

"Such a wonderful match!"

"And so handsome," cooed Mrs. Morris of Morrisania. "I know you came on ahead to settle your father's estate, but the moment Lord Harald arrives in New York we must have you both over for elevenses. It's an English custom, you know, and your husband will be so delighted."

"I don't expect Lord Harald to join me," Meridel said, and pretended not to notice how the two ladies cast swift, told-you-so glances at each other.

After an awkward moment Mrs. Morris forced a smile. "Then you're alone. I see. But if you'd really like to speak to a few ladies . . . let me check my social calendar. Where can I reach you? The Brevoort? Very good, a *most respectable* hotel." But it turned out that Mrs. Morris never could quite bring herself to invite a notorious woman to speak in her home to her friends, even if it would give them all such a wonderful opportunity to inspect Meridel.

When Meridel went with Caleb Finch and his wife to see Edwin Forrest in *Our American Cousin,* she sat in the Finch box and exposed her shoulders, the Wayne emeralds draped around her neck. Her hair, now grown back long enough, was displayed in a magnificent coppery coronal. Dozens of peo-ple—people who counted—watched her and whispered, and many came to visit during the intermission. When she men-tioned that she needed an intimate forum at which to collect for the Underground Railroad, and that Henry Ward Beecher would vouch for her, they responded, welcoming the chance to study her.

Before long she had an invitation to speak at the elegant Winston home on Fifth Avenue near Twenty-third Street. The terse Atkinson said "Uh-huh" when she heard she must wait in the kitchen while a magnificent butler escorted Meridel upstairs. Mrs. Amos Winston fluttered away from the aspidistra in her morning room, exclaiming all in one breath about the difficulty of keeping plants in the newfangled steam heat and how scrumptious it was to see Lady Wayne, whom she would remember forever as the little girl who went to see the queen.

Some fussing followed about where Meridel should stand while she made her address. When guests swept in, Helene Winston poured tea for ladies of English descent and hot chocolate for Mrs. Verplanck and others who had Dutch forebears. Meridel sipped the tea and said that Lord Harald was in good health as far as she knew, that, yes, she had enjoyed social visits even "out there," especially to friends in Westport, Missouri. Yes, the Indians still took scalps. No, she didn't hate them; she rather pitied them. Well, no, she couldn't give Lord Harald the latest social news from New York next time she wrote, because she did not intend to write at all.

Someone said into the silence, "Lady Wayne, I'm sure you left Kansas without your husband because the territory's conditions are simply too uncouth for a delicate lady." Meridel smiled.

Two gentlemen astonished the group by walking in. Amos Winston, sparing time from his Wall Street counting house, had brought along a rotund middle-aged friend, Ted Mercer, who made jolly remarks about having blundered into a bouquet of lovely blossoms. At length Meridel rose to be formally introduced and then to stand gracefully in a subdued little bertha she wore around her shoulders—a style favored by Empress Eugénie of France. The men grinned comfortably from their seats in the rear. The prim-lipped women looked her over, but also kept an eye on old Mrs. Harrison Batchelder, a doyenne of New York's upper-level families. Meridel knew that if Mrs. Batchelder approved of her, she would carry other approval in her wake. If she didn't . . . But Meridel, pinned by a rheumy, basilisk stare, did not want to think about that.

"Thank you, Mrs. Winston. Good afternoon, ladies and gentlemen." She had to pause to conquer a spasm of fright. She feared that they would lull her by listening awhile, then overwhelm her with their scorn as a woman who had left her husband. But there could be no turning back. "I thank you all for attending in charity's name, and I thank you gentlemen especially for putting aside you own affairs for the sake of freedom and abolition." Give them a little joke to break the ice, Atkinson had said. "After all, if there is one fact we ladies can be sure of, it is that gentlemen are always too busy."

Delighted with the opening, Ted Mercer called, "Sure, we keep busy making money so our wives can spend it."

The younger ladies tittered, which helped Meridel launch into the speech she had so carefully prepared. "Why, Mr. Mercer, we ladies feel we must clothe ourselves attractively because you gentlemen prefer it so. But you all would have been surprised, I'm sure, if you had seen how I dressed on certain occasions in Kansas. Really, I looked almost like a Five Points woman." Five Points was a notorious slum. "But when I worked among runaway slaves I had to take care not to be recognized. In Kansas, right now, merely to express sympathy with runaways may earn one a shot or a blow with a hatchet. Many a settler's home has been burned by enemies, and many a homesteader has been left hanging from a tree."

Meridel waited till the horrified murmurs had died. She had every ear as she went into an account of her first visit to a secret "station."

"There on the floor slept an emaciated black woman, very young—a girl, really—completely exhausted. I thought she had a bundle of rags beside her. But it was a baby. For a month she had carried her child toward the North Star, hiding by day, slipping along by night past farmhouses where smoke carried the odor of roasting meat. But she dared not beg food for fear of being captured. What did runaways eat? Sometimes insects—grubs—that scuttle beneath rotten logs. But at least that pitiful young mother kept herself free of chains.

Chains! I saw slave catchers capture an old black woman, weigh her down with chains, and force her to trot behind a horse. She was tied to the rider by another chain."

"No!" someone gasped.

"Yes. I saw it. She and others. And on some plantations, a captured runaway is made to labor all day in a twenty-pound neck ring. He may lose an ear as well for they nail him to a post by his ear and whip him, then cut him loose by cutting his ear away."

Mrs. Batchelder raised a jeweled hand to shivering lips. Her eyes no longer glared through wrinkled slits. They were aghast.

"We know that not every plantation owner mistreats his slaves. But it takes only that one word, *slave*, to tell of men and women in hopeless bondage, working all their lives for nothing they themselves can own . . . of children doomed, generation after generation, to bend their backs and dull their minds with no hope of anything better. Again, few slaves are actually chained. But they are all held by chains of custom and chains of law that require anyone anywhere—even in Free States—to take away their desperately won freedom and restore them to shackles. And so the Underground Railroad is, strictly speaking, an illegal enterprise. But we who support it take the side of humanity, of an ultimate justice, of freedom to live outside of captivity."

"Hear! Hear!" cried Amos Winston, who was no longer grinning.

"Now, it is not hard to hide runaways in great cities like Philadelphia or New York. And when they slip away northward they can find stations not too many miles apart. But in the West . . ."

She tried to convey the vast emptiness that stretched between farms on the frontier. She tried to show the increased danger runaways faced in an area where pro-slavery and anti-slavery settlers fought, and to make them see that where population is scattered, charity is also scattered. "I know the bent of your hearts is toward the black people, who strive only to win the rights of human beings, and I tell you that the situation in Kansas is desperate. Our U.R. conductors and others work almost literally with knives at their throats. I know you cannot go and help them. But you can send money to help them break the chains—both the metal chains and the fetters of ignorance and evil." She reached for her bulging reticule and took out a number of thin steel chains she had prepared, each about four inches long. "Here are chains. Symbolic chains. Will you buy them? Your contribution will go quickly to the Underground Railroad in Bleeding Kansas. In return, if you wear these light bits of metal attached to a watch or dangling from a bracelet or a brooch, it will tell that you gave to break the chains that bind slaves. Think of the starving young mother whose shriveled baby looked like a bundle of rags."

Nobody moved or spoke. "These little chains," continued Meridel, "were made for me free of charge by a certain well-known jeweler, whose only complaint was that his men had never before worked in steel, only in precious metal. I ask you to donate for these chains as though they were yards long and made of gold." Meridel stopped, gathering energy. "Araminta Atkinson, are you there?"

Atkinson, who later told her that she had almost had to fight her way upstairs, came in from the corridor, walking with a starchy rustle proper for maids.

Meridel loaded her with the little chains. "Ladies and gentlemen, I ask you to receive your token from a black hand. I ask you to give a black hand your money." She looked around. "Who will be first?" Then, taking a desperate chance as the oldest person in the room moved her head slightly, she said, "Mrs. Batchelder, did you offer? Atkinson, right here."

For a moment everything balanced on Mrs. Batchelder's hesitation. But she bought a chain. Immediately, everyone else dug for money.

Later, back at the Hotel Brevoort, when Meridel and Atkinson counted $310, they knew they had succeeded beyond their wildest dreams. Atkinson hugged Meridel, saying nothing, meaning a great deal.

Meridel recalled that as she'd been about to leave Mrs. Winston's morning room, Mrs. Batchelder had touched her sleeve with a shaky hand. "Our sexton at Grace Church says that Reverend Beecher has no right to send a notorious woman to raise funds. But your husband may have wronged you, and I see you are decent and honest. Do you want to make other speeches for the Underground Railroad? Could I help you in that direction, do you think?''

Meridel made her next speech in a colonnaded house on La Grange Terrace. The white-marble terrace had been built when the aging Marquis de Lafayette had visited New York from his country seat in La Grange, France. ''Old money'' lived there, and Meridel could well believe it when her hostess, Gretchen Van Heerden, extended her hand as though from a snow-capped height. Eight other ladies of impeccable name rustled in and sat sidewise on ottomans to favor their hoops.

They were joined by no less than five gentlemen, who gave up their money-making hours to attend. Of these, three were unmarried; and of those three the most dashingly dressed was Thorncroft Parrish, a potbellied, fortyish man much given to racing his gig for hundred-dollar bets. In addition—as lady whispered to lady—Thorny happened to be the most notorious, high-living, woman-chasing bachelor in town.

Lounging casually in his coat *à la française* with silk lapels, which showed off the new, turned-down stiff shirt collar, he twirled the seals on his watch chain most annoyingly. When others gasped at Meridel's revelations of life in Kansas, he patted his mouth, concealing a yawn. And he watched her. Like a cat watching a mouse, he watched her. Once he made her falter, and she had to be careful not to look at him again.

Success builds on success. These people had come prepared to buy little chains, and when Meridel had finished her speech all but one crowded to press money into Atkinson's hand. The exception, Thorny Parrish, came directly to Meridel with two twenty-dollar bank notes. He held his bit of chain against his silk brocade waistcoat and said, ''Been wanting to meet you. But I warn you, I waste little time being pleasant. Shall I step out of character for your sake?''

''As you wish, sir. But I thank you for your contribution.''

Dumpy, beady-eyed, Parrish's beard surrounded a shaved area in which his mouth seemed forever moist. Meridel had heard he came from a respectable Delaware family who had told him to leave and go his own way to perdition. Meridel had not believed that a man could appear to undress a woman with his eyes. Now, flushing, she believed it. If the rake had wished to make an impression on her, he certainly had. A bad one.

He laughed, saying in his strangely low, insinuating voice, "No, I'll be myself. This chain—fancy me wearing such a thing. Here, take it back, sell it again." He gave Meridel a moment in which to realize he had his own unpleasant ways of making himself remembered. "You red-haired siren," he said. "I was not invited to your reception two years ago. If I had been, you might never have reached Kansas."

Meridel drew herself up, barely able to contain a flash of anger. "What do you mean, sir?"

"I'd have taken you home for myself."

"Really? I happen to have been betrothed at the time."

He twirled his seals. "I don't attach much importance to that. And by the way, have you heard the ditty that the lower classes have invented? 'Lady Wayne, Lady Wayne/Came from Kansas on the train,/Left her husband high and dry,/Dearie me, I wonder why.' Our filthy poor are our true conservative thinkers, no matter how many bastards they produce. But I see through you. The notorious woman whose title nevertheless gets her into good homes."

She lifted her chin. "Are you insinuating that I am some kind of adventuress?"

"Not quite a Lola Montez, perhaps. But if you expect me to believe you are asking charity merely for sweet charity's sake—"

"Sir, you insult me."

"Insults require greater skill in their delivery than mere compliments, and so the insulter should be given credit." As Meridel gathered her skirts, preparing to whirl away, he stopped her. "On second thought, I'll buy back those links. I can give them to my cook. They'll do for hanging pots." As she fumbled angrily in her reticule he said, "Scheming little charmer, you are showing yourself around because you will soon need another rich husband—as soon as your present noble spouse cuts the bonds of matrimony."

"You are a hateful man!" She bristled.

"I've known that for years. But think before you leap. Who would marry a divorced woman, knowing that no hostess would accept either himself or his wife thereafter?"

Meridel glared. "I have no interest in—"

"In remarriage? I wonder. But be that as it may, may I see you home? You hesitate?"

"Only as to whether I should slap you or kick you."

"Neither will serve as well as selling me still another piece of chain. I'll let my valet wear it. Excellent fellow named Trefanec. Viennese. His wife is my cook. If you ever drop in, I can promise you marvelous coffee. If you ever *happen* to drop in," Parrish repeated as he pressed more bank notes into Meridel's hand.

"You are trying to buy me!"

"But only for sweet charity's sake."

He winked odiously and left her. She was still steaming when Atkinson came up to her, smiling from ear to ear, her hands holding two large rolls of bank notes. "You done just fine, missus." The black girl handed Meridel the money. "This will help the cause just fine."

As she struggled to smile back at Atkinson, who was beside herself with joy, Meridel already began to feel better.

The afternoon's contributions, counted onto a table in Meridel's suite at the Brevoort, came to $350. She exchanged a hug and a kiss with Araminta, but she should have been happier than she felt, she reflected. She stood a long time at the window, watching a lamplighter move up Fifth Avenue, leaving circles of wan radiance behind him on the snow. Now that she had proved she could raise money for Kansas, other matters she could not banish from her memory surfaced.

At last she sat down and wrote a duty note to Henry Ward Beecher. She said he'd be pleased to know that her own way of using chains had worked so well. She hoped to have another speaking engagement within a week. Meanwhile she would purchase a bank draft and send her collection money to St. Louis as the man on Massachusetts Avenue had instructed.

The minister replied promptly. Although he congratulated Meridel a certain annoyance showed between the lines. After all, she had succeeded without his help. Now, he said, she must speak to a more general audience, and he would arrange for her to appear at Coliseum Hall three evenings hence. Later she must speak at the huge Broadway Tabernacle. And it would be best, while she was on tour, to merge the funds she had raised, with his, for safekeeping.

A protest rose in Meridel's heart. She was supposed to be collecting large sums from rich people! But . . . the man from Massachusetts Avenue had made it clear that Beecher was to be her boss.

In 1845 Coliseum Hall had housed the great "Infidels' Convention" at which all kinds of reformers had shouted their plans for a changed world. Meridel found she would share the platform with other speakers who kept up the tradition. One would plead for temperance and another for womens' rights.

As she sat waiting her turn on the platform, she became aware of the difference between speaking to invited guests in a genteel home and addressing a crowd. People drove the temperance speaker into nervous stuttering by waving bottles at him and shouting the names of saloons where they wanted to meet him and have a drink. The formidable person who spoke on women's rights found herself shouted down by those—many women among them—who insisted that a female's place was in the home. A loud-voiced man rose to remind the audience that the famous newspaperman Horace Greeley, writing about Susan B. Anthony, had said it would be well if that famous women's rights speaker were led to a quiet place in the country until she had eased the fever in her brain.

When the unhappy chairman had restored order Meridel came up to the podium, but she had to wait while two men who had been punching each other were escorted from the hall to continue their fight outside. Meanwhile she had become aware that only one man in the audience, who sat in shadows toward the rear, had attended in evening clothes. She could not identify his face, but when she saw him twirl the seals on his watch chain she wished Mr. Thorncroft Parrish had stayed home.

As she began her speech, Meridel met cries of "Louder!"

No sooner had she launched upon her topic than she was assailed by boos, and someone threw an egg that barely missed her.

"Keep yer niggers down South!"' roared a man in laborer's clothing. "Comin' up here to take away white men's jobs!"

"And mind your own repitation before you tell others what to do," screamed a woman who must have read a snide newspaper item about a certain person who thought her married-into title could excuse the label *notorious* that she had decided to wear.

A man of some distinction rose and clarioned. "I am a physician, and I agree with Dr. S. A. Cartwright of the sovereign state of Mississippi that Negroes are adapted to warm weather only. Sending them to the North only deteriorates their brains." Someone else shouted, "If they have any!" and Meridel's voice became utterly lost in cries of "Shame!" and hoots of laughter. She wondered if Beecher had purposely thrown her into this melee of tangled alliances.

She kept on doggedly, and at least her little steel chains held the crowd's attention. But then a slim, striking woman got to her feet and stood in silent dignity while people turned to stare at her. She seemed to be in her late twenties, tastefully and expensively dressed, and her comely features were surrounded by a tiny clamshell bonnet of the most modish kind.

"Lady Wayne," she said clearly, "I am Mrs. Woodrow Bentley, Hebe Bentley, a widow from Dinwiddie County, Virginia. I own a plantation there, and I would be at home now, among my darkies who love me, if I hadn't had to come visit some damyankee relations I can't help having." Mrs. Bentley waited, head held high, amid cheers, jeers, and laughter. "I protest against your view of the Southern way of life, where people work in the air and sunshine, while you enslave your own poor to twelve and fourteen hours a day of labor at wages that barely keep them alive. Our slaves are well fed and never lack a roof over their heads and something in the pot. Your frightful hordes of slum dwellers are turned out into the street by rapacious landlords, and I know—I have seen it—they search for bits of food in offal that butchers throw out. As for your Underground Railroad, you are asking people to help you steal valuable property—yes, support crime! If I had my way I would tie you up in your own silly chains and take you to prison!'' She then began to move toward the aisle. "Pardon me, if you please,'' she said to others sitting in her row, speaking with such forceful courtesy that they hastily drew their knees out of her way. As she marched out of the hall she displayed a back as willowy as Meridel's own.

Meridel pushed along with her speech, but she had grown hoarse with shouting. Ushers supplied by the management—who got a percentage of donations—passed collection baskets, but Meridel's heart sank when she saw how many people folded their arms. "Remember,'' she went on tiredly, "that your contribution may go to help repair an old wagon that must carry fugitives hundreds of miles. Or it may make it possible to give black children more meat, eggs, and fresh greens rather than fatback and molasses, to help them grow up with straight limbs, as we believe . . .'' She kept on talking while the baskets went around, but she could not keep defeat out of her voice.

After management took its share of the collection, Atkinson carried out a cloth bag that sagged heavily but only held copper and silver, not bank notes. Meridel wanted nothing more than to return to her hotel and rest. But she found herself cornered by three elderly, ill-dressed abolitionist ladies who had to tell her how much they were on her side.

Then she faced the long, lean, burning-eyed man named Tilton whom she had met at Plymouth Church. He told her that she must learn to raise her voice or she would have no success. "Reverend Beecher says that a speaker's voice should sound like a great harp in midair,'' he scolded. Then what was she to do if she had a voice that didn't carry?

Outside, snow had turned to slush, and to make matters worse, a dismal mixture of snow and sleet was slashing down from the black sky. Looking desperately for a hansom, Meridel found herself facing a stout, short, beady-eyed man who wore a magnificent astrakhan cap and a matching coat trimmed with false cartridge loops in the Cossack style. It was Parrish.

In the dim gaslight he laughed at her. "Poor dear! How much money is your darkie carrying? No more than thirty dollars, I'll be bound, and all of it in small change."

Swaying on her feet, Meridel said simply, "Not quite twenty-five dollars."

"Allow me to double that stingy sum." He peeled notes from a large roll he took from his coat and pressed them into her helpless hand. "And ten more for good measure. Ah, ladies!" He bowed to the three forlorn abolitionists who, after having been most respectful toward Theodore Tilton, seemed half doubtful and half grateful toward him. "No hansoms in sight, and how can I allow you dear ladies to go home in freezing horsecars, let alone allow your beauty to draw the insulting attentions of coarse men. Here is my carriage, and Lady Wayne and all of you—and the girl Atkinson, too; she'll find a little servant's seat—can squeeze in, and I'll sit outside with my coachman. Never fear, I am well furred. We'll proceed up Broadway, and I'll let you off at any convenient cross street. Do get in."

Clever! There was no way to refuse, Meridel reflected. Instead she had to sit, steaming but helpless to express her anger, as they proceeded uptown, dropping one woman off after another, all of them bubbling with gratitude. And no doubt hardly able to wait to tell how they had ridden with the notorious lady-killer Thorncroft Parrish.

Parrish had been astute enough to realize that none of these women was rich enough to live far uptown. From First Street onward Meridel sat alone with Atkinson, ready for the parrying "Thorny" was skillful at but which Meridel was too tired to return.

Just above Washington Square, where Fifth Avenue began, the coach stopped at the Brevoort. Parrish handed Meridel down and offered to escort her upstairs.

"Don't you dare!" she snapped, then felt sorry. She apologized.

"My, my. Reputation is everything, isn't it?" he said. "But I shall certainly attend your next speech. I don't throw eggs, you know. Perhaps I shall bring a basket of roses to toss. Would you like that?"

"No, but I am grateful for the lift. Good night Mr. Parrish, and thank you again," she said and was about to whirl around and leave when he spoke again.

"I want to take you to the charity ball at the Crystal Palace next week. It's being put on by the Hunter Woods Benevolent Society. They care for widows and orphans and such, you know."

"No, thank you."

"It will be the same night as your speech at the Broadway Tabernacle. Not that one affair will keep people away from the other. The Crystal Palace ball will attract a very different group. It will start late and go on into the wee hours, so you'll have time to whisk back here after you speak, get into a ball gown, and then we'll fly to Forty-second Street."

"I trust you'll find female company, Mr. Parrish, but it will not be mine," she cried.

"Consider it. I could fill an important place in your life."

"I don't think so."

"We shall see."

He made as if to kiss her, but stopped as the point of Atkinson's hatpin flickered an inch from his face. He laughed, embarrassed, and turned to enter his carriage, which seconds later drove away at a reckless speed, spattering slush on passersby.

The days following their encounter, Thorny sent her flowers. Every day there were red roses, which etiquette would bar from ever sending to a married woman since they symbolized passion. Meridel, disgusted, threw them out.

At least she had some good news. Mrs. Gregory Schuyler of Gramercy Park wrote to say that the busy season had been keeping her dreadfully occupied, but that she was now experiencing a lull and could arrange for Lady Wayne to make her lovely speech at her home; if the twentieth of the present month was suitable, she would so inform all the Gramercy Park ladies.

So the flutter about Lady Wayne was dying away and the opinion was that Lady Wayne was certainly not encouraging men to make fools of themselves, and her cause should not be penalized. Meridel sent Atkinson quickly with her own grateful note of acceptance. Then she set herself to prepare for her speech at the Broadway Tabernacle, hoping it would not be too much of an ordeal.

The audience did indeed seem less unruly than that at the Coliseum. The Tabernacle was a church and for that reason, perhaps, it drew a better-dressed and better-behaved crowd. Again the back rows became a dim sea of unfeatured faces, but at least in the very front row, a man displayed one of Meridel's short lengths of chain from a waistcoat button.

She felt herself speaking better. She felt her own emotion flow to the audience, and she saw how eagerly people cocked their heads to catch every word. She said, "The girl had a bundle of rags beside her, or so I thought, but then I heard the weakest little wail and I saw it was a baby, its legs all crooked with rickets, and scrawny enough to break one's heart," and she could have heard a pin drop, such was the silence, except when it was broken by a sob. She felt herself on the brink of a small-scale victory as she said, "When you wear this bit of chain—it weighs only an ounce or two—you can tell the world you are helping to break the chains that—"

But many faces had turned from her to stare at the good-looking, fashionably dressed woman who had risen toward the rear of the big church. Hebe Bentley of Dinwiddie County, Virginia, spoke loudly, cool of voice yet poisonous of tongue.

"I ask you again, Lady Wayne, how can people who live in your noisy, dirty cities know of a plantation economy and its needs? Here in New York I reel under the impact of your stinks—yes, your stinks of ammonia gasses and offal-rendering and bone-boiling. Nor, in the South, do we have your miles of fetid slums! I have seen and, yes, smelled the people sitting on the sidewalks gasping for breath on warm summer nights or lying in rows on the roofs—men and women, married or unmarried—lest they die in the wretched holes you call tenements. I choke on your smoke that you say indicates prosperity. Give up trying to force the South into *your* own life-destroying ways. Stop enticing ignorant slaves into climates that kill them, far away from the secure life they know. Why, I could show you hundreds of black people who would cling to their masters in tears if they threatened to send them

North as a punishment—for you punish our slaves and call it freedom. You entice them away from the good life they know, and instead give them poverty and misery and disease." And again, having said her piece, the woman began to move down the row of seats.

Meridel almost called after Mrs. Bentley, but stopped herself. The North was not without sin. Shaking, she began to speak again. But she stopped, open-mouthed, her words like lead lumps in her throat. A chestnut-haired man with a clean-shaven chin—a man not very tall but very broad-shouldered—had stood up to follow the Virginia woman from his seat on her left. For an instant his dark blue eyes were riveted on Meridel, but Dan Forrester's face remained wooden. He turned away and followed his companion into the aisle.

Mrs. Hebe Bentley took his arm and smiled up at him as they proceeded toward the door, looking very much like the blissful couple.

From her deepest being Meridel called silently, "Dan! Dan!" Whatever pain they had given each other—quarrels, scorn, accusations, hatred—should never have been. The love in her heart cried out wordlessly for her lover. But the couple, Dan Forrester and his new woman, Hebe, walked heedlessly to the door, and all Meridel saw of her baby's father, after all the weeks they'd been parted, was his back, retreating, retreating, through the door and out of sight.

Chapter Four

Only the whispers that raced through the church made Meridel realize she had been standing motionless, saying nothing. She gathered her wits and went on with her speech. But when Atkinson at last piloted her outside she knew she had lost her hold on her audience and had drawn a miserable collection.

In the street, the man in the astrakhan coat waited with his roll of bills ready in hand, his eyes gleaming knowingly.

"You wasted your time this evening, didn't you?"

She only stared at him.

"Take this."

She did not know or care how much money he handed her; she gave it to Atkinson.

"That big, good-looking chap who escorted the woman from Virginia—he turned you positively pale. Friend of yours? You're not saying? But never mind. The night is young, and you need to forget your debacle here and do something joyous. I'll bring you to your hotel and call for you when you're ready, and we can be at the Crystal Palace by nine thirty.''

''Crystal Palace?'' She repeated, as if waking from sleep, uncertain of her surroundings.

''Yes. The charity ball. And here are your three friends to come uptown with us and make everything respectable.'' He bowed to the three forlorn abolitionists. ''Mrs. Bailey! How delightful to see you again. Mrs. Coe! Mrs. Parker! You've sincerely made my evening!'' He ushered them, Atkinson included, from the cold street into the shelter of his coach.

Meridel peered down Broadway, where wagons and a few sleighs made slush of what was left of the dirty snow. But why was she looking for Dan? He'd already gone far away with his slave-owning friend, Hebe Bentley. He'd come to the meeting to jeer along with the others.

Parrish took her arm. ''Come along. Remember, it's all for sweet charity's sake, and everyone who counts will be there.''

She stood another moment, irresolute. Suddenly she needed music; she needed to dance, to be gay, to drink, to chatter, to see many different faces and many different objects—anything to make Dan's face fade. But—with Parrish?

But Parrish had asked her, and Parrish stood ready, and the very small note of caution that had entered her mind died away before the crying need of her heart to forget, to forget!

She found herself smiling and heard herself say the words, ''Thank you'' in a taut voice. And she said, wild with despair, ''I'm sure it will be a lovely ball. Do let's hurry.''

The huge, glittering shape of the Crystal Palace had risen far uptown in the midst of farms, empty lots, squatters' shacks and the permanent homes of a few who thought it profitable to live on Forty-second Street and let the city grow around them. But in the five years since President Pierce had opened the glass-and-iron structure, all sorts of grog shops and peep shows had sprouted around it. Horsecars made a special stop, and a freak show, set up in a tent, offered views of a living alligator, a bearded woman, and a three-headed calf.

It was all one to Meridel. Forcing gaiety, knowing she

must be unnaturally bright-eyed, she entered the Palace through an extravagant turnstile that counted every person and told that more than twenty thousand had found their way inside that day. Inside, an immense chandelier with 530 gaslights blazed upon the crowd in the central dome, upon two complete bands of well-known musicians, upon the flags of all nations, upon magnificent statuary and upon a few of the thousands of exhibits that came from around the world to be displayed at the United States' first world's fair.

Meridel left her chinchilla cape in a vastly overcrowded cloakroom whose shelves sagged dangerously and whose female attendants, having to accept more and more heavy coats, seemed on the point of hysteria. Carefully tucking away her numbered ticket, Meridel went out into the midst of dandies with lavender spats and pearl-headed canes, generals, eager young soldiers, and others. Some people had come in disguise, including a Turk in trousers of pink satin and a spangled veil; a saucy, laughing maiden of ancient Greece who wore a most alarmingly transparent chiton; and a lady who wore a black velvet promenade basque trimmed with ermine and who might not have been masquerading at all. To one side, ladies and gentlemen of the best families—who had dressed accordingly—looked on with alarm at the hordes of shantytowners who had come to join the festivities and perhaps push their way to the tables stacked with free food. But even amidst all the distractions, a Worth gown was still a Worth gown, especially since the French couturier's reputation had grown mightily since he had first designed gowns for Meridel, and she drew more than her share of admiring glances.

Ladies were not provided with dance cards, but the *programme dansant* hung large and prominent. Prior to the midnight supper, the two bands, working alternately, would play a quadrille, a polka, a redowa, another quadrille, a schottische, a waltz, an emeralda, yet another quadrille (obviously very popular), and a final gay polka. Parrish claimed her for every dance, and what did she care? Nothing mattered. She tried to feel gay, gracefully accepting compliments, lightly nodding to people she knew. But she felt like a corpse waltzing, like a woman made of stone curtsying in the quadrille or skipping swiftly in the polka. Chatting between dances, she sipped champagne until she became aware that Mrs. William Colford Schermerhorn was observing her with raised eyebrows. She thought, The devil take all these disapproving high society types. She wouldn't apologize to anyone for her behavior. Leaning forward, she asked for more champagne. It was not only her gorgeously tailored green silk dress that drew attention. The high society women and their equally well-attired husbands looked askance at a married woman who had so openly separated from her husband and who danced with, of all people, Thorncroft Parrish. Some whispered to each other. Some made a point of *not* chatting with Lady Wayne and her escort. But if Meridel had made a mistake in allowing Thorny Parrish to squire her to the Palace— and she began vaguely to feel she had—she did not care. Nothing mattered.

At length Thorny led her away from the huge dance floor so they could cool off—he said—and see some of the exhibits. First they paused at a statue called "The Greek Slave." "Chains, you see," Thorny said in a very soft voice. He smiled, trying to be his most charming. The gleaming white statue portrayed a gorgeously shaped girl, dazzling in her nudity, her head averted in despair and her chained hands held out beseechingly.

"Beautiful," said Meridel, admiring the way the artist had rendered the complete vulnerability, the despair of the enslaved.

"Is she not? And I do believe"—Thorny paused to rake his eyes over Meridel's figure—"I do believe that you and she have the same measurements."

"Perhaps," Meridel said, frowning and sweeping her eyes around the room. "Oh, there's the big Corliss steam engine. It powers all the other moving exhibits. My father described it to me."

Thorny merely cleared his throat and took her arm to lead her through dwindling crowds as they approached the end of one of the naves, which was thronged with exhibits. She knew he wanted to corner her. What did it matter? she reflected. When he finally succeeded at the very end of the nave, they were hardly noticed.

"Really," he said, taking her hand, "this place is too much. Let's leave before the worst of the crush in the cloakrooms. We can drop in at my rooms and have coffee, and then . . ."

"I'm tired. Please take me to the Brevoort," Meridel said instantly. It *did* matter that she not encourage Thorny, she decided suddenly.

"But my man makes the most delicious coffee. He's a Viennese, and they—"

"But you promised that after the ball you'd bring me directly home," she reminded him firmly. He had made such a promise on the way over, when he had been on his good behavior. Of course she had not brought along a maid, which wasn't necessary at a public gathering.

"I did say that," he admitted, twirling his seals. "And if I am not true to my word, well, I must pay a forfeit. Poor dear, you are behind in your collections for Kansas." He plunged a hand into the inside pocket of his satin evening jacket and pulled out a wad of bank notes. "Here is a hundred dollars for your cause. You'll admit that even in sweet charity's name that is a considerable forfeit."

"It is, and I thank you in the name of people you'll never see; they'll be endlessly grateful."

"Yes, yes, but I am grateful I don't have to meet them. Meridel"—he drew her toward him—"come to my apartment for just a little while."

"No."

"I've paid my forfeit. Only come home with me, have coffee, chat a bit. I've never had a chance to be alone with you, and really, it will be for only a little while."

"Certainly not. And I don't think we should stand here away from everybody." She noticed how no one was near their spot in the nave and began to get worried.

"I'd like to show you my collection of Chinese cloisonné vases and my—" As she pulled her hand free of his, he blocked her path. "I won't touch you. I give you my word." But when she glanced at him with sharp disbelief, he said, "Very well, if you are in earnest about helping your barefoot ragamuffins—"

"Kindly do not refer to them that way."

"What I mean is, from my apartment wall safe I will give you another five hundred dollars for your—people—if you will merely honor me with a visit for an hour."

"Does it mean nothing to you that you are insulting me?"

"I am not insulting you—I am giving you five hundred dollars for merely honoring me with a visit," he said angrily.

"Sir, I tell you again that you can't—"

"Buy you? This is not just for your company, dear lady, but for the people for whom you work so assiduously. Or was it all talk, your so-called charity?"

Meridel paused for a moment. Certainly Thorny was no danger unless she considered him so, and he was offering a huge sum of money—desperately needed—for a cause that she might be able to do little more for in New York. And then the image of Dan with his new woman on his arm flashed into her mind. But before she could reach any decision, a loud splintering noise sounded and someone yelled that it came from the ladies' cloakroom at the other end of the palace.

As panicked as everyone else in the exhibit hall, Meridel and Parrish ran in the direction of the cloakroom along with dozens of others. Screams surrounded them and one of the attendants ran out, shrieking, "The shelves! They're all coming down!"

"My sables!" "Dear God, my new muff!" With a concerted rush—from which Thorny held Meridel back, warning her of the danger—beautifully-gowned women stormed the cloakroom in time to see the last of the shelves give way. When Meridel at last ventured in, she stood stunned at the sight of furs, coats, muffs, hats, and other items of clothing mixed with splintered wood on the cloakroom floor. Women waved their checks and screamed their numbers to attendants, who could only wring their hands and wail their confusion. The press of bodies began a series of faintings that *The New York Times* was to describe as horrendous the next day. The crush became nearly a riot as male escorts pushed in, anxious to help. But this invasion of an area considered sacred to women triggered the arrival of blue-tunicked policemen, who only added to the confusion. Someone broke a window. Chill rain swept in from the wintry night, dousing everyone and everything, but especially the furs.

Meanwhile half a dozen shantytowners stole behind the counter, where they tossed garments about, shouting, "Now that's me wife's sable cloak that she's had to wear this ten year past, poor thing!" and, "Bedammit, but I'll have me granny's muff afore I take her out in the cold." Before enraged gentlemen could climb over the counter to stop them, they had loaded themselves with sable and broadtail and ermine and had escaped by smashing other windows, thumbing their noses at the crowd-blocked policemen as they made off.

Meridel never knew who ripped her gown down the back. Many dresses were ripped, shoes were lost, coiffures collapsed. Holding her bodice to keep it from falling down, she heard some sensible man shout, "Ladies, go home and leave your cloaks. The police can guard them. Come back tomorrow with your checks and claim what is yours!"

The grab for cloaks inside the Crystal Palace soon turned into a grab for hansoms outside—with few to be found, for the hackmen had expected the crowd to leave later, and the private coachmen, too, had taken shelter where they could warm the insides of their throats. Getting home turned into a lark for the city's "best people." Gentlemen and their ladies who never before had ridden a horsecar rode one that night, singing.

Thorny did not pause to retrieve his astrakhan from the besieged men's cloakroom but draped his evening jacket over Meridel's shoulders and rushed her out of the Crystal Palace. Shivering in the wind, she did not balk at getting into his carriage. He, too, shivered in his waistcoat and shirt sleeves, damning his coachman for not going faster and for not keeping a flask of whiskey for him and some sherry for his lady guests in the coach.

Very tired, Meridel closed her eyes for a moment, or so she thought. She did not open them again until she felt the carriage stop. Dizzy now, she was glad to have Thorny help her enter the Brevoort as she fumbled to keep her dress in place and wondered what the door porter might think, never realizing that quite a few ladies returned from the Crystal Palace that night disheveled and very gay.

But this scented, mahogany-paneled entry, where a gorgeous jade vase stood in a glass case, did not belong to the Brevoort, and she said so.

"Don't be a fizgig," said Thorny, using the current slang to make light of the fact that he had brought her to his own house. "I can't allow you to enter your hotel looking as though you'd been in a barroom brawl, let alone that you'd had a few drinks too many." He told a hovering manservant in black jacket and bombazine waistcoat, "Trefanec, make coffee." Next he put Meridel into the care of Mrs. Trefanec, a thin, quick woman with a Viennese accent like her husband's. "Liese, Lady Wayne shouldn't really be here without a chaperone," Parrish said, "so you chaperone her. Take her to the guest room and give her . . . Yes, my yellow Chinese robe will suit her taste for fine things. Then mend her dress, and if it needs ironing, iron it. Meridel?" He joggled her elbow to get her attention. "I'll have good Viennese coffee waiting when you come down.

In the handsome guest room Meridel noticed another Chinese vase that stood in a niche in a wall, secured against careless maidservants by a band of ribbon. She still felt unsteady as Liese helped her out of her damaged gown and into a robe of cloud-light yellow silk. She felt better when Liese examined the damaged gown—luckily ripped along seams—and said, "Can make good fix, *ja*."

Cautiously, Meridel descended curving marble steps as handsome as the ones at 42 Union Square. No, she thought as Thorny Parrish, in a purple velvet smoking jacket, rose from his seat at a fireplace—no, she had *not* had too many drinks. She had had no more than two glasses of champagne at the Palace, just enough to make her feel drowsy an hour or two later. The coffee would do her good.

Offering her a comfortable wing chair, Thorny poured from an urn that stood on a tripod over a flame. "One lump or two?" He added a spoonful of whipped cream with cinnamon in it.

After a while she heard music from somewhere. Thorny, giving her a second cup, said, "That's from the Schuyler house next door. Horse-mad family with a roomful of blue ribbons. Why do people go silly over horses? I daresay they are indispensable, but I'm glad I never have to touch them."

Whatever Meridel might have said to that remained unsaid. Dan had always been involved with horses. . . . But no, how silly to think that Dan Forrester might be carousing with the other horse lovers next door.

The sensuous, moist mouth asked, "Tell me, what did Queen Victoria and you talk about at Buckingham Palace?"

"Cotton."

Not believing her, Parrish waited with raised brows.

"New York, London. My cousin Lord Blakiston's estate."

"Ah, those broad English estates. But I can't imagine why anyone wants to live in the country when he can live in town. Although, as far as the Kansas wilderness goes, I gather it was not *that* you objected to so much."

"That is right."

"It was your husband. It takes a woman of courage to leave her husband. I admire you, Meridel."

Again she remembered she was fair prey to any woman-chaser. Still, Parrish behaved himself. He gave her more coffee, picked up a blue-and-white Ming vase with a pattern of laughing children, and remarked that it had been part of his family's collection that had "come to him." But Meridel had heard that his marvelous vases had come to him from an older woman who had kept him close to her years ago, after his parents had kicked him out.

And so they talked of this and that while Liese sewed patiently in a corner, never out of sight. Nevertheless, Meridel became strongly aware that Thorny again watched her much as a cat, ready to pounce. At length Liese took the gown upstairs, where she had a special sadiron she needed. But first she escorted Meridel to the guest room and said she would return there with the dress. Thorny called up the stairs that Trefanec and he would bring her back safely to her hotel.

About time, she thought. It was past two in the morning. Hearing music again, she glanced through a window and saw the Schuyler house close by across a narrow planted strip. The handsome dwelling glowed with light, and from its open windows wafted the music and sounds of merriment and tipsy laughter. Someone tried to sing "Auld Lang Syne," but dance music drowned him out. Yes, the horsey people were making merry.

Sighing, Meridel took off the yellow silk robe, waiting in her petticoats and revealing corset for Liese to appear with her gown. Again the Chinese vase caught her eye. Lovely! Its handles were formed of snakelike dragons with tiny wings, and its proportions carried the eye along magically.

Thinking to hang up the robe, Meridel noticed the doors of two closets—unusual in the place of armoires, and very chic. The nearest was locked. The other revealed a collection of women's clothing in several sizes; therefore it did not belong to merely one woman. Well . . . none of her affair.

She sat and waited. Where was Liese? Suddenly she heard someone inside the locked closet! Its door opened and she shrank away. She saw it was not a closet after all, but a washroom placed between two bedrooms. But who—?

Who but Thorny Parrish, tubby, unhandsome, and grinning. He had undressed, and showed his bare shanks beneath a blue Chinese gown embroidered with a pattern of sword-wielding warriors. Bitterly, Meridel realized she had been trapped. Yes, cat and mouse, spider and fly. And his people so accustomed to his ways that Liese surely would not bring the repaired gown till her master was done with his latest female guest.

"Now you've gotten over the coffee you ought to feel quite lively," Thorny said, coming toward her with little steps. "You are beautiful when you are gowned, Meridel, but I like you better in that low-cut evening corset. So enticing. Come, come, let me see those beautiful breasts. Come, show me, inch by inch." She remembered a Kansas field where a fire burned and a sharp-edged stump waited. But this man would carry through his plans.

"Mr. Parrish, I demand to have my dress! You promised to take me home—safely!"

"Why, certainly I'll take you home—after a bit. And I'll wear a mask as though we had come from a costume ball, so nobody will know with whom you kept intimate company tonight. Come, let me unlace you. Don't show me your lovely curves all at once. Just let the pink little crests peek at me." He almost giggled in gloating anticipation.

Meridel remembered how Dan had turned his back on her earlier that night, and how he had walked out of the hall with his latest woman, plainly showing his attachment to her. If she meant nothing to him anymore, then . . . then what did it matter if she loosened her laces? What difference could it make now?

But even a runaway wife had her personal honor. Meridel realized she had backed up against the dragon vase's niche. Her mind worked quickly. "Mr. Parrish, what about the five hundred dollars you promised for the Underground Railroad?"

"Five hun—!" He scowled. "Why you money-squeezing . . . All right, I'll get it. Just don't expect that kind of gift again." He went back through the washroom and returned in a moment, tossing bank notes onto the bed. "That's where the money goes, by ancient custom."

Yes, the motto in Carlotta's establishment had been: Money on the bed before anything happens. Meridel left it there. While Thorny had gone back to his own room she had broken the ribbon that held the vase.

"Thorny, will you kindly get me the yellow robe? It's in the closet."

"My, we are being coy! Very well." He tossed the airy robe at her. "What's that for?" he demanded as she put it on, her back still to the niche.

"The more I wear, the more I have to take off." But to be covered gave her courage.

Delighted, he held out his arms and his own robe fell open, showing him as a paunchy, bull-like creature. "Ah, little sweetheart!" He approached her with the awkward walk of a man in heat.

But she snatched the dragon vase and held it above her head. "Stop or I'll smash it," she said in a quiet, wire-taut voice.

He stopped short, horror twisting his features. "No!" He clasped his shaking hands together. "You mustn't . . . oh no, you daren't hurt my dragon vase!"

Whether he really loved his vases or whether, as she had heard, he was selling them one by one to pay his debts, she did not care.

"Mr. Parrish, if you attempt to touch me I will throw this vase through the window. They'll hear the crash next door"—where the music had now stopped—"and on top of that I'll scream 'Fire!' and Mr. Schuyler will send footmen to help, and—"

"No, no, don't smash my vase!" The arrogant Thorny now seemed like an overgrown little boy, begging, "Please, please!"

"Move away from me. Get behind the bed."

He rushed to obey, still pleading. "It's Tang Dynasty—the seventh century—the golden age of Chinese ceramics. I've been offered three thousand—"

"Where is my dress?" she asked, then decided she had better not deal with Parrish's servant couple, since she might find herself overpowered by the threesome. "No," she said, "I'll wear the robe. I'll say I'm returning from a costume ball." She could walk to the Brevoort in five minutes, shouting make-believe good-byes over her shoulder as she walked in. "Listen, Mr. Parrish. I will leave the vase in your foyer. But if anyone tries to interfere with me before I leave, I warn you I will smash it." She snatched the bank notes from the bed. "For sweet charity's sake," she said fiercely. "As for me, I am not for sale."

The wind was still blowing fiercely, and Parrish's front stoop bore a thin armor of ice. The light silk robe, held closed only by a sash, flapped wildly about. Meridel could hardly manage to hold it shut as she gripped the frigid iron railing and descended the steps in her evening slippers. But she felt free, and she would not mind the short, cold walk to the hotel; most of all, she rejoiced in having extorted an extra contribution from the man who had sneered at her cause.

But then she felt a new fear like a claw clutch at her belly. A group of men and women in high spirits were leaving the house next door.

Nine coaches waited. In the halo of a street lamp, women in swirls of silk and fur stepped delicately over patches of ice on the slate sidewalk. A footman scattered sand to make walking safer. The wind brought Meridel the scents of good wine, good cigars, good perfume. One man, who wore a small horseshoe of diamonds in his stock, leaned against the lamppost and drunkenly sang:

D'ye ken John Peel with his coat so gray,
D'ye ken John Peel at the break of day,
D'ye ken John Peel so far, far away
With his hounds and his horse in the morning.

The others smiled. Two or three joined in. Meridel hoped
against hope that the singer would draw attention away from
her. But she stopped on the icy steps as two women turned
and stared. They quickly called the attention of the others to
her. Meridel forced herself to go on again. How they watched
as she came down step by step, the silk robe billowing revealingly, the petticoats beneath flapping and flying. The cold
air bit at her bosom, which the robe and her scanty corset
failed to conceal.

Every face, male and female, stared at her. The only sound
came from the robe's flapping like a loose sail. Meridel's
breath came hard and fast, the vapor of which the wind
quickly whisked away. When one of the women nearest her
said in a cracked, high old voice, "Ugh! One of Thorny's
females, I've no doubt," she felt as though a world of people
pointed at her shame.

The other woman said, "Such a disgusting creature."
Then, peering, she cried out in amazement and announced all
too clearly, "My God, it isn't . . . But it *is* Lady Wayne!"

Meridel needed no more to tell her she had escaped from
the frying pan into the fire. She lifted her chin and stood there
as though waiting to be shot. The woman who had first spoken was Mrs. Harrison Batchelder, the aged mentor of New
York's genteel society; the other woman, by the same stroke
of ill fate, was Helene Winston, the first to have opened her
home to a certain titled but notorious woman.

"It *is* Lady Wayne," echoed Mrs. Harrison Batchelder,
peering at Meridel from beneath her withered hand.

Someone else asked, "Lady Wayne? No! But is it really?"

A man's voice; a woman's voice; a man's voice again,
saying gleefully, "Lady Meridel Wayne? But surely she
wouldn't—Say, you're absolutely right. She *did*."

Meridel remained seated at the bottom of the stairs, the
billowing robe revealing her in her underclothes as though it
were a yellow banner flown to catch attention. She stared

upward, over everyone's heads, as though she could find mercy in the black sky.

They strolled toward her. The men jabbed their canes at her as though she were a butterfly they wanted to impale on a pin. The women drew their furs smugly around them.

One of the women said, "You can always count on Lady Wayne to dress tastefully for every occasion."

A man added, "Her father was an Irish immigrant. Now, ain't she the *broth* of a colleen—she's in the soup!"

Another man chimed in, "Was Thorny giving a costume ball for one guest, do you suppose?"

The singer left his lamppost to stagger over and say sotto voce: "Maybe so, with music. I heard a little twangy music—the creaking of bedsprings."

The ladies were not supposed to have heard that, but some giggled.

"Costume ball?" mused a man. "If she were coming from a costume ball she'd be wearing a *woman's* Chinese robe, and it would fit her."

"Goodness me," said a woman with an affected squeal, "whatever could have happened to her dress?"

Helene Winston cried, "Gave it to charity, no doubt." Then she added, with a note of anguish, "And to think I invited that . . . *that* into my home."

Meridel's head slowly drooped. She wanted to die.

Dimly, as she shivered in the wind, she heard the people enter their carriages and then one carriage after another rumble away. The ninth coachman sang at her from the depths of the woolen scarf he wore beneath his top hat: "Lady Wayne, Lady Wayne/Came from Kansas on a train. . . ."

Silence, save for the flapping of Thorny's yellow robe. Gradually Meridel became aware that two people had remained behind the others. A couple. The woman, swathed in rich fur, held the arm of a man who gazed downward, his hat brim hiding his face.

Meridel knew that man—knew him by the set of his shoulders and the bigness of his hands and the way he stood. As for the woman; no doubt at all. The comely face wreathed in white fox belonged to triumphant, gloating Mrs. Hebe Bentley of Dinwiddie County, Virginia.

Dan Forrester at last looked up and regarded her in disbelief and pain.

276

Chapter Five

I must run to the hotel, Meridel thought. I will wrap the robe around myself grandly and sweep in.

No, I must run to the East River. It's not that far away. The water will be cold, but I won't feel the chill long after the river closes over my head.

She knew she could do no such thing. She only stood there and watched Dan wave down a hansom whose driver had come belatedly to check the fashionable streets around the square. He returned to stand before her. "Please get into the hansom, Meridel. We'll take you wherever you want to go."

He took the folding seat. Hebe Bentley sat beside Meridel, taking care not to allow their arms to touch. The hackman flipped open the little trapdoor above their heads. When he said, "Where to?" Meridel whispered, "The Brevoort."

Dan got out with her and they stood in the snow that had begun to drift down around them. She said, "I'll be all right, thank you."

He said, his voice tortured: "Good night. I . . ."

She turned quickly, wrapping the yellow robe around her as the sleepy night porter opened the hotel's door.

But she heard Hebe Bentley say from within the hansom, a bit loudly, "Please Dan, let's get back to my apartment. We still have to go over those papers tonight—about the bloodlines of my horses, you know."

Fate sent one stray kindness. The night porter escorted Meridel to the stairs with no indication of surprise, and, being an elderly man, he took the liberty of saying, "Must be fun, those costume balls."

"Oh, dear God!" Araminta Atkinson bit her knuckles.

"You were right. You told me that if I had anything to do with Thorncroft Parrish—"

"Never mind that. Here. Drink." She handed her a cup of steaming-hot tea laced with rum. "All I can see is, it's out of the Brevoort for you, first thing in the morning, before the story gets around town. We don't want the manager asking you if you might not be more comfortable elsewhere."

Meridel wished she could weep.

Atkinson continued after some thought, "Soon's it's light I'll run downtown and arrange with Mrs. Carpenter. She runs a cooperative boarding house for abo people on Desbrosses Street. You won't like the place, but you can stay hidden there until we think what to do next."

"I'm . . . I'm so . . . sorry. At first . . . I got away . . . without damaging . . . the cause. But then . . . I damaged it so badly. . . ."

"But you brought in hundreds of dollars, the biggest single contribution I've ever heard of. Come on. Get to bed." The voice was gruff, the hands gentle as Atkinson led her to her pillow.

The next day found them at Carpenter's Boarding House on Desbrosses Street, near the Hudson. Winifred Carpenter had been put together out of bones, skin, and lank, iron-gray hair. Her character had been molded around a large core of annoyed righteousness. "You're small," she snapped at Meridel. "That will be no excuse for not carrying your share of the work here. And you pay two dollars a week besides."

Her daughter Hortense took after her, her age—thirtyish—and her unmarried state having set her against good-looking women. "Remember," she told Meridel, "the second floor's for females, the third's for males, and males and females may meet only in the public rooms on the first floor. Decorum will be maintained, and I don't know why a respectable boarding house should be expected to take in a married woman who is not a widow. Remember, you are going to *work*."

"Yes." I have been wife to a Skidi Pawnee and I know about work, she thought.

The mother put in sourly, "House rules are: church twice a day on Sunday—although *you're* not allowed to go out, so we can forget that rule. Bible class three evenings a week right in the house. No drinking. No smoking for the men." It was of course unheard-of for a woman to smoke. "You're lucky. Only reason I have a bed for you is that one of the young women has gone off to work in the Lowell mills in Massachusetts."

"I see," said Meridel. She hoped Atkinson had been able to store most of her luggage. She had entered the boarding house with one valise, feeling like a wounded animal taking refuge in a cave. Atkinson had gone shopping for her to buy a more suitable wardrobe than fashionable evening wear.

When Atkinson returned, she not only brought the new, more utilitarian clothes but also the morning papers, in which Meridel read how the shelves had crashed down in the ladies' cloak room at the Crystal Palace, how the night had turned into a great lark, and why, if she had arrived at her hotel in her torn dress, it would not have made any difference.

Not long after putting the paper aside, Meridel found she had little time for reading. Mrs. Carpenter and Hortense put her to work without mercy. But at least work brought forgetfulness—until the end of the day, when the same question burned: *Where was Eric?* Did her little boy run about somewhere, or had they buried his fever-wracked body? Memories haunted her, choking her, misting her eyes, until she fell into exhausted sleep in her little room hardly larger than a closet.

Soon everyone found out her real identity. When she ate with the others at Mrs. Carpenter's sparse table, girls curled their little fingers as they sipped their thin coffee and put on fancy-lady accents as false as they were hurtful. The bachelors said to each other, "I say, eld chep, is it true that Vicky and Albert have had a spat?" They were abolitionists every one, but still willing to mock a high-placed but fallen person. When Mrs. Carpenter passed around the alms plate—for each boarder gave a dime a week to the Underground Railroad— Meridel gave a dollar, hearing the whisper, "Now she's trying to show she's better than anyone else."

Well, did it matter? She had failed in love, had had a disastrous marriage, had lost her child, had even failed the Underground Railroad. Only one thing had not yet happened to her; she had never given way to misfortune, never been broken.

But if she ever broke, she would break completely. She worked, and even looked for extra jobs to do. Lady Wayne became a drudge, a slavey.

One morning, when she was setting the breakfast table, someone knocked at the door. Mrs. Carpenter opened it partly, keeping the night chain on. A messenger had a note but would not hand it to her. Meridel stopped, her heart leaping when she heard the man say, "I've got to give it direct into the hands of Lady Wayne, see? Her name is on it."

Mrs. Carpenter motioned brusquely, and Meridel came to the door. The man slipped the envelope through the gap to her. Could it be a letter from Dan? Meridel's hand trembled so that she dropped it. Mrs. Carpenter stooped to pick it up and made no bones about reading the writing and printing on the back of the envelope.

"D. Forrester, Hotel St. Nicholas," she announced. "Well! If you've been hobnobbing with that Daniel Forrester who keeps company with that Mrs. Bentley who's been trying to break up every abolition meeting in town . . . well! I don't know what you're doing in *my* house!" Meridel had gotten so shaky that she still could hardly hold the letter when Mrs. Carpenter slapped it into her hand.

"Forrester?" said one of the young working men who had come down for breakfast. "Why he's a big Kansas landowner. Reverend Beecher suspects he connives with those dreadful raiding parties that come over from Missouri."

Likely enough, thought Meridel, clutching the letter desperately. Very likely for a man who had printed broadsides that resulted in the deaths of scores of Free State settlers in the *Barataria* sinking. Except that . . . that she loved him! She could not and did not want to help it. She loved him, needed him, would die wishing for the haven of his lips and his arms.

The dining room was filling up. Every eye watched her twist the letter in her hands. Meridel ached to open it away from those prying faces. And yet . . . what could Dan possibly have to say to her? But why had he found her—it must have taken a deal of looking—if he didn't have something important to say?

But loving him did not hide the fact that he definitely sided with the Slave Staters. As everyone knew. Could she, in this company, here with her spiritual brothers and sisters, however uncouth they might be—could she really accept a communication from Dan Forrester's hand?

Where did her loyalties lie?

She stood as though in court and as though she were, all in one, the accused and the judge and the jury. Guilty of dealing with the enemy or not guilty? She alone must say.

She hesitated another moment. Then she lifted her chin. "I must tell you all that I never invited Mr. Forrester to communicate with me. He merely has presumed upon our having met in Kansas, and he happens to be in New York and has seen me. And—and he attended a speech I made for the U.R., but only for the sake of escorting that Mrs. Bentley, and . . . and if you want to know how I am going to treat this most unwelcome letter . . ." Her heart screamed, *Don't!* But her fiercely set mind made her hands rip the letter into two halves and again rip it across and drop the four pieces into a wastebasket.

"Hmph," said Mrs. Carpenter. "I was ready to tell you to go, but you may stay on."

Tired as she was when she lay at last in her bed, Meridel could not sleep. *What had Dan wanted to tell her?* She fought to stay where she was, but in the depth of the night she crept downstairs, found the wastebasket . . . and discovered it had been emptied. Every day the wastebaskets were emptied into sacks that were kept in the cellar until all paper could be burned in one great blaze.

Should she search for the pieces of the letter in the cellar, then? She peered down the cellar steps with her candle, then whirled as she heard footsteps.

"What are you doing?"

"I just came down for a drink of water, Mrs. Carpenter. Forgot to fill my pitcher."

"Well, young woman, take your drink and get back to bed," said Mrs. Carpenter from her ruffled nightcap. "You need your sleep."

The remark came not unkindly. Hortense never let up in her heckling of Meridel, but the older woman had come to know that Lady Wayne was a silent, hard worker, willing to learn every household skill. Meridel had no choice but to return upstairs.

That week came spring cleaning, with Meridel working harder than ever. Hortense told her there was no wind to scatter bits of paper, so she had better hurry and burn all the wastepaper in the backyard.

Atkinson had dropped in from time to time, muttering at the way Meridel worked but seeming to understand why she threw herself into every task. The gaunt black woman accompanied her to the yard and helped empty the sacks into a wire-mesh container. Hortense, who had come out to fuss in the lone flower bed, watched over her shoulder as though Meridel did not move fast enough, and even complained of time wasted when Meridel had to return to the kitchen for a lucifer.

Meridel struck the lucifer on a stone and lit the paper, and as flames began to waver upward, she saw a torn quarter of a white envelope. The bright sunlight of that spring day showed her blue printing: *St. Nicholas Hotel, 512 Broadway, New York City*.

She could grab it through the mesh. But Hortense was almost beside her. The flames crept upward. Hortense said, "Mind you come in directly and don't stay out here and gossip" and went into the house. Meridel snatched out the fragment, and because all four pieces had stayed together she was able to snatch another, then a third, which came out burning and scorched. One of her fingers was seared, but she hardly felt the sharp burn. Atkinson, asking no questions, grabbed the fourth torn bit and stamped on it to extinguish the flame.

Meridel was able to smooth the pieces of the letter and put them together on the brick walk that ran alongside the house. The edges had been charred, but all the writing was visible, although it had blurred somewhat. No, her eyes had blurred. But at last she was able to focus on Dan's strong writing.

Meridel, my dearest:
  I have just had word from Horse Hurlbut. Six months ago our little Eric was alive and well. Silver Leaf left the tribe six months ago and took our son with her.
  Nobody knows where she took Eric. But if he was alive six months ago, and we know she would protect him, I believe he is still alive. I must see you. I have so much to tell you. Come to me at the St. Nicholas quickly, my dearest. We must not ever be apart again.

Dan

She caught at Atkinson. "Eric is alive!" Then came explanations she never finished as she rushed about, knowing nothing but that Dan waited for her to come to him and would tell her again why their little boy *must* be alive and well and waiting for them somewhere. Atkinson told Mrs. Carpenter that Meridel could now leave the house, and made her change from her working clothes into something in which a lady could be seen in a high-class hotel. All the time, Meridel babbled and fell silent, babbled and fell silent. "Eric is alive," she said as they rattled downtown, and "Eric is alive," she said when the hansom stopped at the St. Nicholas. "And Dan loves me and I've always loved him." Her face glowed as though with fever. She could not sit still.

Atkinson still hardly understood but, assuming the deferential attitude of a maid, took her into the huge hotel's marble lobby surrounded by little shops. Meridel went to the desk clerk and almost screamed, "Mr. Daniel Forrester. Where is he?"

The clerk did not know her and looked at her indifferently. He consulted his room file. "We have no one registered under that name."

"But he's here! He told me he'd be waiting for me!"

The clerk smothered a knowing grin. He found an older register beneath the counter, and for what seemed an eternity he turned its pages as Meridel held her knuckles to her mouth in trembling suspense. "Well, ma'am, there he is, Forrester with two *r*'s."

"Where? What room? Oh, quick, please!"

"But ma'am, this is the *old* register. He was in Room 501, but he left two days ago."

Meridel swayed, clutched at the counter. "Where did he go?"

The clerk closed the heavy book with a sound like the crack of doom. "He left no forwarding address, ma'am."

Stunned, Meridel turned away, and Atkinson led her gently to the door. The dreadful thing was that she knew exactly what had happened. Dan had written the letter a week ago and then had waited. Day after day he waited for her while the four torn pieces of his letter lay in the sack. When in five days she had not come to him, he had told himself she did not wish to see him and only then had he left, despairing.

As she now despaired. A black cloud invaded her heart, until nothing else was left. And, in a hansom on the way to the boarding house, as Atkinson held her and tried to soothe her, and her teeth chattered and she said incomprehensible words, Meridel finally broke.

Put to bed, wrapped in blankets—for she could not stop shaking—Meridel smiled faintly at Mrs. Carpenter, smiled in the same way to Hortense, who had come to demand to know why the ironing had not been done.

"She's perfectly well, Mother! Only malingering! And if you think I'm going to let her stay without doing her work—"

"Be quiet," her mother whispered. "Don't you see her glazed eyes?"

"I don't know the whole story," said Atkinson from where she had sat for hours next to the bed. "But I know she's had a bad shock. She looks the way my aunt looked when I came and told her that her husband had been run over in the railroad switching yard."

Meridel said to nobody, "He waited and he waited and he waited and then he went away. And now I'll never find him

284

again. Ever. Never. And together we could have found Eric. We could have found Eric. But Eric is gone forever. My finger hurts," she said, and childishly put her blistered finger into her mouth.

Eventually a Dr. Banks, whom the Underground Railroad people trusted, came to the house. He was said to believe that much of human illness begins in the mind. He looked hard into Meridel's eyes. Despite her protests he routed her out of bed and had her stand on one foot, then the other. He drew a chalk line on the floor and had her walk on it back and forth. He made her close an eye and touch her forefinger to her nose, then the other eye and the other forefinger. He asked her her name, her father's name, her mother's. He made her count to thirty forward and backward. She remained dazed, but she passed all the tests.

"Physically she is well. She has proper coordination and shows no sign of brain damage. Leave me alone with her awhile."

Carefully he questioned Meridel, and when she began talking, telling her entire story, he let her go on for an hour. Then he gave her a drug that put her to sleep and told Atkinson and Mrs. Carpenter, "Luckily she is very strong in the ways that count. Let her rest. She will recover."

"She's obviously gone mad," said Hortense. "We must send her away to Bloomingdale before she murders us all."

Mrs. Carpenter cried, "She stays here! And I wish I had a daughter with half as much sense!"

After some days Meridel was able to sit up in Mrs. Carpenter's deepest easy chair. She insisted that since she had become purely a guest, she would pay five dollars a week for her room and board and would put two dollars into the weekly collection plate. Gradually the other boarders came to visit her. One girl begged her pardon for having mocked her. She became a respected figure. The young people told each other that the reports of Lady Wayne's immorality simply couldn't be true.

Eventually the dam burst in Meridel, and she wept for twelve hours. Dr. Banks said it was a good sign.

The next day Atkinson had to bring her all the newspapers she had missed. She read about a place in Kansas that early explorers had called *Marais des Cygnes*—the swamp of the swans. Here pro-slavery forces had cornered a group of anti-slavery men. They had picked out five and had shot them dead, proclaiming revenge for John Brown's raid. But the balance of power ran more and more in favor of the anti-slavery and Free State groups. Everyone expected the South to make a desperate last-ditch stand that would drench Kansas Territory in blood.

Meridel rose from her chair. "I am going back to Kansas, where I have work to do."

Atkinson protested that she not had regained her strength. But Meridel found her clothing and dressed herself. "No, I am useless here. Out there I may be able to do some good. And also, somewhere in Kansas . . . perhaps my little boy . . ." For a moment she looked at her own arms, held in the shape of an empty cradle. Then, fiercely, she swore, "I am going back where I belong."

The one thing she did before packing her bags, hurriedly, and taking the next train west was to write a note to Henry Ward Beecher and to her other contacts, letting them know where she was going and how the money could reach the people for whom it was intended most quickly. Then she rushed into the dark tunnel that was her future.

Hebe Bentley had a horsewoman's strong hands. Her right hand made a resounding impact when she slapped Dan Forrester hard across the face.

Outside, the great Virginia plantation was awakening amid spring greenery far more advanced that New York's. Slaves setting out for the fields called gaily to one another. A foreman on a horse rode beside them, watching the sky to gauge the weather. Tangy wood smoke seeped into Mrs. Bentley's chamber, where gold-stippled walls and arched recesses surrounded a great eighteenth-century bed that was wider than it was long. Dan lay there motionless, the outlines of his body showing beneath a fine lawn sheet.

"Hebe," he said at last, "I never will say I love you, because I don't love you. I told you from the first—"

"That you love someone else. But she never answered your letter and she never came to you, did she? *Did she?*"

"No," he said, half groaning the word.

"Then she hates you. Have done with her, Dan!"

"I can't. . . . I can't."

Hebe Bentley returned to the bed, sat on its edge, her naked hips appearing pink in the low sunlight. "Dan, I slapped you because—because you frustrate me so. You don't want me, you want my horses. You've told me that, but if you think being told such a thing helps a woman's pride. . . !" She looked away, shadows playing across her bosom. "Dan, think what I'm offering you. Myself and Blue Hills, my plantation. The crops, the slaves, the horses, the house my grandfather built. Everything. Marry me and you become master here."

Silence.

"Dan, you're a Southerner. You know that men like Washington and Jefferson kept slaves. You know that most of us are kind to our slaves, and you have seen that my own slaves really love me. Slavery must be kept, or the South will perish. Dan, marry me," she said with sudden passion. "I am yours already. Blue Hills will be yours, too."

"My future lies in Kansas."

"Dan, six months here, six months in Kansas. And it might be very profitable to raise horses in different climates on different kinds of graze."

She leaned over him. He sighed, turning his face away. She sat up and cried, "To think that I waited for you there in New York!"

"I told you not to wait. You see how uselessly I waited. Meridel hates me. God knows I've given her reason."

"Dan, what else can I do for you that I haven't done? You know I've the best of the Cleveland Bays, and you know I wanted to give them—"

"No, I'll buy them."

"But I'm still the only one who'll give you the long-term credit you need." She waited for his reply, searched his face, and cried wretchedly, "*She* is still with you!"

"Yes, she'll be with me forever."

Hebe went at him with her nails, but stopped and drew away. "Listen to me. Listen well. If I screamed that you forced your way into my bed, men would come running, and they would kill you.''

"Go ahead and scream," Dan Forrester said.

"They'll kill you, I tell you. Don't you care?"

"I'm dead inside anyway."

"Damn you and damn you! Go back to your damned ranch. Go! Go, I said!" After a silence she said to the face that did not seem to know her: "I'll send the stallion and the mares you've bought as soon as you let me know it's safe."

"Thank you, Hebe," Dan said in a dead voice.

"Damn you, get out of here. Quick, before I scream, and—oh!—how I would enjoy seeing them bury you!" She covered herself with a robe, then stared from the window while he dressed. As he was leaving he turned, wooden-faced, and came back awkwardly, hardly knowing what to do—perhaps kiss her good-bye. But she recoiled from him. "Unless you say you'll marry me, don't ever speak to me again!"

Chapter Six

Atkinson had made her promise she would stop and rest in Westport, and Meridel had to admit to herself that she was worn out with the long train ride. Where to stay? Westport now had a good hotel, but she did not stop to consider for more than a minute where she would go.

"*Mamacita, mamacita!*" Carlotta and Domingo took turns embracing her, while Florabelle and Maybelle and Flossie and Linda Lou and Alvina Mae and Hyacinth came running to welcome the traveler home, where she could convalesce.

Her tiredness faded slowly, day by day. Meanwhile she and Carlotta made plans. She would go to Kansas and rejoin her friends of the Underground Railroad—although not in Lecompton. And she would search and inquire for the red-haired little boy who might be in the care of an Indian woman. Meridel would always send word of where she was to Carlotta. And Carlotta would ask the men who came to her house and the many people she know in Westport if they had heard or seen anything of the missing child.

Meridel took up her old tasks, mending clothes for the fugitives. One night, tired of sewing, she sat in her room and read one of Mrs. E.D.E.N. Southworth's melodramatic novels, then all the rage. Tiring of that too, and thinking that soon she must leave Carlotta's house and go to Kansas, she drifted down the back stairs toward the usual evening sounds of revelry. The peephole revealed three men in blue suits with brass buttons. A river packet had moored at the Westport wharf and packet officers, Meridel had learned, patronized only the best bordellos.

The first officer—she could tell his rank by the three gold stripes on each sleeve—dribbled champagne into Linda Lou's bodice while she giggled and squirmed. The second officer, who had two stripes, was trying to tease Flossie into showing him her ankles, but she only shook her head and cast a coy glance upstairs. Everyone had been drinking. The girls drank weak tea that the customers bought for them at a champagne price—but even the customers enjoyed the ruse.

The packet's captain, a ferocious-looking little man, wore four curlicued gold stripes that ran up to each elbow. Standing unsteadily amid the parlor's overstuffed magnificence, he glared at a large sheet of paper. Meridel had heard an angry voice she now assumed had been his. But it was nothing new for customers to bring in newspapers or broadsides to help them damn the dunderheads in Washington.

The captain, dark and French-looking, with a Cajun accent, waved the broadside in wrath, and Meridel glimpsed the black headline. She caught her breath as she realized she had seen it before. The headline read:

LOYAL MEN WHO DEFEND THE SACRED SOUTH!
STOP AND SINK THE TRAITOR PACKET *BARATARIA!*
DROWN THE ABOLITIONIST RATS WHO WANT TO DECEIVE US!

Yes, this was one of those inflammatory broadsides that had so devastated her in Dan Forrester's cellar.

The captain crumpled it and threw it to the floor. "That cursed Forrester! I'd like to choke him until his eyes pop out!"

But the captain was a Southerner! Why wasn't he glad that so many anti-slavery people had died in the wreck of the *Barataria*?

Echoing Meridel's thought, Linda Lou asked, "But Cap'n, ain't you on the Southern side?"

"Heart and soul I'm for the South!" the captain roared. "But the *Barataria* was my boat, and I know what kind of brave men she carried. Not abos, blast it." Meridel reeled with sudden comprehension as he repeated, "Not abos! I wouldn't have allowed 'em aboard!" He kicked the crumpled wad of paper, shouting loudly enough to be heard throughout the big house, "No! I carried three hundred good Southern fighting men! Helped recruit 'em myself in Louisiana and Mississippi!"

"But the paper said—"

"I know right smart what it said. Just what Forrester printed on a press he bought from Slave State men who fished it out of the Kaw River. Then"—he choked—"Forrester tacked up the notice for Missouri men to see. Got them humbugged into believing they'd be sinking a boatload of abos." Behind the wall, Meridel held her hands to her hot face, trying to comprehend. The captain tossed down a drink and ranted on. "Believed they'd be sinking a boatload of abos, I tell you, and so they set my boat afire and sank it and I stayed with her, I swear it, until water filled the pilothouse. Thirty dead! Good Southern riflemen! The rest scattered. We kept it quiet. Tried to find out who fooled us. Well, now we know it was Forrester. And the Border Ruffians know who they have to kill. And the Raiders. And the Blue Lodge men. And they're on their way to his ranch, and if Forrester lives another twenty-four hours . . . by God, I hope they pull him apart with horses. He's a bigger abo sympathizer than we ever guessed. The boys've already sent back word of something found in the badlands part of his ranch—secret caves for hiding runaway niggers! Caught niggers right there on the spot. They called it the Land of Gilead. And we always thought Forrester was one of us pro-slavers, but just keeping quiet to protect his property from the abos and the railroad men!"

Meridel retreated from the peephole and stood with a hand on her tumultuous heart, feeling every beat. Dan had been secretly on *her* side all along!

Dan lay sweating in the long, narrow storage box in the peddler's wagon. He had run and hidden and run again all night to find Hyman the peddler. The man had more than once carried runaway slaves in the same box Dan was hiding in now. For several days Hyman drove at his usual slow, choppy pace toward Westport, stopping often, as he naturally would, to let farm women buy from his stock of needles and pins, bolts of cloth and pots, and other goods. Between farms he let Dan out of the box and gave him a few minutes in which to ease his aching limbs.

Eventually he felt the sway of the wagon as they crossed the Missouri on the Westport ferry. Hyman told him later that he had seen two floating booms of chained logs secured along the bank. After dark, when most river traffic stopped for the night, the heavily built booms would be floated to a spot below Westport where they would be joined to form a formidable barrier that would stretch across the river.

Yes. Abo watchers had spread the word. Dan knew.

Now he heard the rumble and roar of the city. In time the wagon stopped, surely where Romulus and Remus ran a warehouse. Here Hyman noisily replenished the goods he had sold while Dan slipped out of his box and into the warehouse unseen.

The twins gave him a good meal on excellent china. A wealthy U.R. sympathizer—a Señora Arguelo—lived nearby and had sent the food through a secret tunnel.

Romulus poured coffee from a silver ewer. Like his brother, he was a pallid, long-nosed and very serious. What one twin said, the other confirmed in altered words.

They told him that around midnight two packets, the *Sally* and the *Harvey Wingate,* would round a bend in the Missouri below Westport and continue upstream. These two good-sized boats carried anti-slavery people, not merely men and their families, but their plows, their sacks of seed, their horses and cattle. Once these families—more than a hundred of them—were established in Kansas, the territory would certainly become a Free State.

Dan asked, "You're sure they haven't kicked off the Free Staters and put Slave Staters aboard?"

"No," said Remus. "Every person was checked, and the packets have made no stops."

But the Slave Staters had had spies at the embarkation point and knew that if they couldn't stop and sink the two packets, their cause was lost. So Missouri men had prepared the heavy floating barrier of logs chained and spiked together. The packets would only smash their bows if they tried to punch through. No cannon were available, but the Missouri men would greet the *Sally* and the *Harvey Wingate* with bullets from a hundred rifles. Then, when the packets had to stop, a force would sally out in rowboats and set fire to the craft with torches and run blazing small boats against them.

"The packets can't turn without running aground," said Remus.

"They won't be able to turn without stranding on a sandbar, so they can't go back," Romulus said.

"And they can't break the boom, so they'll be sitting ducks. Okay," said Dan Forrester. "Is the equipment ready?"

"It's going to be terribly dangerous, Leonidas," Remus said.

"Leonidas, you'll be in awful peril."

The man who had eyes of midnight blue remembered a tiny red-haired woman with faerie-blue eyes and a graceful way of walking. He remembered a night when she had shown him a baby cooing in a basket. He remembered holding her across his arms at a westward-looking window. He remembered how they had gone to bed in utter bliss. . . .

He passed his hand across his face. "Let's go."

"We must take you to the river."

"Yes, Leonidas, everything is ready down at the river."

The twins loaded a freight wagon with various crates. Dan slipped into one that had an open side. He sat quietly, remembering, as they drove him toward the river. Soon he heard Spanish and broken English and various Indian tongues all mixed together, smelled chili, and heard children skylarking in the muddy streets. He knew they were passing through a section called the barrio.

Children. What had happened to his own son? How old

would the little fellow be now? As Dan counted months, he felt an ache. Suddenly, through a crack in the wagon, he spied a little suntanned white boy slipping out through a hedge, to gaze at the wagon as it passed by. Ah, the rascal! No doubt he lived in the neat cottage behind the hedge and had been told to stay within sight in the garden. Someone had stuck a feather into his red hair. Playing Indian . . .

Dan squirmed out of the crate and leaped up in the wagon. Eric would be about that age. This child had red hair, and . . . *Who had given him that feather?*

As the boy looked at the passing wagon and his father saw his dark blue eyes, Dan cried out, and leaped toward the little fellow. Whispering to the boy, he bent down and gently rolled up one of the child's trouser legs to the knee. •

He did not know what to say or think or feel when he found a scar above the chubby right knee and knew he had found his son.

A broad-faced Indian woman came at him with a knife. Unable to move, Dan barely saved himself with, "I am Forrester. Meridel's man."

Grabbing the boy to her, Silver Leaf stared at Dan, then whispered, "Meri-del say eyes like night, big shoulder."

"You are taking care of Eric?"

"Take care—Lor' Hara' pay—take um far-far on big water."

Somehow Harald Wayne had found the boy and wanted to steal him away to England. He must not! But the twins had stopped their wagon, and they motioned with fearful urgency for Dan to get back into it.

For the sake of Kansas, he must. "Silver Leaf, you know I am Eric's father. Lord Harald isn't. You must not give Eric up to Lord Harald. Silver Leaf, keep Eric for me." Dan motioned at the lowering sun. "But if I don't come back by tomorrow—this sun, so high, this shadow—I will be dead. So . . . so . . ."

"No dead! Where Meri-del?"

"I don't know. New York maybe. But if I come back alive tomorrow, you and I will take Eric and go find her. *Don't let Lord Harald take him away!*"

Dan vaulted back into the wagon, watching agonizedly

through the crack at his cheerful, puzzled little boy, who peered after the wagon as it rolled on.

Down at the river the twins brought Dan to a covered pier that extended into the rushing water. They lifted a trapdoor, and there in the river a log raft waited, secured to a ladder. Dan climbed down and made sure the raft had a steering sweep, two small kegs, and other objects of cargo. Rejoining Romulus and Remus, he checked that he had his pocket knife, honed sharply, and his watch.

"I reckon to push off about half past eleven," he said.

"Yes, allow yourself time."

"Yes, it will take a little time to get there."

"But don't allow so much time that the riflemen can range on you in the dark. There'll be moonlight."

"Yes, the moon will be out. Don't take *too* much time."

"Well," Dan said awkwardly, "thanks for getting everything ready."

"You know the four hiding places along the river that you can swim to later?"

"You memorized the map and you know where you can hide?"

Assuming he was still alive. "Yes," Dan said.

"We'll look in every hiding place tomorrow. We thank you in the name of our sisters and brothers of the Club."

"We won't miss any one of the hiding places. We thank you in the name of all the U.R. people."

"Good-bye, Leonidas. May God protect you."

"Good-bye, Leonidas. May God preserve you."

"Good-bye," Dan said. He did not expect ever to see the sun rise again.

Chapter Seven

She soared among pink clouds, thrilled with happiness. Little wonder that Dan had acted so strangely and never·had confided in her! Of course he couldn't sell the railroad right-of-way, because laying rails through the badlands of Rainbow Ranch would have revealed the most important station this side of the Missouri. The Land of Gilead! Ah, how they would catch up on all the love that had been denied them!

Only later did a sharp inner voice ask, "Where is Dan now?" Raiders and other Missouri men had invaded the ranch ready to kill him . . . and what did her mortal need for his safety count against a hundred ready guns?

She decided to wait and see if she had word of Dan or Eric, wait at the peephole till someone mentioned what had happened at Rainbow Ranch when the angry men stormed in. She did that through three evenings but heard nothing. And yet, if Dan had been found dead, wouldn't some Southerner gleefully tell the news?

On the fourth evening, Domingo ran a game of ghost poker. Serious players stayed in the cardroom, but two of the girls joined two customers and the old gambler in a riotous game in the parlor. The rules were merely the rules of poker with a slight change: one did not bet with anything but ghost money. Meanwhile Meridel had had to give way to Andreas at the peephole, and during that time—as she found out later—she missed the entrance of an important person from her past. He had come in, had chosen a girl, and had gone upstairs. Back at the peephole again, Meridel watched the ghost poker game.

Suitable bottles had been supplied, and Domingo, having drunk deeply, shuffled the cards. Perhaps the influence of *aguardiente* made him drop the pack, but he picked the deck up quickly.

"*Señores y señoritas*, we play stud. One down, four open."

He slid a face-down card to each player. Then came the first open card, and the betting—in ghost money—soon reached a wild-and-woolly stage.

"Bet a million on my card." "Raise you two million." "See you in solid gold," said a third so-called bettor, laughing so hard he almost fell off his chair.

"In gold?" asked Domingo. "*Caramba*. The weight will break the table. I'll see you in ten-carat diamonds."

"Hide 'em. The glitter hurts my eyes."

Silly of course, but many customers liked to "break the ice" before they took a girl upstairs for the real business of the evening. When the four open cards lay on the table, Domingo admitted that he had dealt four "pregnant straights." Everything depended on the blind card that remained hidden facedown in front of each player.

"Betcha my horse, Domingo! As happened to walk in—see 'im? Git up thar on the table, Brownie. And remember, behave yourself, you ain't out on a road!"

Giggles and laughter. Elaborate complaints about the invisible horse's swaybacked condition. But Meridel hardly heard. She could see the first few steps of the red-carpeted staircase, where a man coming down from one of the bedrooms had paused. She could see only his boots. She knew those riding boots with butted fronts and sides in the English style. She knew their cordovan glow. Before she saw his face, she knew the man who slapped his crop upon a boot in an increasingly fast, angry tattoo.

Domingo was saying, "Now we open our blind cards, and—*mira!*"

The old gambler turned up an ace. The others turned up low cards. His ace-high straight won. Cheerfully he called for a cart in which the horse could haul away his winnings. At the same time the English boots descended the remaining steps and Meridel saw whipcord breeches, a Shetland jacket and her husband's handsome Viking face, gone ugly and red with rage.

The laughter stopped. Domingo gasped, "Meester Wayne! Not see so many year—"

Harald shouted, "So, you old greaser, you're still making an ace turn up where you want it."

"I, cheat? Nevair. Only in ghost poker—when I drop cards I make sweetch the deck. And pliz, I am not greaser, Meester Wayne!"

"No, you're a son of a bitch. Now I see you gave me an ace out of your sleeve that time in San Tomás."

"No, nevair. I swear by my sainted mother—"

"Yes, you did, and you know what that ace has cost me." Carlotta appeared with Andreas close behind her as Harald roared, "And now I'm going to—" he raised his crop and rushed.

The fat woman caught his jacket. He turned, slashed at her face, but Andreas caught him in an unbreakable grip.

"Bitch!" the maddened Harald roared at Carlotta as he struggled.

"My word, I keeped it." She winced, her hand on her cheek. "I make you not the trouble, no, not even when you marry big railroad money."

Meridel gulped at that, then realized that Domingo had hastened out of the house, muttering about an appointment at the Lone Star Saloon. Right behind him, Andreas shoved Harald onto the veranda. For the first time Meridel ran from behind the peephole door into the parlor, and saw Harald fall down the front steps, then get up and stumble toward his birch-paneled coach, where Eddoes waited with his gun in hand.

"No shooting!" Harald said breathlessly as Andreas slammed the house door shut.

Despite the red welt on her cheek Carlotta got the girls singing, in an attempt to restore the atmosphere of fun. Meridel retreated from the parlor. What could have been going on when Domingo had dealt Harald an ace—obviously an unlucky ace—down in San Tomás? He certainly bore a deadly grudge concerning that ace. And, Meridel realized in sudden panic, Harald was well aware that Domingo had gone alone in the dark to the Lone Star Saloon.

When she conveyed her fear to Andreas, the huge man snatched a lantern, and they hurried out into the night. The Lone Star's bartender said that, yup, he now carried *aguardiente* but nope, he hadn't seen Domingo that evening. Could Harald and Eddoes have caught the old man? In growing dread Meridel led Andreas back along the street, pausing often to look and listen.

They searched up and down the empty street, and were about to give up when a moan sounded from a secluded, dark alley. Andreas peered around the corner, holding the lantern aloft; the light lit up the alley, and from behind a barrel high-heeled shoes protruded.

"Wayne," whispered Domingo as Andreas lifted him. As they rushed him home, blood left a trail from the terrible wound in his side. At the sight of the old man, Carlotta went into frantic weeping, then had him carried to her own bed. Someone went for the doctor while Meridel, bending fearfully over the gambler, could do nothing for him except press cloths against the gaping hole where a knife had entered deeply.

Mumbling prayers, Carlotta tore her hair, then uttered a cry of elation as Domingo opened his eyes. But he only murmured, "Dying . . ."

"Lord Harald, yes, my treacherous husband, Lord Harald, did this!" Meridel exclaimed.

Although he lay at death's door, Domingo said, "No." And while Meridel stared and Carlotta clapped her hand to her own tear-wet lips as though in warning, the gambler said,

"Harald is not . . . your husband." Carlotta cried out something in rapid Spanish; by its sound Meridel knew it was a protest. Domingo whispered around a spasm of agony, "I must tell . . . my . . . Meridel."

Surely the dying man was in delirium. Meridel wiped his face and bent to whisper, "But Harald *is* my husband. Rest, Domingo, please."

He tried to touch her. "You . . . not married."

Meridel could only say, "*What?*"

"Sometheeng happen . . . in San Tomás . . . I tell." Again Carlotta protested, but Domingo repeated faintly, "*Sí,* I must tell." He tried to speak in English. When he lapsed into Spanish, Carlotta resignedly held his hand and translated the feeble words.

Meridel found out that the San Tomás dictator, Acevedo, had forced the beautiful Carlotta into his bed. Soon he had made her procuress to the *presidente*. She supplied him, and eventually others as well, with girls.

Growing prosperous, Carlotta was thinking of buying a fertile valley in the back country, hoping the new railroad would cross it. But before she committed herself to purchasing it, she enlisted Harald Wayne of the British consul's office, and a money-grubbing United States diplomat named Nickerson to go with her and inspect the faraway valley. Pursued by head-shrinking Indians, the three had had to hide several weeks in a cave. When they returned at last to the capital city, they learned the railroad would not cross the valley, and that the diplomats, who had been granted only a week of leave, would have to be sent home. But Carlotta had acquired a special problem of her own.

"I was pregnant," she told Meridel. "They were both—how you say?—bachelor men. But who makes pregnant? Nickerson or Wàyne?"

"I see. . . ."

While blood bubbled on Domingo's pale, silent lips, Carlotta, trying to control her emotion, went on with the rest of the story.

Acevedo captured the erring diplomats and announced that gringos could not lightly dishonor San Tomás women. Either Wayne or Nickerson must marry Carlotta—or both would find themselves altered in a way that would destroy their interest in the opposite sex.

Acevedo called in Domingo Quesada, known as an honest gambler. Meridel, aghast—for she suspected she knew what had happened—learned how Domingo had sat down with Wayne and Nickerson and had flipped a coin. How he had dealt the first card—open—to Wayne as Acevedo sneered, "First ace wins fair lady." How other open cards slid fatefully across the table, one to Nickerson, one to Wayne, one to Nickerson, one to Wayne, one to Nickerson. From one to the other the cards had been dealt, until Harald Wayne looked at the ace of spades and said, "More than a chap plans on, don't you know."

Meridel gasped, "Carlotta, did you—?"

A mountainous shrug. "*Sí.* Acevedo, he make us married. Yes, *mamacita*, yes, I married Harald Wayne."

"*Carlotta!*"

"And I say, 'Meester Wayne, go away, you not like me, I not want you, only send feefty pounds twice every year, I say nothing we married. Go marry English girl, anybody, I not care.' But I tell him marry-paper—certeeficate?—is register in *alcalde*'s—mayor's—office. Is good marriage. He quick go away, send money. I"—Carlotta hesitated—"meescarriage, you call it. But still married. Earthquake come. All marry-papers—certeeficates, books—burn up. But I still married. Get good English pounds."

Speechless with the knowledge, Meridel heard a rattle issue from Domingo's throat. Carlotta threw herself across the body.

"*Papá*, my precious *papá*, come back to your daughter, don't go away!" But Domingo had left his child forever.

Carlotta wept. When at last she raised her head, Meridel, herself in tears, asked, "But it's true? Really true?"

The madam nodded. From the fat, sobbing face blotched with wet rouge and kohl came the final words of her fateful story: "*Mamacita*, now you see you have no husband, you never have husband. You not . . . only *I* am Lady Wayne!"

Meridel found herself outside, where the moon had traced an edge of silver on the river. She needed air. She needed to think, though the thick haze in her mind kept her from doing so. At last one great thought broke through: she was not married! Harald, a bigamist, had mocked the ceremony in St. Thomas's Church. Slowly smiling, and with a great weight lifting from her heart, Meridel took off her wedding ring and threw it as far as she could.

She must tell Dan! And when she heard boots crunch in the mist she thought for an instant that a miracle had happened, that her lover had found her. "Dan!" she said.

But the man who briefly showed his killer's face before he grabbed her from behind was Eddoes. "Hold her!" said Lord Harald Wayne.

Too confused to be cautious, Meridel cried, "You're not my husband! You married Carlotta!"

Harald snapped, "Don't let her talk. Bring her to the carriage." Eddoes covered Meridel's mouth with a hard hand. She struggled madly, tried to bite, kick, scratch. But two men who didn't care how they hurt one small woman gagged her, bound her, and tossed her into the dark depths of the carriage's oversize luggage boot.

"So!" Harald said. "Domingo lived long enough to tell you that Carlotta Arguelo is the real Lady Wayne. Too bad, but I must kill you, my lovely, faithless elf. Ah, but I can give you a bit of comfort. Listen, now."

Writhing in darkness, she listened.

"I have Eric and Silver Leaf safe here in Westport. My men found Eric and bought him and the squaw for a couple of good horses. Brought them to me. And within the hour—as soon as I attend to your demise, my dear—I'll be on my way with my poor motherless son for the St. Joseph railhead and thence to New York. And thence, of course, to England. And high time, too, because I'm ruined here and I doubly need every bit of the inheritance due me. Eddoes, I think I'll tell my father that my darling wife died of smallpox."

"Nah, lor'ship, better to have no body. I say sink her in the river."

"But . . . a grave?"

"I can get a grave dug and a headstone put up, no questions asked."

"Excellent, my good man. This will not be the first time a river has been useful to me. We must make sure she sinks."

"You bet, lor'ship. I know a place on the river where a lot of old iron lays around."

Before long, Meridel found herself lying bound and gagged on the edge of a deserted pier. As Eddoes went off to find heavy iron to rope to her body, Harald seated himself companionably next to her and lit a cigar.

"Let me see," he said, knowing she heard him. "The schoolmarm is dead and at any rate she could not have made a proper mother for Eric. But that horsefaced titled creature my father wanted me to marry . . . she would do, as long as I can't have you. Better in some ways . . . because the Norfolk gentry would understand my being unfaithful to *her*. You see, Meridel, you can go to your death knowing that I complimented you." He blew smoke in her direction and she gagged.

The black river swished against the piles. "Goodbye . . . goodbye," it seemed to say. Vaguely the moonlight showed Meridel a great, broken, floating tree that turned in the river's current and which stretched out its gaunt branches as though it were a despairing hand. She lifted her own bound hands in mute appeal but Harald only said, "It is very necessary for you to die, poor elf," in false pity. "Ah, here comes Eddoes with a hundred-pound grating on his shoulder."

How quickly it would pull her down through the black water and hold her against the mud. . . .

Chapter Eight

Dan Forrester glanced at his watch, then climbed down to the raft with a hooded lantern. He checked his coil of fuse, and the other equipment he had loaded on the raft moments before, but especially he checked the two kegs of powder. Not *gun*powder, which burns slowly, giving a bullet time to travel up a gun's barrel and release the explosion before it bursts the gun. But two kegs of fast blasting powder. And only someone well-heeled in handling it could do so safely. With his engineering background, Dan was the only man this side of Kansas who could. There were still dangers, such as a stray bullet from an enemy's gun, which could send the raft, with Dan on it, into a cloud of black smoke.

The shrouded moon hung overhead as he worked the sweep to keep the heavy raft near the Missouri side. Mist that clung to the sides of the river shielded him, and even if he were spotted, he might not encounter trouble, since lone men often plied the river late at night. He checked his Sharps rifle and the twenty cartridges he had brought with him, letting the current meanwhile carry him downstream.

Dimly he made out a great floating snag, and thought he saw motion in the water near it. Listening closely, he heard splashing that sounded more like thrashing. He looked sidewise to increase his night vision—and caught the wild, gagged face of a woman with streaming hair whose face was barely out of the water. He saw her hands grasp the snag by one of its branches, but something was keeping her from climbing up the embankment.

The future of Kansas floated on Dan's raft. He dared not stop. But he could not abandon a drowning woman, and he sculled with all his strength to turn the raft.

Just as the woman's branch broke in her fingers, Dan leaped with the free end of his mooring line. Under the water he met a struggling, dress-hampered figure that he pulled upward until they burst through the water's surface. Somehow he kept her face above water while the raft towed them along. He never knew when he realized it was Meridel he had saved. But he could not have hauled himself and a woman to the raft, her weight unusually heavy, their sodden clothes dragging them down, if the woman had not been Meridel.

When he rolled her onto the raft he first cut away the gag to let her retch and gasp. Then he cut her bonds, handed her a flask of whiskey, and left her while he steered and squinted ahead for the black line on the river that he was seeking.

"Dan," she could finally say.

"Yes, sweetheart."

He set the oar and grasped her tightly to him. She did not tell him how she rolled into the river before her captors could weigh her down with iron. It no longer mattered. Instead she cried, "Dan, I'm not married." When she told him why, he could not believe the story and made her repeat herself as she stood next to him at the steering oar.

Joy shook him, and he told her his own news.

"Dearest, I saw Eric today! Active, healthy—in Westport, with Silver Leaf!"

They tried to tell each other everything, told a great deal as they spoke and kissed, spoke and kissed. But that black line became more and more visible, stretching from shore to shore far ahead. This was the log-boom that had been created to stop the packets.

"Meridel, I know hiding places on the banks. I can scull to one, put you in it. I'll go on and—"

"No," she said, her small voice very clear. "I'll stay and help you."

"But dearest, I can tell you where to find Eric, and—"

No, she explained, Harald Wayne and Eddoes had surely witnessed the rescue and would be off with Eric very soon. She could do no good by saving herself. "My darling, do you think that if you're not afraid to die for our cause, I am afraid?"

"But Meridel . . ." He gestured toward riflemen they could see grouped on the Missouri shore.

"Only call me dearest," she whispered, and by the way he caught her to him she knew his love.

They lay embracing on the rough logs in their wet clothing, wrapped in each other's arms, wrapped in love found again, almost feeling the presence of the child that love had made. For minutes that could not be measured—that might have been hours, might have been lifetimes—they kissed and murmured and shared their hard-won understanding. When Dan told her his Underground Railroad name was Leonidas, Meridel nodded, feeling that in some hidden recess in her heart she had always known it. Again they pressed their mouths together in a lingering kiss they knew might mean good-bye. The river rippled as though whispering gentle words as it bore them on toward their fate.

The raft rose on a little wave as the water rushed against the line of chained logs stretching across the river. As they bumped the logs, the first shot whined over their heads. Dan muttered that all the shooting would likely come from the Missouri side. If the *Sally* and the *Harvey Wingate* steered away from the bullets, they might run onto sandbanks near the Kansas shore.

Meridel threw away her dress and petticoats. Her legs now unhampered, she leaped onto the logs just as two huge, dark bulks—the packets—careened around a bend downstream. They showed no lights, but their captains had no way to hide the sparks that flared from the packet smokestacks as they headed for the barrier under full steam.

Dan rushed back and forth from the raft with the water-proofed powder kegs, the ax, the sandbags, and the rest of his cargo. Bullets splashed them with water, or buzzed away westward as they flicked splinters from the logs. Dan grabbed up the Sharps and fired at long range through the increasing mist to let the Missouri men know he could kill. "But they know one man can't get 'em all," he muttered under his breath. He swung the ax and nicked the heavy chains, making weak spots. Working frantically, he used the crowbar to wrench logs apart while Meridel rolled the kegs down into the yawning gaps.

"See, you could not have done that alone," she cried.

Dan prepared the kegs, approving the way their sides touched the water. For safety he set two fuses, cut them short, and scratched a lucifer alight on a bit of waterproof-covered board kept in his pocket. As tiny, deadly dots of fire sputtered toward the powder, he let the logs spring back and arranged the sandbags on top. Using the pitcher to wet the sand, he increased the weight against which the blast would push. The panting of the packets' engines and the clank of their paddle wheels sounded louder. As Dan tossed the pitcher away, a bullet smashed it in midair.

"Meridel, *run!*"

She ran toward Kansas, leaping from log to log while Dan fired at dim figures who came out warily along the boom. Rifle fire from the leading packet stitched the night with red flashes. Meridel ran recklessly on the unsteady logs, until her foot slipped between two logs that caught her in a bruising grip. Dan wedged the logs apart with his rifle, breaking the stock to get her free.

"Run!"

"Not unless you run, too."

"I've got to keep them from reaching the powder and putting out the fuses."

Just then the rifle's broken stock spilled percussion caps from the set-in container. Meridel caught several of the small brass objects. "I'll give you these one by one."

He had to fire from his hip. Still they saw one Missouri man topple into the water. Dan needed only seconds in which to set the percussion cap, insert another cartridge, close the breech, aim . . . but already one of the enemy had kneeled to take careful aim in suddenly bright moonlight. As Meridel screamed, "Dan, duck!" the world disappeared in a thunderous sheet of fire and a frightful impact that sent her whirling.

"I'm Cap'n Burns of the *Sally*," said the bearded face beneath a blue, gold-trimmed cap.

Blinking away blackness, Meridel saw that two women, strangers, also watched her closely. She lay on a berth in a small room—a packet's cabin. The packet vibrated with its engine's effort to push it upstream.

"Dan . . . where's Dan? Did he—"

"Got hit in the head by a flying log, but you held him up until my mate could pull both of you into a small boat."

"I don't remember. But is he—"

"He's all right, or nearly. He's a tough un. Uh . . . keep yourself covered. The ladies here, they undressed you to get you dry and warm you up."

"But the log boom. Did it—?"

"The blast busted it. It opened like two doors opening downstream, and both packets steamed straight up through the middle. Not only that, a dozen logs fell on our foredeck for firewood. We're above Westport now."

One of the plainly dressed immigrant women cried, "You saved Kansas!"

To the man who staggered into the doorway, his head bandaged, his eyes blackening from the blow he had taken, Meridel cried, "Dan, we saved Kansas!"

The attendant ladies and the captain flushed and turned away, because the lovers were kissing and Meridel's blanket had slipped and neither she nor Dan cared.

Then at last, after she had tended to her man a little, Meridel had to tell him that by now Harald certainly had snatched up Eric from the house in the barrio and was taking him to St. Joseph that night, then on to New York and England.

She tried to tell Dan he must rest—they both should rest—

and later they would decide what to do. But Dan got up from where he lay against her bosom, roaring, "Where's her clothing? Even if it's not dry, get it from the boiler room."

Nobody could stop him from going after Eric. A woman gave Meridel a bonnet and a dress near her size, and Captain Burns loaned Dan a pistol and a couple of blankets. A small boat towed on a long slack line brought them to the Missouri shore, and the packet, never stopping, snatched it away as the couple scrambled up the bank.

In darkness thinned by the setting moon, Meridel stared down an empty country road that ran along the river. "How far to Westport?"

"Miles. How's your ankle?"

It throbbed and burned. "Why, just fine. How's your head?"

Dan only replied, "Let's start walking."

They walked . . . and walked, hearing the mindless whisper of the river and the sound of owls far off.

Finally a promise of dawn crept up the sky. Ahead, the road climbed a small hill, and from that direction came the sound of rapid galloping. They hid behind bushes. The bobbing heads of horses appeared prick-eared against the sky, and in an instant, a speeding, swaying carriage whirled down the hill after four hard-driven grays. The coachman's silver-trimmed hat hung by its thong at the back of his neck. He wielded a long whip without mercy.

The Wayne coat of arms flicked into sight opposite the bushes.

Dan leaped into the road and fired at the coachman, but Eddoes had glimpsed him. He swerved the coach and smiled back triumphantly, knowing the bullet missed. Dan dared not shoot at the back of the carriage lest he hit his son. The equipage speeded away.

Meridel ran hobbling after the coach, then faltered and stopped as the coach left her far behind. Trying to comfort her, Dan said that in Westport they could hire horses and ride to St. Joe. She agreed, but in her heavy heart she knew that Harald would reach St. Joe hours before they did. He would tell the local bushwhackers to load their guns and wait for

Dan Forrester. He would turn his back on the forthcoming murder and leave with Eric on the midmorning train.

Yet they must do what they could do. At least few people were about as they entered the streets of Westport in the early morning. Meridel tightened the bonnet around her face, and Dan walked bent with a blanket over his head, as though he suffered from river fever.

They found the barrio and soon stood brooding before the hedge-fronted cottage where Dan had seen and touched—and had had to forsake—their child. Nearby, the high cupola of Carlotta's house flashed as it caught the sun. Had Harald really stopped here? Had he really carried Eric away?

Dan found tracks in the street which indicated that the worst had happened. He showed Meridel where a four-wheeled vehicle and four horses had stood in front of the cottage; it had traveled on and, turning a corner, had then gone northward toward St. Joe. For a moment Dan puzzled over a spot in the street where the dried mud had been swept smooth. Then they heard a cry: "Meri-del!" They turned to see a broad-faced Indian woman running to embrace her long-lost friend in ecstatic reunion.

After a moment of delight Silver Leaf confirmed that Harald had been there. But Eric's second mother bubbled with a strange excitement. She had welts on her face, and explained that Harald had whipped it, as well as her back and arms, trying to make her carry Eric into the coach and go along with them. Yet Silver Leaf showed no sorrow, only joy as, still hugging Meridel and beaming upon Dan Forrester, she brought them back to the smoothly swept place in the street. Brushing the top dirt away with her hand, the Indian woman brought dark streaks and clots into view.

Dan bent over them. "Blood. And . . ." And a fragment of curved, dark-stained bone to which skin and hair clung. *Blond hair.* Meridel gasped and swayed; Dan caught her.

As though from far away, she heard Silver Leaf say, "Lor' Hara' get shoot. Ah-hmmm. Make dead. Lor' Hara' dead."

Silence. Then, more clearly, Meridel heard Dan demand, "Did you shoot Lord Harald because he whipped you? Or"—he glanced at the carriage tracks—"did Eddoes shoot him and take the—"

"No, no. Shoot come from—from—" Silver Leaf waved all around to indicate she did not know where the shot had come from. She tried to reconstruct a scene. "Lor' Hara'—here." He had stood on the swept spot. "By big wagon, much seats." The coach. "Lantern—up." The coach's side-light, which reached as high as a man's head, apparently had shone upon Harald's face. Silver Leaf pointed at the sky. "Moon too. Somebody see um real good."

"He made a good target," Dan reflected. "Some enemy saw him. But where's the body?"

"Sherf take um." The sheriff had taken the corpse away.

"Well," Dan said, "I guess we'll never know who shot him."

But Meridel knew. She glanced up at the cupola, where a sorrow-ridden woman had, perhaps, gone to mourn. She had seen a face in the darkness—a hated face—and had avenged her father's death.

Carlotta. But with all this, where was Eric? Eddoes had galloped off not only with a valuable coach and Harald's belongings and four fine horses, but also with a child for whom the earl of Danemead would pay a heavy ransom. Where had the gunman gone? How long would it take to hunt him down? Would they ever find him? *Would Eric survive?* Meridel's glance met Dan's. His eyes were slitted with pain, his mouth drawn and grim. Blood had seeped through the bandage on his head. Nevertheless, they must start searching instantly. And yet how could they when hundreds of men stalked eastern Kansas ready to shoot Dan down?

Meridel wondered why Silver Leaf was pulling at them. "Come, come!" At any rate, she reflected, Dan would be safer inside. Inside the cottage Meridel sank onto a bench, beckoning Dan to sit beside her and rest after their hours of walking.

But no, Silver Leaf still pulled at him urgently. Silver Leaf hauled Meridel to her aching feet, chivvied her onward. She took them to a room that contained a cot neatly covered with a blanket of Pawnee weaving and, beside the cot, a small railed bed. A child's bed.

A *little* child's bed.

Meridel stopped short. She dared not take the few steps that would show her the face of the child who slept there.

Dan went to the bed, looked, returned, took his beloved by the hand, and led her to their sleeping son.

"Forres'er say keep, I keep."

There'd be so much more to be told later. And time to tell it, because Silver Leaf wanted nothing better than to come and live at Rainbow Ranch.

Meanwhile, although the world had paused, it turned again and life began all new, all fresh.

"Look, he has teeth."

"And my eyes."

"And my hair."

"I'll teach him to ride."

"We'll all ride together."

"You and me and all our children?"

"You and me and all our children . . . Yes, Dan, yes, all our children."

Eric then wanted to go to Silver Leaf's arms, which was natural enough. But from that place of security he looked back at Meridel with his old, angelic smile.

They must hide awhile. It did not matter. While peace came to Kansas they could plan the rebuilding of Rainbow Ranch. Meridel had grand ideas for a house, and Dan's new breeding stock would be coming in, and the railroad could run without hindrance across a Free State . . . and when Dan was elected governor, what a busy, wonderful life they would lead!

Silver Leaf rattled pots in her kitchen, where she was preparing a big breakfast. She had Eric with her. They were singing a little Pawnee chant. Yes, let the eldest child remember the language of the prairie. And she herself would remember the language, and so much more, which Dan would remember, too. Through all their shared evenings they would whisper and remember. And if the world had once again become a golden apple in her hand, as in the story her father used to read her as a child . . .

Why not?